To Vaughn!
Hope you Journey to the Deep Blue!

THE BIANCA C STILL BURNS

A GRENADA NOVEL

[signature]

Dunbar Campbell

Copyright © 2014 Dunbar Campbell
All rights reserved.

ISBN-13: 9781503094581
ISBN-10: 1503094588

PUBLISHER'S NOTE
This is a work of fiction. Names, characters, places, and incidents either are the product of the author's imagination or are used fictitiously, and any resemblance to actual persons, living or dead, business establishments, events, or locales is entirely coincidental.

Cover by well-known Grenadian artist, Michael Steele, an eyewitness to the 1961 Bianca C incident.
Email: gmsteele37@mac.com
Website: http//.www.gmsteele-artist.com

Inspired by the dramatic *Bianca C* incident, when Grenada residents rushed a frantic flotilla of sailboats, fishing boats, and rowboats to rescue hundreds of passengers from the explosion and fire that sank the Italian luxury cruise ship off the Caribbean island in 1961.

Prologue

The Caribbean Sea
Outside the port of St. George's, Grenada
Aboard the Italian luxury liner, Bianca C
Sunday, 22 October 1961
07:00 Hours Local

The explosion shattered the early morning calm. It shuddered through the luxury cruise ship and echoed off the St. George's hillsides. Mario Costa threw aside his silk sheets and rolled off the bed in his cabin.

Had the disturbance come from the harbor or his ship?

He rushed onto the balcony with a pair of binoculars. His sixth-story luxury suite gave him a commanding view of the horseshoe-shaped harbor. The tranquil blue sea basked in mild sunlight and rowboats bobbed without a care along the waterfront. No signs of any smoldering destruction he would have expected to see from such a powerful blast. Not even on the green hills, crisscrossed with sagging telephone lines and peppered with red-roofed houses. The only smoke came from a car rumbling past on the waterfront road. It spewed a lazy trail of gray exhaust in its wake.

Had his mind tricked him out of bed to end another distressing dream about his wife?

Then, with meager relief, he realized she hadn't driven him mad yet. The blast had not been just a product of his strained imagination. It had also alerted others. Several residents pointed from homes nestled in the sloping greenery. He focused his binoculars on a few people in dark suits and hats, probably on their way to church, who paused on the shoreline. They gazed at the ship with stunned expressions.

Mario peered at the cabins below to see what drew the islanders' attention.

Nothing, except—a fleeting whiff of burning plastic?

Just then thick hot smoke engulfed his balcony, choking and blinding him. Alarm bells choroused within the ship. With his arms flailing to find his way, he stumbled back into the cabin and slid the glass door shut. "What the hell?"

"Papa," his three-year-old daughter cried out from her bed, sitting up and rubbing her eyes.

"It's okay, *bambina*. I'm here." He hurried to the nightstand between their beds and grabbed the red phone.

He dialed the number to the bridge hoping for assurance from *Capitàno* Francisco Crevaco, the stocky fatherly captain with forty years of flawless service to the Costa Cruise Lines.

It rang several times with no answer. He hung up and tried again. Finally, the captain's second-in-command answered the phone.

Despite the emergency and even in Italian, the staff-captain sounded cold. "How may I help you, *Messer* Costa?"

"Where's *mio capitàno*?" Mario hollered over the sound of alarm bells.

Running footsteps pounded the hallways below. Screams.

"*Capitàno* Crevaco is on the way to investigate a crankcase breakdown in the engine room," the staff-captain dryly. "It's spilling fuel, but we can control it."

Mario shouted. "I need to talk to him. Immediately."

"You can talk to me," the staff-captain said. "He left me in charge."

"If you're in charge, then give the orders to evacuate."

"Why? I have everything under control."

"Obviously you don't." Mario snapped. "The alarms are going. We have smoke up here and the passengers are in danger. We must evacuate now."

"I see no smoke from here. But if there's fire, I think we have time to put it out."

"You think so? You have seven hundred people on a burning ship and there's dry land just half-a-mile away."

"Evacuation is going to be too slow."

"Don't we have enough life boats?" Mario asked.

"Yes, but we've lost power to lower them."

"Dammit. You're wasting valuable time. Sound the mayday-call now. The local authorities need to know."

"I hate to disappoint you," the staff-captain said. "These backward islanders have no means to assist us."

Mario's irritation scorched his voice. "If I don't hear mayday calls in ten seconds, you're fired."

"As you wish, sir."

A few moments later, three blasts of the ship's horn bellowed. A pause. Then three more blasts.

"One more question," Mario said during the next pause in the mayday calls. "How's access to the safe?"

"If I have to evacuate passengers, I won't have time to get you to your library."

"I'll come get the door keys myself. Just leave them on the bridge."

"Forget it," the staff-captain said.

"Forget the safe?" Mario shouted into the phone. "Who do you think you're talking to?"

"Right now I don't care. I have to go. It's starting to smoke here too. Evacuate now and take care of your daughter."

"You and I will settle this by the end of the day." Mario slammed down the phone.

He'd never trusted the bastard. He should have had the captain fire him when he first heard the rumors three years ago. It was too late now.

The cabin darkened and the smell of burning rubber tinged Mario's nostrils.

His daughter stood on the bed in her flowered nightgown and pointed at the balcony door. "Papa!"

Thick smoke churned onto the balcony, blocking the green hills and morning sunlight. Sheets of black seeped under the door and curled up the pink walls to the mirrored ceilings.

The mayday horns blew three times again.

"Let's go," he shouted.

"But my dolls—"

"Here, take this one." He grabbed her favorite doll and bolted out the front door with his daughter wrapped in his arms.

Maybe his wife back in Genoa wished this on him as punishment for spending his thirty-first birthday on a cruise without her. What else in God's name did she expect?

A stampede drummed the hallways below. Shrieks rang out as loudly as the alarm bells.

Through the fear chilling his bones and fogging his thoughts, he remembered the escape ladder from his private deck. He lifted the heavy latch and pushed the metal door. Fresh air blew in and the island opened up before him. But something had changed in the harbor. It took him a moment to recognize the reason for the white-water turbulence leaving the island.

A ragtag flotilla of rowboats, sailboats, and motorboats raced toward his cruise ship.

He lifted his daughter onto his back. "Hold Papa around his neck. Tight."

Another explosion rumbled in the ship's bowels. The door rattled.

Mario climbed down the ladder to the water level as quickly as his loose bedroom slippers could take him. Screaming passengers choked other ladders around him, most with red life-jackets pulled over bedraggled night clothes. Some jumped into the water. Boats rowed into the pandemonium. The rescuers took women and children first, four or five at a time, then turned back to shore.

A dark-skinned girl in her late teens maneuvered her rowboat up to Mario's ladder.

She stood barefoot in a see-through nighty and stretched out her arms. "Give me your baby, quick."

He kissed his daughter and passed her into the girl's embrace.

His daughter cried out. "Papa."

"You will be okay now," the girl said.

"I go back to ship," Mario yelled over the commotion, his thoughts struggling between Italian and the little English he understood.

"You crazy?" The girl looked at the diamond-studded gold ring on his left hand. "For your wife?"

He tugged at his ring and handed it to her. "Use this get anything you need. Care her for me. How I find you?"

"Just ask for Cammy. Everybody knows me."

"Cammy, *si?*"

"Yes. What's your baby's name?"

"Bianca, like name of ship."

He turned and climbed the ladder into the smoking hull. Bianca's screams, from the arms of a stranger, tugged at his heart while smoke burned his lungs.

CHAPTER ONE

Grand Anse Beach, Grenada
Wednesday, 19 October 1983
11:45 Hours Local

Storm Butler's pulse quickened in the midday heat. A black sedan led a military truck down the road toward his dive shop. Despite his loose t-shirt, shorts and flip-flops, he sweated while he held the scuba tank on the counter. He hand-tightened the valve and watched the vehicles approach.

The car stopped and the truck pulled up behind it. Eight soldiers dismounted with AK-47 rifles. The soldiers took up watchful positions in the shade of coconut trees along the road and on the white-sand beach.

A small military flag on the hood of the car flapped in the steamy breeze. The backseat passenger sat obscured behind tinted windows, but Storm already knew whose eyes blazed at him from the chilly interior of the air-conditioned car. The last person he wanted to see today, or ever.

The one person he'd wished dead since the day he learned what the word meant.

The driver exited and opened the rear door.

A pair of spit-shined boots stretched out of the car, glistening under the noon sun. A tall muscular man stepped out in the green uniform of the People's Revolutionary Army. He adjusted his mirrored sunglasses and star-studded military hat, and marched across the road toward Storm. Sand crunched under the officer's leather soles.

Storm hoped his facetious tone would repel the officer, but knew it wouldn't. "If you're here to scuba dive, you'll need to change your outfit, Reds."

"It's Colonel Reds Slinger to you, boy." Reds halted on the other side of the counter, his skin leathery and rust colored from fifty years in the tropical sun. His thick moustache twitched. "The American Marines never taught you to respect a superior officer?"

"They teach how to earn respect, not demand it."

Reds stuck his thumbs in his military belt. "There are still lessons I can teach you, son."

"I'm not your goddamned son."

Despite the light skin color and wavy dark hair he shared with Reds, Storm believed his mother when she said Reds was not his father. Storm recalled claps of leather across his back, stinging welts that kept him awake, and the promise he made to himself. One day, Reds would be history.

"I hear you plan to stay put on the island," Reds said. "Don't they call it desertion in the Marines?"

"It's called hardship discharge," Storm said. "And I'm sure you know why."

"Sounds like you ran away from the hardships in Lebanon. How do your buddies feel about you abandoning them just as things are getting hot over there?"

Storm folded his arms. He felt torn about being in Grenada while his band of brothers in Company C, 2nd Reconnaissance Battalion faced daily barrages of rockets and mortars in their role as peacekeepers. They operated under rules of engagement, or ROE, which turned combat Marines into sitting ducks at the Beirut International Airport.

Hell, the huge four-story barracks housing the battalion landing team should have had a target painted on the roof for the hostiles manning artillery batteries on surrounding hillsides.

Written by desk jockeys to pass political smell tests, the ROE defied foxhole common-sense and enraged Storm's platoon. Marines only went to war when diplomacy failed, so why did the very designers of failed foreign policy continue to plan military missions? Why didn't they just step out of the bloody way and let the Marines do what they did best, clean up diplomatic screw-ups?

The platoon sergeant, Gunny, had passed out the ROE cards six months ago on their first day in formation outside the Beirut barracks. One of Storm's fellow sergeants rumpled the rule card and shoved it in his pocket. "Who wrote this bull?"

"Listen to this," another Marine yelled. "'*Keep loaded magazine in weapon, bolt closed, weapon on safe, no round in the chamber.*'"

Groans. Marines armed to the teeth but ordered to keep their jaws shut.

The platoon bitched. Most Marines did—about everything. But to survive, they knew following imperfect orders always produced better outcomes when Marines functioned as a team rather than a cluster-fuck of discontent.

Another Marine snickered. "Peacekeeping? Shit, it's like pissing down my back and telling me it's raining."

Laughter.

"Okay, Marines," Gunny had shouted on the dusty Beirut parking lot. "Shut your rag holes. It is what it is. We will follow the rules to the letter. If any of you screw up, your ass is grass."

Anyone with an ounce of camaraderie knew how painful the decision to leave one's platoon in the middle of combat, especially with their hands tied behind their backs for political window-dressing.

But Storm's reason for returning to Grenada burned deeper than leaving his buddies behind. News of his sister's fatal accident had come a month ago, five months into his Beirut deployment. Back-slapping embraces from his platoon cushioned his grief-soaked flights across Europe and the Atlantic to Grenada.

So why waste time arguing with this knucklehead, Reds? He would never understand. Speaking to him about Marines soiled the memory of Storm's brothers in uniform. He knew corporals who commanded more respect and exercised more discipline than Reds would ever experience, despite his bloated rank of colonel.

Three minutes into the bruising conversation and Storm already had enough of Reds for one day. "You always seem to show up when I'm busy."

Reds removed his sunglasses and glanced around the shop. "Preparing for a dive to the *Bianca C?*"

"How many times do I have to tell you, I don't dive past fifty feet with the equipment available in Grenada?" Storm gazed past crashing waves to the blue water that had entombed the six-hundred-foot iron carcass since a year before he was born. "*Bianca C* is in more than a hundred feet."

Reds chuckled, his bushy eyebrows crowning widely spaced dark eyes. "Then you're not much of a diver."

"There are lots of shallow wrecks and reefs for visitors to see. That's how I'll work my business."

"Your mother said you returned to Grenada to put your Marine Corps experience to work. I know diving is not all they taught you. How come you haven't joined our militia to teach our youth to defend the revolution against Yankee imperialism?"

"I'm a businessman now," Storm said.

"Yeah, I have a few of your business types reconsidering their career choices up in Richmond Hill Prison."

"Is this what you promised the people with your revolution?"

"Shut your mouth." Reds slammed his fist on the counter. "Your insubordination will get your ass in trouble again."

Storm bit his lip and stood the air tank on the floor behind the counter. The breeze slapped him with the fragrance of an old memory, soaked with the cologne oozing from Reds' pores. Storm still remembered the nights his mother used to escape her bed to kiss him and his sister good night. After all these years he still couldn't tell which he hated more: the scent Reds left on his mother's skin, or Reds' voice bellowing from the darkness of her room, "Woman, get back here, now."

Storm leaned toward Reds. "I'm preparing for a dive tour in an hour. If you have nothing else to say to me, I'd like to get back to work."

Reds turned to leave, and then stopped. "There are rumors a secret group may be coming to Grenada to dive the *Bianca C*. If you hear anything, it's your patriotic duty to report it to me immediately. If not, you will be arrested as an enemy of the revolution. Don't forget the penalty for that."

"How can I forget, Colonel Reds?"

***

That evening, Storm pushed open the door to his house and stepped into the dark living room. The wall clock ticked the seconds toward the 7:00 p.m.

chimes. Time felt like an empty plate to a hungry soul. The aroma of baked fish seasoned the air, but his appetite retreated at the scent of rum. He inhaled the hollow darkness, and something collapsed within him. It drained his energy and clawed at his chest with grief. He wanted to drop to his knees and howl from the pain. He wanted to punch the walls.

He wanted to kill.

The female figure remained at the window table where she always sat, silhouetted against the gray night sky with a bottle in her hand.

"No electricity again?" Storm asked.

He already knew the answer, yet he waited for his mother's slurred words. She'd carried the name Carmen until Storm's sister Rachael came along, four years before Storm. While everyone else referred to her mother as Carmen, Rachael had been told at home to say Mommy. So her two-year-old mind had merged the names.

Now Storm and everyone else called his mother Cammy.

She'd also told Storm she chose his name because she had delivered him on a stormy July night in the middle of the hurricane season. He often wondered if his birth night had set the stage for the stormy life that awaited his little family, a black-skinned unwed mother with two brown-skinned children.

Cammy had already lost her daughter. Now she numbed herself for more pain to come. She sipped from the bottle.

With electricity out, she must have felt no need to dress up and lay off the rum in case neighbors knocked at the door to buy ice. The ice cubes in her freezer would be too soft for those without refrigerators who hoped to drink cool comfort in the night's humidity. It must be a disappointment they had learned to live with, given the frequency the government pulled the plug on the city to camouflage port activity at night.

"Yeah . . . Cuban ship in," Cammy said. "No lights tonight."

He'd almost forgotten he'd asked her about the electricity. "I wonder what they —"

"Don't even think about going . . . going down there again. We already know what they bring."

She was right, and he knew it. A couple weeks ago, military curiosity had overwhelmed his common sense. Maybe he missed the nighttime reconnaissance patrols through the dusty streets of Beirut, or maybe he wanted to douse his agony with a little adrenaline. He slipped out of the house with his military issue seven-inch kabar knife— just in case. He melted into the shadows within feet of unsuspecting guards patrolling the streets. Thirty minutes later he climbed over the harbor fence and hugged the roof of a container with a bird's eye view of the pier.

Even in the dark, he had identified the twin cannons of Soviet-made ZU-23 antiaircraft guns and eight-wheeled BTR-60 armored personnel carriers rolling off the Cuban ship.

He had no interest in returning to the port tonight for a cheap thrill, or to gather military intelligence no one requested of him.

He prodded Cammy. "You like nights like this, don't you?"

"What . . . the hell you mean?"

"You know what I mean," he said. "Getting drunk in the dark, so you won't see. So you won't feel."

"Ah, shaddup."

"You're going to face the truth one day."

"You face it for me." She chuckled dryly. "I'm no superhuman . . . like you."

"He came by the dive shop with his soldiers today."

"I don't give a shit."

"You asked me this morning to tell you if he showed up."

She lifted the bottle to her mouth and a nauseating gurgle filled the silence.

"Please," he said. "Don't drink anymore tonight."

"I have a plate in...the oven for you."

Her slurs saddened him. He tossed his scuba bag on the couch, the same couch he'd jumped on as a boy. His older sister, Rachael, used to hold his hands while they jumped together, giggling and jumping until Cammy quieted them with a stern warning.

He remembered a night Cammy had again left them alone, swaying her hips in a body-tight dress and trailing the fragrance of perfume behind her. She drove off down Park Lane with yet another *gentleman*, as she called them.

Rachael sat Storm at the dinner table where they colored picture books, played cards, and read from one of Cammy's many Readers Digests left by her stepfather. When they got bored, they jumped and giggled on the couch. But he fell and the crack he heard in his wrist ballooned into pain. Rachael ran down to the rum shop at the bottom of the hill and begged a *gentleman* to drive them to the hospital.

When Storm returned to the empty house, his arm in a white cast, Rachael played Nat King Cole records to soothe his pain. Rachael, not Cammy, had wiped his tears until he'd fallen asleep that night.

No wonder the house felt so empty now. Even with Cammy seated at the window.

That made him feel worse, because he knew Rachael would not have wanted it this way. Sometimes when he cried after Cammy left for the night, Rachael would hug him and explain. "Cammy is doing everything for us."

Back then he never understood how Cammy could care about them when she spent so much time with men who rarely came home with her.

The wall clock chimed while the steeple clock on the Anglican Church echoed its musical gongs across the bay. It still amazed him how parts of her life would crumble, but she never lost sight of time. Whenever her aging wall clock fell out of step with the one on the church steeple, she would immediately get to work. She would stretch over the couch and, with gentle taps of her red fingernails on the minute hand, align her clock with the church clock clearly visible from her window.

She interrupted his thoughts. "Don't just stand there in the dark. Get your plate and come sit by your mother."

He headed into the kitchen and felt for the matchbox on the counter, next to the flour jar. The same place the matches had been kept all those years. He lit a candle and dripped melting wax into a saucer as a base to hold the candle upright.

He opened the oven and his taste buds roared back to life. A crab-stuffed snapper eyed him from a plate stacked with tomato-laced okra, yellow rice, and mixed vegetables. He used to fill himself with steak, potatoes, and salad in Marine Corps chow halls, and still walk away dissatisfied. Then he'd realized how much he missed Cammy's cooking.

"Thanks." Devouring the meals she cooked him gave her more satisfaction than his words. He pulled up a chair across from her and ate in silence.

She clutched the bottle and mumbled, sometimes to herself, sometimes to him. He couldn't tell the difference.

The puffiness around her eyes had not left since Rachael's death a month ago. But even in the candlelight her smooth forty-two-year-old face still held the warmth and youth that attracted his buddies to the picture he'd hung on his barracks wall. They couldn't believe this woman who looked young enough to be his sister was actually his mother.

If only he could do something to heal the pain in her eyes.

Later that night, he held her hand and led her to her room, knowing she would cry herself to sleep. She collapsed onto the bed. He covered her with a thin sheet and kissed her on the cheek. Turning away from her rum vapors, he headed for the bedroom door.

"Wait," she said.

"Yeah?"

"You know . . . if you weren't my son, I would ask you to kill him."

***

Early next morning, Storm sat up in bed and gazed out his window at the gray predawn light, listening to roosters crow the neighborhood awake. He'd almost forgotten their morning calls after the past few years. He had adjusted to rude awakenings by obnoxious alarm clocks, boots marching past his barracks window, and deafening helicopters in duty stations from North Carolina and Japan to Hawaii. But early-morning incoming rockets in the dusty Beirut bunkers hammered his nerves the worst. The whine and impact of 122mm rockets, especially in the weeks before his unscheduled departure, seemed to carve permanent sound tracks on his brain.

The Beirut barracks, which once served as headquarters to the Palestine Liberation Organization, had seen its days of factional fighting before the Marines arrived. The walls remained scarred from gunfire and exploding rockets. Plastic sheets replaced shattered windows and the honeycombed rooms felt more like cave dwellings. One wall down the maze from Storm's cubbyhole, splattered in red and punctured with bullet holes, looked like it had witnessed many executions. Despite the inhospitable accommodations and incoming mortars, his platoon hung a Marine Corps emblem over the entrance to the barracks with a sign saying "Beirut Hilton, Military Discounts Available."

Storm's little room in the Park Lane house sure as hell beat the Beirut Hilton he'd left behind in the 'Root', as they called the city. Located on the other side of the house from Cammy and Rachael's bedrooms, his room still had the musty smell from the ceiling soaked repeatedly by rainstorms. And the thick brown towel on the floor still served as a mat against the wooden splinters that periodically needled the soles of his feet.

Maybe the room was first designed for storage. Exposed support beams and shelves continued to hold his books from the Grenada Boys Secondary School, or GBSS as most people called his high school. His single bed and built-in closet filled the length of the room and left just enough standing room on the towel for him to change his clothes. He'd read that dogs preferred sleeping in narrow enclosures for their increased sense of security. He wondered now if the comfort he felt in foxholes, buckled into flak jacket and helmet, meant he shared the same survival instincts as a dog.

His little room had given him sanctuary during the long nights of drunken abuse Cammy endured from Reds. The nights he first started thinking some people should be dead.

The memories awakened dormant fires he kept secret in his mind. A sea breeze whispered through the trees outside his window, reminding him to whisper those secrets only in his thoughts. Another urgent chorus from neighborhood roosters blended with the sound of running tap water and banging pots to remove him even farther from the dust of Beirut.

The comforting kitchen sounds announced the start of Cammy's day, just as it had during Storm's boyhood years. He still craved the invigorating aroma of her morning *cocoa-tea*, boiled from cheap balls of local raw cocoa that had escaped the shipments to Switzerland. He'd never lost his preference for Cammy's breakfast drink, tempered with evaporated milk and sweetened with brown sugar. The taste lingered on his memory for many more mornings than imported cocoa powder, made from local surplus and returned to the island in fancy overpriced packages.

The importation of such recycled products at exorbitant prices used to trigger local anger. Revolutionary mantras decried the rape of local resources for profits, which flowed into corrupt politicians' pockets and foreign banks. Protest marches against corruption degenerated into street riots. Tear gas blowing through their windows would send Storm into a coughing fit. The growing discontent galvanized calls for revolution to uproot the entire Westminster system inherited from the British.

The armed revolution eventually came, just weeks after Storm fled the island.

He'd read how the people had flocked to the streets to celebrate the overthrow of the iron-fisted dictator. Rachael's letters shouted high praise for the revolutionary gains in school construction, medical clinics, and in literacy programs. Hundreds of students received university scholarships to thirty countries. Rachael chose to remain in Grenada, travelling around the island to teach basic reading and writing skills. She organized zonal councils where people quizzed government ministers and officials about their programs. Volunteers conducted major housing and road repair projects across the island.

For three years the Grenada revolution served the Grenada people. But over the past year it appeared the revolution had stalled.

It failed to deliver the full measure of liberation and prosperity the people expected. Rachael's letters had hinted that a rising military clique was pushing for greater engagement with global cold-war politics at the expense of the people's needs. This new preoccupation with Marxist ideology drove a wedge between the people and the government. The regime promised but never held elections. Increasingly sensitive to public criticism, they shut down newspapers and jailed editors without charges or trials. Rumors about prison torture appeared to be more than hearsay.

People began to doubt the promises of the revolution, and Storm did not have to look far for the reason. The few who dared to speak openly to Storm, like Cammy, wondered if the erosion of confidence in the revolution had anything to do with the rise in power of Colonel Reds Slinger.

But while the revolution failed to keep all its promises, Cammy never wavered in keeping hers—few they may be.

Her soft footsteps approached outside Storm's bedroom door and her steady voice carried no residue from her tortured night. "Morning. You up yet?"

"Good morning. Yeah. Just waiting to smell your cocoa-tea."

She chuckled from the other side of the door. "Give it a minute."

"It's unlocked. Come on in."

"That's okay. Breakfast will be ready after your bath."

Of course he knew she meant after his *shower*. But Grenadians didn't care about the difference. The bathroom, just outside Cammy's bedroom, still had the old rust-stained claw foot bathtub and leaky showerhead. Years ago, Cammy used to fill the tub for him to play with the coconut-shell boats Rachael made for him.

The thought of his sister ignited the burn in his chest. He pulled back the sheet, rolled out of bed, and headed across the living room to the bathroom before the tears could rain on him.

He showered and shaved with cool water, a daily reminder of one American luxury he'd left behind. He changed into a t-shirt and a pair of swim shorts, and then hurried through Cammy's bedroom toward the kitchen.

A sealed envelope on her nightstand caught his attention. He glanced at the address, but breakfast scents pulled him away.

Cammy stood at the kitchen counter buttering a slice of bread on a plate steaming with scrambled eggs, bacon, and chunks of fried breadfruit.

He hugged her from behind and kissed her moist cheeks. "Smells good. You feed me better than the Marine Corps did."

She stayed rigid, as he expected she would. She no longer bore swollen cheeks and busted lips, but her spirit remained battered after years with Reds—and since Rachael's death.

Yet, her generous breakfast plate said everything he wanted to know. Even after another night of mournful drinking, she'd rebounded to tackle her priorities for another day. She stood barefoot on the wooden floor, her shiny black hair rolled in pink curlers, and a thin flowered dress hugging her schoolgirl figure. The same figure she'd blended with her infectious laugh and raw beauty to keep their plates filled and the lights on.

No, she didn't walk the streets.

Didn't have to. They came to her, with gifts, money, and offers of marriage.

But it did not matter to nosey neighbors. Storm had overheard the nasty whispers all his life. They referred to her as a *cared-for* woman, with the same scorn they held for women who sexed drunks in alleys for dingy money.

He still remembered the hurt when a group of his classmates chimed in on Cammy's colorful lifestyle.

"I bet you don't know your father," one said.

Storm punched the kid in his mouth and the teasing stopped—just for that day.

His revenge came when the ringleader's parents split in a bitter divorce, with Cammy rumored as the cause.

Through it all, Cammy had kept her head up, especially after she finally dumped Reds. Each day she blazed a path into the hearts of established gentlemen, her perfumed laughter fading behind her, never looking back at who might snicker, or follow.

Maybe if she had looked back, she might have seen Rachael gingerly testing Cammy's footsteps to men's hearts, wallets, and deadly secrets.

But it was too late now.

"There's more if you want." Cammy joined him at the window table with her own plate of toast and eggs.

"When I left for America, I used to miss our breakfast mornings," he said.

It didn't feel the same anymore. The three of them had shared many mornings at this table. Moments sheltered from the contemptuous stares awaiting them outside. The mornings bonded them in an unspoken vow to replenish each other's endurance. They ate, laughed, and poked fun at each other. He'd captured the energy of those moments in the echoes of their laughter, and locked them into a shield around his core as he stepped out the door and into his daily arena.

"How come you're not eating?" she asked.

"Just thinking." He closed his eyes to relish a mouthful of Cammy's scrambled eggs, salted and peppered to perfection with chunks of tomato and melted cheese.

"About the accident?" she asked.

He continued to eat in silence.

"Did you hear me?"

He dropped his fork onto the plate. "That was no accident."

"Sorry." She brushed back a string of hair hanging over her eyes.

"I'm not mad at you," he said.

"Can we talk about her car instead?" Cammy's eyes, puffy from the crying he'd heard coming from her room last night, told him her heart still bled, and would for a long time.

"What about the car?" he asked.

"Did he say when you could get it back?"

Storm could not remember the last time she called Colonel Reds by name. She only referred to him as *he*. She probably thought having his name in her mouth would be as dangerous as a fish chewing on a hook. Or maybe she feared her own explosion from the disgust and anger his name would ignite.

"I didn't ask him about the car," Storm said.

How could he tell her he wasn't ready to retrieve Rachael's car from the police evidence garage? Sure, he didn't need it. He'd saved enough of his military pay to make a modest down payment on a used pickup to transport his dive shop supplies. And he doubted Cammy would keep a car in which her daughter supposedly died.

His dilemma came from his belief that Rachael's car still ran okay.

He'd heard rumors it did not sustain much damage, just a busted fender and a little river water on the floor. Cammy still believed a major crash had taken her daughter's life. If she saw the car's good condition now, the sudden flood of questions and doubts about Rachael's death might send her into a tailspin.

It would be best for Cammy to accept the truth gradually.

"They'll keep the car as long as the investigation is ongoing," he said.

"It's taking this long to investigate an accident?"

"Maybe." He searched for words to comfort her. "Let's just take it one day at a time, okay? Anything you want me to do for you today?"

"No, but thanks for offering." She sighed. "You have diving trips scheduled?"

"Just one, from the St. George's School of Medicine. A doctor and his wife from Barbados."

"*Bianca C?*"

"I always drive the boat by there and tell the story of the sinking. But no one has asked me to dive that deep."

"You will tell me if anyone does, right?"

"How many times do you have to ask me?" It was Storm who found out and told her a Trinidad company had started to salvage the *Bianca C* propellers eight years ago, even before it hit the newspapers.

"I ever ask you for anything else?" she asked.

Her question stung him. She was right. She never asked for much. As far back as he remembered. He'd been just twelve years old when she got him his first job, polishing brass fittings and scraping off barnacles on a Rum Runner excursion boat owned by one of her gentlemen friends. She never asked Storm how much he earned or what he did with his money. At the end of each workday she only asked if he'd heard any conversations about the *Bianca C*.

Rachael had explained how Cammy's obsession with the sunken ship began the day she'd made several dangerous trips on a rowboat to rescue passengers from the flames. The local people still talked about how Grenadians had embraced the passengers and sheltered them in their churches, schools, living rooms—and bedrooms.

Storm always wondered why Cammy's questions about the ship felt heavier than a light-hearted conversation about any other past event. Did she and the *Bianca C* share a memory neither could release?

He reached across the table and held her hand. "If I hear anything about *Bianca C*, you'll be the first and only person I'll tell, okay?"

She smiled, and he felt like kicking himself in the rear for being such an ass to her.

He glanced out the window past red cascading tin roofs to the early light glazing the harbor below. The same window Cammy said she'd rushed to when explosions and mayday calls dragged her out of bed to see the mortally wounded *Bianca C* in the mouth of the harbor. Today, another ship filled the port, this one with a Cuban flag waving slowly in the lazy breeze and the name *Matanzas* scribbled over its rust-scarred hull.

Judging from the change in the ship's waterline since yesterday afternoon, he knew immediately it had disgorged a heavy burden overnight.

Weapons, armored cars, tanks?

He reminded himself of his inactive military status and turned his thoughts instead to the day ahead.

"I have to stop by the post office to see if my last military check arrived yet. You want me to mail something for you?"

She hesitated. "No, I don't have anything."

He decided not to ask her about the envelope he'd seen on her nightstand, addressed in her hand writing to the Bachero Costa shipping company in Genoa, Italy.

CHAPTER TWO

Storm drove past the port on the way to his Grand Anse dive shop. The Cuban ship, *Matanzas* crowded the harbor behind barbed wire fences. Somewhere on the island, soldiers assembled and tested a new shipment of lethal weaponry under Colonel Reds' command.

But why weapons, when other basic needs suffered from neglect?

The government's experiment with Marxism had failed to deliver the glorious promises of popular revolution. Tourism dollars dwindled and, except for the expanding military, civilian unemployment rose to its highest in decades. The island's lifeline stretched tenuously around the world, via Cuba, to communist countries behind the Iron Curtain. Free powdered milk and odd-tasting cheese for the poor came in packages labeled in foreign languages. Bulgarian trucks crumbled where they had been abandoned on the sides of the road from a lack of parts. Now and then obsolete Russian transformers exploded on telephone poles from overloaded circuits.

Yet, while routine needs suffered, armored personnel carriers patrolled the streets and people trembled in their homes from the barks of deadly Soviet ZU-23 antiaircraft guns test-firing on the hillsides. Grenada had become an armed camp, but people no longer believed it benefited them. If not for the people, then for whom?

Colonel Reds Slinger?

Reds ran the army, but not the government. The Prime Minister, weakened by internal divisions and declining popularity, had one last hope: mend relations with the United States, now under the presidency of an anti-communist hawk, President Reagan. But if indeed the Prime Minister had already stretched a hand of friendship to Washington D.C., why would the Soviet Bloc countries continue to pour in weaponry under darkness?

Something seemed afoot.

Maybe Rachael had died because she enticed an insider to reveal secret plans for the island. It amazed him how she'd learned Cammy's ways so well. By age twenty-five, Rachael had known the political and bedroom secrets of the most powerful, and the most dangerous men on the island.

Storm pulled into a gas station to buy ice and soft drinks for the boat. Then, enveloped in the emptiness Rachael left behind, he parked on the gravel lot next to his dive shop and gazed out the window. Some locals strolled while others jogged at the water's edge. A light breeze blew the sea smell and the hush of soft waves through his window. A few seagulls floated over the flat sea, reminding Storm of the dive tour he'd scheduled that morning.

The dive request had come in an unusual way. Probably slipped under the dive shop door after he'd locked up two nights ago, the note awaited him on the floor when he opened yesterday morning. A torn yellow page from a legal pad, scribbled in pencil:

> *Hi,*
>
> *I am a visiting doctor at the St. George's School of Medicine, on a brief trip from Barbados. My wife and I would like to reserve a dive tour on Thursday, for just the two of us please.*
>
> *Thank you,*
>
> *Dr. Hallam Garvey.*

Most of Storm's customers since he'd opened the shop had first wanted to discuss available gear, dive sites they'd read about, and rates before agreeing to their tour.

Not this couple.

He stacked the bag of ice on the case of soft drinks and lumbered toward the dive shop. He placed the load at his feet to unlock the door. The stubborn lock, in need of another WD40 spray to fight the sea salt, finally gave way. He shouldered the door open and early sunlight lit the way in. Rubbery smells greeted him as he squeezed past scuba tanks on one side and body gear on the other. He plopped down the load against the back wall, next to the ice chest.

When he reached to open the ice chest, a shadow moved across the wall. The hair on the back of his neck bristled.

Someone had quietly followed him into the shop.

Instinctively, he swung around in a defensive stance. With fists up, he kicked away his flip-flops and spread his legs shoulder-width apart.

A big man, easily four inches above Storm's five-ten and fifty pounds heavier, filled the doorway. The morning light rushed in from behind the man. It blinded Storm, reminding him he should have switched on the lights when he walked in.

"Christ man." The man's voice bounced around the shop with the crusty almost-British accent spoken in Barbados, a thirty-minute flight away. "Didn't mean to surprise you."

"Just an old habit I have," Storm said.

"You can't be that old."

"Feels that way sometimes. Would you mind flipping the switch on your right?"

The fluorescent lights blinked on, revealing a muscular black man bursting at the seams of his red tank top.

A silver tooth glittered when his smiled. "The name is Hallam, left you a note yesterday morning."

"But of course. My apologies. Everyone calls me Storm."

Hallam's handshake vibrated up Storm's arm.

"I'm glad you didn't hit me." Hallam chuckled. "I bruise easily."

Storm laughed. "I blocked out the morning as you asked, for just you and your wife. Didn't have a phone number to call you about the rates and your choice of refreshments."

"No local phone number . . . just a brief visit on the island. Can I help you load anything?"

"I got it. I'll load the tanks. In the meantime feel free to try on fins and weight belts. And pull any drinks you and your wife might like. Is she coming?"

"She's waiting for us." Hallam pointed to a shapely woman standing at the dock. "She's got her own fins and goggles."

"Okay, I'll get going with the tanks. My boat is the white Radon 22 with the red roof."

"I know," Hallam said.

Storm grabbed two tanks and barefooted down the sandy beach to the dock.

Warning bells rang in his ears. Something— several things didn't sound right.

Maybe Storm had just become too vigilant from his years in the Marine Corps, and too distrusting after Rachael's unexplained death.

Hallam knew Storm's boat, but showed no interest in rates or dive sites. He didn't even have a local phone number, required by immigration officers. With the number of foreign visitors dwindling, Storm welcomed unscheduled customers to interrupt his strings of idle days at the shop. Yet, Hallam's approach seemed hurried and off-track.

Storm's concerns retreated as he neared the dock. Even under the wide hat and behind dark sunglasses, the woman looked familiar. Her bikini top bulged generously on her petite frame and a light blue see-through sarong hung from her narrow waistline to her ankles. When the wind blew the sarong open, he followed her exposed copper-toned leg up to her hip.

He knew for sure when excitement pounded in his chest. "Jackie? Jackie Benjamin, is that you?"

"Long time, Storm." Curly brown hair rolling under the brim of her hat had replaced the long black braids he used to twirl in his hands, but the music in her voice still stirred up memories of full moon nights and warm lips under cool waterfalls.

Memories he no longer deserved. Could he have made a different choice if he'd had the discipline back then?

He recalled his Drill Instructor in Parris Island teaching the value of discipline. "Discipline weighs ounces," he'd say every day during painful training. "Regret weighs tons. Don't let the lack of discipline crush your ass with the weight of regrets."

Storm's regrets burdened his mood. "Too long," he said to Jackie, wishing he'd chosen less obvious words to let her know he missed her.

She stretched out a well-defined arm to shake his hand. "Four years?"

He stood one of the scuba tanks against his leg and shook her hand in a warm hold. "Still working out, I see."

"You have to."

"Sorry it turned out the way it did."

"We were young and idealistic," she said.

He doubted she understood how little idealism motivated him to do what he'd done. "How's your father?"

Her jaw tightened. "He recovered from his injuries…listen, we don't have time today for this."

Had she returned with Hallam to seek well-deserved vengeance on Storm?

"I just met your husband," Storm said. "Congratulations . . . I didn't know you were married."

"I'm not," Jackie whispered. "But act as if I am. Pretend you and I just met for the first time. Don't ask why."

Storm pushed the Radon 22 throttle off Grand Anse Beach, wishing Jackie were in the cozy pilothouse with him instead of seated at the rear with Hallam's arms wrapped around her like they were in honeymoon bliss.

Storm hadn't expected his return to Grenada to be uneventful, but running into her in such a weird coincidence was more than he wanted. He had received a compassionate discharge from the Marines to support his grieving mother after Rachael's death, with only a few months left to the end of his enlistment. He busied himself after the funeral tending to Rachael's affairs, comforting Cammy, and shopping for a boat to start his dive business. He'd always wanted a Boston Whaler 18, like his platoon used for night operations, with twin Johnson 115s for speed and cushioned seats for his divers. Now, with less money in the bank than he intended, he prepared to scale down his plans.

But Cammy thought otherwise.

He should have known his mother's grieving meltdowns would hardly dent her resolve to stand by her children, especially now she had just Storm left. When one of her businessmen friends, Kester, stopped by the house to extend his condolences, he casually mentioned he had a pickup truck with attached trailer and boat for sale. Storm recalled rumors claiming Kester, a white Grenadian who ran the Cable and Wireless Company, might be one of several men speculated to be Storm's father. Storm's one conversation with Cammy about his father's identity ended with her saying he didn't need a father if he had her for a mother. Almost in agreement with her, he never asked her about his father again. He didn't want her to think she was not a good enough mother.

Kester drove Storm to a luxury home with swimming pool and tennis court in upscale Lance Aux Epines. A three year-old white five-speed Toyota pickup waited in the driveway. A trailer hitched to the pickup held a white Radon 22 with a red roof over the pilothouse.

"Had the boat for five years," Kester said. "But too busy to take her out. Less than a hundred hours on the water. Great for diving. Stable in any condition. Comes with a removable ladder to help your divers climb onboard with all their gear. Name your price."

Storm restrained his excitement. He'd gone deep-sea fishing on a Radon 22 with his buddies off Morehead City, and loved the ride. The bow rode higher than the Boston Whaler, helping to smooth the rocky ride outside the North Carolina Outer Banks.

He knew Kester would accept even a cut-rate price. Instead, Storm offered a fair price to erase any suggestion he expected a discount for the man's relationship with Cammy.

Kester accepted the offer and they nailed down the payment plan over a couple of ice-cold Carib beers.

"You'll like it," Kester had said. "Especially the pilothouse. Nice and cozy in there."

Nothing about the pilothouse felt cozy when Storm raced the Radon 22 out of sunny Grand Anse Bay with Jackie and Hallam in each other's arms. Her purse, squeezed in next to the cooler under the console, looked similar to one her parents had bought for her birthday five years earlier. It only reminded Storm of guilt-laden regrets for what he'd done to her father.

But if she still held it against him, why would she wink at him and squeeze his hand when he helped her aboard? And why the enticing perfume before a dive?

Something seemed amiss.

She gave no indication Hallam had her on the boat against her will. And if they'd run away to Grenada for a quick illicit affair, why ask Storm to take them on a tour? Maybe this was her idea of a payback. If she planned to stab Storm with jealousy, it was working.

The thought pissed him off. "Hold on." He gunned the outboards.

The increased speed only made matters worse. Hallam held Jackie tighter and hollered as if he were a cowboy on a rodeo horse, with his silver tooth glittering in the sunlight and his feet plopped up on the cover of the fish hold.

Hallam and Jackie had no preferred dive spots in mind, and didn't even seem to care, so Storm drove them on a surface tour of his favorite spots off Grand Anse and Point Salines. About twenty prime dive attractions populated the sea within a five-mile radius. A few natural coral reefs had exotic names like *Purple Rain* and *Japanese Gardens*, while several shipwrecks had names like *Veronica L* and *Bianca C*.

He steered the wheel toward *Bianca C*. They would be unable to see the ship a hundred feet below, but for the time Storm commanded their attention, Hallam might keep his hands off Jackie.

Estimating his location by glancing back at the island's green hillsides, Storm shifted the motors into an idle putter and stepped over Jackie's dive bag on the way out of the pilothouse.

"We're above the *Bianca C*," he said.

"Have you gone down there?" she asked.

Storm looked away from her inviting smile and dimpled cheeks. "Just down to fifty feet, once. But I don't have equipment to hold up under the compression beyond that."

He launched into the ship's history he'd memorized during the tours he worked as a teenager. The ship, six hundred feet long, had been completed in 1944 on the south coast of France, but sunk by retreating Germans the same year. Raised again in 1946, new owners refitted it for a maiden voyage to Japan.

"In 1959, an Italian family firm named G. Costa du Genoa purchased the ship and named it *Bianca C* after the owner's daughter," Storm said. "When an explosion set the ship on fire in October 1961, one crew member died from the blast and two others died later from burns. Grenadians, including my mother, rescued more than six hundred passengers in mainly rowboats and sailboats."

"Does your mother still talk about it?" Jackie asked.

Jackie didn't have to ask the question. He'd told her the story many times when they were teens. Even before he'd learned to walk, Cammy recounted repeatedly how the ship's urgent horns had awakened her in early morning. She'd raced down to the waterfront barefoot and in her nighty. She made three trips that day, rescuing about a dozen people in the rowboat her stepfather left her to earn extra money taxiing people across the harbor.

"Yes, she talked about it even last night," he said. "The *Bianca C* continued to burn until a British frigate, the *Londonderry*, arrived from Puerto Rico two days later. They cut the anchor chain and pulled the ship away from the channel, but it was slow work because the huge rudders had frozen from the fires. The towline broke and the ship drifted until she sank right here below us. This is where the *Bianca C* has rested for the last twenty-two years."

Despite Storm's efforts to entertain his guests with shipwreck history, Jackie and Hallam seemed strangely distracted. She gazed over her shoulder at the island, while Hallam glanced at his watch and stared at the southwest horizon.

Storm's misgivings kicked in again and remained on high alert.

She lowered her voice in the tone that used to tighten his jeans. "Do you have music?"

"What would you like to hear?"

"Anything. Make it loud."

Storm backed into the pilothouse. He fingered through his cassettes on the console and pulled his favorite Bob Marley, with songs they used to dance to. He popped it into the built-in player and cranked up the volume.

I wanna love you, and treat you right

I wanna love you, every day and every night

Shit. Now she'd think Storm queued up the song just for her. He let it play.

We'll be together, with a roof right over our heads

We'll share the shelter, of my single bed

When he glanced back, Jackie seemed more interested in words other than Bob Marley's. She removed a sheet of paper from her purse. Hallam whispered in her ear and she began to scribble at a frantic pace.

Storm's suspicions revived. He glanced out his port window at a cargo ship rounding the point toward them.

Jackie rose from the bench and squeezed into the pilothouse, bobbing to the reggae rhythms.

"I like that song," she shouted over the loud music. "May I have a Coke?"

He gazed into her eyes for some sign of her intentions. "Just one?"

She glanced away. "Yes, thanks."

He stooped over the cooler, inches away from the smooth firm legs that used to pleasure his hands and lips.

She took the can from his outstretched hand and nonchalantly handed him the paper at the same time, pointing for him to read it. She turned and casually returned to Hallam's embrace.

Aware of the ship trudging in their direction, Storm unfolded the paper on the cooler.

> *Storm,*
>
> *Please do everything we ask. Act natural and say nothing. We're being watched from shore and your cabin might be bugged. When the ship comes by, take your boat to the ocean side and keep up with it so no one can see us from shore.*
>
> *So sorry to hear about Rachael.*
>
> *I never stopped missing you. It's okay, Hallam knows about us.*
>
> *Love,*
>
> *Jackie.*
>
> *P.S. After you read this, soak it in the cooler. The ink will fade.*

With little time left to think, he chose to trust Jackie. As the cargo ship closed in on them, he followed the instructions to trash the note. He engaged the throttle and sped the boat in a wide turn away from the ship's path. Then he pulled a steep right across the stern and over the waves cut by the huge ship flying a Soviet flag. He turned the Radon 22 right and pulled into the cargo ship's shadow, away from the sunrise and peering eyes on the island.

He glanced back just as Hallam filled the doorway behind him.

This time, Hallam was not smiling. He lifted his index finger to his lips and then signaled with both fists for Storm to keep his hands on the wheel.

Storm's instincts had been correct all along. Hallam and Jackie held plans other than scuba diving. But whatever they intended, Storm appeared not to be the target. He maneuvered the boat to keep abreast of the ship at twenty knots, flashing cautious glances behind him.

Hallam pulled out the black bag, unzipped it, and passed Jackie a hand-sized box with headphones attached. She adjusted dials on the front plate, extended a foot long antenna, and handed the set back to him.

Storm had seen similar gadgets demonstrated in an urban warfare class he'd taken in the Marines. But those were used to detect radio signals from remote controlled explosives. Was his Radon 22 booby-trapped, or bugged? He'd always suspected foul play in Rachael's death, so he reasoned he might also be on someone's list.

But why?

Jackie gave him a reassuring smile and he relaxed a notch.

Hallam adjusted the headphones over his ears and began slow sweeps around the cabin with the detector. He squeezed next to Storm and waved the detector above the dashboard, which housed the built-in cassette player. Hallam adjusted the dials on his detector and then signaled to Jackie. She handed him a Phillips screwdriver. Balanced on his knees as the boat screamed forward, he removed the screws holding the dashboard plate around the cassette player.

He flicked on a small flashlight and scanned the dashboard cavity. Holding the flashlight in place, he signaled to Storm and pointed at a silver button linked to an exposed wire and taped to the inside panel.

Then Storm read the label on Hallam's handheld box: TL-2000 Bug Detector.

Goddammit. Someone had bugged his frigging boat.

But why did Hallam and Jackie suspect this? And why did they take a risky trip to the troubled island to alert Storm?

Hallam replaced the dashboard plate without disturbing the bug, and continued the sweep around the rest of the boat with Jackie. They had accompanied the cargo ship to within view of the St. George's harbor when Hallam finally gave the okay that no other bugs infected the boat.

In case anyone watched from shore, Storm wheeled his boat slightly northwest away from the ship's path and pointed the bow to another popular dive spot called the *Valleys*. One of Storm's favorites, the five-mile reef interconnected an underwater series of sandy valleys. Even though the Radon 22 had disappeared behind the cargo ship for a few minutes, it might appear they were all along heading for a dive with snowflake eels and angelfish in the *Valleys*.

Storm stalled the boat and dropped anchor on a sandy bank along the *Valleys*. He popped in another cassette at high volume.

"Would one of you tell me what the hell's going on?" he asked when he joined Jackie and Hallam at the rear of the boat.

Hallam glanced over his shoulder toward island. "Go through the safety rituals you give before your dives. Just act normal, and I'll explain."

For the benefit of any peering eyes on shore, Storm conducted an animated demonstration of buoyancy control, tank handling, and mask clearing, while Hallam explained their suspicious behavior.

"We're on a joint operation by the U.S. embassy and the Barbados police. Top secret. I am an undercover officer with the Barbados police. My name is Hallam Garvey. If anyone asks, Jackie is Mavis Garvey, my wife. But we're not married. Everything you see is pretend."

Storm restrained his relief.

Jackie smiled knowingly at him. "Hallam and I just met a few days ago at a meeting in the U.S. embassy. They arranged the cover with the medical school, along with passports showing us as a married couple. And if anyone doubts I'm from Barbados, I can fake a Bajan accent too."

"But why you?" Storm asked her.

"They believe you'll trust me before you trust a stranger."

It bothered Storm people he hadn't met knew about him and Jackie. And they were right. Storm trusted her. But he doubted she trusted him anymore, especially after what he'd done to her father.

Storm still remembered the ball of fire, the heat on the handle of the car door, and the acrid scent of burnt clothes and flesh.

"He's healed now," she said as if she'd read his last thought. "Just a couple burn scars on his back and neck. He walks with a limp."

He shut his eyes for a moment and swallowed hard against the punishment rising in his chest. "I hear he's in Richmond Hill Prison."

"Yes, since the first day of the revolution. No trial. No visitors. No doctors. And he has diabetes."

"Your mom?"

"In Miami," she said. "I'm doing this for both of them."

"I'm sorry . . . for everything." He hoped she understood how deep his regrets clawed at him.

"I know, but let's forget the past for now. We have to be cautious. If Reds finds out who I am, I'll be in Richmond Hill Prison too."

Storm lifted a buoyancy vest and tugged at the straps. "Don't you think Reds will recognize you if he sees you?"

"This is my first time back in four years. Maybe I've changed."

"You're a woman now, gorgeous. I still recognized you."

She blushed. "That's different. My hair has changed, and I've never come face to face with him."

"You'll still have to be careful."

She looked over her shoulder at the hilltop Richmond Hill Prison. "I just want my father out of there."

Storm had always promised himself if ever the occasion arose for him to take back that night, he would. If Jackie and Hallam had travelled from Barbados to recruit him for a prison break, then maybe this was his opportunity to repay the debt gnawing his insides.

The last four years collapsed into a moment of decision. While he'd escaped Grenada, she'd faced the fiery tempers of a revolution he helped ignite. She'd become more of a woman than he'd expected. Determination chiseled her jaws and firmed her lips, but the brown-sugar appeal in her eyes still sweetened his desire for her.

If he turned his back on her again, the burden he'd carry the rest of his life would feel heavier than any sea bag he'd lugged in the Marines.

"What can I do?" he asked.

Hallam pretended to examine a weight belt. "We need you to come to Barbados in the next couple days. It's too dangerous to talk here in Grenada. If asked by the authorities, tell them you still have discharge papers to sign and a final military check to collect from the U.S. embassy."

"I've been expecting it in the mail." Storm pulled on a buoyancy vest and snapped the buckles. "Why didn't you just mail me a letter asking me to come to Barbados?"

"We mailed two letters."

"Never got them. Been checking the post office."

Hallam nodded. "When you didn't write or call, we figured they'd intercepted your mail. It's the reason Jackie and I flew over to see you."

"What kind of operation are we talking about?" Storm handed Jackie the buoyancy vest and reached for his snorkel gear.

Hallam looked at Jackie.

She pulled off her hat and sunglasses as a gust blew by. "You'll have to come to Barbados to find out. All I can say is this is bigger than you or me."

The plea in her eyes and voice reached into him, and torment from his sleepless North Carolina nights seeped out. "Why didn't you write back—"

"Oh, Stormy."

Only Jackie ever called him that, and a part of him craved to hear it again.

"Okay you two." Hallam doused the rising emotions. "You'll have enough time in Barbados to patch things up. For now, I just need your word as a Grenadian and a Marine, to meet us in Barbados in two days. Once you hear the plan, the decision to join us is up to you."

Storm glanced at Jackie. "You can count on me." He lifted a weight belt as he usually did to explain negative buoyancy.

Hallam laid out a set of cautionary steps for Storm. No confidential discussions in the dive shop or at home. No phone calls or letters to Jackie from Grenada. Always be at home before sunset, especially when Cuban and Soviet Bloc ships entered port. And never leave the house before sunrise.

A sea gull squawked overhead and small waves clapped against the boat.

"We have a deal," Storm said. "Now let's do some scuba diving in case anyone is watching from shore."

Hallam chuckled. "We don't know how to scuba dive."

Later, after Storm conducted an hour-long impromptu scuba diving class with Jackie and Hallam, he led them on several shallow dives, one diver at a time so as not to over-tax his rescue skills.

On the last dive with Jackie, Storm held her hand and guided her down twenty feet to the rainbow-colored reefs. He showed her how to relax and blow tiny bubbles with the regulator out of her mouth. And then for the first time in four years, surrounded by curious angelfish in turquoise water, they kissed.

Three hours later, Storm cranked the motors and headed back to shore. The memory of Jackie's kiss lingered—until the Radon 22 pulled up to an unfriendly welcome on the dock.

Reds stood with a squad of armed soldiers in combat greens. "Very long tour, Comrade."

Storm jumped onto the jetty. "In case you're wondering, we didn't dive the *Bianca C*."

"Offload your cooler and bags. I need to inspect your boat and your passengers' passports."

That's when Storm remembered the TL-2000 Bug Detector in the black bag.

The soldiers watched Storm and Hallam lift off the cooler. Jackie followed with the black dive bag and her purse. Storm hoped Jackie's wide-brimmed hat and dark sunglasses shielded her face from Reds' eyes. If Reds recognized her, he would surely conclude her passport was a fake. But worse, the electronic detector in the black bag would immediately raise the alarm. Storm thought of tossing the bag into the sea, but even a blind diver could find it in ten feet of the clear blue water.

The soldiers stacked the cooler, bag, and purse on one side of the jetty, then shuffled Storm and his passengers at rifle point to the other side.

Reds ordered three soldiers aboard the Radon 22. One of them opened and shut the squeaky cover to the empty fish hold. Another entered the pilothouse with a screwdriver, probably to ensure the bug had not been disarmed. Four others stood guard on the jetty, their AK-47s chest high and index fingers on the triggers.

Reds marched up to Storm. "Where are their passports?"

"Colonel Reds, I have never been instructed to check the documents of my diving parties. But I would guess they're from Barbados, judging from their Bajan accents. That's if you want my opinion about—"

He stomped his boots and barked. "I don't want your damned opinion. Show me some documents or else all three of you going to jail."

"Colonel, sir," Jackie stepped up to Reds and a crisp Bajan accent crackled. "Our passports are in my purse over there if you will allow me to retrieve them."

Reds stared at her. "Have I met you before?"

She pulled off her hat, and curly brown hair bounced on her head.

Shit. What was she doing? Even if Reds did not remember her, he might recognize the family resemblance. But then again prison life would have erased the picture of health father and daughter once shared.

Storm braced for trouble.

"I don't think we've ever met," she said to Reds. "My last time in Grenada was ten years ago when I had chicken pox and my daddy brought me here to recover, so my Bridgetown friends at the Codrington school wouldn't laugh at me. It was the most awful thing. The itching and the scabs were —"

"Enough." Reds snapped, his bushy eyebrows twitching. "Go get your passports."

Jackie strutted across the jetty and returned with her purse. Reds yanked it from her hand.

"Hey," she protested. "That's no way to handle a lady's purse."

Storm smiled inside. Jackie's spunk reminded him of the day they'd first met. She had told him he should either cut his wild hair, or have it braided.

Reds stuffed his hand into the purse, rummaging through its contents. He pulled out a small pill bottle. "What's this?"

Jackie glared at Hallam. "My husband snores at night. It's the only way I can sleep."

Reds replaced the bottle and pulled out the passports. His shifted his stare under raised eyebrows between Jackie, Hallam, and the passports. A minute ticked by. The only sound came from waves slapping the jetty and wind whispering through the passport pages.

Finally, Reds tossed the passports into the purse and handed it back to Jackie.

He turned to one of his soldiers. "Lieutenant, bring me the black bag."

Storm counted the seconds, thinking of a way out. The bug detector would surely mean jail for the three of them. But was there something he could do? Too many trigger-nervous soldiers stood around. Reds would be happy for the excuse to see Storm floating in blood.

The lieutenant plopped the bag next to Reds' boots.

Reds unzipped the bag and frowned.

CHAPTER THREE

Cammy hurried across Tyrrel Street in the afternoon heat and down the piss-scented alleyway to the waterfront road. The flip-flops slapped at her soles and a sea breeze blew the thin dress against her damp skin. She needed to buy a few figs and corn flour to complete the fish broth with dumplings she planned for Storm. Since he had just one dive tour today, she expected him home early. She'd expected Rachael to return home too. Watching Storm leave the house this morning reminded her of the night Rachael walked out the door for the last time.

Cammy wondered if a mother ever recovered from the loss of a child.

Storm had quickly stepped into Rachael's role since his arrival from Beirut, helping Cammy at every turn. On his way out the door this morning, he'd asked Cammy if she wanted him to mail anything for her. Had he seen the letter on her night stand? With dismay, she now remembered the letter remained in the same spot. It would certainly raise his suspicions if he returned home to see it still lying there. She picked up her pace, with shoppers and blaring cars congesting the outer boundaries of her thoughts.

She used to be craftier about protecting her children from humiliating secrets. Maybe she'd been too busy shielding Rachael and Storm to recognize that the dangers came not from the lies she hid, but from the life she lived.

Guilt sharpened her grief and she embraced an aching reminder. She would rather die than let Storm meet an early end like his sister.

A voice interrupted her from behind. "Miss Cammy?"

Cammy turned.

A girl about Rachael's age pulled abreast. "Just keep walking. I been meaning to talk to you, but I don't want nobody see me come to your house. I know—"

Two armed soldiers in green uniforms marched past.

"I went to school with Rachael," the girl said.

"Yes, I remember. Pauline, right?"

"Yes." Pauline brushed up next to Cammy and lowered her voice. "My brother was there."

"There where?"

"He said the government is lying about Rachael's car—"

Another soldier marched toward them, but seemed more interested in sweeping a lust-filled gaze over Cammy and Pauline.

Pauline continued. "I need to talk to you in private."

"Come by after dark," Cammy said. "Take the trail behind Marryshow House. Bring a plastic bag and small change. If you get stopped tell them you were coming to buy ice from me."

"Okay." Just as quickly, Pauline disappeared into the pedestrian traffic.

Back at home Cammy slipped the envelope beneath her underwear in the dresser drawer, wondering why Storm had not yet returned. Maybe he'd gotten last-minute customers. Since she did not have a phone, he couldn't call her. She missed the days when her life felt more certain. Now even the circumstances around Rachael's death seemed in doubt.

Like Cammy did each time she'd opened the drawer after the funeral, she walked her fingertips over the folded white shirt and striped tie Rachael had worn during her years at the Anglican High School. Pride rose in Cammy's chest, but by the time it warmed her cheeks with fond memories, the tears began.

She shut the drawer and retreated into the kitchen, recalling the day three-year-old Rachael had welcomed a screaming Italian girl of the same age into the house. While the *Bianca C* burned outside the harbor, within view from the window, Rachael hugged little Bianca like a sister, and patted her head when she cried for her Papa. Why had her Papa given his daughter and a valuable ring to a stranger, and then returned to the burning ship?

The handsome Papa did come for his princess that day. Neighbors led him barefoot, bare-chested, and dripping wet to Cammy's house. Black hair as lush as the Grand Étang forest covered his head and chest.

"Mario." He spelled out his name in broken English, and thanked her in strings of words peppered with *grazi*.

"Where's your wife?" Cammy asked, afraid she might still be on the smoldering ship.

"Italy . . . I believe."

She knew then not to ask any more about his wife, or about the reason he'd returned to the ship. When Cammy attempted to hand him back the ring, he asked her to hold on to it until the time for him to leave the island.

In the meantime, she opened her house, and her fluttering heart, to Mario and Bianca.

Cammy led him to the bathtub, apologizing about the half bar of soap and thin towel she handed him. She also found him a pair of pants and a jersey Reds left when he flew to Antigua for his three-week police training camp.

"*Telefono?*" Mario asked after showering and changing.

Again, she apologized and took him on a short walk past the chaos of sirens and shouts, to the Cable and Wireless building on Carenage Road. A crowd of rescued passengers filled the street in front of the doorway, yelling for a turn to use a *telefono*.

When Mario pushed his way into the melee, Cammy hesitated. He held her hand and guided her into the building like he was leading her onto a dance floor. And like a perfect dance partner, she didn't need words to tell her what to do next.

"Kester." Cammy raised her voice toward a face she recognized behind the counter. A faced she'd kissed before.

Kester didn't have to search long to find Cammy waving at him from the sea of Italian faces.

He called her over. "This is madness."

She pointed at Mario. "He needs to make a call to Italy now."

"So does everyone else," Kester said. "But they all left their money on board. Who's supposed to pay for these calls?"

She glanced at Mario. "He will."

Three hours later, Mario finally slammed down the black phone in a private office Kester had secured at Cammy's insistence. Mario had asked her to place calls when English was required, to Genoa, New York, and London. She gathered from the calls that Mario was the owner of the *Bianca C*. The phone shook in her hand, her nerves overwhelmed by the realization that an island girl's voice carried news to the world of a blazing cruise ship: one crew member dead in the initial blast, two in the hospital, and all remaining 671 passengers and crew rescued in local boats by the Grenada people.

All survivors resting comfortably in homes, churches, and schools—while the *Bianca C* blazed.

On the way home, she fought back the dizziness from the sheer excitement. He must have sensed her waning energy. He held her hand again as they walked up to her front door.

Her house became a command center that afternoon, as crew members stopped by with updates for Mario about the ship's condition. One in particular, a balding man in smudged uniform, held loud arguments with Mario in the front yard.

Cammy wished she understood the Italian language. And wished he understood more English.

She made repeated trips to the shop down the street, to purchase on credit soft drinks and ice for the nonstop flow of visitors paying homage to Mario. As it grew dark, she started a chicken dinner with rice and peas, slices of tomato and chunks of fried breadfruit.

Later, she left Mario and the girls in the living room while she caught her breath and took a shower. To her dismay, she realized she'd not gotten to her Sunday laundry. The towel Mario used was the only one hanging in the bathroom. She dried unhurriedly, and hugged the damp towel around her—longer than if Reds had used it first.

Into the night, Mario sat at the window and gazed out at his flaming ship.

Cammy's compassion remained the last thing she could give him.

During the night, as their daughters slept in another room, raw lust ignited between Mario and Cammy. In a language that needed no translation, their bodies and souls exchanged pleasure she'd never known.

But by sunrise, he was gone again, leaving only the echoes of Italian whispers in her ears.

Cammy asked a neighbor to watch the sleeping girls and raced down to the harbor in search of Mario.

Sirens wailed.

She dashed down to the pier. Men in white lifted a stretcher into the ambulance. She recognized Reds' pants and jersey on the man lying in the stretcher, but not the cooked flesh covering half his face. The same face that sought comfort in her bosom the previous night.

An hour later at home, she hurried to answer knocks at the door. A stocky man in uniform identified himself as *Capitàno* Francisco Crevaco. He stuffed a stack of money in her hands, and ran off with Bianca bundled in a blanket.

Rachael cried for her new friend.

Cammy cried too, for the bliss she'd never felt before and never would again. Now, all these years later, she never forgot the emotions she felt the day the *Bianca C* still burned offshore.

Maybe it was the reason she hadn't mailed the letter yet. She didn't want to spoil the memories.

A tap at the door in the fading light reminded her Storm had been gone much longer than she'd expected. If this was he, why didn't he just open the door? Maybe it was a neighbor coming to buy ice, or Pauline stopping by with news of Rachael's accident.

Cammy quickened her steps to the door and pulled it open.

The sight at the doorstep revived visions of burnt flesh. Feelings of loss clogged her awareness. Then, as blackness closed in, the floor rushed up to her.

CHAPTER FOUR

Storm listened to Reds' warnings, still confused about how the TL-2000 Bug Detector had disappeared from Hallam's black bag and the boat before Reds could find it.

"You're free to go, but I'll be watching every move you make," Reds said. "Just don't let me catch you out at night. I will not let traitors like you betray the people's revolution."

"Colonel," Storm said. "I don't see how you help the people by detaining our Bajan visitors here in the sun for three hours while you ransack my boat. This will only scare away people who want to dive our sites and spend their money—"

"Enough! You three better be packed and gone before dark."

Reds turned and marched off the jetty with his squad of soldiers trailing behind him.

Storm waited until the sedan and jeep disappeared toward the main road, and then he turned to Hallam and Jackie. "That was close. But where the hell did you hide the detector?"

"In about a hundred feet of water," Hallam said. "Sorry bloke, but you might be short of a couple weights too, to keep it down."

Storm chuckled, and gazed out at the fading sun. "It's been a long day. You two better be on your way. Need a ride to the hotel?"

"We have a rental car," Hallam said.

Jackie removed her sun glasses. "Actually, I need a drink, but I can wait till you come to Barbados. Our flight is first thing in the morning, so we have to get packed."

"I'll see you in a couple days," Storm said.

"We have a lot of catching up to do." She shook his hand.

Storm watched them drive off, and determined to be home before dark, he set to work. He rinsed off his tanks and scuba gear, washed down the boat, and stacked away his cooler in the dive shop. After a few sprays of WD-40 on the fish-hold hinges and his door lock, he sped home.

In the early darkness, a taxi parked in Storm's usual spot on the narrow street next to the house. He pulled over on Tyrrel Street, just down the hill.

A cigarette glow lit the taxi-driver's face as Storm climbed past.

But as soon as he entered the yard, he knew something was wrong.

The front door stood wide open. Just inside the darkened doorway, a man was kneeling over Cammy with his hands on her.

***

The embassy guard pushed open the gate for Reds' black sedan. The driver accelerated the car up the palm tree-lined driveway and stopped in front of the Point Salines hilltop mansion. A curvaceous young woman in heels and light buttoned-down suit leaned over and opened Reds' door. He stepped onto the brick driveway in the haze of the dying sunset. A steady breeze greeted him with claps from the Cuban flag overhead, horizontal bars of blue and white flanked by a red triangle with a five-pointed star.

"This way, sir." She led Reds across the lobby under chandeliered ceilings and through bands of sunset-red light streaking through bamboo blinds. "Colonel Bravo is waiting."

Reds' boots pounded the tiled floor, reminding him why he always felt robust in military uniform. Uniforms exuded power over circumstances—power to transcend the humiliating poverty that so crushed him as a boy, power over people, and soon, power over his own country.

The girl stepped aside at a doorway and pointed Reds toward a balcony overlooking a quiet bay. A motor boat flying the Cuban flag rocked gently alongside a jetty below.

A mustachioed barrel-chested man filled a chair against the handrail. "*Siente te, por favor*," the Cuban colonel said.

Reds resented that except for the *por favor*, Colonel Bravo's invitation to sit sounded more like an order.

Reds pulled up a chair across from the heavyset officer and accepted a cigar from his hairy, outstretched hand.

"What did you find on the boat?" Colonel Bravo asked.

Reds put a lit match to the tip of the cigar and sucked a few hard puffs. "Nothing."

"You must be smarter than the American mercenary."

Reds' temper simmered. He blew out cigar smoke and watched it vanish in the steady wind. "Just what is your point, Colonel?"

"If you're in his face every day, he'll have nothing for you. You have to watch from a distance. Give him rope to run."

"As soon as you get me reliable information I can sink my teeth—"

"Here's reliable information. He's more dangerous than his sister." Colonel Bravo said. "And you know fully well the problems she almost caused us."

Reds didn't want to revisit that night, so he shifted the conversation. "The electronic bug on the boat is still in place, undisturbed, and we've picked up nothing. Nothing from those in the house either. I have more important security concerns than chasing rumors about the *Bianca C*."

"When our Moscow comrades tell us they've picked up voice traffic about *Bianca C* between Rome, New York, and Barbados, it's no rumor."

"I am more concerned about security at the new airport than a ship buried in the ocean."

The table groaned under Colonel Bravo's elbows. "Airport construction and security is our concern, not yours. You won't see a MIG fighter-jet land here until *I* give Havana and Moscow the green light."

Reds knew better than to dismiss Colonel Bravo's words. The Cuban's reputation had taken on heroic notoriety when he led Operation Carlota in the 1975 Angola offensive against South African and Zairian forces. His rapid-fire successes at driving foreign forces out of Angola convinced a pleasantly surprised Soviet leadership Bravo was their man. They immediately opened the floodgates and airlifted heavy weaponry into the country, including the feared MIG fighters.

Radical revolution in the Caribbean also needed Soviet firepower. Were it not for the commitment of Soviet military hardware in Cuba, Castro's revolution would have been on the ash heap of history in a few short years.

The Soviets also understood Grenada now sat at the same crossroads. Just weeks ago in a Moscow meeting, Soviet Foreign Minister Gromyko had told Reds that between 1974 and 1980, ten countries had moved into the Soviet camp. While the United States was still reeling from its Vietnam debacle, Latin America was ripening for revolution. The Soviet Chief of Staff, Marshal Ogarkov, followed up saying that for two decades Cuba was the only Marxist government in the region. Now there were Nicaragua, Grenada, and a serious battle was underway in El Salvador.

In keeping with the Brezhnev doctrine, once a country became communist, there was no going back. As part of the Latin American strategy to counter U.S. global power, the Soviets needed Reds as much as he needed them. The completion of the new airport at Point Salines was as important to Soviet policy, as it was to Reds' political ambitions. The Soviets valued Grenada's strategic location, within MIG range of Venezuelan oil fields and vital shipping arteries like the Panama Canal. The island, a thousand miles southeast of Cuba, could open the gates for Soviet influence to the entire South American continent, now festering on the verge of revolution.

Grenada held the key. As Castro once said, Grenada's was a big revolution in a small country.

And this was Reds' revolution. "Moscow is fully aware this island is my responsibility," he said.

Colonel Bravo squinted from behind his cigar smoke. "I don't think I should remind you, Comrade. You're not the Prime Minister yet."

Reds leaped to his feet and clicked his heels. "This meeting is over, Comrade Bravo."

Bravo chomped on his cigar. "Just remember *Bianca C*. But keep your distance and contact me before you take any action."

***

Jackie locked the bathroom door of the hotel suite she shared with Hallam, glad to be alone with the hurricane of thoughts roaring through her mind. Her instincts and experience with men forced her to distrust them. Storm was no exception. She recalled her anguish when the family gardener stole her piggybank from her bedroom, leaving a trail of muddy boot steps behind him. And how could she forget when her dad cheated on her mother with a young maid?

But against the black sky of disappointment in men, a few stars shone with hope. When Jackie's mother packed to leave, Daddy begged her to stay. He quit his drinking ways and philandering pastimes. His promotions in the Ministry of Finance led to an invitation from the Prime Minister to run for office in the political elections. He did, and won. Jackie felt confident Daddy's victory came on his own merit, but widespread accusations of election fraud stained the party's landslide, and dulled Jackie's hope to rebuild trust in her father.

Soon after the elections, the island began to slide toward popular uprising, carrying Storm on the crest. She remembered his speech to a gathering on her high school grounds when he encouraged students to join a strike to protest government corruption. His passion electrified her teenage imagination to the point where she forgot she benefited from the very government Storm condemned.

Their chemistry blended from the start.

All through the strikes and riots, they made time to steal kisses in the movie theaters, swim at night on Grand Anse Beach, and dive at Annandale Falls.

Her parents tolerated Storm's youthful idealism and allowed him in the driveway, but never invited him into the house. Storm would lean against Daddy's car and hold her under full moon nights. His chest vibrated with predictions about the historic inevitability of revolution, a revolution to cure all social and economic ills. Those nights ended when her mother would call for her to go to bed.

Then one night Daddy's car exploded, just after he'd left the house to buy cigarettes. The firemen found him burned and unconscious on the side of the road, a safe distance from the blazing car.

Forensics proved he had been dragged to safety, but no one came forward to admit saving him. A Scotland Yard investigation discovered the bomb was devised with demolition techniques taught at a police academy in Antigua. They arrested a former police sergeant turned revolutionary agitator, Reds Slinger, and questioned him under circumstances he described to reporters as torture.

He confessed to building the bomb, but denied planting it. A student recruit planted the bomb, he claimed.

A student rebel named Storm Butler.

When Jackie heard the report on the radio, she felt like her heart had been torn out of her chest and stomped on, yet again. She locked herself in her room, feeling numb to everything except when tears flowed down her cheeks.

But by then, Storm's mother had called up a few favors to fast track his application for an American visa, and a one-way boat ticket away from the island. Jackie later received a brief letter he wrote her during his basic training at Parris Island in South Carolina. He poured out dismay for what happened to Daddy, but revealed nothing about the bomb or about Reds' role in it.

She couldn't force her fingers to write him back. It was the last they communicated, until today.

Jackie should have expected the way their steamy relationship ended. He was too close to her, and too much of a rebel.

He had to choose.

With Reds' prodding and deception, Storm must have chosen the rebel's cause over her. Maybe the plan had gone bad. Had Storm expected Daddy to be in the car? There was so much she wanted Storm to explain, in person.

At least it would help mend the broken trust still aching in her heart.

The same distrust that kept her alert for the deceptions she had learned to expect from men.

Like tonight on her way into the bathroom. She thought she heard Hallam unlock his briefcase and grab the phone.

She turned on the water but left the door slightly ajar as Hallam dialed numbers.

Then he spoke up. "May I speak to Colonel Bravo? He's expecting my call."

***

Storm raced up the steps, barreled through the doorway, and head-locked the man kneeling over Cammy. He rolled the man across the floor and prepared to put the military choke on him.

"No!" Cammy struggled to her knees. "He's my friend."

Storm released the man and rushed to Cammy's side. "What the heck's going on?"

"I just fell . . . he was helping." Cammy sat up. "Get the light."

Storm flipped on the living room light and studied the stranger. He sure as hell didn't look like he belonged in the islands, in blue suede suit, open-neck white shirt and black patch over his right eye. Well-tanned, he emitted a cologne scent, which blended richly with the aroma of Cammy's spicy fish broth.

The man stood, combed his fingers through lush salt-and-pepper hair and adjusted the eye patch. He looked about fifty years old. "Sorry, maybe I leave now."

"No, please don't." Cammy rose to her feet and turned to Storm, her voice shaking. "Get him something to drink."

"No trouble." The man cleared his throat. "I . . . I came to say thanks."

"Sit." Cammy showed the man to the couch.

"I just wanted to give to you this." He reached into the breast pocket of his blue jacket and pulled out an envelope, yellow with age. "Please read it."

She stared into his eyes, her own on the verge of tears. She hesitated, but eventually reached for the envelope with trembling fingers.

Storm glared at them. Who the hell was this guy?

"Excuse us." She grabbed Storm by the arm and led him into the kitchen, whispering in his ear. "He's an old friend."

"I don't care to meet any more of your gentlemen *friends*." He'd long ago grown exhausted trying to remember all the names of Cammy's male friends who drooled after her. "What is he doing here?"

"He came to thank me for a . . . a favor from long ago."

Embarrassment warmed his neck. "I don't want to hear it."

She snapped. "Don't be rude."

"It's none of my business."

"I need to freshen up a bit." She calmed down. "Just keep him talking."

Storm was sitting alone in the living room when Cammy came out a few minutes later. She wore the dress she'd worn in the picture that drew lustful glares from his Marine buddies, her bosom bursting around an eye-catching cleavage, and smooth dark legs exposed above her knees.

Her glow vanished. "Where is he?"

"He left when we were in the kitchen."

"You just can't let him go." She tightened her fists. "He'll get hurt again."

"He's a grown man, for Christ's sakes. He had a taxi."

He felt like adding maybe the man was headed where he belonged, with his own family. But Storm knew he would regret it even before the words reached Cammy's ears.

"You don't understand," she said.

"You're right, I don't. And I never will."

A tap on the open door interrupted his disgust.

Storm pulled open the door. A familiar young woman in her mid-twenties stood just outside, sweating in the night's humidity and glancing nervously behind her.

"Let her in," Cammy said. "She's Rachael's friend."

That's when Storm remembered Hallam's warning. Reds might have also bugged the house.

***

Jackie wrapped a towel around her damp hair, afraid if she wiped the steamed bathroom mirror, she might see in her eyes the same fear pounding her heart. Just outside the door sat a man with whom she shared a hotel room, and whom she had trusted with her life—until thirty minutes ago.

She'd believed Hallam worked undercover for the Barbados police and the American Embassy in a covert operation against the Cuba-supported Marxist government in Grenada. An operation that might free her father from prison.

But why had Hallam just secretly phoned the top Cuban commander on the island? She'd picked up Storm's name and mention of the *Bianca C* out of Hallam's muffled phone conversation with Colonel Bravo, but could not decipher the rest of it.

If Hallam betrayed the operation, her hopes to free her father from prison would evaporate, and worse, both she and Storm would be in mortal danger. She had to warn Storm.

She retreated into her robe, sat on the toilet with the cover down and held her head. What should she do now? Even if Storm had a phone, she couldn't call because it would be bugged like his boat and house. She had memorized the phone numbers to both the Barbados police and the U.S. Embassy in Barbados. But the American handler firmly instructed them never to call from Grenada. The warning still rang in her ears. Since the American Embassy in Grenada had been shut after the revolution, if anything went wrong in Grenada, she and Hallam would be on their own.

But now it also looked like *she* was on her own.

A sudden knock on the bathroom door almost launched her into the ceiling.

Hallam's voice boomed from the other side of the door. "You're quiet in there."

"Yeah," she said. "You know us women and our hair after a day at the beach. I'll be right out."

"Take your time," he said. "I'm going to run down to the beach bar for a taste of the Grenada rum punch. I'll be back in thirty minutes so we can have dinner in the restaurant downstairs."

"Okay. I'll be ready when you get back."

Just the break she needed.

When she heard Hallam slam the front door on his way out, she rushed from the bathroom and headed for his briefcase where he left it on his bed. The locks clicked, and she opened the briefcase. She fingered her way through an *Islands* magazine and travel brochures the handler had given them in Bridgetown, but found nothing suspicious. She peeked into the side pockets. A folded piece of paper caught her attention. She opened it and her pulse raced at the sight of the Cuban commander's name, Colonel Bravo, followed by a Grenada phone number.

Steve, the lean and intense American handler in Bridgetown, had repeatedly warned them about Colonel Bravo, assigned to Grenada by none other than Fidel Castro. Colonel Bravo's cunning proved valuable in manipulating governments from behind the scenes. He had personally set the trap that flushed out a CIA agent who had held the second highest position in the ruling Angola Revolutionary Party. Bravo shot him immediately.

So why had Hallam, on a Barbados police mission with the CIA, phoned Bravo like they knew each other?

"Found what you're looking for?" Hallam filled the open doorway behind her.

Jackie dropped the paper into the side pocket and quickly shut the briefcase. "Sorry, I . . . I was just looking for our flight information for tomorrow."

Her heart pounded.

He marched over to the coffee table and snatched up her ticket and itinerary. "Here it is where it's been all along."

"Thanks . . . silly me."

He snapped. "I don't like snoopy fingers."

"Why are you acting like you're hiding something from me?" She braced for an answer she might not like.

"We're in this together, but listen to me very carefully," he said. "There's a lot more going on than you know, or should know."

"What are you saying?"

"The Americans pulled you into this for one reason. To recruit your boyfriend so—"

"He's not my boyfriend." She pulled the robe tighter around her and snatched her papers from his outstretched hand.

"If the Americans believe for one moment you know anything else or you're sniffing around their plans, they will scrub the entire operation. Then your father would rot in prison, or worse, face a firing squad."

His threat felt like a bee sting. She understood so little about this spying and espionage business. Was Hallam a double agent, just trying to scare her into silence, in case she'd seen Colonel Bravo's phone number in the briefcase?

Maybe the Americans already knew and approved of Hallam's contact with the top Cuban military officer on the island, as part of a larger plan. If so, then their warnings about Colonel Bravo must have been designed to smokescreen her from the rest of the operation. When they returned to Barbados, she could confide her suspicions to Steve at the embassy. But if Hallam was right, her father's eventual release from prison could be jeopardized if she revealed she knew more than she should.

"You have nothing to worry about," she said. "I just want my father's freedom."

"Good." His silver tooth glittered with his smile, and his posture relaxed.

She decided to help calm him even more. "Remember we're supposed to be married. Let me get dressed and we'll have dinner together." She winked at him.

"Great. I can't wait to try the rum punch."

What if she was wrong and Hallam was in bed with the Cubans? Maybe she should tell Storm. She couldn't wait until he showed up in Barbados. His sister Rachael had already died under strange circumstances. Might Storm be next? Hallam had mentioned Storm's name and the *Bianca C* in the muffled conversation with Colonel Bravo. What would a ship buried in a hundred feet of water have to do with Storm?

Jackie would never forgive herself if something happened to him that could have been avoided had she warned him about Hallam's double-dealing.

She would have to talk to Storm tonight, and the only way to do so would be to go to him.

But how could she slip away from Hallam and get to Storm's house four miles away during a nighttime curfew with armed soldiers on every street corner?

She didn't know how, yet.

CHAPTER FIVE

His finger to his lips, Storm signaled for quiet first to Cammy and then to Rachael's friend standing at the door in the darkness. If she had information about Rachael's death, he couldn't take the chance of someone listening through electronic bugs hidden in the house. He gestured to Cammy to step outside and led them both down the steps. They crossed the narrow walkway and passed through a broken-down gate into the kitchen garden. Cammy and the girl sat on the wooden bench, hidden by rustling corn stalks and pigeon-pea trees shivering in the evening breeze.

The girl's eyes seemed to plead for an explanation for Storm's weird behavior.

"Wait here," he whispered. "Don't say anything yet."

Storm slipped out of the gate and followed the chicken-wire fence bordering the garden. If someone followed the woman, they might still be in the vicinity. He peered around the back of the garden and into the shadows of the neighbor's hedge, alert for any signs they were under observation: rigid human contours against vegetation, body odor, or cigarette smoke. He completed the perimeter around the garden without detecting anyone, and then felt foolish for doing so.

Hell, he didn't even have a goddamned weapon. If he'd found someone, would he have crawled up behind the unlucky bastard and broken his neck? Then what? Bury him in the garden?

He still wanted the truth about Rachael's death. Maybe she had stumbled onto some murderous plot brewing under the already strained surface of Grenada life. His suspicions about the government's role in her death sank deeper roots after the boat trip to the *Bianca C* today. Why had Reds bugged Storm's dive boat and the house? Did he fear both Storm and Cammy might learn Rachael's secrets? And what might all this have to do with the American effort to recruit Storm into a covert operation planned a hundred and fifty miles away in Barbados?

The situation had too many moving parts that did not fit together, and they raged at him faster than the rifle-propelled grenades he'd faced in Beirut. The Marine Corps had taught him how to control the complexities of enemy reconnaissance and combat execution.

Improvise, adapt, overcome, they taught.

But this felt different. On this island he called home, he knew these people, shared their blood, loved some, and hated others.

His instincts felt oddly scattered.

He needed time to clear his thoughts. The drink he had planned to relish his reunion with Jackie today would have to wait. He reluctantly pushed her from his thoughts and walked back into the garden.

Rachael's friend was sitting with her head low, wringing her hands while Cammy held her around her slender shoulders.

He explained why the house was no longer a safe place to speak. "Did anyone see you come here?" he asked.

"I don't think so. I took the trail behind Marryshow House."

"Good."

The sprawling two-storied house, a stone's throw from the garden, once belonged to Theophilus Albert Marryshow, a local hero who rose from newspaper-boy to newspaper-owner and leader of the struggle against British colonialism in the early 1900s. His creole pride showed in the mixed French and British architecture of the house. Marryshow died in 1958 and his house quickly faded behind disrepair and thick vegetation. But when a community group restored it in 1972, Storm claimed the secluded back yard for shooting birds with slingshots and smoking his first cigarettes. Later, the rewards became sweeter when he learned to entice girls with promises of private tours around the historic grounds.

If Rachael's friend had used the trail behind Marryshow House to get to Storm's house tonight, no one could have seen her from the street.

"I don't know if you remember me," she whispered.

"Yes." He remembered her now. Pauline Holas.

He was maybe ten years old when she started visiting the house to play and study with Rachael. He recalled the girls took a break from their studies to dress up like Hollywood actresses. They borrowed Cammy's decorative stones from her Singer sewing machine drawer, leftover items from the carnival costumes she occasionally sewed for extra money. Rachael locked the bedroom door behind her, but left the French shutters open beside the door.

Storm peaked past the thin curtains hanging over the shutters.

Still in her white school shirt, Pauline loosed the top buttons, cupped her breasts in her palms, and squeezed them together with a glittering stone nestled in her cleavage. "I am Elizabeth Taylor." She giggled at her reflection in the mirror.

Her display brought warmth to his face and groin.

Rachael laughed and rolled around on the stones scattered across the bed.

Pauline lifted her skirt to her hips, exposing smooth legs and white panties. "See, I have million-dollar legs too."

Storm ran off. Something was happening behind his zipper he couldn't control.

Soon thereafter, Pauline's visits came to an abrupt stop. Storm never knew why and often wondered if it was because she might have seen him peeking at her.

Now twelve years after their Hollywood display, Rachael was gone, along with Pauline's teenage giggles.

A solemn tone weighted Pauline's words in the garden. "I saw her that night. She was dressed up for a party. She said an inner circle of government and military people were going to honor her for her work in the Women's Council. I never saw her again."

"Did someone at the party tell you what happened?" Storm asked.

"No, but my brother saw the accident," Pauline said. "He's a soldier and was on patrol when it happened."

"What did he see?" Cammy asked.

"The cars . . . he saw the car drive off the edge of the road and roll down the embankment toward to the river."

Storm detected hesitancy in her voice. "Did it flip over?"

"My brother said it stayed on the wheels and banged into a rock in the river."

"That's all?" he asked.

"He was one of the first to reach the car." She turned to Cammy. "He just wanted me to tell you she did not suffer. She looked peaceful."

Cammy stood. "Rachael would be happy you came here to tell us." She embraced Pauline and headed back to the house.

It pained Storm to see his mother so defeated, her head slumped and her feet dragging into the house. A half bottle of rum awaited her under the kitchen sink, enough to fog the grief for another night.

Storm turned to Pauline. "It was brave of you to come here tonight. Maybe you should spend the night here instead of walking home alone. I could give you a ride, but Reds warned me to stay off the streets at night."

"Thanks," she said. "But there's more I didn't want your mother to hear."

He waited.

She wiped her eyes. "There were two cars stopped at the scene before the accident. When Rachael's car rolled down the embankment, the other car raced off in the opposite direction. My brother did not see who was in it."

"But the police said she was speeding," Storm said.

"The only car speeding was the car heading away from the scene. There weren't even tire marks to show she tried to hit the brake before the car went off the road."

"Damn."

"There's something else. My brother was one of the first to reach the car. When he lifted her out, the back of her head was wet. He thought it came from a splash of river water. It was dark, but later, when he held his flashlight to his hand, he saw blood."

"An injury to the back of her head while she's driving forward?"

"Yes. The car was not seriously damaged. She had no blood on her face, just the back of her head."

So why did the police insist on a closed casket funeral? Reds himself had said Cammy would not want to see how badly injured Rachael was.

"Did your brother hear any gunshots?" Storm asked.

"No gunshots," Pauline said. "But he wondered how Reds knew about it so fast. He showed up five minutes later with a truck and a squad of soldiers. They took her body and the car away. The next day the government radio announced she died in an accident."

He exhaled a deep breath. "Everything you say makes sense now."

"One more thing," she said. "My brother said her skin was dry and cold, like she was already dead hours before the accident."

That murdering son-of-a-bitch Reds!

***

Jackie counted three sleeping pills in the bathroom and dropped them into her shirt pocket, within easy reach for when she needed them for Hallam's drink. She fixed her collar, turned off the light, and stepped out.

Hallam stood waiting outside the door, soaked in Old Spice cologne, his black muscleman shirt stretched tight around his barrel chest and bulging biceps. "Ready?"

"Yes." She stared at him suddenly doubting three pills would put down a man this size. She'd trusted him until an hour ago. Now she engineered her demeanor and decisions with cold calculation under a veneer of innocence. "Silly me, I just remembered something. Excuse me."

She returned to the bathroom and walked out a minute later. "See anything different?"

He gazed at her, a little too long. "Hmmmm. You still look just as great."

"We're supposed to be married, remember?" She giggled, waving her left hand in front of him to show off the wedding band Steve had loaned to her in Barbados.

She had removed it for the boat trip, but now it was her best excuse to cover her return to the bathroom for two more sleeping pills. She hoped her eagerness to role-play as his wife at dinner might just help him to forget he'd found her rummaging through his briefcase.

But it could also give him the wrong idea.

She held his arm as they walked out of the room and headed down the flight of steps into the lobby, furnished with wicker chairs, flowers, and paintings of sunny coastal scenes. A musician standing under a fake coconut tree pinged calypso notes on a steel drum. An elderly couple shuffled to the music on the polished dance floor, while a few people lingered around the dimly lit bar in subdued conversation. The barman, in a shirt blazing with colors, paused in the middle of mixing a drink to gaze at Jackie.

Did her tight jeans and heels enamor him, or did Colonel Bravo and Reds have spies watching them in the hotel?

A smiling waitress approached. "Are you here for dinner, or would you like to sit at the bar?"

Jackie reminded herself to act like a wife and allowed Hallam to answer.

"Dinner," he said.

She let Hallam lead her into the sparsely occupied dining area, an open balcony overlooking the white-sand beach. The sea breeze flapped the tablecloths, blended the rustle of coconut leaves with the wash of the gentle surf below, and soothed her thoughts.

She recalled another night she'd had dinner in this restaurant, the night her father had taken the family to dinner here about eight months after the car bombing. Eight months after Storm left the island. Under the watchful eyes of bodyguards, the three of them sat in the far corner, her mother in a flowered dress, and her father in open navy-blue jacket and collared red shirt. Still recovering from his injuries, he hung his cane on the back of his chair, and struggled into the sitting position. After dinner, his eyes glistened in the lamplight and his voice shook as he held Jackie and her mother's hand, his own disfigured by burn scars. He apologized for every pain, embarrassment, and tear he ever caused them. He announced he had advanced diabetes and needed his family around him more than ever before.

The car explosion had broken his body and cracked open his spirit for a new man to emerge.

Within months, revolutionaries overthrew the government, locked her father up in Richmond Hill Prison without medical care, and exiled her mother to Miami. Jackie fled to Barbados to finish her university studies and to pray for the day when she would again meet the kinder man her father had become.

Maybe having dinner here with Hallam tonight was an omen of good fate. It made her feel closer to her father. When the waitress invited her to choose among the empty tables, Jackie pointed to the same corner table her father had chosen four years ago.

They sat and Jackie immediately set to work on her plan to see Storm tonight.

She turned to the waitress. "Would you please bring us two of your famous rum punches? I'll have a small and my husband will have a large, of course."

Jackie smiled at Hallam.

***

Pauline sniffled then bent and lifted the hem of her dress to her eyes. "Maybe I should go now."

"Please stay the night." Storm touched her hand lightly.

She flinched, but did not withdraw her hand.

He remained seated next to her on the garden bench allowing the painful reality to sink in that Rachael's death was no accident, and Reds might have planned it—even done it. He gazed up at the sky for relief. Star light struggled against the glow from the city lights below. An occasional sea breeze blew up the hillside, taming the humidity but hardly calming the rage building in his chest. Two gunshots in the distance reminded him guns now dictated what people said and did on the island.

He studied Pauline in the dim night. She was five years older than him. Her full lips still glowed with the succulence that used to awaken his boyhood desires. But her eyes seemed less certain, like a flickering candlelight in a losing fight against the wind. He used to daydream about his lips on hers. Now all he wanted to do was to hold her, to protect her the way he wished he could have protected Rachael. But her reaction to his touch warned him off.

She broke the silence. "I knew it the day Rachael brought him home from the riot."

"Who . . . what are you saying?" Storm asked.

"You were on the Cadet Corps camping trip that weekend."

"I remember there were riots against the old government then."

"She . . . Rachael rescued him after the shootings and convinced your mother to hide him in the house for two days."

"Rescued who?"

"Duncan."

"Duncan? Prime Minister Duncan?"

"He wasn't Prime Minister then. He was twenty-eight, she was eighteen. But I knew something was going on."

Pauline reminded Storm of the day thousands of students joined the street demonstrations led by Duncan to protest police brutality. Government thugs attacked the marchers with rocks, tear gas and bullets on the harbor road, a five-minute walk from the house. One of the attackers shot Duncan's father in the back, killing him instantly. Duncan's security men raced him out of the area and Rachael led them to the house, up Tyrrel Street, to the trail behind Marryshow House, and then over the low fence on the side of the garden.

"She led them the same way I came tonight," Pauline said. "Your mother was worried about Reds showing up, but she hid Duncan and a bodyguard in the house for two days. Rachael took care of Duncan like they were married. Of course he already was. She cooked for him, washed his clothes, and when the radio announced his father's murder, she consoled him and they cried together. I knew it then."

"Knew what?"

"She loved Duncan."

Storm had suspected Rachael of living a secret life. Like Cammy, she would dress up and leave the house saying she was going out, but Storm never knew with whom. She never brought any boyfriends home either. Rachael had carried out an illicit affair with Duncan, a married man.

It would devastate Cammy to know how well Rachael had followed in her footsteps.

Pauline had more to say. "On the second day Duncan hid in the house, Reds showed up unexpectedly. He had a key. He was still a police officer and still loyal to the old government. He drew his gun to arrest the men, but your mother and Rachael protested. In the uproar, Rachael ran outside and returned with a cutlass. She told Reds 'the only way you will arrest them is to kill me first.' "

The commotion attracted neighborhood attention, and a crowd of Duncan's supporters began to gather in the yard. While Rachael and Reds faced off, Duncan and his bodyguard slipped away through the crowd. When rumors started the next day that Duncan had escaped from Reds, the police chief fired Reds.

"That's how he turned against the old government," Pauline said. "But he never forgave Rachael and Duncan for causing him to lose his job in disgrace."

Now Storm wondered if Rachael had turned down offers for overseas scholarships to remain close to Duncan. "And you think this has something to do with Rachael death?"

"Rachael died because of her loyalty to Duncan."

"Wasn't she also in a relationship with a PRA captain?"

"I think she used the captain to get information about Reds and the military. The captain disappeared a week before she died. I believe he gave her information she was not supposed to know. It gave Reds the chance to even the score. But I don't think he's finished yet. You might be next."

***

Jackie excused herself from the table after their fish dinner and made a hasty visit to the lobby restroom, leaving Hallam behind to order a second round of rum punches. She'd kept the dinner conversation lighthearted, partly to calm any suspicions he might still harbor after catching her in the act of fingering through his briefcase, but also to sooth her nerves.

The time had arrived to execute her plan.

She stared at her reflection in the restroom mirror as she removed the pills from her pocket, fearful her face might betray the doubts flooding her thoughts. Her coffee-toned complexion, inherited from her bi-racial parents, seemed flushed from the sun exposure on the boat today. Her eyes reddened a little, maybe from sadness and fear. She hoped Hallam dismissed it as the effects of the rum punch.

She counted the five sleeping pills. Would they be enough to knock him out for the night? Maybe, but mixed with rum punch, the potion might also kill him.

What would be worse, a fatal overdose or Hallam awakening in the middle of the night to see her gone from the hotel room? She knew whom he would call first. Colonel Bravo, the spy hunter and executioner.

It came down to Jackie or Hallam.

She couldn't take any chances. Storm had to be warned tonight. Hallam and the top Cuban military officer on the island had their sights on him, and, for some strange reason, on the sunken *Bianca C*.

If Hallam died from an overdose while Jackie went searching for Storm, her conscience would not suffer.

She returned the pills to her pocket and hurried back to the table.

Hallam was already sipping his second rum punch.

"You really like those, eh?" She forced a smile and reached for her glass.

"Tasty, but the damn rum is well disguised."

"My mother used to make those," she said. "The right mixture of lime and pineapple juices could hide the taste of the rum. Be careful. It can sneak up on you and put you to sleep for a long time."

"It will take a lot more than these weakling drinks to take me down." His silver tooth glittered in the lamplight.

Jackie waited for his drinks to send him to the men's room so she could deposit the pills. But he continued to slurp from his glass. The ice cubes clinked away the seconds. She needed at least half of his drink to dilute the pills, or he might detect a change in the taste.

She had to act now, and fast. "How about some dessert?"

"I'm okay, but don't let me stop you."

She pulled the plastic menu from the middle of the table and opened it so Hallam would not see her retrieve the pills from her pocket. Just then another sea breeze blew into the restaurant. She loosened her hold on the menu. It blew out of her free hand and landed on the floor next to him.

"Oh silly me." She tightened her fist around the pills and rested it behind her glass.

"I'll get it." He bent over to pick up the menu off the floor.

In one swift motion, she dropped the pills into his glass.

An hour later, Jackie turned the key in the lock to their room and pushed the door open.

Hallam stumbled past her. "You're right . . . about those damn rum punches." He collapsed face-first onto the bed.

Within minutes the sound of his snores vibrated the room.

She set to work to make his dreams comfortable. She rolled him onto his back and removed his shoes. The ceiling fan creaked at high speed but failed to generate the airflow they'd had in the restaurant. She slid open the back door and a salt-scented gust pushed into the room, unabated by a coconut tree stretching past the second story balcony.

Jackie turned off the fan and left the sliding door open.

She entered the bathroom and changed into t-shirt, shorts and sandals, the new pair with thick soles and deep tracks: comfortable to run in and easily removed if she had to swim. She fastened the Velcro leather straps, wondering how best to leave the hotel room without being seen. Stepping out the front door at midnight would be foolish.

After turning off the room lights, she climbed over the balcony rail, embraced the coconut tree, and shinned down into the uncertain night.

***

The phone jolted Reds awake. Irritated, he grabbed it off his nightstand. "Colonel Slinger here."

"Sir, it's me . . . from the hotel."

He recognized the barman's voice, edged with urgency.

"Did they leave?" Reds asked.

"No, we're still watching, but—"

"Dammit, your orders were to call me *only* if something happened."

"I see something you must know, sir."

"What?"

"She put something in his drink when he wasn't watching. She was holding him tight on the way back to the room."

Reds remembered the young woman saying she carried sleeping pills to overcome her husband's snores. Maybe the big Bajan had other bedroom shortcomings that needed medical encouragement, especially since his passport showed he was twelve years older than his bride.

Reds chucked. "They're on their honeymoon. He might need a boost to keep him busy tonight."

The barman laughed. "Just wanted you to know everything I see, Colonel."

"Okay. But remember if any of them leave the hotel, follow them and see if they lead us to the Yankee Marine. I think they were more than just dive customers. If we catch them together again, especially at night, they will have a lot of explaining to do."

"No problem. We're watching."

Reds hung up the phone, realizing he should have reminded the barman to have another guard watch the rear second-story balcony. But whether his targets from Barbados used the front or back door, they would be detected. The Bulgarians, the best in espionage and reconnaissance, had taught Reds. And he in turn had taught his men well.

The Bulgarians might have failed in the 1981 attempt to assassinate Pope John Paul, but that did not diminish the many unpublicized successes Reds learned about during his six months in the Bulgarian capital, Sofia.

His training advisor, a young dark-haired major named Sergei Vasiliev, arranged a week of R&R for Reds at a sunny Black Sea resort. After the first few days of Russian vodka, Cuban cigars, and Scandinavian women, Sergei took him for a long walk along the shore. The conversation blueprinted Reds' future with more certainty and glory than even he could have envisioned on his own.

The Cuban and Bulgarian leadership, with Soviet permission, offered to groom him in secret to be Grenada's next Prime Minister—in case something bad happened to Duncan.

Reds' instincts warned him not to ask what might happen to Duncan. He didn't have to ask. Duncan's lukewarm allegiance to Soviet Bloc countries and waning commitment to Cuban-style Marxism had left former comrades less optimistic about his future, and more enthusiastic about Reds'.

Two crabs could not live in the same hole. Duncan had to go.

Duncan's future dripped with blood while Reds' future blazed with power.

Reds only had to prove to his European friends he had the steel *cojones* to make life-and-death decisions to help the rising tide of global communism.

First there was Cuba. Now there were Nicaragua, Grenada, and a serious battle was underway in El Salvador.

Sergei had repeatedly reminded him of Lenin's words, "The revolutionary dictatorship of the proletariat is rule, won and maintained by the use of violence, by the proletariat, against the bourgeoisie, rule that is unrestricted by any laws."

But while Marxist-Leninist philosophy hammered solid bricks on the road to his future, Reds also had a past to rectify.

No one, man or woman would humiliate Reds without punishment. Maybe his seeds lacked the potency to bear children, but did Cammy have to seek out foreign men to swell her belly with those little brown-skinned devils? And then to drive a final nail into his groin, the bitch had walked around St. George's, head held proud and high, showing off her babies, and telling his friends Reds could never have good-looking babies like hers.

Her verbal stabs at his infertility had bled his soul. He wanted a wife and children, a family to call his own—not the fractured home life he'd grown up with that still awakened him with aching memories of whips and hunger. He wanted to marry Cammy, for her to bear *his* children. Children he could mold to look up to him and admire him the way he craved a real father.

True, he'd slapped Cammy around a few times after a couple of drinks. After all, real men had strict ways to keep their women in line, to get their respect, and to show how much they cared for them.

But when he offered to marry her, she laughed in his face.

Despite Cammy's painful rejection, and her continued glee at his lost chance at fatherhood, he stuck around. His hard-earned dollars kept her ravenous children's plates filled and their boney bodies clothed, more than his mother's faceless men ever did for him.

And his reward for shouldering Cammy's burdens during those early years? One night after she pushed him too far again, she ran screaming with her bloodied mouth to a neighbor's house and called the Chief-of-Police. The Chief ordered his goons to kick Reds out of Cammy's Park Lane house like he was a mange-infected dog.

Within days, she replaced him with a privileged high-society snake from Lance Aux Epines.

Those bitter days turned his heart cold and changed his life's purpose with steeled dogmas. Authority was the weapon of the privileged. For the privileged class to be crushed, Reds must become the authority. With authority, he would control his reality. But if reality dictated he could not have a family, he would exercise his authority to ensure neither would Cammy.

Tonight, the path to complete authority stretched unobstructed before him while Cammy and her bastard children fell perfectly into his plan to eradicate the dismal past behind him.

To impress his European mentors with his ruthless decision-making, he simply had to demonstrate unequivocally how much he shared the same hunting instincts like Colonel Bravo.

Cammy and her little flock presented the best targets.

One down. Two to go.

If anyone left the hotel room tonight, they would be the unsuspecting bait to hook Reds' next big fish, Storm.

***

Jackie glanced over her shoulder as she soft-footed her way north in the tree line shadows along the sandy shore. Was the noise behind her the sound of the wind cracking through a tree, or a footstep breaking a twig? Maybe she should have risked taking the rental car instead, and if caught just put on the dumb act. She ruled out driving through the well-patrolled streets, especially since Reds had warned them to stay in the hotel after dark. She would certainly be stopped and arrested. But even if she drove to Storm's house and back to the hotel without incident, how could she explain to Hallam the additional miles on the meter after he'd locked the car in the hotel parking lot for the night?

The sound of crashing waves and the swift brush of sea breeze on her face nudged her back to the present. She had two options left. Somewhere along the beach, she would have to steal a rowboat to take her to the St. George's harbor. Either that, or do something she hadn't done since she was sixteen years old: swim the two miles from Silver Sands Beach to the harbor. Back then she'd taken second place in the annual swim race under sunny skies, and earned a congratulations kiss from Storm.

She picked up her pace at the thought of Storm. But at the same instant, the warming memory of his kiss collided with a dreaded shout from the bushes on her right.

"Halt!"

CHAPTER SIX

Storm cautioned Pauline that she faced danger if she walked home alone at night, but she repeatedly declined his offer to sleep in the house. He wished he understood her reluctance. Maybe the thought of sleeping in Rachael's bed was too uncomfortable, especially after the past few hours in the garden rehashing Rachael's life—and death. So he suggested she sleep on the couch.

Pauline fell silent and fixed her gaze at the dark house.

A patrol truck on the waterfront road rumbled past and then faded in the distance. The howl of a dog reminded Storm life still existed out there in the slumbering city. This was not the rambunctious Grenada he remembered. The memories from his early years still hung on his mind like laundry on a clothesline in the windy sunshine. A thrill ran down his spine as he remembered sliding down the steep Park Lane on pieces of cardboard slicked at the bottom with yellow breadfruit slime. One day he overran the intersection next to Marshall's rum shop and slid into the busy Tyrrel Street— directly into the side of a passing car. He earned a couple bruises and a few laughs from his friends.

The aches subsided by nightfall, especially after they shoplifted chocolate bars from the *Rock 'n Roll* grocery. They fled the waterfront store and raced up to the little park overlooking the port. They licked the sugary loot off their fingertips while a Norwegian cruise ship, looking like an alien city of lights, floated into the horseshoe-shaped harbor.

The night's fun came to an abrupt end when a friend's mother found them sitting on the grass slapping mosquitoes and surrounded by loose chocolate wrappers. She grabbed her son by the ear and pulled him aside.

"What the hell you doing playing with he?" She shouted, gesturing at Storm. "Next thing you get the disease he mother have from all her men."

Storm raced home, humiliation burning his chest. Cammy tried to console him, but he could no longer deny the reality. Cammy's lifestyle had erected barbed restrictions on his own life.

Storm's friends soon stopped visiting the house to skim over *National Geographic* magazines left behind by Cammy's asthma-ridden stepfather. And when Storm met Jackie a few years later, not even she would come to visit him at home.

Pauline's visits to Rachael had also stopped. But was her reason the same as that of Storm's friends? She continued to gaze with disdain at the house at if it was the last place on the planet she wanted to enter.

"You know so little." Pauline held his hand when he asked her if Cammy's reputation was the reason she stopped coming to the house. "You promise not to tell your mother what I am about to tell you?"

"I promise."

"One day I came to visit Rachael," she said. "Reds was home, alone. Rachael had taken you to the library. Your mother was shopping in town."

"Yeah?"

"Reds raped me on Rachael's bed. That's why I can't go in your house anymore."

Two nights ago, Cammy told Storm in a drunken slur if he were not her son, she would have asked him to kill Reds.

After tonight Cammy did not have to ask.

The Anglican Church bell rang the twelve gongs of midnight while Storm laced up his jogging shoes. He'd decided against wearing his old combat boots is case soldiers caught him walking Pauline home. It would be so easy for the authorities to claim they had arrested him in American military uniform.

He entered Cammy's room expecting her to be asleep. She was sitting up in bed, the yellow envelope from the one-eyed visitor on the pillow next to her. She held a letter to her chest in the dim lamplight. On her night stand, the black Sony radio he'd sent her from North Carolina played Ray Charles' version of *Rainy Night in Georgia*. Rum vapors soaked the air.

She looked up at him with eyes puffed, either from the contents of the now empty bottle standing next to the radio, or from crying again. Maybe the letter from the man triggered her tears this time, but Storm had no interest in her affairs with this 'old friend', or any other.

Before she could say anything that might be picked up by an electronic bug hidden in the room, he turned up the battery-operated radio and whispered in her ear. "I'll be right back. I'm going to take Pauline home."

"No." She grabbed his arm. "Don't go out there. Let her sleep in Rachael's room."

"She can't."

Just then, the lamp went out.

Shit.

He backed up to the door and felt for the switch to the overhead incandescent bulb. He flicked the switch up and down several times.

Nothing. Another unannounced blackout.

Storm had neither the time nor patience to argue with Cammy tonight. He now knew why he could not convince Pauline to sleep in the house. The poor girl would likely relive every sordid moment of her torture, without sleeping a wink.

He returned in the dark to Cammy's bedside and whispered. "Pauline can't stay. We'll be okay. I'll come back after sunrise."

Cammy sank into her pillow. "My heart can't feel anymore." She clutched the letter to her chest. "I couldn't stop Rachael from leaving. Now I can't stop you either. Just go."

He hated to walk away from his mother in her despair, but the anger blazing in his veins left no room for empathy.

He pulled the front door shut behind him and walked into the garden to look for Pauline—but she was gone.

Dammit!

He hurried out the gate and glanced up and down Park Lane.

No lights. No one in darkness. No footsteps.

She lived in Paddock, about fifteen minutes away. To get there, she would take either Tyrrel Street, or the lower Carenage Road. Regardless, he doubted she would get far without being caught by patrolling soldiers.

Storm bolted down Park Lane toward Tyrrel Street.

***

Jackie froze at the sight of the dark form stomping out of the bushes along the beach. A young soldier took shape in the night haze, his rifle pointed at her. Waves of fear crashed on her thoughts. Imprisonment, torture, and maybe worse awaited her.

"Don't move." The soldier ordered.

She mustered all her strength to remain calm and to pronounce her best Bajan accent. "I was just out for a walk."

"You from Barbados?" he asked.

"Yes." Relieved her first verbal offering had softened the soldier's attitude, she sprinkled a little charm. "Just visiting your lovely island for a couple days. Thought I would enjoy the sea breeze tonight, just like you're doing."

"What you doin' is more fun." He chuckled. "But you not supposed to go out after dark."

"Sorry, I didn't know Grenada had an official curfew."

"It's not official, but . . . what hotel you staying at?"

"Hotel?" If she told him the Spice Island Hotel he would turn her back in the direction she just came from and her plans to warn Storm about Hallam would be scuttled. But if she gave the soldier the wrong answer and he escorted her to a front desk employee who couldn't identify her, she would be in even deeper waters.

She decided to take the chance. "I'm at Silver Sands Hotel, just ahead."

"Better go back to your hotel before you get stop again. Plus we have lot of clouds. It could rain."

"Okay, thanks for protecting the beach. Goodnight." She turned and shuffled off in the sand toward the electric glow of the Silver Sands Hotel, glancing back just once to see the soldier still watching her.

She wiped beads of sweat off her forehead. Even if she found a boat now, the soldier might see her drag it into the water.

Damn.

Her spirit dampened further when she approached the two-storied hotel. The beach chairs and umbrellas congesting the beachfront earlier in the day were gone. Also gone, the rowboats that had been pulled up to the white picket fence bordering the hotel. The huge flamboyant tree guarding the rear entrance seemed to celebrate her misfortune, casting a dance of shadows over the bare sand.

Her confidence sank. What should she do now? She could not return to her hotel on the opposite end of the beach. The soldier might stop her again, and what would be her excuse this time?

If she swam from the beach to the harbor it would take her at least two hours against the night tide and strong breeze blowing ashore. And with the thick clouds hanging over the island, a sudden squall would be likely. She hated even more the thought of swimming in the blackness, not knowing what jaws lurked below.

Panic tightened her throat.

Would she do this just for Storm? He'd abandoned her when she needed him the most, while her father—and her trust—lingered on life support. A part of her still hungered for the truth about what happened that night. But a deeper emotion longed for Storm's passion, his zest for life, which had survived his many punishing setbacks. Maybe her motivation tonight came from the thought of his embrace.

She quickly squashed the excitement. Her father's freedom from Richmond Hill Prison meant more to her. It might ultimately depend on her getting information to Storm. He needed to know that the top Cuban Communist enforcer on the island knew about their conversation on the boat today, and the source was Hallam.

Hallam might be a traitor.

She must see Storm tonight, even if she had to swim to —

Was that the outline of a small boat bobbing offshore? She peered out at the sea where a channel of light from the hotel tamed the darkness. As she focused on the object, her doubts vanished and her energy reignited. A rowboat floated less than ten yards offshore, probably with oars inside. She hoped it had an anchor rope she could easily untie.

In case the soldier was still observing her, Jackie strutted onto the walkway meandering between a swimming pool and the hotel's beachfront entrance, out of his line of sight. Her sandals crunched on the sandy concrete. She worried the sound might attract additional attention. There could be other soldiers lurking in the darkness around the hotel.

She followed the walkway until she left the hotel, its yellow glow, and the soldier behind in the distance. On the sand again, she removed her sandals and plowed into the darkness along the shore. Even if the soldier was still watching, the curtain of light between him and Jackie would surely distort his view.

Keeping low, she slipped her hands into the sandals, crept into the warm water, and floated toward the boat.

She paddled up to the anchor rope stretching from the bow.

Then dismay seized her. Chain.

How in God's name could she cut or untie a chained anchor? Or lift it without attracting attention?

She pulled herself up and into the wooden boat. In the darkness, her fingers found the roundness of oars stored on the sides. She crawled through fish-scented water on the floor to the bow and traced the chain by hand. The chain ended at a wooden bracket on the inside of the bow—padlocked.

Maybe she could not cut chain, but she could surely break wood. She grabbed one of the oars and shoved the handle into the space between the bracket and the frame. The bracket groaned when she pulled down on the oar, but it held firm. She hung her entire one-hundred-and ten-pound weight on the oar and lifted her feet. The bracket resisted a moment, then cracked, and completely gave way before Jackie had time to steady her feet. She fell back onto a wooden seat, and instantly felt the burn of sea salt on her scraped back. The bracket splashed into the water, dragging the extra chain behind it.

She stayed down and eyed the shoreline to see if the noise had attracted unwanted attention. No one broke the shadows along the beach. No lights reached out to the boat.

Now free from the anchor, the boat started to drift back to shore—into the spotlight of the Silver Sands Hotel.

Just then, the entire island blackened. Lights out again. Maybe another arms shipment tonight.

Jackie grabbed the oars, braced herself on the wooden seat, and guided the craft away from the shore. Somewhere in the dark distance ahead, St. George's harbor and Storm's Park Lane house waited.

The Bianca C Still Burns

***

Cammy tossed the letter on her pillow and leaped from her bed. Even in the dark, she found the empty rum bottle on the nightstand, and threw it against the wall. It exploded and the shattered pieces rained across the wooden floor.

"Why me?" She collapsed to her knees and held her head.

She'd long lost count of the number of times she'd asked herself that question. She must have been quite young the first time. She had lived those early years in the countryside village named Post Royal. There was nothing royal about the meager existence her mother scratched from the hillside lot left by her grandmother. Even then, Cammy had promised herself she would never grow calluses and wear out her fingernails on any activity that delivered nothing but stale sweat, constant hunger, and a leaky roof.

She never knew her biological father, a fisherman lost at sea before her birth. But when her stepfather came down with asthma, eight years after abandoning her mother and moving to the city, Cammy's mother sent her to take care of him— an alcoholic asthmatic pedophile.

She was thirteen.

And when she ran away from his Park Lane house to return to her home, the welts on her back from her mother's whipping taught her a lesson she never forgot.

Life is about choosing which pain you must live with.

Her mother either doubted every word Cammy said about her stepfather's abuse, or simply did not care. So Cammy took the slow bus ride back over the mountains to her stepfather in the city, to earn the tear-soaked dollars her mother needed to drown her soul at the Post Royal rum shops. When his eyes and lips swelled from his asthmatic attacks, Cammy boiled water and covered his head over the pot with a towel for the steam to unclog the mucus in his lungs.

But she never stopped praying for him to die.

And when the rum swelled his organ with perverted desires, she turned her face away from his pungent grunts, stared up at the exposed beams, and silently cried.

As the years sapped his feeble health, he must have realized how much he'd taken from her, and how much he owed her. When Cammy turned seventeen, just after he'd lost a leg to diabetes, he signed the house over to her. The next day she returned from the shop to a note on her bed.

He had boarded a ship to return to his native Guyana to gasp his last congested breath alone.

No apologies, no pleas for forgiveness, no letters. Just a note and a pain-filled house that years later continued to attract new pain she no longer chose.

Even rum failed to comfort her, and the scattered pieces of bottle around the bedroom floor reminded her that jagged edges of her life still gnawed at her nerves. She struggled to her feet, reminding herself to sweep the floor before going to sleep. But she doubted she could sleep now. She worried about Storm, playing with death somewhere out there tonight.

"Why me?" Her thoughts rolled with images of the one-eyed visitor at her door earlier. She couldn't bear to think his name. Would he knock on her door again? She had no way of finding him. He hadn't given her a hotel name or phone number. He just showed up and disappeared, like he'd done so many years ago, this time leaving an old letter in a yellow envelope. An old letter reviving her past like nothing else had.

The naked lust, the bliss, the perfection, bundled into a shooting-star moment.

Yes, it came and went in a flash. But the memory never faded. In fact, it grew into a secret she protected from everyone else.

His letter haunted her with remorse. If she'd received it years ago, she might have made wiser choices. He'd written it the year the *Bianca C* had sunk, but for reasons she was yet to know, he never mailed it.

Maybe the same reason she never mailed hers.

The ship lay buried for twenty-two years under a hundred feet of sea, but the visit tonight reminded her the past could never be buried deep enough to keep secrets from floating to the surface.

Finally, it seemed, the *Bianca C* had begun to let her secrets bubble up from the sea floor.

Cammy needed to prepare for more pain to come.

She lit a candle and swept the shattered bottle off her floor.

***

Storm raced along Tyrrel Street in the humid darkness, as fast and silent as his jogging shoes could take him, hoping to reach Pauline before patrolling soldiers caught her—or him. He could not think of a worse time for either of them to be on the streets. Reds had already warned him to stay indoors, and the colonel's suspicions would surely ignite if they arrested Pauline and forced her to admit she'd just left Storm's house at midnight. Reds might immediately guess the reasons for her visit under cover of darkness: to tell Storm about her rape and to reveal what she suspected about Rachael's murder.

Murder?

It struck him he'd finally accepted it as fact. His sister had been murdered. He'd always known the government's explanations did not add up. But Pauline confirmed it tonight. His temple pulsed and the first bead of sweat rolled down the side of his face. Rachael's murder left a painful cavity in his soul.

Now it screamed for retribution.

In the distance to the right, the outline of a Soviet ship he'd seen earlier took shape against the gray sky. It filled the harbor with a mechanical hum that blanketed the sound of his footsteps on the road. Electric power to the city had just been turned off, but subdued spotlights guided the port's activities. The coincidence of a Soviet or Cuban cargo ship in port, nighttime power outage, and the rumblings of heavy trucks throughout the night no longer bewildered city folks.

Cammy had repeatedly warned him never to be caught roaming about on nights like this. Anyone found, especially on streets close to the port, faced certain arrest and vicious interrogation.

He'd already jogged a half mile, but still no sight or sound of Pauline. He peered into the darkness, looking for a female shape, but the night had driven everyone off the streets.

Everyone except him.

Just then, headlights rounded the corner ahead. He darted into bushes on his left and dropped to the ground. A truck rolled slowly up the road in his direction. He eyed the Bulgarian truck through a filter of vines and weeds. It crawled to a squealing stop a few feet away. Five soldiers with AK-47 rifles jumped off the back of the truck.

Four of them spread out to the far side of the road. One hurried across the street toward him.

Fuck. Storm wished he'd taken a knife with him.

He could surrender and plead ignorance. But time still remained for him to leap to his feet, hammer his fist into the soldier's groin, and snap his neck.

In seconds, he could mow down the entire squad with their comrade's rifle before they could say Lenin.

Instead, Storm wondered how many of them he'd sat next to in school.

He hesitated, knowing damned well he would not have done so in Beirut.

The soldier halted two steps away, in Storm's kill zone.

Storm waited behind the vines for the dreaded command to stand with his hands up. But Rachael flashed across his mind and sealed his decision.

He would fight. Every muscle in his body juiced up on adrenaline. He would kill.

The seconds slowed.

The soldier let his rifle hang from his shoulder, reached for his crotch, and lowered his zipper.

A shower of warm beer-scented piss sprayed the vines above Storm's head and trickled down his neck.

***

Jackie's arms ached but she kept rowing. The city lights had suddenly plunged into black an hour ago. Now she worried about navigating her way along the choppy channel into the horseshoe-shaped harbor. The Americans in Barbados had briefed her and Hallam about nights like this when the government would shut off the city lights to offload military hardware.

From her swim days, she recalled that shallow reefs bordered the channel, shallow enough to puncture the boat. But then soft lights in a beehive of activity at the pier guided her safely into the port.

Blanketed in darkness, she rowed past a droning cargo ship moored at the pier. On the deck, iron cranes stretched like long arms into the dim sky carrying containers larger than many of the houses on the island. A speaker barked commands in Russian. Heavy machinery squealed, absorbing the splash of her oars in the fuel-scented sea.

Her confidence lifted. She could reach the shore undetected.

She maneuvered past the pier and headed toward the shoreline bordering the Tanteen soccer field. A rattle of stones greeted the boat at the shore. She jumped into cool water up to her knees. She'd thought of letting the boat drift away, but it remained her only safe means of returning to her hotel before Hallam awakened from his rum-punch slumber.

An abandoned boat in the harbor tonight might also raise the alarms.

The traction of her new sandals held firmly on the slippery ground as she pulled the boat up the low embankment. Waves slapped the boat and a dog barked in the distance. A steady breeze flowed from the black hillside.

Storm's house sat five-minutes away, through streets she hadn't walked in years.

He'd already lost his sister under suspicious circumstances. Now it appeared Hallam had used Jackie to bait Storm into a plot with more tentacles than she first believed. Why had Hallam met with American agents in Barbados one day, and then secretly called the top Cuban officer on Grenada the next? Maybe Storm had special knowledge about the *Bianca C* that made him a target. He'd become a deep sea diver in the Marines, but he'd never dove the sunken ship—at least he said he didn't.

Maybe he knew more than he'd told her.

She sighed.

It wouldn't be the first time he had not been truthful to her. The first time, her father almost burned to death.

She froze at the sound of an approaching truck. It rumbled to the street bordering the far side of the open field. Headlights pierced the dark. Jackie dove on the muddy ground on the side of the boat, just under the direct line of light. Then high beams painted the night phosphorous-white. So bright, she expected the driver would notice if she blinked. A low wave lifted the rear of the boat and splashed her bare ankles. The boat rocked in a tug-of-war with the retreating wave.

Fear tightened her chest.

If another wave came, she would have to let the boat go. If she stood to grab hold of it, the soldiers would certainly spot her. But worse, the soldiers might drive across the field to rescue the boat—and find her too.

Another wave rolled up, this time over her legs and shorts. The boat floated. She held her breath. The wave receded, taking the boat with it.

Laughter erupted from the truck.

She remained flattened to the soft ground and blinked away sweat burning her eyes. The high beams turned off but the truck remained at the intersection in a low growl. The next couple minutes felt like hours.

Finally, the truck turned and thundered off toward the port.

Jackie glanced back. The boat had vanished in the dark sea.

When she could no longer hear or see the truck, she crawled up the embankment and rolled onto the grassy field. She gazed up at the sky and evaluated her predicament. She'd lost her boat ride back to the hotel, and some poor fisherman might have lost his livelihood. A twinge of guilt gnawed at her. Maybe the boat would be found adrift and returned to its owner.

At this moment, she had bigger headaches.

She pushed the light button on her watch—one o'clock in the morning. Little time remained for her to find and warn Storm, and then to figure a way back to the hotel before Hallam awakened from his stupor. It would be out of the question for Storm to try to drive her back to the hotel past watchful street patrols.

Dismayed by the risks awaiting her, Jackie decided to focus on her first goal: getting to Storm's house without being caught. Her scruffy appearance, the pasty feel of fish-scented mud on her cheeks, elbows, and knees would certainly not impress him, but that was hardly a concern. Well . . . maybe. She doubted a full bottle of her Chanel No.5 perfume would subdue her odor. She considered a brisk swim to wash off, but the harbor water would only trade her current aroma for a petroleum scent and a shivering night in clothes drenched for a second time.

She rose to her feet and sprinted low across the soccer field. On the far side of Tanteen Road, she melted into the shadows of the hibiscus hedges lining the sidewalk. The sweet fragrance of flowers calmed her as she hastened past the landmarks from her school days. The bakery overlooking the port still emitted the aroma of the best bread she'd ever tasted and the *shack-shack* tree across from Bobby's Tire Shop still waved its seed-filled rattles in the wind.

She recalled a kiss from Storm under the tree, after a movie at the Regal theatre.

The memory had distracted her just as she passed the deep shadows on the side of the tire shop. Without warning, two hands lunged out of the darkness and seized her. One hand sealed her mouth, shutting off the scream at her throat. The other hand roped her midsection and swept her off her feet into the alley.

She struggled against her captor.

A mixture of fear and repulsion seized her. Fear for her life and repulsion by the stench of piss.

A familiar voice whispered in her ear. "Shhhh. Pauline it's me, Storm. Soldiers are coming our way."

Storm! Why does he think I am Pauline? And why does he smell like a drunk who'd pissed on himself?

***

"You scared the hell out of me." Jackie hissed at Storm in his yard thirty minutes later, after they had evaded the street patrols and sneaked up Park Lane.

"Scared? You could have gotten *killed.*" He struggled to control his worry beneath a thin coat of anger.

"And why would you be grabbing Pauline out here on a night like this?" she asked.

The sprinkle of irritation in Jackie's tone reminded him of her teenage possessiveness over him. She might have remembered Rachael and Pauline were friends during their years at the Anglican High School. But did Jackie now think Storm had a romantic interlude with Pauline?

He quickly explained Pauline's visit earlier that night and his search for her. "I hope she made it home okay."

"You mean . . .?" Jackie asked.

"Mean what?"

"You and Pauline…"

"No, my dear." He welcomed the feeling Jackie had not totally discarded him from her heart.

Even in the dark, the warmth in her eyes seemed unscathed by the distrust that had yanked them apart for the past few years. Except for the underwater kiss today, it seemed an eternity ago that he'd stood this close to her, alone. Her presence rekindled passions he'd refused to surrender. He held her hands. But the temptation to kiss her quickly retreated as a breeze stirred his collar.

She sniffed the air. "What the hell were you drinking?"

He explained with a chuckle how the soldier had urinated on him. "If I find that bastard . . ."

"We both need a shower," she said.

"Did you leave your hotel just to invite me to shower with you?"

He expected her to laugh, but her mood dampened abruptly.

She glanced away. "Something strange is going on." She recounted the night's events, beginning with Hallam's phone call to Colonel Bravo. "They talked about you and the *Bianca C*."

"Damn."

"Is there anything about the ship you haven't told me?" she asked.

"I can't think of anything. Believe me."

"Have you gone down to the ship?"

"Would love to, but we don't have the equipment on the island to do it." He gazed at her. "We're both in this together. Would you ever trust me again?"

She looked away.

Maybe his question had reminded her about her father. Only Storm could have planted that bomb. And only Storm could tell her the truth. But would she believe him?

Her distrust and disappointment had not yet hardened into rejection, or else she would not have risked so much to come all this way tonight to warn him.

"I am proud of you," he said. "You were brave tonight."

"Storm, I missed you so much. But . . ."

"I'm so sorry for what happened to your father. It was not supposed—"

She placed her finger to his lips and whispered. "Are you sure you want to tell me now?"

"I waited four years to tell you the truth. I don't want to wait anymore."

"Okay."

"That night, I had only gone five minutes down Old Fort Road after I said goodnight to you. I heard a car coming down behind me." Storm had looked back as the car rounded the corner. Just then the road shook with a bang. A ball of flames lifted the car and slammed it into a tree on the side of the road.

He knew immediately.

He sprinted up to the flames, grabbed the hot door handle and rolled Jackie's father out of the car. Lights came on in neighborhood houses. Someone shouted to call for help. Jackie's father sat up and moaned with his hands to his face.

Storm knew he would be in grave danger with the police if he stayed. Confident medical help was on the way, and Jackie's father had not seen him, he had raced down the road with anger exploding in his chest and tears filling his eyes.

"I told Cammy everything," he said. "The next day I was on the Federal Palm boat to Trinidad, and a week later I was on a plane to America. Not sure how she did it, but I was too afraid, too ashamed to ask."

"So it was you who saved Daddy? Oh Stormy. I wish I had known."

"I thought you would know the whole truth and never want to see me again."

"A few days later the police arrested Reds and he said you planted the bomb in the car. Please . . . please tell me you didn't."

"No one was supposed to be in the car. Reds made the bomb. He instructed me to place it in the car when I visited you. I had it in a paper bag and hid it in your driveway when I came to visit. When you said goodnight and turned in, I placed the bag on the floor behind the passenger seat. The car was unlocked and the windows down—"

"Why?" She thumped his chest. "I trusted you. Why?"

"It was not supposed to hurt your father. I am so sorry."

She sighed and wiped her eyes.

He swallowed hard. He realized he might never have the chance again to tell her everything, so he continued. "Reds said the bomb was set to go off at 3 o'clock in the morning while everyone was asleep. He lied. The bomb did not have a timer. It was made to go off when the car vibrated on the road. Jackie, you could have been in the car the next day . . ."

"Or it could have gone off in your hands. But why, Storm? Why did you go along with his senseless plan?"

"Reds said if I planted the bomb, he would leave the house and stop beating Cammy. I did it for her."

***

Mario Costa adjusted the patch over his left eye, blind now for more than twenty years, and scanned the blueprint of the *Bianca C* spread across his yacht's cabin table. He'd thought about mooring in the St. George's marina for the night. But then the harbor master had tugged him by the sleeve and suggested otherwise. If an aging luxury yacht pulled into the harbor on the night a Soviet ship delivered military hardware, it would certainly raise suspicion.

Mario decided instead on the freedom and safety of international waters outside Grenada.

He was on a mission, not on a vacation.

But disappointment had already set him back. His unannounced visit to Cammy had ended in disaster. He'd stood at her door, unable to recall the words he'd memorized for two weeks across the Atlantic. So mesmerized by how well she'd preserved her youth and beauty. Had she fainted from the sight of his eye patch and scarred face?

And her son. Where did he come from? Mario did not stand a chance against those arms. He couldn't blame the boy. Anyone who'd seen Mario kneeling over Cammy would have assumed she'd been attacked.

He returned his focus to the *Bianca C* blueprint. Several years earlier, a company from Trinidad had salvaged the propellers. A letter from Cammy first alerted him about unusual activity around the site. Through the binoculars he'd sent her in 1963, she'd spotted cranes hoisting the huge propellers into the cargo hull of the Trinidad ship. The salvage work received little media coverage, but Cammy was able to read the ship's name. A few cables and phone calls led Mario to the owner of the salvage company. He sent Mario a full report of the

Bianca C's condition. The proud ship stood upright under a hundred feet of water, visited only by nurse sharks and moray eels.

The confidential report from the salvage company reassured Mario that at least one of his two reasons for returning to Grenada still awaited him.

His other reason remained elusive and probably petrified after his first clumsy attempt at Park Lane tonight. He smiled when he tried to imagine what his friends in Genoa would say if he told them his dashing one-eyed good looks made an island girl faint.

An Italian woman might at least expect a bouquet of red roses and a bottle of wine before feigning lightheadedness.

Regardless, he'd come too far, after too many years, to turn back.

She'd been his North Star, but never knew it. Even before the *Bianca C* went up in flames and crashed to the sea floor, Mario's personal life had also begun to sink. The *Bianca C* loss compounded his failures, and the loaded Beretta in his Genoa desk drawer seemed his final exit.

Cammy didn't know the terrible legacy of suicide in his family. The last Costa to choose that route was his own father. Mario had found him in the study. Gray and red splattered on the wall. The last and most vivid picture of a man gifted with immaculate business skills but burdened with a genetic disposition for depression. All it took was a temporary setback to tip the scales.

But on Mario's most catastrophic day, Cammy rowed her boat into his life. She sparked a tiny flame in him that flickered occasionally but never went out. While a hundred feet of water drowned the fires on the ship, her letters in the ensuing years kept alit his frail will to live.

Cammy's words did not fit into the artificial intellect his ex-wife preferred in Genoa. His ex-wife's pretentious circles memorized and regurgitated the dusted off thoughts of others in tired conversations. In their company, wine became his remedy.

Cammy's words flowed with emotional purity unscathed by formal education, but energized by island turmoil. Dipped in pain, her simplicity resonated at his human core, like nothing and no one else did.

She touched a part of his soul not even his wife had ventured to seek during their miserable marriage.

It would have surprised no one if Mario had chosen his father's fate. In fact, those who knew him expressed surprise and admiration for the way he faced the unforgiving headwinds that had taken others in his family.

But then none of his friends or family knew about Cammy. Her words had become his secret lifeline. She usually ended her letters with: "the island misses you more today than yesterday."

The last letter he'd received from her a couple months ago described heavy rains flooding the streets and triggering landslides across the island. "It rained," she'd written, "like an island weeping for a long lost friend."

Her words over the years did more than encourage him to improve his English. They unlocked his reason for living—and kept locked the Beretta in his desk drawer.

He didn't have to guess how she felt about him. But at the same time she discreetly left him the breathing room he desperately needed to manage the personal blows that ambushed him after the *Bianca C* went down.

His wife had never reached his soul with words or feelings, even before he discovered her affair with the *Bianca C*'s second-in-command, the staff-captain. Her most memorable words came in the divorce papers she served in his hospital bed, the same day the best doctors in Genoa gave up on saving his eye from the burns. The ugly divorce, which dragged him to the precipice of bankruptcy, turned out to be just the beginning of his troubles.

When the *Bianca C* sank, he should have guessed his own daughter, Bianca, would face the same dismal future as the ship he'd named after her.

The struggles gobbled up his years in chunks, and mocked his will to live.

No one but Mario had known of the steady North Star giving him the direction and hope he needed to stay afloat—and to return to Grenada.

A knock at his cabin door interrupted his thoughts. "Come in."

The door squealed open and a young crewman leaned into the cabin. "Signore Costa, we're outside Grenada's waters now. Have you decided to press on to Barbados tonight? We can be there in four hours."

"No, let's float out here for the night. I have to make one more visit in the morning."

"Yes, sir." He turned to leave.

"One more thing," Mario said. "Send this message to our man in Barbados." He tapped his finger on the *Bianca C* blueprint while the crew man pulled a pen and small notepad from his shirt pocket.

"Ready to copy," the crew man said.

"Send in code: Confidential. Looking for a commercial diver."

Mario had recruited one of the best divers in all of Italy. But after a night of drinking in a Miami nightclub and mouthing off about his diving exploits, the diver jumped ship for another offer on a Bahamian island. Mario and his crew spent an additional week island-hopping the best dive shops in the Caribbean, from the Caymans to the Grenadines, without finding another diver willing to execute Mario's plans.

Tonight by radio, he'd received the name of a recruiter in Barbados. Maybe this fellow would find him the candidate he needed.

Mario continued. "Diver must be expert in underwater explosives and demolition. Trust-worthy. Military experience with prior top-secret clearance preferred. Compensation negotiable."

"Got it." The crewman exited the cabin and left Mario alone with his thoughts.

***

Storm squinted at his watch. At 3:30 am, the port would still be busy and patrols on high alert. "We have to get you back to the Spice Island Hotel before Hallam awakens," he said to Jackie.

"I can wait and take the first bus at sunrise," she said.

"Too late, and too risky." He held her hand and led her into the house to the small living room couch. He whispered in the darkness. "Sit here, I have an idea."

He made his way into the kitchen and slid his hand along the counter toward the matchbox and candles. He lit a candle. Jackie glowed in the soft light and she smiled at him—which only made him feel like shit.

He wondered if he could live long enough to repay her for his mistakes.

She'd risked everything tonight. Drugging Hallam, stealing the boat, and hiding from soldiers, just to warn Storm he could be in danger. Despite the smears on her cheeks, the sweaty cap on her head, and muddy sandals, her eyes held the same gleam that once sent desires swimming through him. His guilt retreated and his heart raced.

An hour later, Storm squeezed in behind the wheel of his Toyota on Park Lane and shut the door with a click no louder than the strike of a match. His watch showed 4:30 am, one hour to sunrise. One hour before anyone dared to venture outdoors.

But he had no choice.

He glanced down to his left at Jackie's petite frame curled up on the floor of his truck. She just fit under the cooler jammed between the dashboard and Cammy's lap. Cammy wore a pair of jeans and a rumpled t-shirt, with a cap pulled over her head. She'd barely had time to wash her face and change after Storm had awakened her to explain the situation less than thirty minutes ago.

The cramped cabin stunk of stale beer and piss, but Storm kept the windows up to preserve the stench.

He released the handbrake and the truck coasted down Park Lane. "Here we go."

"Me girl," Cammy murmured to Jackie. "We'll get you out of this. Don't worry, eh."

Even if they made it to the hotel without patrol stops, Jackie would only have a few minutes to shower and dress before waking Hallam for the hour-long drive to Pearls Airport. If he suspected she'd left the hotel, they could all be in danger.

A nauseating wave of dread reminded Storm of his sister's death just one month ago.

He turned left on to Tyrrel Street and headed south toward Grand Anse Beach. The electricity blackout still covered the island, but now shark-gray skies prepared for sunrise. Heavy cranes at the port continued to lift military cargo against the skyline. The soldiers who roamed the area two hours ago seemed absent from the street.

He drove about twenty miles per hour, just fast enough to not appear in a suspicious hurry. Loose scuba gear, a couple of tanks, fins, and snorkel masks, rattled under the tarp in the back. He popped in a reggae cassette to ease the tension, but kept the volume low. Except for his headlights pushing aside the black curtain ahead, no other lights shone anywhere.

He stretched down and rubbed Jackie's head. "We've passed the port and we're in Tanteen now. Anglican High School is just ahead."

She held his hand and kissed his palm. "Thanks."

It took another two minutes for Storm to drive past the high school asleep on the hillside to the left. The road meandered through the round-about intersection toward the dingy-white Regal cinema. His headlights awakened the blackened windows, and they glared back at him from behind forbidding wrought-iron gates.

The truck sputtered along the winding road through Paddock and entered the stretch of Belmont Road Storm used to walk to get to the beach on sunny days. Wood-framed rum shops and single-story houses elbowed each other along the street front. The rambunctious Belmont neighborhood used to express its pride with blazing carnival costumes, intoxicating steel drum music, and bloody knife fights. Body scars contained the chapters of men's lives.

Storm wondered how many of these once-proud Belmont men now cowered in their beds at night rather than face new weapons more menacing than switch blades. Or how many of them might actually be the soldiers patrolling the streets this night.

The Belmont stretch ended abruptly at a sharp turn to the left. On the right, barbed-wire gates blocked the road leading up the peninsula to the once glamorous Islander Hotel, now the Prime Minister's headquarters. One guard sat alone at the gate, an AK-47 held upright between his legs.

Storm hoped the man would be weary at the end of the night shift and too busy counting the minutes to sound the alarm at the sight of a civilian vehicle. The guard glanced passively at them and then at his watch in the headlights, but remained seated.

Storm relaxed a little. He calculated they were halfway to Jackie's hotel, with the riskiest areas behind them. In the distance over the hotels, a hint of red. Sunrise had begun to roll in.

He shifted gears and picked up speed.

Just then headlights turned the corner a hundred yards ahead. The height and width of the beams looked like those of a truck. A car followed. Remembering Grenada traffic rules, Storm held the wheel to the left and slowed.

The truck gave no indication the driver had seen him—or cared. It rumbled in a direct charge toward them. A head-on crash with the truck would be deadly for all three of them.

He had one option.

"Hold on!" He slammed on the brake and jerked the wheel to the left. The back of the Toyota slid sideways across the loose gravel. The pickup stalled with his door in the path of the speeding truck.

He braced for the impact, of either metal or bullets.

The truck squealed to a stop a foot from his door. About eight soldiers jumped from the back. They fanned out across the street with their rifles.

The car pulled up and one of the soldiers opened the back door.

A tall soldier stepped out and barked. "Search them."

Storm waited until the soldier reached the door, then he lowered his window.

Colonel Reds sniffed the night air. "I knew I would catch you. But did you already piss yourself?"

CHAPTER SEVEN

Reds could hardly believe his luck. The bitch and her belligerent son had underestimated him, and insulted his intelligence once too often. Now they sat helpless in his clutches. He had felt it offensive when Colonel Bravo insisted the previous evening that Storm was more valuable to them alive than dead. Bravo expected Reds to allow Storm, a Grenadian trained by Yankee Marines, to roam the island like a free animal. Reds doubted the Cuban colonel would have allowed this to happen in Cuba.

To hell with Bravo.

Reds had waited years for this moment. He grinned seeing the young bastard squirm next to his slut-mother. Storm blinked in the glare of the army truck headlights while Cammy sat helpless in the passenger seat burdened with a white cooler in her lap. A soldier held an AK-47 pointed at her head.

Perfect.

"Leave her in there," Reds ordered. "I want her to see him die with the smell of his piss up her nose." He pulled his Makarov 9mm from his hip holster and aimed it at Storm. "Get out."

It would be so easy to report the events on today's radio broadcasts: *Two traitors shot to death in a failed attempt to ambush a security patrol during curfew hours. They blocked the road with a Toyota pickup truck, but the soldiers reacted quickly. Both attackers were killed before they could use the rifles and hand grenades found in their cooler.*

Those two idiots made it so easy.

Storm eased his door open. It stopped against the bumper of the army truck. "There's no...no room to get out."

A dog barked across the street.

Reds stepped closer to Storm's door. "Get out now, or I'll put a bullet in your skull."

Storm slurred his speech. "Your soldiers…will have to reverse the truck."

"So you can turn and speed off? You still think I am stupid?"

"I can't very well do that… with a gun on me."

"You're drunk," Reds said. "Get out."

Storm squeezed a leg out the door.

Cammy reached over and slapped him over the head. "You drunkard. I warned you about leaving too dammed early to open your dive shop."

Storm's head bobbed from the slap in feigned intoxication. He pulled his leg back in.

"And turn off that stupid music." She punched him on the shoulder.

Reds laughed. "You stink too, boy. Still pissing yourself after all these years?"

Cammy always stood in his way when he wanted to whip Storm for wetting the bed as an infant. She would remind him her children were not his. "When you can have children, you can belt them."

How little she realized not having his own children relieved Reds of one torturous burden she would bear. He never had to bury a child—but she had.

His redemption had come with her daughter in a sealed coffin.

And he had just begun. He now held both Cammy and Storm on Belmont Road, trapped like mice in a cat's claws.

More dogs barked. House lights came on and curtains shifted.

A streetlight flickered down the road.

Dammit.

Electricity had been turned on. He hadn't expected the Soviet ship to offload this early.

Reds glanced up at orange rays slashing the gray sky. The first civilian traffic might show up any minute. Not enough time to do this his way.

The radio on his belt crackled. "Silent Visitor to Top Dog. Silent Visitor to Top Dog."

Shit. Colonel Bravo's voice at 5 o'clock in the morning surprised him. Russian Vodka usually paralyzed the fool in bed until past 8 o'clock.

Reds pulled his radio. "Come in, Silent Visitor. Over."

"Are you in a secure position? Over."

"Affirmative. Over."

"A loose boat was discovered banging into the cargo ship. Anchor chain broken off. One of your patrols reported seeing a wave take it off Tanteen shores. Looks suspicious, especially with our shipment last night. Check out the Tanteen location. Over."

Reds hated how the Cuban kept one step ahead of him, and always with a condescending tone. How did Bravo get all this information before him? Grenada soldiers reported up the chain of command to Reds, not Bravo. On paper the Cuban filled an advisor's role, but he acted like a commanding general.

The radio crackled again. "Top Dog, do you copy? Over."

Reds spat his words. "Yes, yes. On the way to Tanteen. Over and out."

He clipped his radio to his belt without awaiting the reply. Just like the Cuban to screw things up.

Reds turned his attention back to his catch. What should he do now with Storm and his mother? Storm looked pathetically distraught and smelled like he'd been drinking all night. He was certainly in no mental or physical state to be involved with any boat in Tanteen. He could barely drive.

Could Cammy's idiotic son really be part of a clandestine plot against the Grenada government? Whatever cloak-and-dagger suspicions Bravo invented about Storm and the *Bianca C* must be a figment of the Cuban's imagination.

Yet, something didn't feel right about Storm and that Barbados couple.

Especially, the doctor's young mouthy wife.

Cammy slapped Storm again. "My only son, back in Grenada to become a drunk. Shame on you."

At this rate, mother and son might kill each other before sunrise. But that would only rob Reds of the pleasure he craved—to have them die at his hands.

A soldier marched up. "Nothing in the truck, sir. Only dive equipment in the back and food in the cooler."

Storm hiccupped. "Can . . . can we go now?"

"When I get both hands on you, you'll pay," Cammy shouted at Storm. "Getting me out of bed for this shit."

Reds chuckled. "If you had listened to me, you would have straightened out his ass years ago." Turning them loose to go after each other's throats might just be a good thing. He faced his soldiers. "Let's roll. Tanteen."

The army truck roared and reversed away from the Toyota door.

Reds stood back from the stench and glared at Storm. "You're a loser. If your mother hadn't always gotten in the way, I would have straightened you out a long time ago. Get out of here before I change my mind. There won't be a next time."

Storm mumbled. "Th . . . thanks."

The Toyota jerked forward and sputtered past Reds.

Reds shouted. "I hope you drive off the cliff before you get to Grand Anse."

***

Reds stood on the Tanteen shoreline and scratched his head. A quarter-mile to his right, a red hammer-and-sickle flag flapped lazily over the freighter parked at the pier. A mechanical hum floated over the field. Why would anyone steal a rowboat in Grand Anse to spy on a Soviet freighter in St. George's harbor? A better-prepared mission might have used one of the yachts moored in the lagoon area as a base of operations for a scuba diver with clandestine equipment. Reds paced the muddy landing while his soldiers fanned out in the pre-dawn gray to search ramshackle buildings along the field.

A young lieutenant marched up and saluted. "Sir, you must see this."

Reds followed the lieutenant to an embankment.

The lieutenant pointed his flashlight at a narrow groove carved into the mud. "This is where the truck patrol said they saw the boat float away last night."

Small waves rolled up the embankment, but not high enough to erase the unmistakable evidence someone had pulled up a boat here in recent hours.

"There's more," the lieutenant said to Reds, kneeling and pointing a twig to shoeprints around the groove. In the flashlight glow the shoeprints displayed well-defined tracks of a new pair of shoes or sandals. An X marked the instep, and at the heel, a circular seal. "Looks like the same person made all the prints."

"We'll find him," Reds said. "Call investigations and have them lift his prints. I need pictures too."

"Sir," the lieutenant said. "It might not be a man."

"What are you saying?"

"There's something else about these prints, sir. Look at the size."

Reds scanned the prints.

"My wife is a size six," the lieutenant said. "These are about the same size prints she leaves in our back yard. It could be a woman. A heavier man would also leave deeper tracks."

"She must be a strong woman." Reds raised his eyebrows. One person— a woman? Only a strong woman could have rowed this distance and still have leftover strength to drag the boat up the embankment. If a female agent wanted to spy on the Russian freighter, why had she waited till nightfall to get to St. George's? "And why drag the boat up, if she didn't need to?"

"That's the point, sir. I think she needed it. She had to get back to Grand Anse, but her plans failed when the waves took the boat away."

Reds twirled his moustache. The lieutenant floated interesting theories. The pieces still didn't add up to a well-planned espionage operation. But Reds hated to overlook obvious clues Bravo would later dangle as more proof of his superior intelligence. If a compelling reason demanded the spy returned to Grand Anse the same night, what could it be?

The lieutenant broke the silence. "Sir, did you notice something about the Bajan woman when she came off the boat yesterday?"

"You mean that smart-mouth bitch?"

"Yes. Storm and her husband lifted off the cooler, but she carried the black bag."

"So?"

"When we searched it, it was filled with diving gear and weight belts."

Reds' impatience warmed his temples. "Get to the point, soldier."

"She was strong. Maybe strong enough to pull the boat. And small enough to wear size-six shoes."

"Assuming you're right, she's either still stuck in St. George's, or found another way to get back to the beach."

The lieutenant glanced across the field to the road. "I think she's still here in St. George's. No other boats were reported missing and patrols did not report any civilian traffic last night on the roads between St. George's and Grand Anse."

Until Storm and Cammy.

But after a thorough search, the soldiers had found nothing suspicious in the Toyota. No way could anyone else have hidden in there.

The lieutenant faced Reds. "One more thing about—"

"Snap to it, soldier. I don't have all day to listen to your ideas in trickles."

"If she's the one, she definitely has a reason to return to Grand Anse in a hurry. Her immigration documents showed that she has a morning flight to Barbados. She might try to take the first bus back to the hotel."

The lieutenant might be wrong. But what if he was right? Early light chased away the gray and morning dew glistened across the field as far as the street. A crowded Volkswagen van sped past. These small buses— named *One More* because regardless of how crowded, the drivers always found room to squeeze in one more passenger—would be the best choice for someone without a car to get around.

"There goes the first bus to Grand Anse," the lieutenant said.

A cold fear chilled Reds.

"Let's go." He ran to his car, shouting at his soldiers. "We have to get to the Spice Island Hotel before she does."

***

"The Spice Island Hotel is just down the beach from here." Storm pulled the Toyota to a stop at the end of the narrow gravel road facing the sea. The first sunrays glazed the surface of the blue water ahead and small waves washed ashore in soothing rhythms that bore no semblance to the harrowing moments they had just survived with Colonel Reds.

A few early-morning walkers strolled along the white sand. Storm and his Toyota would be unrecognizable from that distance—thick sea-grape trees crowded both sides of the road and overhead in a shadowy canopy.

"Quickly, let's get you on the way," he said, worried Hallam might already be awake, even after Jackie recounted the number of rum punches and sleeping pills the big man had consumed.

Storm pushed open his door and sprinted over to the passenger door. It squealed open. He grabbed the cooler off Cammy's lap and stacked it against his scuba gear in the back. He helped Cammy out and extended his hand to Jackie. She grabbed his and squeezed her way up from the floor.

"Phew. Felt like I was trapped in a filthy men's room." She stepped onto the road and inhaled deeply with her arms stretched above her. "The fresh air smells good too. What a ride. I'll need a full body massage after this."

Storm twisted his jaw and rubbed his shoulder. "Yeah, me too. I didn't know my mother had such a punch."

Cammy chuckled. "Sorry, Son. But it fooled Reds, right?"

They laughed, but not for long.

"Okay, let's go," Storm said to Jackie.

"I'm going alone," she said.

"No way."

"If anyone sees us together, we're both in trouble. If I'm alone, I could pretend I got lost on an early morning walk."

Jackie made sense. But he couldn't let her go alone and didn't want to argue with her about it.

"Okay, but stay away from the hotel entrance," he said. "You think you can climb the coconut tree up the back balcony?"

She pulled down her cap and flexed an impressive pair of biceps that budged the sleeves of her t-shirt. "What do you think?"

"You're ready." He kissed her cheek. "I'll see you in Barbados in a couple days."

Even without sleep for twenty-four hours, her eyes brightened. "I'll be waiting."

She gave Cammy a warm embrace and sprinted down the beach toward the Spice Island Hotel, her sandals kicking puffs of sand behind her.

Storm waited until Jackie disappeared in the morning haze then turned and handed Cammy the key to the dive shop. "Take the truck back to the shop and open up like it's a regular day. I'll jog back and meet you there."

"What you want me to say if Reds shows up looking for you?"

"Don't worry," he said. "You handled him well back there on Belmont Road. Just tell him I had too much to drink last night, and went for a swim to recover."

"Are you going swimming?" she asked.

"Not yet. I'm going to the hotel. Just in case Jackie gets an unpleasant surprise."

***

Jackie peered through the hibiscus hedge alongside the beachfront. Two men, trying to look inconspicuous, watched the hotel entrance and her second-floor room. She'd seen her father's security men on duty often enough before the revolution to recognize their watchful gestures. One man leaned against the gate to the unoccupied swimming pool puffing a cigarette, while the other paced the brick driveway leading up to the main entrance. Both men faced the stair cases leading from the central lobby area to breezy hallways and ocean-front balconies upstairs. The third hallway on the left led to Jackie's room, overlooking a splashing water fountain and the beach. Her blue front door remained shut the way she'd left it last night.

While the Spice Island Hotel had unhindered sea views from the front, the rear balconies opened up to majestic views of the island's lush mountains. Luckily for Jackie, Grenada's construction laws forbade the building of hotels higher than coconut trees, just two floors. To get into her room undetected, she only had to climb the coconut tree stretching past her rear balcony, a foot from the wrought-iron rail.

But she first had to evade the eyes of the watchmen at the front, and maybe others watching the rear balcony.

At six o'clock in the morning, few people meandered around. A couple dressed in flowery colors stood next to suitcases in the open lobby. A cab pulled up. The driver jumped out, loaded up the luggage and departed with the couple. They most likely were headed to Pearls Airport, about an hour of misty, winding mountainous roads away. And probably to board the same eight o'clock flight Hallam and Jackie needed to catch to Barbados.

She and Hallam still had to pack, check out, race to the airport, return the rental car, and allow time to shuffle through customs and immigration.

But before any of this could happen, Jackie still had to get into her room and take a shower without awakening Hallam. She sniffed her shoulders. Her body odor alone would reveal her night of sea water, sweat, and stale piss. She had to have a shower.

She thought of circling the back of the slightly elevated swimming pool to the rear balconies—where her coconut tree waited—but the open spread of immaculate lawns offered little visual cover from the man standing at the pool gate. Maybe she could pull down her cap and pretend to be just a tourist on an early morning walk, but the men would probably see through that.

She could also retrace her steps back down the beach and fight through the brush to the back of the hotel. But that would be a dangerous waste of time. Any minute now, Hallam might shrug off his rum-punch and sleeping-pill hangover to find her gone.

An absence neither he nor the watchmen would be able to explain.

Suddenly, she missed Storm. He would know exactly what to do. She told herself to calm down. Take a few deep breaths. Pick the least risky option.

But which one?

She didn't have to think about her choices for long.

To her horror, the scene unfurling in front of the hotel decided for her. A black sedan raced down the driveway toward the hotel. A rumbling army truck followed. Both vehicles screeched to a halt at the entrance and soldiers jumped out.

Reds slithered out of the sedan and gestured loudly at the man by the pool gate. The man stomped out his cigarette and hurried away from the pool toward Reds.

Reds barked at the man, who then pointed up to Jackie's room.

The unwatched lawn opened up before her. A straight line from her position to the back of the hotel lay in a blind spot to the armed men gathering at the entrance.

While Reds grilled the watchmen, Jackie squeezed through a space in the hedge. To avoid looking suspicious to anyone else who might be watching, she walked past the pool in a casual stroll—in sandals that slipped on the moist lawn grass.

At each step she expected to hear a soldier yell the alarm. At each breath she took, she expected to hear Reds' growl. But instead seagulls chatted over the beach behind her. The army truck idled and its fuel-scented exhaust drifted past in the breeze. Male voices grumbled in urgent tones.

She turned the corner to the back of the hotel. Up ahead, the coconut tree waited for her, five unoccupied balconies away.

She picked up her pace.

Three balconies to go. She stiffened her legs to compensate for the wet grass.

Air conditioning units vibrated against the walls and green lizards scattered. Twigs crunching under her footsteps sounded as loud to her as fireworks.

She reached the tree. Upstairs, the sliding door she'd left open last night remained open. The drapes floated lazily in the sea breeze.

Good.

Her heart drummed. She took a breath and hugged the tree. She positioned one foot against the side. Her sandals slipped down the tree trunk. She tried the other one. It slipped too.

Damn.

She looked down. Wet mud and sand from her sandals pasted the trunk. Tanteen mud mixed with beach sand and grass dew.

She had no time to scrape off her sandals.

A door opened three balconies ahead of her. She remained still behind the tree with just enough room to peek past it. A big shirtless man stepped out. He hocked and spat over the rail. Then he lit a cigarette and took a long drag.

Shouts echoed from the front of the hotel. Heavy boots drummed on concrete pavements. The man turned away to face the other end of the hotel.

Now—or jail.

She kicked off her sandals and hugged the tree again.

She planted her bare feet against the trunk—just as a pair of sweaty hands grabbed her ankles.

CHAPTER EIGHT

Mario gazed through his binoculars at Grand Anse Beach from the deck of his yacht and replayed in his mind the cryptic message he'd received from Barbados around midnight. "Proceed with an abundance of caution. Local situation hostile. Use discretion and maintain secrecy."

Why such warnings to a routine request for a commercial diver on an exotic Caribbean island? The message also gave him directions to a dive shop on the beach, but not the name of the shop or the diver.

Strange.

Strange too how other divers he'd contacted on his cruise from Miami to the Leeward Islands backed away, even when he doubled his offer. The headline news about the harsh revolutionary government had probably scared them off. Maybe the same fear kept visitors away. Only a few people strolled along the white-sand beach. A man threw a stick for his dog to fetch. A couple strolled hand-in-hand.

A girl hurried up the beach toward a hotel.

Suddenly she dropped low and crouched behind a hedge.

Mario sipped the last of his dark Turkish coffee and adjusted the lens on his binoculars. The girl peeked toward the hotel lobby. A black car and a green truck raced unto the driveway to the hotel, past a sign that said *Welcome to the Spice Island Hotel.*

The vehicles pulled up adjacent to the hotel lobby. Armed men jumped out of the vehicles. Two other men rushed up to the group. A tall man in their midst seemed to be giving orders, his hands waving and pointing. Meanwhile, the girl squeezed through the hedge, crossed the lawn, and vanished around the back of the hotel.

Mario lost sight of her, but kept his binoculars focused on the men. They split into three squads, about six men in each. The tall man led one squad upstairs to the second floor and disappeared down a hall away from Mario's view, while the other men took off in opposite directions toward the ends of the hotel.

The armed squad on the ocean side rounded the corner facing the lawn and followed the path the girl had just taken to the back of the hotel.

Strange indeed.

Mario waited a few moments to see what might happen next, but gave up when his crewman climbed to the deck.

"*Signore* Costa," the crewman said. "The dinghy is ready to take you ashore."

"Thank you." He placed the binoculars next to his empty coffee cup. "Did you radio immigration to report our return?"

"Yes. The officer said he still has us on record from yesterday. But he wants us to keep our passports ready and available in case the coast guard pays us a surprise inspection."

"Good. Let's play by the rules."

The midnight warnings and the hotel episode he'd just witnessed heightened Mario's concerns. He needed to exercise extra vigilance to prevent the local situation from turning on him.

He couldn't let that happen now—not after waiting all these years.

***

Jackie's nails hurt as she clutched the tree in desperation to pull away from the sweaty hands gripping her ankles. She turned to see who was holding her, and almost passed out from relief.

She hissed. "Storm, what're you doing here?"

"Shhhh." Sweat dripped past his eyebrows. "Loosen your hold and step on my hands. I'll push you up."

Footsteps and shouts echoed around the corner.

Storm's push propelled her a few feet up the tree, high enough to stretch out her right foot to the ledge of the balcony. Steadying her hold around the tree with one arm, she gripped the rail with the other. She released the tree and pulled herself over the rail.

When she glanced down, Storm was gone.

More shouts.

She squeezed past the balcony table and parted the drapes. Hallam lay across the bed on his back. His mouth gaped open and his jaw trembled in snores almost loud enough to rattle the paintings on the wall.

She stepped into the room. Her knees shook as she tiptoed on the carpeted floor toward the bathroom.

Heavy footsteps pounded the hallway outside the front door. Loud bangs on the door vibrated the walls.

Reds' voice filled the room. "Open up in there."

Hallam moaned and lifted his hands to his head.

Jackie dropped to her knees and scampered across the floor into the bathroom.

More bangs on the door. More of Hallam's groans followed.

She locked the bathroom door behind her, switched on the lights and stripped off her clothes. She turned the shower on full blast and tossed her clothes into the tub.

Heavy hammering on the front door.

She stepped into the tub and let the water soak her from head to toe.

A crash, the sound of splintering wood, then shouts in the room.

Hallam yelled. "What the hell…you doing?"

"Where's she?" Reds shouted.

"Where's who?"

"Don't play stupid. Your wife."

"In the shower, dammit. We have a flight to catch this morning."

"Get her out, now."

Hallam sounded indignant. "Did you hear me? She's taking a damn shower."

Jackie opened the shampoo bottle and emptied it over her head. She lathered and scrubbed her hair, face, and armpits furiously.

Reds hollered. "I don't give a shit what you say. Get her out or I'll break down the fucking door."

"Over my dead body," Hallam said.

Metallic clicks.

"Okay, okay," Hallam said. "Put down your rifles."

Soft taps on the door. "Sweetheart?"

Hallam played the married couple role well. But why?

Shouldn't his entanglement with Bravo also include Reds? A trickle of confusion seeped into her distrust for Hallam.

She pretended she didn't hear him, and squirted liquid soap over her body.

He tapped the door again, and shouted a little louder. "Sweetheart? Can you hear me in there?"

"Yeah. It's hard to hear you with the running water. I'll be right out. Just rinsing my hair."

Loud knocks on her door.

"You in there," Reds said. "Come on out now."

"Colonel Reds? Is that you?" She watched the last muddy brown on her shorts and t-shirt flow down the drain. "What a nice surprise. Did you come to say goodbye?"

"If you don't come out now, you'll be the one saying goodbye—forever!"

She'd stretched Reds' patience to his limit. If he'd killed Rachael, wouldn't he also kill Jackie if pushed too far? "Hallam will make you a cup of coffee while you wait. I'll be right out."

Satisfied she'd washed away all evidence of her night, she turned off the water, then squeezed and hung her clothes on the thin line stretched head-high across the tub. Those would easily fit in a plastic bag for the flight to Barbados.

She wrapped her hair in a towel. A quick application of deodorant and a double-spray of Chanel N°5 cologne restored the final touches of the femininity she'd discarded last night.

"No more warnings," Reds said. "Come on out now or we'll break down the door."

"Please, Colonel," she called out. "This is not a strip show. Let me get on some clothes and I'll be right there." She slipped on her underwear and wrapped herself in a bathrobe.

Reds was standing at the door when she pushed it open.

He barked. "It's about goddamned time."

Other soldiers crowded the room and one stood guard at the front. The front door hung on one hinge. A wooden panel, which held the lock, lay splintered on the floor.

Hallam stood across the room next to the bulky television with two soldiers pointing their rifles at him. "Watch your language with my wife."

"Shut up." Reds turned to his soldiers. "Search everywhere. Bathroom cabinets, under the bed, her suitcase. Everywhere."

She lifted her hands in feigned innocence. "Maybe I can help you find what you're looking for, if you tell me what it is."

"Good idea," Reds said. "We've all had a long night and don't want to waste any more time. Where are the shoes or sandals you wore last night?"

Oh shit!

If anyone looked over the balcony, they would find her sandals sitting at the base of the coconut tree. Maybe Storm had taken them—if he escaped in time.

Fear clouded her thoughts.

She struggled to remain in control.

"Sandals?" She reached into the closet next to the bathroom door and pulled out the pair of blue open-toed dress heels she'd worn to dinner with Hallam. "You mean these?"

"Do you think I am an ass?" Reds' moustache twitched. "You know the ones I am talking about. The ones with flat soles you wore last night to steal a boat and row it to Tanteen. You left us some nice prints in the mud."

Hallam laughed. "This is an amazing story. Tanteen? Colonel Reds, you're mistaken. Christ man, my wife's been here with me all night."

Jackie chuckled, relieved to have Hallam support her story, even though he'd been so comatose last night, he would have slept through a hurricane.

"Colonel," she said. "I am not sure who you've been talking to, but I've not heard such an outrageous thing in a long time." She stepped aside from the bathroom door way to allow a soldier to enter. "But please search as quickly as you can. We have a flight to catch."

Reds fisted one hand into the palm of the other. "You don't go to the airport until I say you go to the airport, understand Miss Bigmouth?"

The soldiers scrambled around the hotel room, lifting mattresses, peeking under the beds, and emptying closets. One soldier pulled out a pair of black slippers from her suitcase.

Reds inspected the soles. "No, not these." He threw them back into the suitcase and glanced around the room, his face wrinkled in thought. He marched across the room to the sliding doors at the rear balcony. "You always leave your sliding doors open with the air conditioning running?"

"My husband had too much to drink last night," she said. "I let the fresh air in this morning to help him wake up."

"Is that so?" His eyebrow lifted. "So how did he know you were here all night?"

Shucks.

She bit her lip and remained silent.

"It's simple, Colonel," Hallam said. "When I got up to use the rest room at 3 o'clock this morning, she was still in bed with me. How drunk do I have to be to not notice *her*?"

Reds stomped his boot on the floor. "I ask the questions around here. Not you."

Why did Hallam lie to save her skin? Maybe his link with Bravo had nothing to do with Reds. It finally struck her she might be wrong about Hallam. He'd been on her side all along—at least in a face-off against Reds.

Would Hallam have played the same game to protect her if Bravo had been standing in the room interrogating them?

Her thoughts froze when Reds slid the drapes open and marched on to the balcony.

Three steps and he reached the rail. He stared at the coconut tree running an arm's length past the balcony.

Please don't look down.

Reds started to lean over the rail when his radio crackled.

***

Mario climbed out of the inflatable dinghy and up the step ladder on the Grand Anse Beach jetty. His crewman shifted the gear in reverse and revved the outboard motor.

"I'll radio you when I'm ready," Mario shouted at him.

"I'll be waiting onboard, *Signore* Costa."

Mario stood at the end of the jetty and watched the dinghy cut a whitewater trail back to his motor yacht, a parting gift from his brothers who'd gently booted him out the door of the Costa Company fifteen years ago. He adjusted his eye patch and squinted at his yacht, anchored a hundred yards offshore on a sandy trough to avoid damaging the reefs. Even from this distance, the hand-me-down yacht pleaded for a paint job to replace the dirty coat she'd worn for years. Since he'd lost his lavish homes to his ex-wife in exchange for visitation rights with Bianca, he called the yacht home.

If his mission to Grenada succeeded, should he buy a super luxury yacht? That was what his father would have done. Yet, surrounded by opulence and glitter, the old man had used a bullet to end the emptiness gnawing his insides.

Mario recalled when he too had craved the glitter. He'd showered his glamorous wife with expensive sparkle that made men green with envy at their frequent social events. Tuxedo nights at the *Teatro dell'Opera di Roma*, candlelight dinners at the romantic *Restorante Matricianella* in Lucina, sunny cruises to magical ports as far apart as Naples and Barcelona in the Mediterranean to Curacao and Caracas in the Caribbean. The young couple savored each other's company—at least he'd thought so.

But from the very day his father died, new business responsibilities poured down on Mario like the avalanche he'd survived on the Swiss Alps. His fingers ached from signing papers. Time once reserved for his wife shrank. The number of opera nights and cruises dwindled—for him, but not for her.

She kept up the social charade without him, and with new gusto. Her cruises went from three-day trips to Barcelona with friends and family, to two-week escapades in the Caribbean by herself. She shopped like it was an Olympic sport, and she the reigning champion. His desires had to scratch past crystal wine glasses and fur coats for fleeting sensual pleasures with her.

Then came the night he couldn't extract from his thoughts. The night she returned from a Caribbean cruise and called out another man's name while in a naked embrace with Mario.

Later the same year Mario became a father, and the giggling little bundle he named Bianca saved his life.

Each time the handgun in his desk called for him, the image of Bianca's radiant smile soothed his mind and relaxed his trigger finger. When Bianca turned two he personally supervised the painting of her name on the white hull of his new ship and took her on the maiden voyage from Naples to Guaira in Venezuela.

His wife stayed home, but he convinced himself as long as he possessed wealth and could spend precious minutes to share it with Bianca, he needed nothing else.

Then the *Bianca C* burned and sank, taking his wealth with it.

"He's suicidal," his wife shrieked in court as he sat numb with an eye patch and bandaged face.

Her hysterics worked on the gowned fatherly judge deciding his future.

When Mario shuffled out of the courthouse and into the cloudy day he felt lucky to still have one eye, the shirt on his back, and a few supervised visits each month with Bianca. The loyalty he expected and his final trust for his now ex-wife took flight in the northern Po Valley winds chilling Genoa that day.

But today, he still trusted his yacht. She never failed him. The yacht provided him a warm bed on those painful nights when he puked out his guts on cheap wine. She floated him away to the middle of the Mediterranean when he needed to escape the memories. If his plans went well here in Grenada, he'd reward her for the years of loyalty. She deserved a complete paint job, new aluminum rails, interior panels, and new cabin curtains. He'd already invested in a modern communication upgrade with an advanced radar system.

He stared out at the ocean graveyard entombing his *Bianca C*. The grief tightened his chest. He'd finally returned to Grenada to regain his life and his wealth. But if he had to choose one, he would choose life over wealth.

He turned away from the sea and hurried off the wooden jetty, pulling down his cap to shield his eye from the morning glare. Small waves whispered along the shoreline and a few sea gulls argued overhead. The warning in last night's cable worried him.

Use discretion and maintain secrecy.

To his right a young woman stepped out of the water, her wet dark skin shimmering in the early sunshine. The direction of the Spice Island Beach Hotel seemed to command her attention as she glided up the shore on firm slender legs. She pulled back her medium-length hair and twisted it. Water trickled over her slender shoulders, past the strap of her red bikini top, and down the exposed curves of her back and waist. She rolled a rubber band off her wrist and fastened her hair into a neat bun. Her bare feet massaged the sand in graceful steps toward a thatched-roof shack nestled in a cluster of coconut trees.

He could not clearly see her face from this angle, but a memory of quick bright eyes and full inviting lips raced his heart.

From a safe distance, he followed her footsteps in the sand.

She pushed open a front door on the side of an open counter and shut it behind her.

He stopped at the counter and waited for her to come around. Only then he noticed the overhead sign, *Storm's Dive Shop.*

When she walked up to the counter, her hand went up to her mouth.

He stretched out his hand. "Cammy, it's me. Please don't faint again."

CHAPTER NINE

Jackie listened intently as Reds' radio crackled, hoping the interruption would pull him away from the rail, and away from a view of the lawn below. Just minutes before, she'd kicked off her sandals to climb up the tree to her balcony. A climb she could not have made without Storm's help. Now her sandals probably lay in the open, with sole prints linking her to the stolen boat found adrift in the St. George's harbor.

"Silent Visitor to Top Dog," Reds' radio crackled again. "Silent Visitor to Top Dog. Come in. Over."

Jackie recognized the gruff voice with the Spanish accent on the radio.

Reds grabbed his radio. "What the hell does he want now?" He made an about face on the balcony.

Thank you, Colonel Bravo. Jackie slowed her breath so as not to miss any of the conversation.

Reds lifted the radio and barked into it. "Top Dog here. Over."

"What's your 20? Over."

He paced the balcony and glanced into the crowded room. "Spice Island Beach Hotel. Over."

"So I heard." Colonel Bravo's pause stretched the seconds. A breeze swept through the room, flipping the pages of an island magazine on the coffee table. The broken front door screeched on one hinge. "Explain how you go from investigating a suspicious boat in Tanteen to breaking down hotel doors. Over."

"This is not the time or place. Over."

"I have a 10:00 am with the PM at HQ. It may be a better time and place to discuss. Over."

PM at HQ?

Jackie watched the color drain from Reds' face. She quickly deduced Bravo had a meeting with Prime Minister Duncan at the headquarters and wanted to use the occasion to dress down Reds. But how did Bravo know so quickly that Reds and his goons had invaded the hotel room? Maybe Bravo had eyes and ears planted all around the island.

"My schedule is booked," Reds said. "Over."

An uncomfortable silence swept through the room. Jackie glanced at Hallam where he leaned against the television with armed soldiers at his sides. He winked blood-shot eyes at her and one side of his face cracked into a slight smile. Even in his hangover daze, he was obviously enjoying the radio tug-of-war between Reds and Bravo.

But she held on to her caution. Hallam still had to explain his own hush-hush phone discussion with Bravo.

What would a Bajan undercover policeman on the CIA payroll and a dangerous Cuban Colonel have to do with Storm and a sunken ship?

She looked at her watch. It would be a miracle now to meet their flight on time. If they missed the flight and became stuck on the island another day or more, Reds might be at liberty to prey on them again.

But at least Colonel Bravo would be scrutinizing his every step. She'd expected those two were allies. If Jackie was wrong about this, what else had she misread?

Colonel Bravo snapped. "My next report to Havana will detail our communications problems. I hope we can resolve it before then. Over and out."

Reds shut off his radio and slammed his fist on the balcony table. "Dammit." He stomped into the room and signaled his soldiers with an up-and-down pump of his fist. "Let's get out of here."

The soldiers filed out the doorway leaving him in the room with Hallam and Jackie.

Reds pointed his finger at Hallam's face. "There's something fishy about you two, and I intend to find out. You can escape back to Barbados, but Storm and his mother are mine. The minute they engage in any counter-revolutionary activity, it will be nasty. You'll read about it in your Barbados newspaper."

He marched out of the room, crushing wooden splinters from the broken door under his boots. The door squeaked in the breeze.

When Reds' steps faded down the hallway, Jackie rushed across the room to the balcony and leaned over the rail.

Her sandals were gone.

Thank you, Storm.

"What are you looking for?" Hallam asked.

"I'll explain later." She glanced at her watch. "We have to get going to catch—"

The phone rang. Hallam frowned at Jackie. She shrugged.

Maybe the front desk inquiring about the damages?

Hallam picked up the phone. "Hello." He nodded a few times. "Yeah, she's right here."

He handed the phone to her and she immediately recognized the voice on the other end.

"Senorita, this is Colonel Bravo from the Cuban embassy." His tone had switched from the abrupt radio conversation with Reds to a melodic delivery Jackie would have expected from a suave Latino playboy asking her to dance. "My humble apologies for what you just endured."

"Thank you, sir. We're okay."

"I understand you have an early flight. Is there anything we can do for you?"

She seized the chance. "Yes there is, sir." She explained all Hallam and she still had to do to catch their flight, plus this new unpleasant business of reporting a damaged door to the hotel manager.

"Don't worry about anything," Colonel Bravo said. "Just pack your bags. I'll have my personal driver come by in a few minutes to take you both to the airport. And I'll see to it that Colonel Reds handles the rental car and pay for the damages to the room."

***

Storm covered up Jackie's sandals in the brush and pushed his way through the undergrowth away from the Spice Island Hotel, replaying in his mind the radio conversation he'd heard between Reds and Bravo. He'd stayed hidden in the tree line away from the searching soldiers but close enough to hear their words.

The friction that filled the air left no doubt the two men despised each other, even as they appeared to be working toward the same military goal. Cuban and Soviet shipments of armory clearly operated with Reds' complicity. His soldiers protected the harbor and patrolled the streets to maintain secrecy. Could the arms buildup on the island be connected to the weird phone conversation Jackie had overheard between Bravo and Hallam the previous night?

Storm didn't have a clue why they associated his name with a ship buried for twenty-two years under a hundred feet of water. He'd seen the rusting hull from a distance, but never got close enough to touch it.

Surely Hallam's secret phone conversations with Bravo had betrayed trust the Americans had in him. But why? The Marines had taught Storm the four key reasons agents turn against their own. 'MICE' stood for money, ideology, compromise, and ego or extortion. Had one of these been used to turn Hallam against his American handlers?

Clearly, Reds had been left out of whatever plot entangled Bravo and Hallam. The radio conversation left Storm no doubt that the hotel incident had stretched further any rift that previously existed between Bravo and Reds.

Relieved when Reds finally left the hotel without arresting Jackie, Storm hurried back toward his dive shop. Just in case Reds decided to make another unannounced visit.

Storm retraced his steps across the bushy terrain to the narrow road, and then cut left onto the beach. More people strolled along the powdery white sand or mingled in the shallow blue water than an hour earlier. No one seemed to pay attention to him when he kicked off his jogging shoes and dove into the water in his shorts and t-shirt.

He turned around to scan the length of the beach. Two people sat in front of his open shop, maybe Cammy and another of her many annoying male acquaintances. No sign of Reds and his soldiers.

One fully dressed man sat in the shadow of a coconut tree with a pair of binoculars hanging from his neck.

Storm chuckled. If the man worked for Reds, his Grand Anse report might read: "Storm went for a swim. But so did twenty other people."

Satisfied his piss stench had been washed away, Storm grabbed his shoes and raced up the shore to his dive shop.

Cammy, in her red bikini, sat on the sand in front of the shop. Next to her—close to her—sat a man wearing a blue cap crested with the green, white, and red *Italia* flag. Probably to deflect the kind of negative attention a Stars and Stripes USA cap might attract.

When they turned to face Storm, he recognized the man with the eye patch.

Cammy and the man stood. Lush salt-and-pepper hair flowed out from under the cap and gleamed in the morning sunlight. The wind flapped his embroidered jersey around his lean physique, but the sleeves held their well-pressed creases. So did the creases on the khaki Bermuda shorts, which matched with his brown sandals.

Standing about equal height to Storm, the man dusted the sand off his hand and extended it to shake Storm's.

"This is Mario," Cammy said. "You met him last night."

Storm watched Mario's hand and hesitated. He hadn't the time to be sucked into another of Cammy's toxic friendships with men like Reds who'd walked in and out of her life as far back as he remembered.

Other more pressing concerns competed for Storm's attention: Reds haunted him, Americans wanted to recruit him in a dangerous operation, and he wanted to patch things up with Jackie by helping free her father from prison.

He had no room for another round of pretentious handshakes and smiles from men, local or foreign, who just wanted to bed his mother.

"Is there any reason I should meet you?" Storm asked, tasting the bitterness in his words.

Cammy hissed. "Storm!"

Storm glanced at Mario's outstretched hand. "It's not personal," he said to Mario. "I hope you understand you're not the first man my mother introduced me to. I just don't like memorizing the names of men who walk in and out of her life like she's a doormat."

Cammy's eyes burned at him with pain he'd only seen when she grieved for Rachael.

She faced Storm with rage simmering her words. "You can't be my son." She raced into the shop and slammed the door behind her.

Mario turned red and withdrew his hand. Emotion trembled in his European accent. "I am terribly sorry. I came here because someone with high regard for your diving skills recommended I talk to you. Cammy . . . your mother was just telling me about the diving you did in the American military."

Storm might have lost a potential customer, but so what. He'd had enough of these men. Wasn't that how she brought Reds into her life? Thick discomfort hung in the air, even in the sea breeze chilling Storm's damp clothes to his skin.

He turned to leave, but Mario's words stopped him. "Your mother is hurt."

"There's enough hurt to go around," Storm said.

Mario looked briefly over his shoulder at the sea, and then back at Storm.

"I came a long way for a dive, young man," he said. "Right now it's more important for you to go back in there and tell your mother how much you love her."

Storm stared at Mario's face to see if it might betray a hint of humor behind the strange words none of Cammy's men ever used. Burn scars, like the ones Storm had seen on some combat veterans, covered one side of Mario's face from below his eye patch to his jaw line. The other side of his face, clean shaven and tanned, radiated with compassion—and patience.

Mario continued. "I can only imagine how you feel. You lost your sister, and you don't want to lose your mother. She's all you have left." He held Storm by the shoulders. "You don't have to hurt her to keep her. Go back in there and tell her your fears. You'll both feel better. I'll be back in an hour. We can talk about diving later."

Mario turned and headed down the beach leaving Storm bewildered—and feeling like he'd just stepped barefoot into a deep pile of warm cow crap.

✳✳✳

Nothing seemed to calm Jackie's confusion. Not even the cool Grand Étang mountain breeze blowing through the open window of the Mercedes sedan on the drive to Pearls Airport. She sat in the back seat with Hallam, staring at the small Cuban flag shivering over the hood. Something didn't quite fit, but the harder she tried to sort things out, the more puzzled she became.

Earlier, the Cuban embassy driver had sped them away from the hotel, through sluggish Belmont traffic and up the steep Lowthers Lane to bypass the St. George's congestion. In the distance, the dark forbidding windows of Richmond Hill Prison glared down at her. The long green-roofed structure dominated the hilltop with high walls and razor wire.

Somewhere in there, her father battled diabetes without proper medical attention. She ached for him. The promise by the Americans to gain his freedom had convinced her to help recruit Storm in their secret plans for the island.

Now, premonition clouded her thoughts.

Nothing she'd learned so far made her feel she'd see her father soon—or ever again. Might her involvement with the Americans jeopardize his life, rather than free him? And had she gotten Storm entangled in more danger than she'd been led to believe, just one month after his sister's death? It felt like she'd led him into a growing web of deception, with Hallam, Bravo, and Reds about to devour themselves and those around them.

But why?

Bravo's unexpected generosity also faced Jackie's scrutiny. His cool phone conversation assured her the plane would be waiting and they would leave Grenada safely. Yet, something he'd said bothered her, and the annoyance fluttered around her brain without delivering an answer.

As they drove higher into the lush Grand Étang Mountains, the Cuban driver glanced back in his seat. "*Senora*, I can turn up the windows if the breeze gets *muy frio*."

The cool air helped keep her awake after the long sleepless night. "It feels good, thank you." She chuckled at the thought of being called *Senora*.

That's it. It finally hit her.

The driver referred to her as *Senora*, assuming she and Hallam was a married couple.

Bravo had called her *Senorita*. He must have known they were not married, but let it slip.

If Bravo knew this all along, then he knew their passports were fakes. Hallam must have also betrayed to Bravo her identity, the Americans' plans, and Storm's agreement to join them.

Then why hadn't Bravo arrested them, or at least instructed Reds to do so?

The only explanation making sense to her was that Bravo was playing the same clever game he perfected as an agent in Angola.

A cat and mouse game, where in the end he always walked away as the victor and his opponents always ended up dead.

CHAPTER TEN

Storm stood next to Cammy outside his shop, watching Mario fade down the beach in the morning haze. "I had no idea Mario was the one who handed you his daughter while the *Bianca C* was burning. I'm sorry I overreacted."

Cammy embraced him. "You're a possessive son. And I love you for it."

"I love you too." He held her tight. "I just wish one good man would stay in your life."

She chuckled. "When the right one comes, I'll keep him."

"So what's Mario doing back in Grenada without his family?"

"He doesn't have a family. His wife divorced him and took everything."

"His daughter Bianca must be grown now."

"He has no one left. She's gone too, died a few years later from a blood disease. They tried to use Mario's blood to save her, but the tests revealed he was not Bianca's father."

When Mario returned to the dive shop about an hour later with sweat dripping from his forehead, Storm was ready to bury his own head in the sand. Instead he handed Mario a cold orange Fanta from the ice chest as a goodwill gesture.

"This should cool you down," Storm said.

"Thank you," Mario said. "Great beach for walks."

Cammy chimed in. "When we live here all our lives, it takes visitors like you to remind us what we have."

"I will do all I can to remind you." Mario downed half the bottle before pausing for a breath. "Perfect."

"Is now a good time to discuss your dive?" Storm asked.

Mario gazed out at his yacht. "Many years ago, a young mother saved me and my daughter from a burning ship. She sheltered us and fed us. Then she refused my money." He faced Cammy and Storm. "I would like to invite you both to dinner on my humble yacht tonight. We can discuss the dive then."

Cammy shook her head. "Oh . . . but it's not safe for us to be driving around at night."

"Then come before sunset and stay the night. I have enough beds for you both. The sky will be clear tonight and the moon will be bigger."

"Okay." Cammy looked at Storm and smiled like a teenaged girl asking for permission to accept her first dance invitation. "Okay?"

"Okay," Storm said.

"Terrific." Mario said. "I hope you like red wine with your lobster."

Storm chuckled. His preference for red wine with seafood dinners in Morehead City restaurants used to bring surprised looks from his friends and servers. White wine just never appealed to him.

At least he had something in common with Mario.

He watched Cammy accompany Mario in a casual stroll down to the jetty to await his dinghy. For two people who hadn't seen each other for twenty-two years, they seemed like they'd never been apart. He wondered how letters alone could have sustained their friendship over the years.

But another nagging thought dragged his attention away from them.

Mario hadn't said yet which site he wanted to dive. Storm could only guess that if Mario, the owner of the *Bianca C,* returned to the island after such a long time, he might want to dive his own ship.

If so, then the phone conversation between Bravo and Hallam made more sense. They must have discovered in advance that Mario would be asking Storm to dive the ship.

But who else but Mario could have given them that information?

***

Reds lay in his bed listening to his cat purring on the pillow next to him. In all his years, Toompin was the only living creature who'd never judged him. They had bonded since the night he rescued the shivering kitten from rain and hunger. Toompin slept long hours, but dedicated every waking minute to pleasing Reds, either depositing shredded lizards and bloody rats at his back door, or massaging his chest while he watched television. And when he collapsed in bed after long hours of defending Grenada's revolution, she would knead his hairy chest with her claws and purr against his heartbeat until he fell asleep.

Toompin was the only one who knew Reds had a heart.

While Toompin brought him comfort and reassurance, people poisoned his dignity with stinging humiliation and disappointment. Bravo, Cammy, Storm, and now the young lieutenant.

Trained in Cuba and Bulgaria, the lieutenant should have given Reds more intelligent advice this morning. Instead, he'd planted seeds and theories that triggered Reds' mad race down to Grand Anse with his soldiers. They'd stopped the crowded bus and searched it, for naught. Then they rumbled into the Spice Island Beach Hotel, smashing a room door and inspecting shoe soles in a frantic search for a female spy.

This resulted in yet another degrading confrontation with Bravo and a repair bill for a broken hotel door. Reds could not stoop to apologize to the hotel manager, as Bravo demanded, so Reds ordered the lieutenant to do so with his tail between his legs. It served the lieutenant right.

And to cap it all, Bravo had insisted Reds show up to a closed-door meeting with Prime Minister Duncan, probably expecting Reds to crawl through the door and sit meekly at the table with a dead man.

Hell no.

Duncan's days were numbered.

Reds would rather lie in bed with Toompin and muster his own thoughts around his plan to seize power.

All he had to do was exercise patience, but he must be more cautious going forward.

Too much was at stake.

Politically, it was only a matter of time. Prime Minister Duncan's recent visit to Washington had signaled his displeasure with the ideological direction the island had taken. This raised alarms among Grenada's Eastern Bloc friends and elevated Reds as their favored candidate to assume power—in the event Duncan met an untimely demise.

Militarily, all the pieces were falling into place. Even as Colonel Bravo seemed oddly confrontational with him, the Bulgarian conduit regularly kept Reds apprised of the progress. Their last phone call a couple days ago had filled Reds with optimism. The main armaments delivered at the port were already in secret locations around the island. The runway, even with an incomplete terminal, stood ready to accommodate the Soviet's largest aircrafts. The Ilyushin-76s were probably already fueled in Havana and ready to take off with the final installments of the plan.

Excitement raced through Reds' veins when he repeated Marshal Ogarkov's words to himself. "For two decades there was only Cuba in Latin America, today there are Nicaragua, Grenada, and a serious battle is underway in El Salvador."

The Marshal of the Soviet Union then emphasized how countries like Grenada must be in solidarity with the Soviet Union to prevent American imperialism from turning back history.

Fifteen years ago, Neal Armstrong had landed on the moon saying "One small step for man, one giant leap for mankind." Reds' next steps might be in a small country, but for the future of mankind, he would stand shoulder to shoulder among the giants of history, the architects of historical inevitability—and world communism.

So why had Bravo suddenly turned antagonistic toward Reds, especially in recent weeks after *Bianca C* became the centerpiece of their conversations?

Maybe Bravo intended to test Reds' resolve and commitment.

But hadn't Reds already passed the test in Rachael's case?

Events of the past couple days dimmed Reds' vision of his future. Separately, the Bajan couple, *Bianca C*, Storm, and Bravo, all seemed like petty annoyances in the grand scheme. Yet, together they looked ominous, like hurricane clouds gathering on the horizon.

Toompin climbed on to Red's chest and purred. A fruit-scented breeze blew through his window, carrying the sound of a ripe mango crashing down from the backyard tree. His grandmother used to warn him about the dangers of living life like a ripe mango.

"Stay green," she would say. "When you're ripe, you fall and spoil."

What would she say today, if she saw him now? As Chief of the Grenada People's Revolutionary Army, he'd earned this white hilltop mansion with guarded gates, swimming pool, and cocktail parties with world leaders and generals. The walls around his room shimmered with military regalia, medals, and framed certificates. He even had a soldier just to shine his boots and iron his uniforms. The smell of leather, shoe polish, and starch blended in an assuring fragrance.

He adjusted his pillow, crossed his legs at the ankles, and gazed at the shine on his boots. His grandmother was no longer around to belt him for wearing shoes in bed, but he would remember her advice. He would remain green. He would remain on guard. He would remind himself to seek his own counsel and never trust anyone—not even Bravo.

People were unpredictable, unreliable, and vulnerable to mushy emotions. Reds' world required structure and unquestioning obedience in order to correct human flaws. All his personal failings traced back to his lack of absolute control. Cammy, Storm, and the lieutenant immediately surfaced on his mind.

Toompin's purrs calmed him.

He'd just begun to doze off when his private phone rang. "Yes?"

He listened intensely to the man on the other end of the phone.

"Storm and his mother had a conversation with the owner of the big yacht," the man said. "The owner's immigration papers have his name as Mario Costa. But when Mr. Costa returned to his yacht, Storm closed up his shop early and went home before lunch."

"Interesting."

"Storm's mother act like she know him long time."

"What do you mean?"

"She talked to him for a longer time. And she walk with him down to the jetty."

"The whore always walks with men. So what?"

"It all add up when you see the name of the yacht."

"What's the name?"

"*Carmen*."

"You sure?"

"Yes, sir."

The ominous clouds began to gather again, and a renewed sense of urgency kicked in.

"I think tonight is a good time to pay the *Carmen* a surprise visit."

***

That afternoon, Storm pulled Cammy by her hand to help her up the step ladder from the dinghy tied alongside Mario's yacht. Storm had tried to persuade her that wearing a dress on a windy yacht might be a bad idea, but he knew he'd lost the argument after she spent an hour in front of the mirror in her favorite dress. She'd worn it for Mario the previous night, but he'd already disappeared out the front door. Storm knew she would not let this chance escape again.

A picture of her in the same body-hugging halter dress with plunging V neckline had found a convenient home on his barracks wall in North Carolina—too convenient for drooling Marines who refused to believe such a shapely young woman could be his mother.

He always enjoyed the glee Cammy radiated when she dressed-up to hold center stage for men's attention. But he forbade his thoughts from imagining what it meant when she had them alone behind closed doors. Now in the late afternoon sunshine, in her blue and white dress Cammy looked perfectly matched with the blue sea and Mario's white yacht.

"Welcome aboard." Mario's eye-patched smile emitted delight as he reached out to hold Cammy's other hand. Her glittering tropical-fish earrings jingled when he embraced her.

Mario's hair shone in the sunlight and his black Polo shirt hung casually over tan slacks, a more subdued appearance than Storm expected from the former owner of a luxury cruise ship.

Despite Mario's warm hospitality, Storm remained suspicious.

How had Bravo and Hallam known in advance that Mario would be attempting to recruit Storm for a *Bianca C* dive? And most puzzling of all, what about Mario's plans that attracted such secretive phone conversations between Bravo and Hallam?

Jackie had risked her life to tell Storm about the phone call. Storm owed her the answer—and a lot more.

Mario led Cammy and Storm on a tour of his aging yacht. Storm followed them on the full walk-around deck, unable to avoid seeing the gentle way

Mario clasped Cammy's hand to guide her down the stairwells and hallways. She seemed relaxed in the new surroundings, as if she'd spent more time aboard luxury boats than Storm knew of.

He'd seen the name *Carmen* painted on the front of the boat, but if she'd noticed it, she said nothing. He decided to keep tight-lipped to hear if Mario would slip an explanation.

"This yacht has been my home for many years," Mario said. "Ninety feet long, five guest cabins, and powered by twin diesel engines."

Creaky floors and smudged walls tainted the otherwise generous layout of the yacht's comfortable interior living area. The lounge embraced sparse furniture, coffee table, couch and loveseat, all in faded tropical colors. Thin curtains struggled to keep out the afternoon rays spraying over a built-in breakfast nook and glittering against glasses and bottles in a well-stocked bar across the lounge.

Double doors led to a spacious dining area on the aft deck. Frayed corners of a light blue table cloth fluttered in the sea breeze on a table surrounded by eight mismatched chairs.

Just in time, mouth-watering seafood smells floated from below deck and quickly restored Storm's assurance in the old yacht.

Mario took them down a narrow stairwell and past the galley manned by a crewman wearing an apron splotched with cooking ingredients. "My chef will give you a little taste of Italy, lobster lasagna. We took a taxi fifteen miles to Gouyave where we found the largest fresh lobsters."

Storm guessed from the bouquet of flowers on the dining table upstairs Mario had been shopping for more than just lobsters.

Mario opened squeaky doors into cozy cabins furnished with double beds and desks. "These cabins need a woman's touch," he said to Cammy. "Let me know if you see any changes I can make."

Cammy stepped into the fifth cabin and crossed the floor to the windows. She held one of the curtains, yellowed with age and sagging on a rusty spring-tension rod. She swiped the curtain with her palm and powdered material drifted like dandruff in the sunrays.

She turned to Mario. "I can sew you some new curtains. My Singer sewing machine will be happy to do that for you. You will need new rods too."

Storm recalled Cammy sewing school uniforms and wedding dresses to earn extra money, especially after she had Reds kicked out of the house. She also sewed dazzling costumes for her male friends who played in carnival bands every February, on the two days before Ash Wednesday. Storm remembered the day Rachael fitted one of the costumes around him while Cammy was gone. Rachael folded the sleeves of the oversized black silk cape, trimmed in red and decorated with fake diamonds, and led him to the mirror. The glass nuggets, like the ones she and Pauline had played with on the bed, had lit up his reflection with an aura that seemed to transport him to a new world.

Cammy's sewing skills would certainly give Mario's yacht a badly needed facelift.

Mario chuckled at her proposal. "We have a deal, but only if you agree to one condition."

She strutted back across the cabin toward him with a tease in her eyes. "What exactly do you have in mind, Mr. Costa?"

"Let my crew bring your sewing machine on board so you can work here."

"And," she said, tapping her chin with her index finger, "why would I want to do that?"

He laughed heartily. "So I can supervise you, of course."

She giggled and they shook hands. "Deal."

It bothered Storm that they did not discuss the price.

Under a moonlit sky, red wine flowed amidst a delicious dinner of triple-decker lobster lasagna with garlic bread, fresh garden salad, and skewers of local fruit. The sea clapped gently against the yacht, swaying it to soft Italian music from overhead speakers. In the distance, St. George's twinkling lights reminded Storm of the late night he sailed out of Morehead City on the USS *Iwo Jima*, bound for the Lebanon deployment. He tossed back the last of the wine in his glass and glanced across the table at Cammy. Mario sat at the head of the table to her left while she sat across from Storm. He couldn't recall the last time he'd seen her glow with such contentment. While bottles of rum had failed to drown her month of grief over Rachael and years of torment with Reds, it seemed dinner and laughter with Mario had rejuvenated her.

With a light touch of his hand to her elbow, Mario excused himself from the table and disappeared into the lounge.

She leaned over the table and sniffed the bouquet of flowers. "Do you think he bought these just for me?"

Storm laughed. "I hope he didn't buy them for me."

They were still laughing when Mario returned carrying a red binder.

"I feel left out of the joke," he said.

Cammy giggled. "We couldn't tell if you bought the flowers for Storm or me."

"That will be the mystery of the night. If you don't figure out the answer by morning, I'll tell you."

He had a crewman clear the table then spread out a three-foot long blueprint from the binder.

"This is the *Bianca C*," Mario said.

Storm leaned over the blueprint, a maze of lines labeled in Italian. A red circle at the front of the ship drew Storm's attention.

Mario pointed his finger in the middle of the circle. "This is where I want you to go."

"Me? What about you?"

"I don't scuba dive much anymore, son."

Just then the crewman marched up and whispered in Mario's ear.

Mario quickly refolded the blueprint and returned it to the red binder.

"Stay here." He nodded toward shore. "Looks like we have unannounced visitors." He hurried into the lounge area with the binder tucked under his arm.

Storm glanced over his shoulder in the direction of a speeding motor. A boat raced toward them with the spotlight on full blast.

CHAPTER ELEVEN

Confused, Storm watched the boat with a Cuban flag pull up aft of Mario's yacht. Why were Cubans patrolling Grenada waters?

While one man on the boat controlled the helm, the other, a burly man, adjusted the vinyl fenders at the side to cushion the hulls when they touched.

"Good evening, gentlemen," Mario shouted.

The burly man leaned forward. "Colonel Bravo from the Cuban Embassy. Permission to come aboard, sir."

"Permission granted, *mi amigo*," Mario shouted back. "As long as you have a couple extra Havana cigars."

Colonel Bravo laughed. "I might have more than you asked for, *Capitàno*."

Storm wondered if the *mi amigo* meant the men knew each other, or was just the friendly manner in which seafaring people greeted each other.

Bravo had also referred to Mario as *Capitàno*, not *Capitán*. He already knew Mario was Italian, either from his accent, or from Bravo's access to immigration documents.

The colonel and his crewman tossed ropes onto the *Carmen*. Mario's men held the ropes while Colonel Bravo climbed aboard the groaning deck ladder. Bravo barked instructions in Spanish to his crewman, who then retrieved the ropes, revved his motor, and pulled away from the yacht.

The boat whipped around and sped back to shore.

It looked like Bravo had invited himself on the yacht with plans to stay a while.

Clearly, Mario had not expected new company. He had reacted in surprise when the boat pulled up, quickly disappearing to conceal his *Bianca C* blueprint.

Something within the red circle on the print had drawn Mario back to the island after twenty-two years. Whatever it was, it had also attracted hostile attention— from a CIA turncoat and a Cuban executioner.

Storm watched Bravo's every move. The colonel turned and faced them with a chewed-up cigar stump sticking out of his mouth. Completely bald, he had a thick shoe-polish black moustache stretching across his round face like a belt of dark cloud across a full moon. His short-sleeved safari shirt, with button-down pockets and shoulder flaps, ballooned around his stomach and hung almost to his knees.

Storm did not have to guess why one side of Bravo's shirt protruded slightly from his bloated waist. Bravo carried a handgun, probably the standard issue pistol for the Soviet KGB, the Makarov 9mm. With a magazine clip of eight rounds, Bravo carried enough firepower to take out all six of them on board, including Mario's three crewmen. He'd have two rounds to spare and surely another magazine saved in one of the many pockets in his shirt and khaki shorts.

When Storm glanced up, Bravo was watching him with squinted eyes. A half smile wrinkled one corner of Bravo's mouth.

He retrieved a wrapped cigar from his top pocked and handed it to Mario. "As promised."

"Hmmm." Mario twirled the cigar under his nose and shook Bravo's hand. "*Grazie mille.*"

"You're welcome. True Cuban gentlemen never make a social call without blessing their guests with one of our finest." He extended his hand to Cammy. "And who is this beautiful lady?"

"Excuse my bad manners," Mario said. "This is Cammy Butler and her son, Storm. My name is Mario."

Bravo kissed Cammy's hand and shook Storm's. "You're a well-built young man. Are you with the People's Revolutionary Army?"

"No, sir."

"Ah, you speak differently. Have you been to America?"

"Briefly." Storm wondered how Bravo detected the trace of an American accent after just two words. From the secret phone conversation Jackie had picked up between Hallam and Colonel Bravo, the colonel obviously knew more about Storm than he wanted to reveal. The colonel already had the answers to his questions.

"Army?" Bravo asked.

"Marines."

"Maybe the Grenada militia could use your skills?"

Cammy spoke up. "Right now he's too busy running a dive shop."

Storm chuckled in silence. Cammy would never let Storm forget he was her son.

"Shall we sit a while?" Bravo asked.

Mario led them back to the dining table, lit more by the full moon than the yacht's feeble overhead light bulbs. "If I had known you were visiting tonight, I would have saved you some lobster dinner."

"I am sure we'll have other occasions." Bravo filled the chair Cammy had earlier, across from Storm.

Mario pulled over another chair for Cammy to sit next to him at the head of the table while one of the crewmen served a round of red wine.

Mario got to the point. 'To what do we owe our gratitude for such a pleasant visit?"

"Mr. Costa, we like to make our foreign guests feel at home here in Grenada."

Mr. Costa? Mario had not told Bravo his last name.

If Bravo intended to feign a casual visit and to convey the impression he had no hidden interest in them, it wasn't working—thanks to the information Jackie had given Storm.

Storm's spirit lifted when he remembered he'd booked his flight to Barbados tomorrow afternoon. While he expected his two-day trip to be taken up with meetings at the American Embassy, he hoped for some private moments with Jackie.

Bravo struck a match and cupped his hands around it to light Mario's cigar. When the tip of the cigar flared, it glowed against Bravo's eyes—the coldest eyes Storm had ever seen.

"I want you to have a pleasant visit," Bravo said. "But we have some paranoid people on the island. I don't want any of them to intrude."

"I'm sure it'll be okay," Mario said.

"I'm not so sure." Bravo pulled two business cards from his top pocket and handed one each to Storm and Mario. "Call me if there's anything I can do for you. There's very little I can't do here because—"

The sound of a speeding boat slashed through their conversation.

"Hmmm." Bravo glanced at his watch. "I'm not expecting my driver this soon."

The boat slowed and glided closer to them. A Grenada flag slapped gold, green, and red over the helm. Three solders staggered on the rocking boat, their AK-47s in wild aims at the yacht.

A fourth soldier held a megaphone in one hand and a pistol in the other.

"Everyone, stay where you are," Colonel Reds shouted.

CHAPTER TWELVE

Bravo's cigar stump remained unlit. But when Reds' boat blasted the *Carmen* with a blaze of white spotlight, Storm thought he saw smoke rise from the Cuban's nostrils.

Bravo pushed back his chair, the legs scratching the wood floor with his weight. He rose slowly to his feet, like a cat about to spring on an unsuspecting prey. He reached below his shirt and withdrew his Makarov.

The safety clicked.

Shit!

Storm pulled Cammy to the floor. "Get down," he whispered to Mario.

They crawled under the table and into the living area. Mario directed them behind the bar. They huddled low. The crewmen's footsteps hurried past them and down the stairwell.

When Storm looked around at the dozens of wine bottles stacked around them, he realized how unsafe it would be if AK-47 bullets from Reds' soldiers began to puncture holes around the yacht.

Storm felt naked. "Do you have any weapons?" he asked Mario.

"Yes, in a desk back in Italy. I don't like guns."

Four years of packing an M16 rifle, M7 bayonet, and a handful of fragmentation grenades had fed Storm's sense of invincibility. Now with a firefight about to ignite in front of his face, he felt helpless. The most he could wish for if hell broke loose was to grab a couple of the wine bottles, dash down to the engine room, and refill them with gasoline. A Molotov cocktail or two might give Reds a taste of the fiery trap he'd set for Jackie's father four years earlier.

Storm peered out from behind the bar for a clearer view of the deck.

Bravo stomped toward the step ladder, his boots pounding the floor.

"Comrade," he shouted at the boat nudging against the *Carmen*. "Turn off that light, or someone will die here tonight."

"Colonel...Colonel Bravo?" Surprise floated Reds' voice to a high pitch. "I didn't expect—"

"Turn off the fucking light, now." Bravo lifted his handgun and pointed it at the boat.

Two shots rang out.

Glass shattered, and moonlight reclaimed the yacht.

The breeze blew in a sniff of gunpowder.

Cammy squeezed Storm's hand. Mario wrapped his arm around her waist and held her close.

Metallic clicks from the boat.

"Hold your fire!" Reds shouted.

Italian music strummed on with the soft claps of the sea against the hull.

Bravo lowered his pistol. "I hope you have a logical explanation for your rude intrusion into a pleasant evening."

"I didn't expect—"

"What were you expecting, Comrade?"

"This is...not the time and place... to talk." Reds' words stumbled in the night.

"Havana will hear about this," Bravo said. "I'm ready to leave. Take me back to the jetty."

"I have questions for these—"

"We're leaving now!" Bravo's voice cut through the sea breeze with a razor-sharp edge Storm had last heard from Parris Island drill instructors.

Storm stood and helped Cammy to her feet. Mario held her hand and the three walked back onto the deck.

"Sorry to see you leave in such a hurry, Colonel Bravo," Mario said.

Bravo shook his hand and then Cammy's. "I hope we meet again under better circumstances."

He turned to Storm, and, with his back toward Reds, shook Storm's hand in a vice grip. "Call me if you need anything," he whispered. "*Anything.*"

Bravo marched to the step ladder and lowered himself onto Reds' boat.

Reds holstered his pistol and glared at Storm from the bobbing craft. "Unpack your bags. I canceled your flight to Barbados. Surrender your passport to Internal Affairs by nine o'clock in the morning. You'll never leave this island."

Disheartened by Reds' pronouncements, Storm watched the boat lights shrink toward Grand Anse Beach. Something more powerful than ideology had come between communist comrades, Reds and Bravo. Powerful enough to have them draw guns on each other. It even pulled the Cuban spymaster into an alliance with a CIA operative.

Whatever it was rested a hundred feet under water, in the red circle of Mario's *Bianca C* blueprint—where Mario wanted Storm to dive.

***

Reds towered over Bravo, but the Cuban's rock-solid demeanor gave Reds pause as they faced off on Grand Anse Beach. Bravo's bald head shone in the moonlight and sat like an inflated basketball on imposing shoulders—almost like he didn't have a neck.

It was Bravo's fault Reds had made such an embarrassing entry at the yacht tonight. Reds had planned a full search of the yacht for evidence of espionage he could pin on Storm and Cammy. This was Reds' jurisdiction, his authority, his duty.

He waited until his soldiers retreated up the beach from the heated conversation to come.

"Why the secrecy?" he asked Bravo. "If you had informed me of your plan to visit the yacht, I would have delayed the search until morning."

"Did *you* alert me of *your* plans?" Bravo barked, locking his arms across his barrel chest. "You've tested my patience long enough. You have your day-to-day security functions. I have mine. If you keep stepping on my toes, someone will get hurt and it won't be me."

Reds slapped the handgun on his waist. "Are you threatening me?"

"I don't make threats." Bravo stepped closer to Reds, his cigar breath staining the air. "I keep them."

"Is that what you call socializing with counter revolutionaries out there on the yacht? They are trained by the Yankees and are dangerous."

"I have dealt with dangerous people all my life. Right now, you are becoming one of them."

"You expect me to let Storm roam the island free to thumb his nose at us?" Reds yelled.

"His sister was your responsibility," Bravo shouted back. "Now he's mine, dammit. They are all mine to dispatch when the time is right. Just stay out of the way. Got it?"

Bravo turned and marched onto the jetty where his embassy boat waited.

The boat cut white water toward the Pointe Saline peninsula until the night swallowed it up. Even with Bravo gone, the relief Reds expected did not materialize.

And he knew why.

He turned his attention to the *Carmen*, floating offshore. The gall of that one-eyed Italian to name his yacht after a Grenadian woman—Reds' woman. The sight earlier of Mario on the deck with Storm and Cammy spun turmoil on Reds' mind. Anyone who didn't know them would think they were a family. But Reds knew better. This multicolored trio wore a disarming innocence to mask the kind of danger Bravo would never understand. They posed a danger, not only to Reds' political ambitions, but to his fragile dignity.

Pressure bulged at his temple and he felt like exploding when the last light turned off on the *Carmen*.

He'd missed his opportunity on Belmont Road earlier this morning. He had them trapped like mice in the white pickup. But in the interest of prudence, he'd let them escape. And now his punishment came in a tidal wave of fury crashing over him.

Cammy was about to pleasure the scar-faced Italian—pleasure she'd denied Reds for so many years.

He turned and headed up the beach to where his driver awaited him. "Take me home."

Tonight more than any other, he needed to feel the claws of his cat Toompin dig into his chest.

Reds glanced at the nightstand clock again. It was 3 o'clock in the morning. He'd lost count of the number of times he'd rolled over to check the time or the number of sleepless minutes that had slipped by since he'd collapsed on the bed after the Grand Anse debacle.

Despite the creaky fan overhead, the humidity soaked his brow in sweat and mosquitoes buzzing at his ears aggravated him. His simmering anger must have repulsed Toompin. She kept her distance from him and fell asleep at the foot of the bed. Images of Cammy wrapped in the arms of another man congested his thoughts.

All that mattered to him seemed out of his control.

His only hope had come in whispered promises from his Eastern Bloc comrades. In cities from Havana to Sofia and Moscow, they'd promised him eventual authority over his own island, ample reward for his loyalty to the Soviet doctrine of expansion.

And most comforting, they had expressed supreme confidence in Colonel Bravo's role, perfected in Africa, to usher in Reds' ascendance to the top of the political ladder.

All appeared to have been progressing as planned—until Bravo's obsession turned to Storm and the *Bianca C.*

The *Bianca C*, Bravo had told him, was part of a CIA plot. The Americans had infiltrated an agent onto the island to plant a network of listening devices on sunken ships outside the harbor, starting with the *Bianca C*. These devices could be calibrated not only to measure the traffic and weight of ships entering and leaving the St. George's harbor, but also to signal the results to American submarines lurking in international waters.

The agent, Bravo had said, was already in place and awaiting delivery of the electronics.

The agent?

Storm Butler.

Reds' very own Storm. The kid Reds had failed to groom as a son—the boy who squealed like a little pig whenever Reds belted him for insubordination. The same boy who couldn't properly follow instructions to bomb a minister's car just four years ago.

Storm, now trained by the American Marines, had returned to the island to threaten Reds' plans for control. But if Storm posed such a danger to the island's security, why was Bravo so adamant in protecting him? Maybe Bravo was laying a trap, allowing Storm to run free and expose other conspirators on the island.

But that was no reason to leave Reds out in the cold.

To hell with Bravo.

How dare he tell Reds what he could and couldn't do on his own island?

If Bravo wanted to be the one to eventually kill Storm, Reds couldn't give a shit.

What truly mattered was, if this espionage crackdown on Storm and Cammy became an international incident, Reds would not be left out of the glory. He would ensure he received proper credit for preparing the lamb and its mother for slaughter.

But first, he had to tighten the screws around them.

Bravo had allowed the Bajan couple to escape back to Barbados. Reds would not make the same mistake with Storm. Without his passport, Storm would not be able to leave the island.

Then let the games begin.

Bravo would play his game, and Reds would play his. No toe-stepping with the Cuban anymore. Reds intended to break that belligerent Marine before Bravo did.

But Reds would leave nothing to chance. Before he made his next move, he would call his Bulgarian comrade in Sofia to find out if Bravo had also been keeping secrets from them.

CHAPTER THIRTEEN

Storm paced the floor of his cabin. Since Reds had cancelled Storm's flight to Barbados, the entire plan to meet with embassy staff was out of the question—for now. Storm would be unable to sign his final discharge papers from the Marine Corps, or to receive his last check. But these seemed minor next to his real concern, Jackie. Since she'd left for Barbados the previous morning, he hadn't communicated with her. Maybe if he called the embassy, just to say he could not travel to sign his discharge papers, Jackie would eventually get the news from her American handler. But the embassy might then drop Storm from their plans, leaving her alone and vulnerable to Hallam's double-dealing with Bravo.

Storm had to stay engaged. He must still get to Barbados, but how?

Bravo's words rang in his ears. *Call me if you need anything. Anything.*

Why the feigned generosity? Storm needed to be careful. Rachael might have fallen for similar ploys.

He pulled open the curtain. Moonlight glazed the surface of the water all the way from the yacht to the beach.

Grenada's mountains stretched into the glowing sky, as if reaching out for relief from the darkness engulfing the island's future. A far cry from the exhilaration he felt when Cammy called him in North Carolina with the news Duncan had finally overthrown the old dictator left by the British. The revolution promised liberation, education, jobs, and justice. And the government radio regularly touted the many benefits the revolution delivered: university scholarships to Cuba, free medical clinics staffed by Cuban doctors, and more schools than under the old dictator.

But free benefits had come with a punishing price.

The government banned political parties and newspapers, promised but held no elections, arrested hundreds without trial, and shrugged off accusations of torture. No wonder then Jackie felt so compelled to free her father. Suspicious disappearances and murders, especially of those with political connections, went unsolved—like Rachael's case.

His conversation with Pauline two nights ago left Storm with the firm belief Rachael's death was not an automobile accident like the radio said, but murder—and Reds was behind it. Storm had not seen or heard from Pauline since she'd run off in the night from Park Lane. He knew her neighborhood, but scouting it and knocking on doors asking for her might raise eyebrows and put her in more danger.

Grenada suffocated with fear Storm had not known in the years growing up on the island.

Glittering revolutionary promises competed with a grim reality. The power-to-the-people slogans that galvanized the population against the dictator now looked like cunning distractions to disguise the revolution's true objective: power *over* people.

Storm should not have been surprised, especially when characters like Reds began to climb the ranks of power. Under the revolution, Grenada, previously an agricultural island and popular tourist destination known for its welcoming population, began to look like a military base. It surprised him how quickly the People's Revolutionary Army became the largest employer of the youth. Patrol trucks outnumbered banana trucks on the narrow streets leading to the port. Military camps sprang up overnight. Storm worried about what other plans the government harbored with secret night-time deliveries of military hardware.

Had Grenada also raised American concerns? In recent months, President Reagan warned that the new airport under construction in Pointe Salines was a Soviet air base, secretly designed to handle MIG fighters.

Storm had driven by the site, busy with Cuban and Grenadian construction crews, but he couldn't identify any of the structural features he'd been trained to look for in a military airfield. The site had no parallel taxi ways, hardened aircraft hangers, signs of underground fuel tanks, or defensive surface-to-air missile platforms—basic infrastructures needed to stage Soviet fighters. But he did see several American students, from the nearby medical school, freely jogging the length of the runway in telltale outfits like Texas Longhorn t-shirts and Nike caps.

It would have been so easy to infiltrate CIA agents among the 800 American students to verify the true intent of the airport. Maybe Reds allowed American students unfettered access to the airport for just that reason: to disarm American concerns about a secret airbase.

For now, all the president could point to as evidence that the airport would be used for MIG fighters was a statement Reds had made at a press conference. In an unguarded moment of caustic bravado, Reds had claimed that if he ran the country, he would give the Soviets rights to use the airport as a military base if they chose.

Why invite American hostility before the runway was smooth enough to even land a two-seat Cessna? Reds' arrogance seemed fueled by powerful assurances originating outside the island.

Logic seemed to have dissipated in the boiling chemistry of geopolitical suspicion.

Storm felt he needed to know more, and do more.

He had to get to Barbados, to calm his nerves, and maybe to relax American jitters with all he'd observed so far.

That's when the idea struck him. There might still be a way to get to Barbados.

He would plead his case to Bravo and hope that the Cuban could twist Reds' arm.

Storm's proposal would be simple: allow him to fly to Barbados to sign his discharge papers from the Marines, and he would be free to join the Grenada Army—if Bravo could convince Reds.

Storm would deal with the consequences later. After all, he wasn't the first Grenadian to swap the American uniform for Cuban fatigues.

***

Cammy lay on the bed in the cabin Mario had selected for her and listened as his door across the narrow hallway screeched open. Footsteps paused. She held her breath in the darkness, waiting for the handle to turn, or even to hear a tap on her door. Maybe he would push it open and ease into bed with her, his warmth comforting her, his hands caressing her legs. If only she could again taste the freshness of his foreign breath as his mouth possessed hers. She craved for his excitement to fill her. Instead, her heart sank when the footsteps headed away from her door and toward the stairs leading to the upper deck.

The dark ceiling gazed down at her until her pulse slowed. She rolled out of bed and slipped on an oversized t-shirt he'd left hanging on the bed post when he showed her the cabin earlier. She retraced Mario's footstep up the stairs to the deck.

He was standing at the rail gazing at the island. "I am glad you came," he said without looking back.

"What time is it?"

He turned. "Perfect time for us."

Under the moonlight, his disheveled mop of hair hung over the most handsome face she'd ever seen. Flawless skin and a gentle gaze dignified one side of his face while a black eye patch watched over the rugged skin on the other side.

He kissed her and her world stopped in a moment of perfect passion. She held him and returned his kiss like their lips belonged together. His mouth sought her neck. She let him, rolling her head back.

The stars twinkled with a gleeful reminder. For more than twenty years she'd dreamt of this—to return to the arms of the only man who'd touched her soul before he touched her body.

CHAPTER FOURTEEN

Cammy spent the next hour cuddled into Mario's embrace, holding him around the waist as they gazed at the glowing sea. "I didn't think I would see you again," she whispered.

"I never stopped thinking of you. But coming any time before now would have been a mistake. I just wasn't ready."

"I understand."

Mario had opened his heart to Cammy on the beach the previous morning. She tried to imagine the torment he'd endured with his wife and the excruciating recovery from his burns. Cammy treasured the trust he showed her, and eagerly returned it. She reached into the pocket in her shorts.

"Remember this?" She handed him the diamond-studded ring he'd given her the day twenty-two years ago when she'd rowed up to the burning *Bianca C.*

"My God. You kept it all these years?"

"I wanted to mail it to you, but you said it would get lost."

"Yes, of course. I think I wrote you an angry letter telling you never to mention the ring again."

"Must have been while you were going through the divorce."

"I haven't put on a ring since then."

"You can now. Your divorce is behind you."

He handed it back to her. "Hold it for a couple more days until I get one for you."

Her heart fluttered. "What do you mean?"

He gazed back in the direction of the *Bianca C.* "I have a few diamonds in a safe on the ship. If Storm can find them, one might fit you."

***

Storm rolled out of bed and dressed before sunrise. He had a busy day ahead. Internal Affairs agents would be expecting him to surrender his Grenada passport, or else they might be breaking down his door to find it. If Reds had the power to remove Storm from flights leaving the island, what good would a passport do?

Storm needed someone with equal or higher authority to allow him to travel. Puzzling events had been closing in quickly around him, but they only triggered more questions than answers, answers that probably awaited him in Barbados.

None of the pieces so far fitted together. Reds was involved in Rachael's apparent murder. The Americans in Barbados had a plan to bring down the revolution. Bravo and Hallam had secret phone conversations about Storm and the *Bianca C*. Last night's confrontation between Bravo and Reds left no doubt that those two hated each other. And after twenty-two years, the owner of the *Bianca C* had returned to dive his ship, equipped only with a red circle on a blueprint.

However convoluted the pieces, there had to be a common thread linking them all together.

Someone in Barbados held the thread, and Storm intended to find that person before he planned the *Bianca C* dive.

He damned well wanted no unpleasant surprises awaiting him under a hundred feet of water.

Barbados had to come before *Bianca C*.

He could request Prime Minister Duncan's permission to travel, using Duncan's prior friendship with Rachael as a pretext to meet. But Rachael was already gone. Duncan had been powerless to protect her. He was Prime Minister in title only.

Storm needed someone like Bravo. Bravo had been suspiciously generous in offering to help Storm with anything he needed and had even raised the possibility of him joining the army. Would Bravo override Reds if Storm agreed to enlist in the Grenada Army?

Storm knew several former classmates who held ranks in the army and in government, but since his return to the island, they'd avoided him like he had leprosy.

He couldn't blame them. Times had changed.

More Grenadians lived in America than in Grenada, but since the revolution Grenada had crossed over the ideological divide.

A Grenadian returning to Grenada from America with military ties invited the kind of contempt reserved for traitors.

Except Carl Marrow.

It was widespread knowledge Carl had served as an American soldier and had returned to the island after the revolution to help train the local militia.

Storm had attended the boys' school with Carl's brother, Denver. Storm intended to find Carl today, at least to find out what to expect in the Peoples' Revolutionary Army—before Storm called Bravo with the offer.

He glanced around the cabin one last time and pulled open the curtains, which reminded him that, with everything else loading his thoughts, he'd promised Cammy to get her sewing machine delivered to the yacht, so she could get started on Mario's new curtains.

He let himself out of the cabin and followed a succulent breakfast aroma to the galley where the chef manned a flat grill sizzling with bacon and omelets. A silver percolator on the side belched coffee-flavored steam while a humming exhaust fan sucked grill smoke up a vent.

"*Buon giorno*," the chubby Greek chef said.

"Good morning to you too, my friend." Storm shook the man's hand. "Thank you for such a pleasant wake up call."

"I hope you like the taste as much as you like the smell," the chef said. "The others are already waiting topside."

Storm was surprised to see Mario and Cammy seated next to each other on the deck holding hands in the soft early morning light.

Mario released her hand and stood abruptly like he'd been caught doing something Storm would disapprove of. Storm wished there was a way to tell Mario he'd rarely seen his mother as content as she'd been in the last day. If Storm had to write a prescription to cure her withdrawal since Rachael's death, the remedy would be Mario.

"Good morning." Storm kissed Cammy on her cheek and shook Mario's hand. "Up early?"

Cammy smiled. "Actually we enjoyed a few hours of full moon. Now we're waiting for sunrise."

Mario stretched across the dining table and pulled a piece of paper from under a coffee mug. "We received a strangely coded message from the same diving company in Barbados that recommended you for the *Bianca C* dive. Came in overnight, digitized on an unusual frequency. Took my radio operator a couple hours to decipher it, but even in English we can't make sense of it. See if you can figure it out."

Storm read the message:

No passport no problem. Improvise, adapt, and overcome. Immediate. SF.

No shit.

Only a Marine could have written that message.

How many times in the last four years had he heard *improvise, adapt, and overcome?* The sign off on the message, SF, stood for Semper Fi, the Marine Corps motto derived from the Latin term Semper Fidelis. *Always faithful.*

The message was clear. Even if Reds had scrubbed his flight plans and cancelled his passport, the agents from the American embassy in Barbados still wanted to meet with Storm.

He just had to figure out how.

Just then, a new question began to stab him. How did the American agents know that he would be on the yacht?

After breakfast, Mario retrieved his red folder and rolled open *the Bianca C* blueprint on the table. Storm stood next to Cammy and zeroed his sights on the red circle. It appeared to be on the upper level of the ship. He calculated it to be about one hundred feet down, since the ship was sixty feet high and sitting in a hundred and sixty feet of water.

Mario pointed at the red circle. "This is what I wanted to talk to you about the night before our visitors showed up."

"What's there?" Storm asked.

Cammy chuckled. "A diamond ring."

"Yes," Mario said. "Along with a small family of diamonds. I had them in my personal safe here in the upper study on our last voyage in 1961." He pointed at the third window on the port side of the top level.

Cammy held Mario's hand. "Is that where—"

"Yes I was burned trying to get there. I passed out from the smoke, but the Grenadian harbor master pulled me to safety."

Storm squinted at the blueprint. "A safe underwater for twenty-two years. We'll be looking at rust, fire damage…does anyone else know about this?"

"No." Mario glanced over his shoulder. "Not even my crew. They think I am just here to recover some old artifacts."

Once again, when Storm thought he knew the answer to one question, other puzzles popped up. It troubled him that Mario still had no clue agents from the Cuban embassy in Grenada and the American embassy in Barbados already knew about a planned *Bianca C* dive. Hallam and Bravo might also be after the diamonds. But if Mario was able to keep the secret from his own crew, how had others in the Caribbean known the purpose of his trip even before he arrived?

"I'll need to upgrade some of my equipment for a hundred feet," Storm said.

"You mean you'll do the dive?"

"If I can get everything I need. At a minimum new pressure gauges, twin-cylinder harness, independent regulators and new seals."

Mario shook his hand. "Great. I have a collection of brand new scuba equipment downstairs. I'll show you when you get back from the passport office."

"One more thing. We might need plastic explosives, maybe C-4."

"Take that off your list. I already have more than we need."

"Where?"

"Right here on the yacht."

While one of the crewmen drove Storm by dinghy to the jetty, Cammy remained behind, to measure curtains. The arrangement suited Storm. He didn't want to explain to her why he might spend half the day looking for a

PRA soldier who'd served in the U.S. Army. So far as she knew, he had to surrender his passport, get some work done around the house, and return with the sewing machine after lunch.

He felt no qualms leaving her with Mario on the yacht, even with the C-4 explosives on board. Storm had been trained in the planting and triggering of plastic explosives, and knew they were extremely stable and virtually impossible to set off by accident. If Reds searched the yacht and found the explosives, he would assume they had clandestine intent. But Storm doubted Reds would return to the yacht so soon after his confrontation with Bravo last night.

Storm's initial suspicions of the Italian had also subsided overnight. Clearly, the *Bianca C* was Mario's only goal on the island—besides Cammy. He was even more in the dark about Bravo and Reds than Storm. And it appeared embassy agents must have borrowed the diving company's radio frequency to deliver the cryptic message to Storm last night. Hell, the message totally confused Mario.

Storm hurried up the beach to his dive shop. He opened the door, turned on the lights, and looked around in case someone had slipped another written note under his door, like Hallam had a few days ago. Maybe even one from Pauline saying she was okay.

But there were none.

He grabbed his inventory clipboard off the counter and made a list of items he might need for the *Bianca C* dive. Grenada stores were sadly lacking in advanced scuba gear, so if Mario did not already have those in his inventory on the *Carmen*, Storm intended to buy them in Barbados—if he got to leave the island.

Regardless of the quality of Mario's dive equipment, Storm intended to use it as a backup argument for permission to travel to Barbados.

He locked up the shop and drove in sluggish traffic to their Park Lane house. His passport and flight ticket sat where he'd left them next to his packed bag on the living room couch.

The Internal Affairs office was already open when he walked through the door at 8:45 am with his passport.

The uniformed agent standing behind the counter grinned. "We were expecting you."

"Can I have a receipt, anything in writing to show the date and time I brought it in?" Storm asked, holding on to the passport.

The man stopped smiling. "You joking or what?"

"No, I am not."

He raised his voice and reached out to snatch the passport from Storm. "You know who you talking to?"

Storm grabbed the man's wrist. "I don't give a shit who you are. Call Reds."

Another agent pushed through a swinging door behind the counter and reached for a holster at his chest. "We got a problem here?"

Storm recognized the new agent, a former classmate. "It's me, Storm from GBSS."

"I know who you are." Rigid jaws and tired eyes pushed away the boyish look Storm remembered from their school days. He turned to the first agent. "Man the phones, I'll take it from here."

Storm released the man's wrist and faced his former classmate. "I just need some document showing I delivered my passport."

The classmate waited until the other agent disappeared into the back room. "Let me give you a piece of advice, Comrade Storm. In Grenada you don't demand. Only we do."

All hope vanished that their school years together would have paved the way for a civil discussion. "I am disappointed to hear that's what the revolution has come to."

"This could end nasty." He unsnapped the holster, but left the handgun in. "This isn't the Grenada you left four years ago. Hand over the passport and be on your way."

Storm walked into the morning sunlight empty-handed and sad.

***

Thirty minutes later, Storm pulled his pickup into the intersection facing Carl Marrow's house. He glanced around to see if he could find a parking space. But he quickly changed his mind about parking when he recognized the former American soldier crossing the narrow yard adjacent to the house. Carl, tall, dark brown, and handsome, also looked as sharp and proud in his olive-green PRA fatigues as his brother, Denver, used to look in his GBSS Cadet uniform. Carl shut a gate behind him, and marched down Lucas Street.

Storm coasted his pickup down the street and braked alongside Carl.

"Good morning, Lieutenant Marrow. Want a ride?"

Carl turned and looked at Storm, but kept walking. "Storm Butler, right?"

"Yes." He waited to see if Carl would accept his offer.

Carl glanced around. "It won't be a good idea for me to be seen driving around with you."

"I want to talk to you about joining up with the PRA. Both Colonel Reds and Colonel Bravo thought I should."

"They did, huh?" He checked his watch. "I'm early for duty on the fort. See that restaurant at the bottom of Lucas Street with the outdoor tables? Drive ahead and I'll meet you down there. It's better to be seen in the open."

Storm found a parking space just past the traffic box where a sharply dressed police woman directed traffic with white-gloved hands. Carl was already seated under a green Heineken umbrella outside the restaurant, five car lengths away. Storm liked the location, which overlooked a police woman and a noisy intersection: a perfect spot to carry on a private conversation without raising suspicions.

He shook Carl's hand and pulled up a chair.

"My brother used to talk a lot about you," Carl said.

Storm had known Carl casually over the years, but had been Denver's classmate and friend since they attended the Wesley Hall primary school just up the street. They target-practiced with slingshots on discarded bottles, acted in a play together, and even teamed up in a few back street skirmishes against students from other schools. When they passed the GBSS entrance exams, Storm and Denver had immediately signed up for the cadet corps, which taught them to drill with British .303 rifles.

Carl chuckled. "Denver's favorite story was the campaign speech you made for him at school when he ran for the student council."

Storm laughed at the memory. As Denver's campaign manager, Storm had delivered a speech to the student body in the assembly hall, the last of a dozen campaign managers promoting their candidates that morning for student council positions. He dreaded delivering the tail end of a long string of monotonous speeches that left the audience fidgeting. He climbed the podium and gazed down at the students in their uniforms—gray flannel slacks, white shirts, and striped ties locked in tight Windsor knots around their Adams' apples.

When Storm finished his speech, he yelled out: "Show your appreciation to my candidate. Give him some claps!"

Storm's call for applause, tainted in sexual connotation, ignited the all-male audience in laughter. Denver had won his student council position by a landslide.

Storm and Carl were still laughing when the waitress showed up. "All you not drinking yet but you feeling good already?"

"Good memories do that." Storm ordered them a Coke each and returned to the conversation. "I lost touch with Denver after I left Grenada."

"People were saying you bombed the government minister's car and jumped on a boat to Trinidad. That's when Denver grew real serious about revolution. He became president of the student council and started a student union for all secondary schools on the island. He led student demonstrations against the old dictator, made anti-government speeches, and got caught up in a few riots. Sometimes he would leave at night, and not return until morning. My mother was always worried."

"He was only seventeen."

"You are both the same age."

The waitress served their drinks and returned inside.

Carl continued. "Remember the school kept an armory of old British .303 rifles for cadet-corps drills?"

"Yes." Storm recalled how the armory, adjacent to the basketball court at GBSS, emitted a lingering smell of grease and metal.

"One night all fifty of the rifles disappeared. The next morning secret police broke down our front door and dragged Denver away in his school uniform. No one knew where they took him." Carl sipped his Coke and swallowed hard.

"Take your time." Rachael had written Storm about the arrest when he was in North Carolina, but without the details now angering him.

"That night they returned him." Carl's voice shook and his eyes moistened. "Rolled him out of a truck at the front gate. A bloody mess. He had rope burns around his neck and his eyes were red. He hasn't been the same since. Even though he survived, I lost my brother that day."

"Where's Denver now?"

"When my father got us papers to go to America, he left the island and buried himself in academics. The last I heard he was working to become a professor in Africa."

"And you?" Storm asked.

"I wanted to return to Grenada to help even the score, so I joined the American Army for the training. Probably the same reason you joined the Marines. But just my luck, I was stationed in Germany when Duncan finally staged the revolution. Once I was discharged, I came back and signed up with the PRA. Now I'm not so sure it was a good idea."

A speeding car backfired and Carl jumped.

Storm hesitated, but he knew he eventually had to ask Carl about the PRA. "What should I expect if I submit papers to join the PRA?"

"Are you discharged from the Marines?"

"Not yet. I am on hardship leave since my sister died. I have to go to Barbados to sign my final discharge. But Reds canceled my flight and Internal Affairs took my passport this morning."

"Shit." Carl glanced around and whispered. "That's not good. Forget about the PRA."

"I am hoping Reds will return my passport to travel if I join up."

"Listen to me. If there's one thing the American military taught us, it was discipline. Discipline and paranoia can't co-exist. The PRA is soaked in paranoia right now."

"Paranoia?"

"Yes, from all directions. The Grenada Army worries about an invasion. The American Navy just conducted its largest exercise since World War II, off Puerto Rico. A dress-rehearsal invasion of a fictional island country called Amber and the Amberines. Obviously, it's a pointed gun at Grenada and the Grenadines."

"Someone needs to tell them most of the Grenadines belong to St. Vincent, not Grenada," Storm said.

"True, but it still makes the PRA nervous about the old dictator returning from exile. And now there are rumors of a split between Reds and Duncan. Soldiers might have to choose sides. Soon, comrades might be shooting comrades."

"It can't be so bad."

"It is my friend, but don't expect to hear about it on the news. Most of the high-ranking officers are still in their twenties. Young, inexperienced, and paranoid. When the shooting starts, it would be better for you to die as a civilian than as a soldier. One day people will curse this uniform."

CHAPTER FIFTEEN

Reds leaned over the polished desk in his study, lifted the red secured phone and dialed the long distance number he'd committed to memory.

It rang twice, followed by a click, and then a female spoke in Bulgarian. *"Dobar wecher."*

He glanced at the wall clock in his soundproof office. Grenada's time was 10:00 am. It would be 16:00 hours in the Bulgarian capital, Sofia. He'd learned to say good afternoon in Bulgarian since his first visit to Sofia three years ago. *"Dobar wecher."*

She must have identified the source of the incoming call or recognized his accent. She switched to flawless English. "Foreign office, how may I help you today, sir?"

He'd reached the right place. That's where he'd met Sergei Vasiliev, on Reds' first tour of Eastern European capitals immediately after the Grenada revolution. The foreign office was actually the First Head Directorate, under the Committee for State Security, best known for planning the assassination of dissident writer Georgi Markov in 1978. Sergei's delight brightened his smile when he hinted that one of his comrades had shot Markov with a poisoned umbrella on a crowded London bridge.

"This is Colonel Reds Slinger from Grenada," Reds said. "Is Secretary Sergei Vasiliev available?"

"But of course, Colonel Slinger. He would be happy to hear from you. Just a moment please."

Reds imagined her with deep brown eyes, long dark hair, and a smile that would melt Antarctica. Sergei always had a string of girls like her waiting to entertain visiting dignitaries such as Reds. He wondered how much better his Sofia visits would be after he seized the reins of power on the island. A blended memory of city lights, the scent of women's perfume, and smooth white skin on silk sheets excited him.

But it also left him unprepared for the cold voice that came on a few moments later.

"Colonel Slinger. I hope you call with news to lift spirits on this side."

Reds prepared to disguise specifics with tone and innuendoes. Even on a secured phone, he never knew who else might be listening. "Well...actually, I was calling to verify all parties are happy and working with the same blueprint."

He waited to interpret the messages coming from the other end of the phone.

Sergei cleared his throat unhurriedly. "Frankly, our friends like the blueprint and have used it before with success. But they have grave concerns the top dog might chew it up."

Our friends? A lump caught in Reds' throat. *Chew it up?* Moscow had anxieties Reds might bungle the plan to remove Duncan from power.

Something or someone must have changed their minds. What the hell could have happened since his last conversation with Sergei two weeks ago?

Reds tried to calm his rising panic. "Concerns can seem a little exaggerated from a distance."

"Comrade, the observations are up close," Sergei said. "The observer thinks the blueprint lines are losing focus."

"Blurred lines can always be corrected. Maybe I should meet with the observer?"

"You already do, every day. He's your silent visitor."

Silent visitor? Bravo! His reports to Havana must have already made it all the way to Moscow via Sofia. He'd probably complained that Reds had not been following his orders to back off of Storm, a CIA operative. But who was Bravo to be barking orders to Reds, the top military officer in the Grenada Army, and soon to be the Prime Minister?

"Personal distractions can lead to a bad product," Sergei said.

Personal distractions? Had the SOB Bravo also reported Reds' diligent pursuit of Cammy and her counter revolutionary son as personal?

"Could the problem be the observer's vision is a little distorted?" Reds asked.

Silence

"Hello?"

"I heard you," Sergei said. "We will no longer talk about him. The problem is yours, not his."

How could Reds guide the conversation to Bravo's preoccupation with the *Bianca C* without aggravating Sergei further? Did Sergei know anything about a CIA plan to install listening devices offshore? Or was this just a decoy the Cuban made up to keep Reds off balance?

Reds decided to cast his own bait. "The observer seems more involved in the deep sea than the blueprint. He thinks there's a big catch waiting for him."

"So we hear. Fishing is his business. Leave him alone."

So there was a CIA plot. Bravo had been right all along. Or had he also pulled the wool over the Bulgarian's eyes?

"Colonel Reds," Sergei said. "You have work to do."

Reds took a deep breath and slowed his thoughts. "There are just perception problems. I can change them."

"Trying to erase old perceptions will leave ugly scuff marks everywhere. My advice is to forget the old. You need to carve out new dramatic lines, to make the old vanish."

"Is that what our friends said?"

"I know what they like. Decisive, bold lines, clean but final. Until then, the remaining goods are on hold."

Goods on hold. Reds needed the secret shipments of armored personnel carriers and anti-aircraft cannons to counter internal resistance against his takeover. But future shipments included heavier armaments for a Soviet Brigade like the one in Cuba, to discourage an American-inspired invasion. Reds needed Soviet boots on Grenada to fully secure his power.

"Take a look at the model our friend's neighbors used," Sergei said.

Soviet neighbors? Of course, Afghanistan. Just four years earlier, the Afghanistan Deputy Prime Minister Hafizullah Amin seized power and had his own Prime Minister suffocated by a pillow while he slept. Had Sergei just given Reds approval to apply the Afghanistan solution in Grenada?

"It's a model that might work well for you," Sergei continued.

It worked well all right—for the Soviets.

Within ninety days after Amin's takeover, Soviet paratroopers executed him and installed another puppet head-of-state to do their biddings. Then the floodgates opened. Soviet tanks rolled across the border and overtook the entire country.

But Reds was no fool. This would be like inviting a centipede into his bed. At first it might snuggle against human warmth. But it always rewarded its host with a ruthless sting.

Reds didn't want to die like Amin, staring into the barrel of an AK-47.

He knew the mistakes Amin had made. The Soviets referred to Amin as a "bloodthirsty spy of American imperialism." They scorned lukewarm allegiance to their goal of international communism. But Reds' commitment to Marxist-Leninist revolution was unquestionable. Sergei knew it. The Soviets knew it. Reds was one of them. Maybe they were waiting for Reds to deliver the final killing blow to Duncan before they would throw their big cards into the game.

Carve out new dramatic lines. Decisive, bold lines, clean but final.

"I understand," Reds said. "I'll keep you posted."

He ended the call with Sergei and dialed another number. Excitement drummed in his chest. His time was rapidly approaching. He twirled his moustache and counted the seconds.

A male voice answered on the sixth ring. "Military command."

Reds snapped. "You're supposed to pick up the phone immediately. Call a secret meeting of the military council to meet at Fort Frederick in two hours."

"The full council, sir?"

"Yes, all sixteen."

"Any code words for this meeting?"

"Yes," Reds said. "Tell them the code word is gallows."

"Gallows? Like the gallows used to—"

"Yes, dammit! The gallows used to hang people."

CHAPTER SIXTEEN

Carl's warnings troubled Storm as he drove back to Park Lane in horn-blowing late morning traffic. The government news braying from the car radio gave no hint of the internal strife brewing just beneath the island's strained surface. The radio announcer droned on in the rising humidity about Prime Minister Duncan's promises of future tourism dollars from the new airport, affordable food from treaties with Eastern Bloc countries, and Colonel Reds' steadfast promise to defend the people against counter-revolutionaries. "The PRA will tolerate no manifestations whatsoever of counter-revolution. Counters will face heavy manners," the announcer warned.

When the next news item started with "Another car bomb in Beirut", Storm turned off the radio in disgust. He didn't need to hear the government's interpretation of an international situation, when they couldn't even report Grenada's declining situation truthfully.

Carl's conversation confirmed Storm's suspicions: the revolutionary government wavered precariously on the brink of a violent split, with the popular Duncan on one side and the devious Reds on the other. If Carl was right, and Storm had no reason to doubt him, the army was equally divided.

An implosion seemed imminent. And that made it even more urgent for Storm to meet with the embassy in Barbados.

Shifting conditions in Grenada could impact whatever plans the Americans had to stall the Grenada revolution and free Jackie's father from prison. Guilt still gnawed at Storm for the pain he'd caused her father. He had given his word to Jackie he would do whatever was required to help, but he still had no idea what the American plans were. If it involved a prison break, it had better be soon. A Reds' coup over Duncan would make such a plan virtually impossible.

Storm also needed to purchase upgraded scuba gear for the *Bianca C* dive, even as a nagging suspicion told him the dive was somehow linked to the American plans. Why else would the same company, which recommended him for the dive, also send him the embassy message?

But this still left one side of the triangle jagged with danger: the connection between Hallam and Bravo. They shared an interest in Storm's dive to the *Bianca C*— even before Mario offered Storm the job.

Maybe someone had leaked word to Bravo and Hallam that the *Bianca C* was a treasure trove of diamonds. And if they knew this, they probably also had plans to seize the diamonds, when or if Storm surfaced with them. How else could he explain Bravo's eagerness to offer Storm any assistance he needed—*anything*.

Storm needed to talk to Mario so they could devise a plan to protect the diamonds. Mario described them as a small family of diamonds. What the hell did he mean? Would a small collection of diamonds be sufficient motivation for a Cuban spy hunter to team up with a CIA agent?

What a stroke of clever intuition that Jackie decided to listen in on the men's phone call. With a wave of admiration for her, Storm recalled that she'd spent a night rowing a boat and dodging armed patrols to let Storm know.

She'd promised Storm not to give Hallam any hint she'd listened in on the phone conversation with Bravo. If Hallam got wind of it, her life could be in jeopardy. They'd left the island for Barbados over twenty-four hours ago. Despite the urge to hear her voice and be assured of her safety, Storm had no secure way of contacting her.

He had to get to Barbados soon, to find Jackie and to let the embassy know about Hallam.

And, it appears, others wanted him there just as urgently—*improvise, adapt, and overcome.*

While Carl's premonitions rang alarming bells, Storm's only clear option was to start the paperwork to join the Grenada Army. It might convince Bravo and Reds he was serious about wearing the PRA uniform. Storm hoped, given the risk of allowing an active duty Marine to enlist in the PRA or allowing him first to travel to Barbados to sign his official discharge, they would choose the latter.

The last ingredient Reds and Bravo might want to add to the potent mix threatening the island would be another sprinkling of divided loyalties.

Even then, Storm might still find himself caught in the crossfire of the deepening conflict. How bizarre, the image of him in Cuban uniform firing a AK-47 while he still had Marine combat uniforms and a sea bag stowed in a Beirut locker.

No one in his platoon would believe this shit. They would probably have some wisecrack about it. Storm chuckled at some of the colorful but profound sayings he'd heard over the years.

Even the young boot from Iowa had his share. Still nineteen and medicating his acne with Noxzema, he'd occasionally join in a game of blackjack with Storm's squad. When the conversation turned to the desk jockeys who designed the peacekeeping mission, the kid finally got his chance to add to the bitching repertoire. "My grandfather always said if you make sausages don't shake hands with the manure collector. Damn, looks like the manure collectors in D.C. pushed their way into the Marine chow hall without washing their hands. We'll be lucky if we get out of here with just the shits."

Now it looked like Storm had been shaking contaminated hands as well. But among his concerns, diarrhea sat low on the list.

As dangerous as his options appeared, enlisting in the People's Revolutionary Army offered the best chance to get to Barbados. All he hoped for today was permission to get on a flight—for Jackie and her father, for Mario and his diamonds, and for Grenada.

Even if it meant he'd have to shake hands with people he distrusted. He would use their tools of deception, and hope he would be better at it than they were.

He would deceive Bravo and Reds with feigned loyalty for their cause. After all, hadn't Storm demonstrated his faith in the revolution when he planted the bomb four years ago?

So many things could go wrong. For now though, he couldn't think past the next couple of days. He'd deal with the *'what ifs'* later.

First he had to deliver the sewing machine to the *Carmen* for his mother.

He drove up Park Lane and backed into the driveway. The house seemed undisturbed, but his home had lost a little of its welcome in the past few days.

It saddened him, especially when he opened the top drawer of the sewing machine and saw the black velvet bag. It bulged with Cammy's glittering fake gemstones that he, Rachael, and Pauline used to play with.

He rolled the sewing machine on squeaky wheels to the door and lifted it onto the back of his truck. He braced it with his cooler and returned to the house for his dive bag.

A heavy truck rumbled down Park Lane and squealed to a stop at his driveway. Footsteps pounded toward his open door.

Three soldiers rushed in with AK-47 rifles.

Storm dropped his bag.

The lead soldier, in baggy uniform and probably Storm's age, pointed his rifle at Storm's chest. "Going somewhere?"

"Yes," Storm said. "To my dive shop in Grand Anse."

"Heard you been around town asking questions about the People's Revolutionary Army."

It amazed him how quickly his conversation with Carl had travelled. "True. I want to join up."

"We don't accept Yankee traitors in our army."

"Both Carl Marrow and I served in the American military, but we're still Grenadians."

"One traitor is enough."

"You'll have to ask Colonel Reds about that. Both he and Colonel Bravo from the Cuban embassy suggested I enlist."

"We'll see. In the meantime walk lightly. We'll be watching you."

"By the way," Storm said pointing at the soldier's rifle. "Your magazine is not inserted all the way. It's likely to stress the magazine spring and cause jams."

The soldier slapped the magazine into place, pointed the muzzle away from Storm, and blasted Cammy's wall clock to splinters, leaving a fist-sized hole through Rachael's bedroom wall. "Works now. Thanks for the tip."

After the soldiers drove off, Storm locked up the house and sped toward Grand Anse. He pulled into the first gas station he came to and parked next to a payphone at the side of the building. He sat in the pickup, staring in the review mirror to see if anyone followed. Satisfied he was alone, he stepped to the phone and dialed the number on the card Colonel Bravo had given him last night on Mario's yacht.

A woman answered. "Cuban Embassy, *buenos dias*. Who would you like to speak to?"

"Is Colonel Bravo available?"

"He's in a meeting right now. Can I have him call you back?"

"I am on a pay phone. He's expecting my call. Tell him it's Storm, and it's urgent."

"Okay. *Un momento por favor.*"

Colonel Bravo's gruff voice filled the phone a few moments later. "Glad you called, young man."

"You asked me to contact you if I needed your help."

"Say no more. Meet me at the embassy in an hour."

The phone went dead.

When Storm pulled up at Grand Anse Beach thirty minutes later, he was relieved to see one of Mario's crewmen waiting on the jetty. They loaded the sewing machine onto the dinghy and roped it to the seats.

"Tell Cammy I'll be back in a couple hours." Storm glanced at his watch. "I have a meeting in fifteen minutes."

"*Si, amico mio.*"

"Also, tell Mario I might want to test his diving equipment at fifty feet over the *Bianca C* if I get back before sunset."

The crewman nodded. "We'll prepare to lift anchor." He accelerated the motor with a full twist of the throttle and sped offshore toward the *Carmen*.

Storm jumped into his pickup and raced back to the main road. He turned right toward Lanse Aux Epines and had just passed the sugar mill on the way to the embassy when the reality struck him. He was an active duty U.S. Marine about to meet in the Cuban embassy with one of the top communist spy hunters in the western hemisphere.

He wondered who else knew about it.

***

Cammy stood on the sun-baked deck of the *Carmen*, peering through the binoculars at the speeding white pickup and clinging to the relief Mario's presence gave her.

"Do you worry about him?" Mario stood with his arm around her waist, a steady breeze whipping around them.

"Only when he's not diving," she said. "He has more enemies on land than in the sea."

"I am glad he's agreed to dive for me. I think he'll be okay. He's tough and intelligent."

Cammy almost said "Yes, like his father."

Instead she walked away and poured herself a rum and Coke at the bar.

***

The sight of thirty or so Cuban soldiers in olive-green uniforms guarding the gate and walls around the embassy surprised Storm. His basic embassy-duty training in Parris Island taught that the host country held the responsibility for external protection of diplomatic personnel and facilities, while the embassy country exercised interior security. About six Grenada soldiers, in Cuban uniforms, but distinguished by shoulder straps, shorter sleeves, and East-German styled helmets, stood outside the gates. They huddled in the shade of a coconut tree in hand-waving conversation that suggested disgruntlement in their midst.

They paused and stared at Storm as he rolled up to the gate in front of an 'Entrance for Visitors' sign. He did not recognize any of the men, and hoped they did not recognize him either.

Two armed Cuban soldiers approached his pickup while several others remained at the gate.

One of them stopped at Storm's window. "The embassy is closed today."

Odd. So why all the extra security around the compound?

Maybe this was an omen for him to return to his struggling dive shop and forget this whole convoluted mess. How the hell did he get mixed up with the Cuban and American Embassies? Even the plan to dive the *Bianca C* smelled so odorous it attracted both Bravo and Reds to Mario's yacht with guns drawn on each other.

After the strains of last few days, the smart thing to do might be to stay low and avoid these people. But then it would mean turning his back on Jackie and dumping his best chance to dispel his guilt for almost killing her father.

And poor Cammy would be devastated if her son turned down Mario's offer to dive the *Bianca C*. Even as she grieved for Rachael, she'd made such a gallant effort to help Storm set up his dive shop so he could anchor his skills in Grenada—and also, he guessed, so she could mother her only surviving child.

Mothering defined every sacrifice Cammy made. Every man she entertained, every dollar she tucked into her bra, every steaming pot she labored over, was for her children.

If Storm succeeded in his job for Mario, maybe recovering a ring and handful of diamonds on the *Bianca C*, it would be Cammy's biggest reward—proof her son was home for keeps, that he could make a go at the business. Abandoning her dream now would stack another betrayal on his twenty-one-year-old conscience—more guilt than his sanity could shoulder.

No. Regardless of the danger and uncertainty awaiting him, turning back now was not an option.

From behind the wheel, Storm looked up at the Cuban soldier. "Colonel Bravo is expecting me. I just spoke to him on the phone."

The soldier stepped away from the pickup and pulled a radio from his belt. He engaged in a few moments of radio conversation in Spanish before returning to Storm. "Pull to the other gate." He pointed down the main road to a narrow gravel driveway that disappeared around the embassy wall.

The guard at the side gate was already pushing it open when Storm drove up. He guided Storm to a parking space next to a palm tree.

Storm climbed out of his pickup and locked the doors.

"This way." The guard led the way across a stone path and up several concrete steps to a heavy wood door. "I must search you for weapons first."

The guard frisked Storm, but it was brief since Storm was wearing only a light t-shirt, shorts, and jogging shoes. The guard unlocked the door with keys hooked to his belt and pointed Storm toward a female receptionist in an open lobby of marble floors, dim ceiling chandeliers, and large portraits of Fidel Castro. The aroma of tobacco smoke lingered in the air.

The embassy might have been closed for business on the outside, but not on the inside. Embassy staff hurried in and out of offices with stacks of paper and colored folders, casting nervous glances at him. Phones rang in unseen offices. Four men in white four-pocket shirt-jacks and dark slacks stood at the entrance of a hallway. Storm assumed them to be armed, given the awkward bulges at their sides.

Two attractive women, one dark-skinned and apparently pregnant, the other a blonde in a red dress, sat in subdued conversation in a dimly lit living area adjacent to the hallway. A Grenadian soldier with a rifle stood alone facing down the hallway with his back to Storm.

The Cuban embassy appeared to be under siege.

The receptionist, seated behind a polished wooden counter, tapped her pen on her desk to gain Storm's attention. "Mr. Butler?"

"I'm sorry."

She pointed to a leather couch bordered by sprawling potted palms and facing the soldier. "Please have a seat over there."

"Thank you." Storm walked over to the couch and sat down before recognizing the soldier across from him.

Carl Marrow in PRA uniform.

***

Colonel Reds Slinger glanced around the long table at his council of sixteen military and intelligence officers, excitement drumming in his chest. He'd groomed these cadres for more than five years now, indoctrinating them in Marxist study groups, pushing for their promotions, and approving their training courses in Cuba and Eastern Europe. Young, eager to please, with jealous clutches on the power he'd granted them. He knew they were prepared with iron will to exercise new levels of power and authority over life and death. He'd sharpened their loyalties to perfection—not like the insubordination drilled into Storm by his mother.

Soon those two would pay.

Reds called upon his senior officer, twenty-five years old. "Lieutenant-Colonel, give us a status summary of the military situation, both personnel and hardware."

The lieutenant-colonel flipped a folder open. "We have eight of our Soviet BTR-60 armored personnel carriers on full tanks and ready to go. We have four Soviet ZU-23 anti-aircraft guns installed, tested, and operational. We currently have fifteen hundred regulars and three thousand reservists under arms. Our army is better trained and larger than all our neighboring islands combined. We can suppress popular resistance and repel any mercenary invasion."

"How is morale?"

"The pay raise you authorized during Duncan's visit to Washington has kicked into their pay checks. They know you will look after them better than Duncan did. Morale is high."

Reds turned to another young officer. "Major, give us the political situation."

"Our delegation met with Duncan a few days ago to propose the power sharing plan to resolve the deepening crisis with the revolution. The joint-leadership plan was simple. Duncan would continue his work with the masses and to strengthen the party. You as the top military commander would assume full authority for national defense and foreign affairs. At first Duncan appeared to agree, but one of his advisors called this morning to say Duncan is doubtful power sharing will work. He said the change-of-mind came after consultations."

"Consultations?" Reds slammed his fist on the table. "Consultations with whom? I am the only one he has to consult with."

"Our intelligence report might have the answer."

Reds turned to the major. "Go ahead, Major. What do you have?"

"Colonel, we have some concerns about the Cubans."

"Get on with it."

"They have six hundred construction crew, most trained as reservists in Cuba with combat experience in Africa, plus fifty military advisors. The military advisors showed up unannounced at our camps this morning, but they were not scheduled to conduct any training today. We also just received word from our troops at the Cuban embassy gate that the ambassador ordered all Grenadian soldiers be replaced by Cuban soldiers. Then Duncan showed up with a full bodyguard detachment for a high-level meeting with the ambassador."

"Dammit." If Duncan now received advice from the Cuban, it could only mean they no longer considered Reds a reliable ally. They could kiss his Grenadian behind. Regardless, who needed the Cubans when he had the Russians?

"There's more, sir. The last report I received ten minutes ago says the two men who served in the American military, Carl Marrow and Storm Butler are also in the embassy."

"Those treacherous bastards! I knew it. We don't have much time. We have to move now. Code word gallows is in effect immediately."

***

Storm sank into the couch wondering why Carl was avoiding eye contact with him. They'd had a Coke and a friendly conversation just a few hours ago. So why had Carl suddenly turned cold and distant?

Storm didn't have to wait long for an answer,

The creaks of heavy doors opening drifted up the hallway.

The four bodyguards unfolded their arms and gazed around the lobby. Carl tightened his rifle across his chest.

One of the bodyguards approached Carl as footsteps in the hallway pounded toward the lobby. "Take the rear."

Unable to see down the hallway, Stormed assumed from the bodyguards' preparation that the footsteps belonged to high level officials, probably just concluding a meeting with the ambassador. Storm was not surprised to see the first set of footsteps belonged to Colonel Bravo. Bravo stepped into the lobby, followed by three men.

Storm recognized Duncan immediately, but not the other two men. Duncan strolled tall, with well-groomed afro and beard, radiating a commanding yet disarming presence. His voice boomed against the walls, and his laughter captivated Storm's attention. No doubt, Rachael must have been enveloped in Duncan's charisma. She'd probably taken risks for him—risks which led to her death.

The two women at the end of the lobby rose from their chairs and walked up to Duncan. The pregnant woman held his hand and they embraced. Storm assumed she was the teacher he'd heard about, in love with Duncan and probably now carrying his baby. If she'd been in competition with Rachael for Duncan's affections, Rachael's death probably brought her more relief than grief.

The woman in red stood next to a dark-skinned man Storm assumed to be the Cuban ambassador. Storm had read in North Carolina that the Cuban ambassador had married a gracious American woman, equally dedicated to her Marxist beliefs as she was to her American heritage. Now Storm believed this woman to be the ambassador's wife. Bravo kept a discrete distance, nodding agreements when the discussions drifted in his direction, and avoiding eye contact with Storm.

After farewell hugs and kisses with their embassy hosts, Duncan held the pregnant woman's hand and headed to the front door surrounded by his four bodyguards.

Carl followed, brushing past Storm with a hiss through clenched teeth. "Leave the island. The shit is about to hit the fan."

Fifteen minutes crawled by since the visiting entourage departed the embassy, leaving Storm alarmed by Carl's cryptic behavior. Should Storm have taken the warning seriously and returned to the *Carmen*? It might raise Bravo's suspicions if Storm left abruptly before they met.

Bravo had immediately disappeared down the hallway with the ambassador and the woman, probably to recap the earlier discussions. Bravo had not acknowledged Storm's presence and it left him worried that showing up at the Cuban embassy might be a bad mistake.

He glanced at his watch, just as footsteps tapped in the hallway. The woman in red, no more than thirty-five, strutted in elegant steps toward him. Storm's concerns vanished, leaving him only with embarrassment at the scanty t-shirt and shorts he wore.

She stretched out her hand and smiled with dimples outshining the chandeliers hanging from the ceiling. "Hi, my name is Debbie. I'm Ambassador Villa's wife."

Her North Carolina accent sounded like it floated unscathed onto the island in a bottle. Her hand felt like a warm glove in cold weather.

"It's an honor to meet you, Mrs. Villa," he said, relieved he hadn't stuttered.

"Please, call me Debbie. I believe you're here to see Colonel Bravo?"

"Yes. I hope he's still available to meet today."

"Of course," she said. "When he mentioned you are a former U.S. Marine and were stationed in North Carolina, I told him I would chat with you for a few minutes while he confers with my husband. I was born in North Carolina. Speaking with anyone who's been there is a rare treat. It takes me home to my fondest memories in an instant. You don't mind talking to me, do you?"

He smiled. *This woman could melt the goddamned cold war.*

They sat, and she had him relive his Parris Island experience and his introduction to the Carolinas.

"I missed Grand Anse Beach," he said. "So every chance I got I drove to Atlantic Beach off Morehead City." He recalled the endless miles of windswept sand dunes and the patrolling flights of squawking seagulls.

"Oh my!" She squeezed his hands. "I grew up in Morehead City. I used to love the drives with my parents along Atlantic Beach."

He decided not to tell her about the bars he'd been kicked out of in Havelock or the apartment-rental agreement cancelled in Morehead City because of his brown complexion.

"I enjoyed catching crabs along the inlets," he said.

She laughed. "My father used to take us at night. With just one chicken leg as bait and a net, we would catch enough crabs to fill a bucket."

They were still laughing when Colonel Bravo walked up, chewing on an unlit cigar stump.

He grinned. "Sounds like you two have known each other a long time."

"Feels that way," she said. "Lovely to have met you, Storm." She shook his hand and headed back down the hall.

Bravo immediately returned to business. "Follow me."

He led Storm away to the far end of the lobby and down a dark musty staircase. They entered a narrow office, which looked more like an interrogation room, with a thick door and combination locks. Bravo turned on an incandescent bulb, casting dim light over a small table with a black phone. He locked the door and pulled up a chair. "Grab a seat."

Storm sat across the table from Bravo. "Thanks for agreeing to meet with me on such short notice."

Bravo ignored the niceties and offered no apologies for keeping Storm waiting. The Cuban wore a cigar aroma almost as thick as his weathered skin. The edge of his voice bristled with his years of cunning. "When you work for a man like Mr. Costa, you deserve to have all the support you need."

"I need Reds to return my passport. I have to buy some equipment upgrades in Barbados to do the dive for Mr. Costa. Can you help me?"

"Out of the question. Things are changing fast and you have to act now. Forget the passport. Forget Barbados. Assume you can get what you need without going there."

Was Bravo aware of Storm's plan to meet with U.S. Embassy personnel, and also attempting to block communications between them? Maybe the Cubans had intercepted the message sent to the *Carmen* last night.

"I can't get the scuba upgrades here in Grenada," Storm said. "I was also considering joining up with the PRA, but I'll have to sign my discharge papers at the embassy first."

"My friend, forget everything you thought you knew when you walked in here. Nothing is as it appears."

"I'm not sure I understand."

"The obstacles between you and your goal are illusions. Fog clouding a city block can be condensed into one glass of water. Focus on the glass."

"Colonel Bravo, this isn't fog. Do you realize the risks I take by coming to you? I am still active in the American military. I could be court martialed for sitting here with you."

"Lucky you, my young friend. If my boss upstairs hears this conversation, I could be shot. He thinks you're just here to ask me to pressure Reds for your silly little passport. Now you and I know very well, there's a lot more going on." He stuck his index finger first at Storm's chest, and then at his own. "You and I need each other."

What could Bravo need from Storm, if not the diamonds? But Mario had given little indication the diamonds added up to more than a few trinkets, hardly enough for a man like Bravo to risk facing a firing squad.

Was Storm missing something else here?

He had to tread carefully.

"You see this phone?" Bravo pointed at the phone sitting on middle of the table. "Suppose I say there's going to be someone on the other end who can get you everything you need, would you trust me?"

"Everything?"

"Everything, including a pretty young lady who can't wait to see you again."

Jackie? It almost sounded more like a threat than a carrot. And how the hell did Bravo connect Jackie to Storm?

Of course, Hallam must have revealed everything to Bravo.

That sonofabitch Hallam.

Storm felt ambushed by the path the conversation had taken. But then again, Bravo seemed fully assured of himself, as if he saw right through Storm's façade, and knew a whole lot more about the shit Storm was about to step into. Despite Jackie's warning about Bravo's cold-blooded record in Africa, he had nothing to gain from Storm's demise—for now. Reds might, but clearly he and Bravo hated each other's guts.

Storm and Bravo shared distaste for Reds. *The enemy of my enemy is my friend.*

And that was enough for Storm. "Without any other options, I'll have to trust you."

Bravo dialed a long distance number. In the quiet room, the dial tone sounded as close as if Storm held the phone to his ear.

A male answered. "You got him?"

"Yes." Bravo handed the phone to Storm.

"Hello," Storm said into the phone. "Who am I speaking to?"

"Hallam."

CHAPTER SEVENTEEN

Jackie's intuition sounded the alarm when she sat in the restroom and read the coded note Hallam had handed her across the bank counter an hour earlier. She'd not seen him since they landed in Barbados from Grenada at noon yesterday. He instructed her at the airport to return to her normal routines in the capital, Bridgetown. She lived a boring routine between her teller job at the Barclays Bank and her Taekwondo classes. He would contact her again once he'd met with Steve, their American handler from the embassy.

She couldn't wait to tell Steve that Hallam was in bed with Bravo, the top Cuban intelligence officer in the Caribbean. Yes, the same murderous skulk Steve had warned them about before the Grenada trip.

Even before she unpacked her suit case from the Grenada trip, she hurried out of her flat to find a phone booth down the street. Using her home phone or showing up at the embassy unannounced was out of the question. It violated all the security protocols Steve had spelled out for them.

She called his embassy number several times. No one answered. She returned to the phone booth again before going to sleep, but still had no luck. She spent half the night tossing around in bed, worried about her father and Storm.

By the time she arrived at the bank for work next morning, a migraine squeezed her head in a vise grip and her stomach cramped unmercifully. So when Hallam showed up in a business suit pretending to be a customer, she didn't have the will to return the pretense with a smile. When he passed her the note between his Royal Barbados Police Force paycheck and a deposit slip, she almost threw up.

An urgent tone seeped through his low flat words. "Our friend can't wait to see you again."

The only 'friend' they had in common was Steve. In fact, Jackie's friends would be surprised to know she'd been meeting at the embassy with these men. Her friends would be even more flabbergasted to learn she'd just spent the last few days sharing a hotel room in Grenada with this hunk of a man almost twice her age now standing in front of her. It felt like she had two lives, two sets of friends, and both invisible to the other.

"We'll meet at the time and place in the note," he said. "Read and destroy it on your next break."

She completed his deposit without saying a word and watched him swagger out the front door with the ease of a man on his way to his baby's christening.

But Jackie knew better. Hallam shared secrets with a dangerous man.

She tucked the note into her skirt pocket, wondering if he'd ever killed anyone like Bravo had.

Now seated in the restroom stall an hour later, she read the encrypted note and translated the instructions in her mind:

After work, go straight home. Make no outgoing calls, and ignore any incoming ones. Leave the house at exactly six-fifteen, drive around the city several times to shake off anyone following. Drive thirty minutes to the safe house with the directions below. We meet at seven o'clock sharp tonight.

The directions led to a desolate house at the bottom of a windy bluff overlooking the Atlantic. By seven o'clock, it would be dark.

She assumed they were to meet Steve there, so he could debrief them on any intelligence they'd gathered during the Grenada visit. But it was the first she'd heard of a meeting with Steve outside of the U.S. Embassy in Bridgetown. They'd met several times around a polished oak table in the embassy basement on hectic Broad Street, just two blocks away. Four solid walls surrounded the soundproof room and an armed Marine stood outside the locked door.

They'd also not met at night before.

So why would Steve want to meet tonight way out there, behind God's back, as islanders would say, when the embassy was just a few blocks away?

If Hallam suspected she knew about his conversation with Bravo, he wouldn't want her talking to Steve. Surely by now Hallam knew she'd uncovered his double-dealing. He'd caught her rummaging through his briefcase at the hotel, minutes after he'd gotten off the phone with Bravo.

The smooth-talking Cuban colonel also tried to convince her that his effort to get them to the airport on time was his diplomatic way of apologizing for Reds' behavior. But she didn't fall for it, especially when he referred to her as *señorita*. Steve had worked meticulously on their cover as a married couple to get them in and out of Grenada without suspicion. If Bravo knew they weren't married, then he knew everything else.

Only Hallam could have divulged the information to Bravo.

The Grenada operation would be in jeopardy. Her father might never again see daylight. And Storm could be in danger at this very moment.

All because of Hallam.

Jackie could end his undercover career—or his life. So why would he risk having her expose his treachery to Steve?

Maybe Hallam planned to kill her tonight.

He could dump her body into the roaring Atlantic surf, never to be seen or heard from again.

The 7 o'clock meeting sounded like a death trap.

She needed Storm now more than ever. A trickle of fear whispered in her thoughts that she would never see Storm or her father again. She had never felt so alone.

Her hands trembled when she tore up the note and flushed the pieces down the toilet.

CHAPTER EIGHTEEN

Storm listened carefully to Hallam on the phone in Bravo's office, hoping to detect any trace of deception beneath the words.

"We don't have much time," Hallam said. "For now forget everything you think you know."

Forget everything you think you know? Those were the same words Bravo just used!

Storm remained on guard, aware Bravo could also hear the conversation.

"I am listening," Storm said.

"I know you wanted to travel to Barbados to purchase new equipment for your dive, but with changing conditions, you may have to improvise."

"I am not aware of any new conditions."

"I'll get to that in a minute. For now, give me a list of what you need for the dive."

Storm gave him a full list of all the equipment and parts he might need for a hundred-foot dive. He trained for hundred-foot dives in the Marines, with specialized gear designed for military operations and not available on the commercial market. He'd gone down to fifty feet in the second-hand tanks and buoyancy control devices he used in his dive shop, but didn't want to take any chances with deeper pressures.

He'd heard enough about the tragedies from worn seals, leaking hoses, and malfunctioning gauges that still read positive air pressure even as divers took their last breath on an empty tank.

"I can cover the equipment with payment from Mr. Costa and my last check from—"

"Money is not a problem," Hallam said. "We'll get you the best of everything you need, but if necessary, you'll have to adapt."

So far Hallam had used *improvise* and *adapt* in his conversation. Was he trying to slip a message past Bravo's filters?

Bravo seemed detached from the conversation. He struck a match and lit his cigar stump. The air in the small room grayed with smoke.

"I am still not sure where this conversation is going." Storm squeezed the phone against his ear to hear Hallam's words clearer, but also to muffle any of the conversation escaping into the room. "I just came here to have my passport released so I could get to Barbados."

"We're all on the same page. But you don't need to go to Barbados to get it all done. Together, we'll *overcome* any obstacles."

Damn! *Improvise, adapt, and overcome.* Hallam must have known about the message sent to the *Carmen* last night. He'd used Marine Corps lingo, but shit, he'd also parroted Bravo's words.

Who the hell was Hallam working for?

Everything Storm thought he knew began to wobble. *Forget everything you think you know.*

If a Marine had prepared Hallam for this conversation, might he be listening on the other end?

Maybe Storm should return an acknowledgement—to test his theory. He hoped Bravo didn't know the first line of the Marine Corps hymn, *From the Halls of Montezuma to the Shores of Tripoli.*

"Listen," Storm shouted into the phone with feigned anger. "I need real equipment to get down a hundred feet. This isn't a goddamned swim on the shores of Tripoli."

Hallam paused. "Aye, aye, sir."

I'll be damned. Hallam either had a Marine next to him scribbling key words for him to say, or he was a master at deception. Was Hallam a Marine himself? No. Storm would have detected that the first time they met. Clearly he wanted Storm to know whose side he was on, despite his link with Bravo. And he wanted Storm to get the message, sneakily, without Bravo's knowledge. Regardless, any more foot-dragging or word games on the phone might raise Bravo's suspicions, even as he chewed his cigar and blew smoke to the ceiling.

"How do you plan to get me the items I need?" Storm asked Hallam.

"You'll have to convince Mr. Costa to drive his boat to Palm Island in the Grenadines, St. Vincent territory."

"No way. That's about sixty nautical miles from here."

"Fifty nautical miles. It'll take you four hours with an easy cruising speed. Colonel Bravo will get you coast guard clearance. We'll be waiting for you at the south-west bay. Be there at 1:00 a.m., tonight."

"Are you out of your fucking mind?" Storm asked.

"Be there."

The phone went dead.

With Bravo walking alongside him, Storm realized Hallam had not mentioned Jackie's name once in the conversation. In the interest of time? As they crossed the lobby toward the exit door Storm wondered how deep the shit was that he'd gotten into. The harsh reality was that the time to climb out of it had long passed. He could have refused Hallam's offer two days ago on the Radon 22. But saying no to help free Jackie's father would have tossed Storm back into the guilt tailspin he'd been trapped in for the past four years.

"I have a son a few years younger than you," Bravo said. "I'm not sure I can stand by and watch him get into such deadly business."

Deadly business?

"What do you mean?"

"Oh…diving wrecks at a hundred feet. He's in high school in Havana. Never had any problems with him…until recently."

Storm waited to hear more, but when an embassy employee hurried across the lobby within earshot, Bravo changed the subject.

"I'm sorry we can't help with the passport," he said just loud enough for the woman's benefit.

Sorry my ass. Easy for Bravo to say.

Since going to Barbados was out of the question, Storm now had to convince Mario to drive the *Carmen* fifty nautical miles north tonight to an uninhabited island.

And Storm still had no idea if they were heading into a deadly trap like the one Rachael had driven into on her last night alive.

***

Standing in the bustling Fort Frederick Command Center, Reds twirled his moustache and reread the message from the Cuban Embassy:

> "*Safe passage requested for Italian yacht Carmen and passengers from Grand Anse to Palm Island tonight at 19:00 hours. Final phase of international investigation. B.*"

Reds grinned when he realized the information intentionally left out of the message. "It's about bloody time Bravo got off his cigar and did something."

The message gave no return date and time for the *Carmen*. It meant one thing. They were about to embark on a one-way trip. Cammy, Storm, and the eye-patched Italian would not be returning.

The timing could not be more perfect. Reds planned to be preoccupied with Operation Gallows tonight. Let Bravo take care of Cammy and her counter-revolutionary son. Palm Island would be a great place to end their hollow lives without implicating Reds.

Reds still had one thing in common with Bravo: their preference for explosives to dispose of enemies and evidence. He hoped Bravo chose an explosion loud enough to hear it fifty miles away.

He turned to his assistant. "Send this to Colonel Bravo immediately: '*Congratulations. Palm Island permission granted. Please confirm when investigation is concluded and a bottle of Grenada's best rum will be on its way.*'"

The assistant marched off toward a bank of flashing communication equipment manned by soldiers with headphones.

Reds called over another soldier. "Pull the men watching the yacht off Grand Anse. They won't be needed there anymore. Repost one of the agents to Duncan's headquarters and the other to his house."

He paused, bursting with a sense of invincibility. The two things he wanted most now rolled in perfect harmony toward fulfillment.

By dawn tomorrow, he expected Duncan dispatched into history to make room for Reds' ascension as boss of the island.

Just as sweet, Cammy and her little clique would be gone from Reds' life forever.

The Bianca C Still Burns

***

"This is the most *ridicolo* story I have ever heard," Mario yelled when Storm climbed aboard the *Carmen* thirty minutes later and explained why they had to pull anchor and head to Palm Island tonight.

Mario had given his three-man crew a well-deserved break at the Spice Island Hotel on Grand Anse Beach, so Storm felt free to recap the day to both Mario and Cammy around the table on deck. That's when Storm realized he'd sunk so deep into this shit with Bravo and Hallam, he'd become resistant to the stench. It made him wonder if he'd missed any blind spots that might return to crucify his ass.

"Let me see if I understand this madness," Mario shouted at Storm. "The CIA and Cuban intelligence know about the *Bianca C* diamonds. And from behind the scene, they want to help us find the stones, right?"

"I think so."

"You believe Bravo is helping us because he wants to steal the diamonds?"

"Everything I've heard and seen so far makes me believe so."

"So why doesn't he just get his own dive crew to find them before we do?"

"My guess is the logistics of the search make it easier if we do all the work up front, then all he has to do show up on a boat with a couple of soldiers and take the goods. Even now, we're being watched from shore, but he doesn't know where your diamonds are on the *Bianca C*. He'd have to find men and time to search a ship two football fields long and seven stories high."

Sarcasm ribbed the edge of Mario's voice. "Okay, so we know Bravo's motivation. When you were on the phone at the *Cuban* embassy with the *Barbados* double-agent, did you ask him why the *Americans* are helping us? Certainly he knows *everything*."

Storm ignored the prods. "I expect them to tell us when we meet them on Palm Island tonight." He withheld his belief American involvement had more to do with destabilizing the Grenada revolution and freeing political prisoners like Jackie's father. But what could possibly link the diamonds to a covert political operation? "Bravo will arrange coast guard authorization for the trip, supposedly for us to pick up diving equipment."

"So this plan calls for you to order more gear when you haven't even seen or tested the ones I brought?"

"I was going to use needing gear as an excuse to go to Barbados, but now Hallam is using it as the reason for us to meet them on Palm Island instead. No one knows what you already have on board."

Storm didn't want to say openly that they might still need the gear he'd ordered from Hallam. Storm hadn't yet inspected the new equipment below deck, but he had doubts about Mario's financial ability to purchase the most reliable gear for the mission.

Mario might have been wealthy years ago, but besides the new communication radar, nothing on the yacht hinted of the glittering opulence befitting this once magnificent yacht. The *Carmen* needed a new coat of paint and the splintering planks above deck had already served their best years in the sun long ago. The discolored canvas canopy over the deck table and the aging ropes coiled on the deck appeared to be in a race to see which would unravel the most threads in the sea breeze.

Mario couldn't even afford the kind of quality staff members who had once graced the yacht in formal wear and charming European etiquette. Although the pot-bellied Greek chef stirred aromas that could awaken the appetite of a sleeping shark, when he labored in the galley he bellowed seafaring songs punctured with English obscenities. And when he served his steaming delicacies, he smiled with tobacco-stained teeth, sported overgrown nostril hairs entangled with his moustache, and burped gases foul with stale garlic.

After buying new curtains that Cammy promised to sew free for him, Mario probably wouldn't be able to buy a decent pair of fins.

Without the gear Storm listed for Hallam, this dive might be in trouble before it started.

Mario squirmed in his chair. "So in addition to us collecting scuba gear we don't need, we will meet with the CIA to *hopefully* discuss a plan to protect the diamonds from the Cuban who *might* want to steal them. Is that what you're saying?"

As crazy as Mario made this sound, he'd laid out the situation well with all its bizarre pieces.

"Yes, essentially," Storm said.

He adjusted his eye patch. "Young man, it's a hot day, but I am accustomed to heat. It can't distort my reasoning. I'm not taking my boat anywhere tonight. Forget it."

"Then find someone else to do your bloody dive."

Mario snapped. "I will."

Cammy, seated in her red bikini next to Storm, had been quiet throughout, but now she shouted at them. "Stop it you two. Stop it now. You're not listening to each other."

Mario calmed down and turned to her. "My dear, I don't want to get you upset, but here's what I've heard for the past thirty minutes. Your son knows about the diamonds. And he's spent the day meeting with PRA soldiers, a Cuban spy, and on the phone with a CIA double agent."

"True," Storm said. "But I have not told a soul about your diamonds."

"So how did everyone else find out?" Mario asked. "As I see it, you were the *only* one I told who's left the boat today."

"Wait one goddamned minute. Are you accusing—"

"I just want answers," Mario yelled.

"The only answer you'll get from me is I will not be responsible for your safety and diamonds once I get off your yacht."

"There must be more to this than you're telling me and your mother."

"We're wasting time," Storm said. "I am not going to risk my life and hers for some rusty heirloom that's been in your family for two-hundred years."

Mario jaws tightened. "If I didn't care for your *madre*, I would—"

"You would do what?"

Cammy stretched over to slap Storm on his head. "Where's your respect?"

Storm grabbed her arm in time. "Maybe this is something you two need to talk about. We only have a couple of hours before nightfall."

Mario adjusted his eye patch. "If it's agreeable to you, I will pay you to test the equipment to see if they are appropriate for this dive."

"Agreed. When I return, you can tell me if you changed your mind about Palm Island."

"My decision is final. We're not going to Palm Island tonight, or ever."

"Fine." Storm pushed back his chair and stood. "When I resurface, you pay me for the tests and we go our separate ways. Get someone else to find your precious little pieces."

He marched off past the bar toward the stairwell with Cammy's plea fading behind him. "Storm, don't…"

***

Cammy felt vulnerable with Mario after Storm heavy-footed it down the squeaky stairwell and disappeared below deck. Earlier, she slipped into her red bikini for a refreshing swim around the yacht with Mario. They climbed aboard and towel dried, but before she could change into casual blouse and shorts, he used his heart-stopping accent to talk her into staying in her skimpy swimsuit. But Mario's restrained admiration for her cleavage and dark legs did not make her uncomfortable—no, she welcomed those tender moments, especially while she ran her fingers through the shallow waves of soft black and white hairs on his chest.

Her despair rose from deeper roots, stretching more than twenty years into her past, to the days when the *Bianca C* flames belched thick smoke across the horizon of her memory.

Her heart drummed. The bond she hoped for between Storm and Mario stood on the verge of a painful and permanent fracture.

She knew what it meant.

The day had finally come to free the secret she'd cradled all those years. But it also came with fear. The fear a mother bird might experience just before its chick took the first leap from the nest.

It could end in an agonizing crash.

Especially now that the growing rift between Mario and Storm might snap the branch holding the nest.

Cammy left Mario at the table and headed to the bar to make him a gin and tonic. Her hand shook when she stirred the tinkling ice cubes in the drink. She poured herself a half-glass of straight rum without ice and returned to the table.

Mario took the glass. "Thanks."

The touch of his hand on hers still electrified her, but his voice sounded heavy with regret.

Regret at meeting Cammy? Regret for his toxic argument with Storm?

She swallowed a mouthful of rum and gazed out at the sunny green island, letting the rum warm her insides before speaking. "I've never had any reason to doubt my son."

"He's been under a lot of stress." Mario sipped his drink. "I wish he'd kept his mind on the dive, instead of getting caught up in all the intrigue plaguing the island."

"He didn't make this up. You know…about Bravo and Hallam."

"Maybe not. But I didn't come all the way from Italy to join up with CIA and Cuban agents."

"Can we at least go to Palm Island to hear what they have to say?"

"My dear, you're as hardheaded as your son. I'm staying in Grenada until I find someone else to do the dive."

"Suppose what he said is true?"

"I'm supposing it's not."

"I believe him."

He raised his voice. "You do because he's *your* son. Why should I believe him?"

"I'll tell you why you should believe him." Tears rolled down Cammy's cheeks like the first drops of water from a dam about to burst. Then the words gushed out. "Because he's your flesh and blood. Mario, Storm is your son too."

✳✳✳

When Storm pulled open the door to the storage locker next to the *Carmen's* engine room, the rubbery smell of scuba gear greeted him like the scent of a new car. The hangers held three dark blue long-sleeved wetsuits, a small, medium, and large, made by the Camaro Company out of Austria. Just like the Italian to choose a European brand, a reputable brand nonetheless. His choice of dark blue colors showed he understood how colors like yellow, white, and red, appear more visible to sharks.

Three wetsuits, but one buoyancy vest with connected regulator and pressure gauge meant one thing: Mario planned for a solo diver. Unsure of the diver's suit size at the time he purchased them, he invested in three available sizes.

Storm pulled off the medium suit and held the material to his face with a deep inhale.

His Marine recon squad regularly chorused "I love the smell of neoprene in the morning" an improvement over another he'd heard from DIs in Parris Island, "I love the smell of napalm in the morning." But of course napalm was the jellied gasoline used with devastating effect in the jungles of Vietnam.

He loved the smell of neoprene too because it reminded him of his first scuba dive when he was twelve. He tried to remember who gave him his first try, among the many unnamed faces Cammy brought into their lives for explosive bursts of adventure followed by dashed hopes.

Any one of these men, including Reds could be Storm and Rachael's father.

Most never stuck around very long, so Storm made little effort to remember their names.

Maybe Cammy waited all her life for the 'right' one.

She had befriended a visiting American diplomat from Trinidad who also had turned out not to be the right one. Storm forgot his name too, but most likely he was the one who strapped the first tank on Storm's back. The diplomat, in a neoprene suit, helped Storm adjust the older model double-hose regulator and showed him how to clear ear pressure by pinching the nose shut and blowing into it with his mouth closed. The man showed him how to avoid jaw fatigue by relaxing the bite on the mouthpiece and reminded him that the breathing cadence for a double hose is a long slow inhale followed by a long slow exhale

When Storm sank into the sea, the tranquility and beauty so contrasted with the turmoil Reds instigated above water, he knew in an instant what he wanted to do for the rest of his life.

On the diplomat's return to the island with his six year-old daughter the following year, Cammy arranged a coastal ride for them on the *Rhumrunner* party boat. Distracted by the loud music and back-breaking limbo dancing, no one saw the girl fall overboard—except Storm.

Before he had time to think, he grabbed a life jacket, jumped in, and swam up to her. His jump alerted a crewman and the boat turned around in time to rescue them.

Five years later, when Storm stumbled into the house sweating soot and oozing gasoline fumes from the car bombing, Cammy knew who to call at midnight. The next day Storm boarded the Federal Maple inter-island ship on a one-way ticket to Trinidad. A week later, he flew to San Juan carrying a United States green card sporting a picture of him in an unruly afro. He also had a seething attitude.

He took a taxi directly to the Marine Corps recruiting office and signed on the dotted line.

Life had become too dangerous not to know how to fight. What he hadn't expected was how much the Marines would teach him to fight and dive—really dive.

Now on the *Carmen*, he caressed the new dive suit, checking the collar, sleeves and ankle cuffs for the tight fit that limited water seepage. He tried on a pair of gloves but put those aside since he had no plans to encounter anything but fifty feet of water today.

Mario shopped for a solo diver, probably because maintaining secrecy would be easier with one diver than with two or more. But solo diving faced general scorn among professional diving circles. Trained in the solo skills of self-sufficiency and redundancy, Storm realized Mario's choice of gear clearly showed he too understood the requirements and the danger solo divers faced.

Among the six eighty cubic-feet aluminum tanks, complete with new valve covers and shiny O rings on the dive rack, Storm tugged on a yellow canister. He recognized the container of spare air manufactured by Submersible Systems. He'd read a recent article about a solo diver whose life the canister saved when the main tank ran out of air, even as his pressure gauge showed a positive reading.

Mario obviously invested heavily in the best equipment available, gear to assure the success of the mission, and the safety of the diver. Why would he spend this much money to recover a few gems worth more in sentimental value than in cold cash?

If Mario meticulously cut corners to afford this dive, Storm now understood his reluctance to waste fuel on a useless night trip to a deserted island. It would be a disappointment, with all the great gear in the locker, if Mario could not find anyone else in Grenada willing to solo dive at that depth.

As much as Mario wanted the *Bianca C* dive to be strictly his operation, this was no longer the case. The dive now became inseparable from whatever secret plans the Americans and Bravo hatched.

Those plans probably stretched from the *Bianca C* to the American embassy in Barbados, with tentacles leading to Reds, the Grenada Revolution, and political prisoners in Richmond Hill Prison.

Storm's commitment to Jackie reminded him not to let Mario's indignation or his obvious affection for Cammy throw him off course. He intended to test the gear in the waters above the *Bianca C* for an hour and allow Mario the time to digest everything they discussed topside.

Whatever it took, he would try once more to get Mario's agreement to take the yacht to Palm Island tonight.

The Italian did not know what Storm knew, so Mario's skepticism was understandable. But pretending no danger existed could lead to deaths, including Cammy's.

Even if Storm and Cammy walked away from Mario as if he never existed, Storm's deep entanglement with Bravo and Hallam prevented him from escaping unscathed. If it became necessary, Storm would play hardball. Maybe he would even get in Mario's face to read him the riot act, anything to get him to go to Palm Island tonight.

Storm didn't want to upset Cammy, though. She seemed as hooked on Mario as he seemed on her, and it confused the hell out of Storm, in a pleasing kind of way. She looked happier and more at peace in the last couple days than he'd seen her in months—except for the recent episode when Mario insinuated Storm told Bravo about the *Bianca C* diamonds.

It seemed alien for Storm to be considering his mother at a time like this. His Marine DIs had always hammered the lessons of calm, calculating discipline in times of pending danger. Emotion, especially the type linking Marines to their mothers, had no role in combat. Now, her affections for Mario complicated it even more.

If Mario still refused to drive the *Carmen* to Palm Island, should Storm consider taking his Radon 22 instead?

He quickly quashed that idea.

His primary and secondary gas tanks would be dry halfway to Palm Island. He also needed to buy additional five gallon containers as reserve. Even if he had the cash to buy fuel before the gas stations closed for the night, he kept remembering Hallam's instruction to have Mario take his yacht up to the deserted island—not Storm's Radon 22.

Why did it have to be the *Carmen*?

While Storm busied himself inspecting the gear below deck, Mario maneuvered the *Carmen* above the *Bianca C*, a mile offshore from Grand Anse. Mario and Cammy were in a subdued conversation behind the wheel when Storm climbed on deck with his tank and buoyancy vest. On Storm's second trip from below deck with a handful of gear, Cammy watched from the helm while Mario left his seat to pressure check the tank and strap it onto the buoyancy vest. Once Storm tested a few breaths with the regulator, he suited up with the dark blue set and strapped on his weight belt. Mario lifted the tank and vest on Storm's back to allow him to fasten the straps across his chest.

Mario snapped the spare-air holster to the vest and inserted the yellow canister. "I'm glad you decided to use this. What do you think about what we have so far?"

We?

"You have the latest and best." Storm pulled his dive glass over his head and squeezed into the fins he'd owned since North Carolina. "Whoever does the dive for you will be in great shape."

"We're right above the *Bianca C* bow, so you should see her around fifty feet."

"I was about sixteen my last time that close to the ship," Storm said. "You could just begin to make her out."

"We'll track your position with this buoy." Mario showed him an inflated orange bladder buoy along with a flying red-and-white dive flag. An automatic feeder held a roll of a hundred and fifty feet of nylon rope, if Storm needed this much tow line to return to the buoy. "We'll keep our engines in a slow idle within view of the flag."

Storm hooked the tow line to his shoulder ring. "Thanks, you thought of everything."

"Good luck." Mario shook his hand and surprised him with an embrace. "When you return let's talk about Palm Island again."

Storm looked at Cammy to read the reason on her face for Mario's abrupt change of mind. She gave Storm a glancing smile, and he understood.

A little sprinkle of her magic and Mario changed his mind.

The disgust soiled Storm's thoughts. By the time he began to feel pissed off, he was already off the swim platform and into the water with a splash.

She couldn't help herself.

To her this was just another day, another man, and another favor earned for her family.

Storm hated that his mother still had to live like this, but as the blue water embraced him, a tranquil sense of appreciation made him smile in his face mask. He didn't have a perfect life, but she'd made it an amazing one. And he loved her for all she did for him and Rachael.

No one did it better than Cammy.

She intended to get them to Palm Island tonight, because her son thought it important to go.

***

Jackie used her pounding headache as an excuse to leave work at 4 p.m. She walked out of the bank and into the afternoon heat. Even with sunglasses on, she squinted in the afternoon glare.

She had one last chance to see Steve before heading to the strange meeting Hallam instructed her to attend tonight. It was a simple plan: get to a payphone close to the embassy and call Steve. Tell him it was urgent. Have him meet her so she could tell him that Hallam's link with Bravo had compromised the Grenada mission—and Storm's safety.

She blended into the pedestrian crowds on Lower Broad Street and headed east across McGregor. She hurried past the embassy, glancing around in case she recognized Steve's narrow face and wire framed glasses in the crowded entrance.

No such luck.

Up ahead, around the bustling taxi stand on the corner at Bolton, a phone booth stood empty. She squeezed into it and opened her bag in search of coins.

Footsteps hurried up to the booth and someone filled the doorway behind her. "Need some change, ma'am?"

She glanced back. "Hallam! Are you following me?"

"Steve would be displeased if I report this," Hallam said. "You've been jumping from phone booth to phone booth all over Bridgetown since your return from Grenada yesterday."

"Yeah? What *else* haven't you told him yet?"

"What are you talking about?"

"I'll tell you just as soon as you tell me why the hell you've been following me around."

He tucked a couple of coins into her hand. "The three of us will talk about it tonight. Be there, seven o'clock. We have a busy night ahead of us."

Busy night?

He strolled away in jeans and a loose khaki shirt. The man changed clothes as often as he switched loyalties.

Just then the right side of his shirt lifted in the breeze.

Hallam had a handgun tucked into a holster on his waist.

***

From about fifty feet away the *Bianca C* loomed dark and imposing on its white-sand bed. Sea depth and silt runoff from the island's rivers combined to diminish visibility in the foggy blue water. It did not surprise Storm. This month, October, typically received some of the heaviest rainfall of the year. And just one day after the full moon, the fluctuating spring tides helped trigger currents that stirred up the silt. Even so he could still see farther than in most of the waters he'd dived in North Carolina, Texas, and Hawaii.

The ship stood upright on her keel as if to defy the fire, water, and time threatening her dignity. Her fate had been sealed since that Sunday morning twenty-two years ago when engine room explosions shattered the morning calm and mayday sirens awakened St. George's with urgent wails for help.

But even in defeat, her six-hundred feet of magnificence still graced the ocean floor.

The sight reminded Storm of another ship of matching length he'd visited in Hawaii. This ship had also met a tragic end on what too started as a peaceful Sunday morning, exactly twenty years before the *Bianca C* sank. The USS *Arizona*'s mortal blow came, not from accidental explosions, but from a deadly early-morning ambush by Japanese planes. Her air-raid alarm sounded at 7:55 a.m. At 8:06 a.m. a Japanese bomb triggered a volcanic eruption in the forward magazine. At 8:15 a.m. the broken ship dropped forty feet to the bottom of Pearl Harbor with a thousand men trapped on board. Her upper deck remained above water and, like the *Bianca C*, the USS *Arizona* burned for two days.

Forty years later, the bodies remained entombed in the ship. On his last training exercise to Hawaii, Storm visited the memorial built above the sunken ship. Bubbles of thick bunker fuel oil still bled each day from the half-million gallons on board.

Unlike the USS *Arizona*, the *Bianca C*'s wounds allowed her to delay her demise— just enough time for Grenadians to launch their hastily assembled flotilla of local boats and anything else that floated. Within two hours they plucked six hundred and seventy grateful souls from the quaking inferno, most still in pajamas.

Cammy used to recount to Storm and Rachael how the *Bianca C* anguished in the fiery throes of death for two days. Within view from Cammy's living room, the ship stood watch over the port from the channel while flames devoured her bowels and smoke bellowed out from her shattered windows.

Cammy would gaze out to the sea. "It was like *Bianca C* was watching to make sure we had enough warm food and beds on the island for her passengers. She boiled the sea water around her and blew hot air on shore, with no concern for her own needs. Sometimes her insides rumbled like a hungry stomach. Her side plates turned cherry red and her paint peeled from the heat. She glowed at night like a huge lighthouse to remind us she was still there, watching over her flock."

The British frigate HMS *Londonderry* arrived from Puerto Rico two days after the initial explosions to help prevent the sinking ship from choking the channel. They boarded the *Bianca C* and attached a tow line.

"They tried to drag her into deeper water," Cammy said. "But she protested."

The ship resisted when they dragged her into the strong winds, her rudder frozen. Finally, at exactly noon, two days after the fire started, too broken hearted and wounded to fight anymore, she chose her burial site.

Cammy would point from the living room window through which she witnessed the sinking. "It's a mile offshore from Grand Anse." Maybe from there, she would explain, *Bianca C* could still watch the horse-shoe harbor that embraced her shivering passengers and the hillside homes that sheltered them for a week. "I cried when she gave up and sank."

It seemed to Storm Cammy had been crying since then, either for lost love or lost lives.

Had she felt the *Bianca C*'s loss so deeply because they shared the same resilience? Like the *Bianca C*, Cammy had suffered fire in her soul and abuse to her body, but never faltered in her commitment to her children.

Maybe Cammy had recognized in the ship the same altruism guiding them both.

"She sank with secrets," she used to say with a glass of rum in her hand.

But she never explained more, and Storm had been too young to know what to ask. On some days she sat at the window for hours with the powerful binoculars she'd received in the mail glued to her eyes, watching the *Bianca C* site as much as it watched her.

While the USS *Arizona* sank with fuel oil that still bubbled to the surface, the *Bianca C* sank with secrets.

After twenty-two years, the *Bianca C* secrets had also begun to bubble to the surface. With deadly consequences, Storm worried.

***

At 4:30 p.m. Reds had his driver return him to his hilltop house overlooking the airport construction, trying to appear as calm as a duck on water, but paddling like hell below the surface. Today would be Reds' last day as just a military commander. Tomorrow he would be General Secretary of the Central Committee, Commander-in-chief of the Armed Forces, and Prime Minister of the island. But his success required stealthy planning. So this evening as part of his strategy, he would maintain his normal routines with as little fanfare as possible. Once home he would examine every step again, to ensure the takeover reflected his brilliance in policy making and military planning.

Nothing would be left to chance.

He pushed open the front door and gazed back from his hilltop view of the new airport that replaced a hundred million cubic feet of Grenada soil. The runway, built by Russian trucks, Japanese bulldozers, and Cuban labor, stretched nine thousand feet along the spine of the Point Salines peninsula and stood ready to welcome the largest and fastest Soviet jets.

Only one thing might please him more than to see Soviet Ilyushin-76 troop carriers landing with soldiers to consolidate his victory—Cammy's disappearance from his world.

Her very presence on the island, with her son and that one-eyed Italian, provoked his ugliest moods.

Reds shut his front door behind him and hurried past the kitchen. Earlier, he'd called his cook to order a seafood dinner with a bottle of the best Bulgarian white wine, a gift from Sergei. Now the pots smothered the air with the blended aromas of lobster, garlic butter, and island spices. On another day with less on his mind, he would have stopped in the kitchen, slapped the young cook on her firm behind, and sampled a few of her dishes. But tonight he marched straight down the hallway to his study. He locked the door behind him, collapsed into his black leather chair, and placed a secure phone-call to his intelligence chief.

"Anything else on the subject?" he asked when the intelligence chief answered.

"The Italian was the owner of the *Bianca C* before it sank."

Reds twirled his moustache. "Tell me something I don't already know."

"He spent a night in Cammy's house while the ship burned."

During those days, Reds attended advanced police training at the Antigua Police Academy. Cammy announced her pregnancy soon after Reds returned from Antigua, but by then Mario Costa and his passengers had already departed the island six weeks earlier. That bitch must have taken the Italian off his ship and straight into her bedroom. Even before she delivered, Reds began to feel the change in Cammy's attitude. She distanced herself from him, answered his inquiries with abrupt responses, and rejected Reds' sexual advances with cold mockery.

He dismissed her changes as typical of pregnant women. But months after Storm's birth, just as Reds began to embrace the pride bonding father to son, Cammy's scorn finally exploded.

Maybe he'd had too much to drink that night. His fists did little to subdue the garbage spewing from her mouth. He left her unconscious on the floor, while four-year old Rachael screamed at him with her crying baby brother in her arms.

How dare Cammy threaten his manhood? How dare she deny he fathered her children? Her belligerence started when she met the Italian. He turned her against Reds. If Mario Costa also fathered Storm, then the Italian's demise tonight would be even sweeter. Reds regretted one thing. He would be too busy tonight to witness Costa go up in smithereens along with his bastard son and the boy's slut mother.

Reds' intelligence chief interrupted his rage. "We still don't know why Mr. Costa returned to Grenada. Everything we see says he is dead broke."

"Too bad. When Bravo is done with him, he will be more dead than broke. And if Bravo does not do the job, I will."

"What about the other girl?"

"What girl?" Reds asked.

"The one we picked up two nights ago."

"Ah, yes."

"Have you seen her naked?" the chief asked.

"What...what do you mean?" A memory of raw sexual power over a teenage virgin aroused Reds.

"She has quite a body," the intelligence chief said. "It will be a shame to see her go to waste. She's gotten the usual, stripping, cold water, a little roughing up, but I don't think she knows anything about the boat we found floating in the harbor."

"Hold on to her a couple more days. I might still have use for her if Bravo fails me."

They chatted briefly about the plans for tonight, but the ten year-old memory of surrendering flesh, finger nails slicing his back, and exploding groins still fanned Reds' desires. The episode released years of pent up rage and almost restored everything Cammy had denied him—almost.

He prepared to end the conversation. "I'll be here all night. Keep me posted."

"Yes, sir."

"By the way, what's the girl's name again?"

"She was Rachael's classmate. Pauline."

***

Cammy wished she could dump a bucket of water on Mario's rising anger.

While Storm tested the scuba gear below the surface of the sea, Mario stomped around the wheelhouse of the *Carmen* shaking his head and snapping the elastic band to his eye patch. "Why didn't you tell me before? It could have changed so much for us if I knew he was my son."

"You expect me to believe because I got pregnant from a one night stand with some rich man, he will pack his bags to come get me?"

"Yes."

"Mario, that's the oldest trick in the book: 'I'm carrying your baby. Marry me or send money.'"

"But you did carry my son." The wooden floor creaked under his footsteps. "I...I could have sent you money for Rachael and Storm to—"

"Dammit," she yelled. "I don't want your money. I told you that too when you offered to pay me just to watch activities around the *Bianca C*."

How could he know the emptiness gnawing her insides so deep, money would never reach? Even on Christmas mornings, when her children opened the few presents she could afford, the empty boxes and strewn wrapping paper only reminded Cammy of her own discarded needs. Her tree lights twinkled.

Christmas carols echoed out of neighbors' windows along with mouth-watering aromas of baked ham and rum cake.

But while neighborhood children squealed at play with their new toys, Rachael and Storm muffled their delight to avoid awakening the thug snoring in Cammy's bed.

Maybe she should have used Mario's money to pave her way out of Reds' life. But he knew how to badger his way into her room with his police uniform and authority. Mario's money might have only bought her larger empty boxes and more rumpled wrapping paper.

Her agony came from unmet craving. She craved for what she once held for a fleeting moment, and then lost: a taste of bliss from the only man to caress her spirit and fill her soul.

Maybe her dream flourished only in the womb of her imagination, wishful thinking that belonged only in the mind of a simple island girl, its sustenance a drain on her energy.

A sudden onset of exhaustion overwhelmed her and she collapsed in the worn rattan couch facing the back of the pilot seat. Maybe the years of wishing and hoping, yearning and wanting had run its course and finally sapped the last of her energy.

Submission and grief burdened her words. "I never knew what it was to have a real father. I punished my own children with the same curse. In all my life, my heart and home felt whole just once. That was the day you spent in my house. I don't want your money."

"Did you read the old letter I gave you yesterday?"

"Ye," she said. "It just reminded me how much our secrets stole from us. We both felt the same way, but hid it from each other."

"Then what more do you want from me?"

"I wanted you, Mario. But you were fighting too many demons with your wife in Italy to be available. It's too late now."

He stepped away from the wheel, knelt in front of her, and held her hands. "Why do you think I named this boat after you? You're so wrong, *amore mio*."

***

Swimming fifty feet below the *Carmen,* Storm surrendered to his fascination with the *Bianca C.* Cammy's stories of raging fires and heroic rescues converged with the magnificence before him in an intoxicating moment. He decided to violate the most important lessons hammered into his brain in scuba school: plan your dive, dive your plan, and unless you absolutely had to, never, never dive alone.

On impulse, he decided to descend to the *Bianca C,* fifty feet below his planned depth—alone.

Three white-spotted eagle stingrays swam by, flapping their wings and wagging their venomous barbed stingers as if to remind Storm he'd better test his gear again. It worried him that the ship's allure had so distracted him he'd almost forgotten his agreement with Mario to test the new dive equipment at fifty feet.

Could this be an early sign of impaired thinking divers experienced when they slipped into the dangerous narcotic state of nitrogen narcosis? The Martini effect, or 'rapture of the deep', as his Marine buddies used to call it, affected people differently, most often beyond a hundred feet but occasionally in shallow waters as well. He sought comfort in the thought that the *Bianca C*'s upper decks sat no deeper than ninety feet.

He also recalled how fatigue and stress-induced adrenaline aggravated the hallucinatory effects and flawed decision-making.

Fatigue and stress?

Hell. He hadn't had a full night's sleep in days. And scuttling between Reds, Bravo, and Mario hadn't exactly felt like a honeymoon.

He removed his regulator from his mouth and tested it against the water pressure, watching the bubbles expand like balloons up the channel of foggy blue light. He reached behind him and turned the air valve off then on again, with little resistance. The buoyancy bladder exhaled and inhaled air with equal ease. The spare canister delivered a strong flow of air, even though the mouthpiece felt a little awkward.

But he didn't give a damn about comfort. The little yellow puppy might save his life one day.

He tugged at the nylon tow line trailing from his shoulder ring to the flagged buoy on the surface, via the safety reel floating just above him. The reel fed more line at Storm's pull, and when he released it, the reel took back the slack in a smooth rewind.

His confidence in the equipment grew, and so did his respect for Mario.

Finally, he released just enough air from his vest to allow the negative buoyancy he needed. He exhaled slowly and equalized his ear pressure, pinching his nose and blowing into it. When he glanced down, he felt like he floated in air above a ten story building, and could fall any minute.

Feet first, he began the slow descent toward the *Bianca C.*

She welcomed him from behind an undulating curtain of blue, her main structure unyielding to the rigorous punishment she'd endured. Despite her torturous life, she'd become a home to a plethora of aquatic life on the sea floor, just like she'd once provided a home to pleasure-seeking passengers on the ocean surface. She nurtured a thick coat of Marine vegetation from which blossomed colorful fan and branch corals in the steady currents. Giant sea sponges stood watch over the lush gardens as rainbow colors of fish darted in and out of portholes and windows. Turtles grazed leisurely on the greenery.

Even after twenty-two years, her foremast, wrapped in scarfs of vines, and circled by adoring barracudas, jacks and mackerels, still stood upright and proud above the winch house.

A large school of barracudas grinned at Storm with razor-sharp teeth but kept their distance. Curious yellowtail snappers swam up to him in the glimmering shaft of light and then scurried away in a yellow cloud.

Maybe one day he would get to take Jackie on this dive. She adjusted well on her first dive a couple of days ago, even allowing a brief kiss at twenty feet. It reminded him that if Mario agreed to go to Palm Island, and if Bravo kept his promise, he might see her again tonight.

When a wave of euphoria swept through Storm, he remembered not to get carried away at this depth. The pressure gauge showed two thousand psi. At a hundred feet, he had about fifteen minutes to absorb the scenery before heading back to the surface at a controlled pace. Panicked resurfacing at a fast pace led to decompression sickness. The bends, as divers referred to it, caused joint pains in the lucky ones, but paralysis and even death in unlucky divers who surfaced too rapidly from depths like Storm now dove.

He preferred an ascent rate of thirty feet per minute with an additional ten minutes of interval stops. His watch showed 4:45 p.m.

He should be on his way up by 5:00 p.m., just enough time to locate the third cabin from the port side on the upper level.

Mario had said he'd converted the cabin into a personal library. The library provided him solitude with a cigar and a good book while his daughter Bianca took swimming lessons in the pool. He'd also installed a safe at the floor level in the rear bulkhead of the library. It hid behind a five-foot long wet bar, which supplied him with all the cognac he needed to disconnect him from his painful marriage.

Storm floated over the bow toward the upper deck, counting the windows from right to left. He felt like he was face-to-face with the windows of a high-rise building, in an increasingly stronger current sweeping across from starboard to port.

Excitement bubbled inside him. He drew closer to the third window, dark on the inside at first but clearer with each thrust of his fins.

He doubled his effort to stay on course in the current and grabbed the upper window ledge to resist the steady drag.

With one hand clutching the ledge, he unsnapped his flashlight from the front of his buoyancy vest, glad he carried it in case he needed light for closer inspection of his gauges. He waved the light across the cabin. Encrusted rods and cables dangled like spider webs from the ceiling, lifelines to a hanging colony of green algae, white feathery ferns, and yellow mushroom polyps. Against the back wall, the weakened skeleton of Mario's bar clung together in an awkward pose of twisted metal, still dutifully hugging the rusty sink with boney limbs.

Storm unhooked the tow line from his shoulder ring. The last thing he wanted now would be to cut the rope, or worse, to get entangled in the obstacle course awaiting him in the cabin. He found an empty bolt hole in the middle of the upper ledge of the window. When he snapped the hook into place, a metallic ping echoed sharply around the cabin.

With the flashlight in one hand, he tightened his grip on the window ledge with the other and prepared to squeeze into the cabin.

Movement on the cabin floor directly below him caught his attention. He didn't have to look closer.

Twelve feet of bulky gray rose from the shadows with dead eyes and dorsal fins.

His euphoria changed to naked fear.

Oh shit!

He almost spat out his regulator.

He'd disturbed a resting shark.

✳ ✳ ✳

Mario tapped the seat of his leather armchair behind the wheel. "Come here my love," he said to Cammy. "You can be my pilot while we wait for Storm."

"Glad to." She uncrossed her smooth dark legs and left her glass on the end table. When the sun began its dip toward the horizon and the cool breeze picked up, she'd changed into her jeans shorts and loose white blouse tied around her narrow waist.

For a moment regret burdened Mario's conscience. Why did he wait so long to return to Cammy? But when she placed her hand in his to help her settle into the seat, regret for the past vanished to make room for the pleasure of the moment.

He kissed her. "Lesson number one: never take my seat without kissing me first."

"*Sì, mio capitàno,*" she said.

The music in her laugh flowed into aching parts of him he'd hidden from sound and light for years.

"Where did you learn that?" he asked.

"I listen to how your crew men talk to you."

Her surprises made him marvel at the many layers of her human texture. Much of it accommodated pain but still left ample space for her to embrace slivers of humor. Her joys and pains, dreams and losses, and yes—her loyalty, blended in a rich tapestry of humanity. Next to Cammy, his ex-wife's glittering pretenses now seemed even shallower and brutally selfish than he'd first thought after the bitter divorce.

When Mario lost sweet Bianca from her blood condition at such a young age, his agony tasted like an overdose of bad medicine. The tests confirmed he'd not been her biological father. Even as he fought off his ex-wife's attempts to siphon his dwindling wealth, he worried he might die one day without leaving a trace of himself behind.

In the meantime, Cammy had kept vigilant watch on the *Bianca C* with the only thing she'd ever accepted from him, a pair of binoculars that took three months to reach her by mail. He asked her to write him whenever she observed suspicious activities around the ship. Yet, it seemed she wrote even when a sea gull flew over the site.

How he grew to love seagulls.

But little did he suspect she'd given birth to his son and raised him into a splendid young man, an ironclad secret she'd protected until today.

And after Storm disappeared below the surface to test the dive gear, Cammy compared the picture of him she always carried in her purse, with a picture Mario kept of himself. They both gasped at the similarity between Mario as a frolicking young man on the beaches of the French Riviera, and Storm with his Marine friends on a North Carolina beach.

"Oh my God," she whispered.

Even as Mario's copper tan gave him a slightly fairer complexion than Storm's, they both shared the same angular jaw lines, lush eyebrows, and steady dark eyes.

Cammy would never know the depth of the gift she'd given Mario, and neither would he. He couldn't reach that far within himself. In an instant, she'd given him more life than he ever thought could exist in him.

He would have given her his last lira for keeping his dream alive, but she never asked for a penny.

Even while she survived abuse and grief, she kept her life-doors open for one more drink, one more laugh, one more kiss.

He kissed her again.

With one hand still holding the wheel, she placed her other palm gently on the burned side of his face and returned his kiss with a girlish moan, her eyes closed.

He hated to stop. They still had to look out for Storm, and to discuss how to break the news to him.

Storm had a father, a father who wanted him as a son.

"Storm should be popping up over there any time now." Mario pointed to the flagged orange buoy a short distance away and glanced at his watch. "We're just coasting around in a circle."

She circled her index finger around his lips. "Around and around. Hmmm… sounds like fun. And easy."

He kissed her finger. "Here comes the difficult part, the second lesson. Hold the wheel in position and don't move while I taste your neck."

Her playful squeals filled the cockpit and his heart.

He had never felt so alive, now that he finally had something to die for—a family.

His own flesh and blood.

***

Face-to-face with the monster, Storm released the window ledge. He let the current drag him swiftly away from the shark without transmitting any distress signals that might excite its appetite. Glancing back to ensure it had not followed, he grabbed the next window. This time, with the current threatening to pull him away, he scanned his flashlight around the neighboring cabin, more thoroughly but quickly, for additional hostile tenants.

Except for a few mangled furniture pieces, the floor looked bare. Satisfied this cabin held no hidden danger, Storm squeezed in, careful not to snag his regulator hose or bang his tank on the upper ledge. He jammed the slimy remains of a broken chair across the window—just in case the shark came knocking.

Of the original wall separating the two cabins, only a see-through fence of scrambled poles, cables and rods remained, dissecting the view of the shark next door. The shark's twelve feet stretched the length of the cabin. Ceiling cables hung like dreadlocks along its head, filling the window opening Storm had just escaped. The tail brushed the rear bulkhead above Mario's bar. The beast easily weighed over three hundred pounds, even without the foot long remora suckerfish clinging to its back.

The longer Storm observed the shark from the safety of the neighboring cabin, the more his nerves calmed. The rounded dorsal fins and unusually long tail identified it as a nurse shark. Its docile nature seemed at odds with the two elongated barbels hanging from its snout, making it look like a cross between a saber tooth tiger and Count Dracula.

Despite their ferocious bearing, nurse sharks preferred to eat more bite-sized meals than their great white cousins, which had gained nerve wracking notoriety in the movie *Jaws*.

But nurse sharks lived twenty-five years. And while most sharks had to keep moving to have a fresh supply of seawater to replenish their oxygen intake, nurse sharks were capable of pumping seawater across their gills while resting in place.

This one next door probably stood at the front of the shark line to claim Mario's library as its private room the minute the smoldering ship crashed on to the sandy ocean floor twenty-two years ago. Now, after a lifetime of tranquility, the poor thing must have thought it awakened from a bone jarring nightmare. What else could explain the glass-faced, tank-backed alien that invaded its luxury spa with dazzling unnatural lights and pinging metallic echoes?

Given its attention on the now empty window, the shark probably questioned its sanity.

Storm glanced at his watch and pressure gauge. He had five minutes to initiate a slow controlled ascent to the surface with decompression stops. After coming this far, he hated the thought of returning to the *Carmen* without confirming the presence of a safe next door. Entering Mario's cabin with a terrified shark might be suicidal.

Even nurse sharks attacked humans when provoked.

But damn, Storm had already provoked this one.

His best bet would be to encourage it to exit peacefully through the window. As a nocturnal feeder and with dusk approaching it might soon leave on its own to begin its nightly feast. Storm had no time to wait. He still had to retrieve the tow line hooked just biting distance from the shark's mouth.

He quickly dismissed the idea to abandon the tow line and resurface in dying light. The rising currents and shifting tides could drag him miles away from the rendezvous buoy before his head broke the surface. Sure, he could ditch his tank and weights to lighten his swim to the *Carmen*, but in his dark blue suit, he doubted Cammy and Mario would see him after sunset. And if they continued to 'live boat' overhead, circling the buoy to find him, Storm risked getting run over by the clunky yacht.

Even if he signaled with his flashlight, it would guarantee a hostile response from the Grenada military, already jittery about an invasion. He could see the headlines: *U.S. Marine shot while practicing invasion signals off shore.*

The same reception might await him if he chose to crawl out of the water on a dark beach instead. Some trigger-nervous PRA soldier would drop him instantly with a burst of hot AK-47 lead.

All Storm's trepidations would vanish if he could just get the shark to leave quietly.

Cammy always said she felt better about his safety below water than above. He wished he could hear her say it just once more.

For Storm to hear his mother's voice again, the shark had to go.

It held an alert gaze at the window, poised to fight off another nightmarish intrusion.

Storm tried to recall what he'd studied about sharks' avoidance behavior. Different shark types had their own unique responses to stimulations. Nurse sharks responded to sounds made by small prey like shrimps. Loud sounds like the banging of metal might scare it off, but it could also invite a toothy sand tiger shark.

He'd also read that sharks feared bubbles, except the great white and tiger sharks. Most sharks typically avoided swimming above scuba divers, the source of rising exhale bubbles.

Seconds slipped by. Storm's pressure gauge needle shifted toward red. He might afford just one bust of air through his regulator to scare the shark away. If that failed, he would escalate to noise.

He wrenched a foot-long metal leg from a broken chair and swam up to the cluster of cables and poles separating him from the anxious shark.

CHAPTER NINETEEN

Among the quarter-million people living in Barbados, Jackie knew only two she could talk to about her predicament. She couldn't find one and didn't trust the other. The one she didn't trust wanted her to meet him at a desolate house on the turbulent Atlantic coast tonight. Now she'd stumbled onto his double-cross with the Cubans in Grenada, Hallam might want her dead. If she decided not to go to the house, and missed a legitimate meeting, she risked jeopardizing the mission to free her ailing father from prison.

If only she could find Steve, the handler from the American embassy in Bridgetown, the only person she trusted to protect her or erase her suspicions.

For operational security, Steve instructed her never to use her home phone to call him and never to show up unannounced at the embassy. So since her arrival from Grenada yesterday, she tried to call him several times from payphones, but without luck. The phone just rang and rang. When she walked past the embassy an hour ago, no one at the entrance or in the immediate lobby area even closely resembled Steve in his wire-framed glasses.

Hallam probably handed her change to make her call at the phone booth earlier because he knew Steve would not answer.

Now she wondered if Hallam already eliminated Steve, and planned to kill Jackie tonight.

How did it come to this?

Two weeks earlier, Steve walked into the bank where she worked as a teller. Lean, rigid, and about fortyish, he wore jeans, safari shirt, and wire-framed glasses with flipped down shades.

He handed her a deposit slip and cash, with a business card on the top of the stack. He delivered words as short as his blond crew cut. "Call me. It's about your father."

When the revolution toppled the iron-fisted regime four years ago, they jailed her father, a former government minister. No trial, no family visitation, only occasional Red Cross packages. It seemed her father would wither away and die, a lonely man in prison. But Steve raised her hopes that the Americans might want to help.

She met with him the same afternoon, in an embassy basement room with four plain walls and an armed Marine Guard outside the locked door. Steve introduced her to Hallam and they sat around a polished table without paper or pens.

"We can free your father but we need your help. No guarantees." Steve explained they had plans in Grenada but needed one additional member on the team. They wanted her to go to Grenada to meet that candidate and convince him to join the group.

"Who?" she asked.

"Storm Butler."

She leapt from her chair, her heart quaking and her eyes flooding. "He tried to kill my father, dammit!"

"Misguided teenaged vandalism. We did our own investigation for his green card."

"Tell that to my father."

"Storm did it for his mother, not for Reds," Steve said. "It was supposed to be a parting favor for Reds to stay away from Cammy."

She sat back in her chair, each moment of those terrifying days cascading over her thoughts and sapping her will to argue. "I might need to play a violin for the rest of this story."

"It's the truth. Reds lied to Storm, told him the bomb would go off in the car while everyone was asleep in the house. But Reds designed it with a vibration trigger. Someone had to be driving to set it off."

"My father could have died."

"Yes," Steve said. "You all could have. If Storm had stumbled while carrying it, he too could have died. He was the one who pulled your father from the burning car and saved his life."

"If Storm has the guts, then let him tell me to my face. I've waited for four years."

Steve glanced at Hallam. "Now we're getting somewhere."

Hallam's face stretched with a silver-toothed grin.

Jackie still had more questions, especially since Steve had all the answers. "So why is Storm back in Grenada?"

"He's awaiting a hardship discharge from the Marine Corps, to be with his mother. His sister Rachael died recently in a suspicious accident."

"Oh God, no."

Now two weeks later, after going undercover in Grenada as Hallam's wife and convincing Storm to join a plan she knew nothing about, her father still lingered in prison, and she feared for her life with no one in Barbados to help her.

The loneliness closed in around her.

It had taken two emotional weeks to admit she missed Storm over the years. But it might be too late now to tell him how much she wanted him back in her life.

She probably had only two hours left to live.

CHAPTER TWENTY

Worried he could slice his regulator hose against the barbed end of a hanging cable, Storm removed the regulator from his mouth and stretched the hose at floor level, five feet below the shark. The standard twenty-eight inch hose barely made it past the clutter of cables. He squeezed the release. Precious air poured out, but the current through the window dissipated the bubbles between the cables. Nowhere close to the shark's head.

The shark held its position without flinching.

Damn. What a waste of air.

He returned the regulator to his mouth and pulled out the yellow canister, filled with three cubic feet of air. Just enough for a minute of breathing at a hundred feet, but at least he could stretch his arm further than with the primary regulator.

He waited to time a slowdown in the current and then squeezed the release.

Bubbles floated and expanded past the shark's eyes. This time, the shark accepted its temporary eviction notice with grace. It moved forward and out of the window like a sluggish truck exiting a tunnel.

Bingo.

It cleared the opening, turned left and coasted in the current past the second window without even a glance in Storm's direction. It disappeared in the fading light around port side with the remora suckerfish still hanging on to its back.

"Happy feeding," Storm wanted to shout to both of them.

His watch showed 5 p.m. and the needle on the pressure gauge just crossed below fifteen hundred psi. He could still stretch a few minutes for a quick inspection of Mario's library. Rather than exiting the second window and re-entering the third again, he decided to save time by squeezing past a clutter of cables hanging against the bulkhead next to the shaky bar.

He made it through and found himself staring at the open window. If the shark returned at this moment, he'd be trapped. The seven-inch kabar knife he'd carried from Beirut and now sheathed at his leg would be no match for a killing machine.

He would have to block the window as well.

He tugged at the bar. Whatever rusty bolts still held it in place, finally gave up. The frame came loose, and so did the sink, falling with a clang and generating a louder echo than the earlier ping that had awakened the shark.

Several blue fish scattered.

Now he worried other monsters heard the noise.

He easily lifted the bar with its hollow legs and shut it like a gate against the window opening. He secured it in place with a few rapid knots of the tow line and turned back with his lit flashlight pointing toward the bulkhead.

The light pressed forward past the forest of hanging cables to the fallen rusty sink on the floor. Over the sink, the unmistakable round dial of a combination lock peeked out like the eye of a Cyclops.

Storm's heart drummed. He dived to the safe and shifted aside cables for a clearer view.

Just as Mario had described, bolted rivets held the medium-sized two cubic-feet safe to the floor. His blueprint showed a two-inch steel casing, but the structural integrity of the safe itself would be severely compromised after the heat of the fire.

Most safes withstood twelve hundred degrees for an hour, but steel lost half its yield strength at five hundred degrees centigrade, and ninety percent by a thousand degrees. The ship probably burned at higher temperatures. Mario received his facial burns on this deck, five doors down the passageway from this library. Pictures Storm had seen of the ship showed thick smoke gushing out of these very windows. And Cammy described the glow reaching even the upper decks for two nights. The safe's steel casing and door must have glowed from the heat as well.

Also, rapid cooling of steel, after the ship sank, further altered its internal grain structure forever. All welded parts, especially around the hinges, would be melted or cracked. The combination lock, the weakest part of the safe, probably disintegrated from the heat first, especially with its plastic, spring-loaded washers. The braided gaskets around the perimeter of the door, like those used in ovens, would have burned next, leaving gaps around the door that might allow Storm to use his crow bar if needed. Only diamonds, fire-tested from prehistoric volcanoes could have survived the *Bianca C* inferno and twenty years of harsh seawater salinity.

Almost disguised by the grimy rust-colored encrustations, the aged safe would be a warped, brittle box, waiting for a controlled blast to reveal its contents.

Storm glanced at his watch and pressure gauge. At 5:10 p.m., he had eleven hundred psi left and ten minutes to get to the surface. At this depth and level of physical activity, he would drain air at around a hundred psi a minute.

Not good.

Although he doubted anyone would be knocking on the safe soon, he covered up the combination lock with the bucket and shifted a few hanging cables over it for special effects.

He retreated to the window and loosened the ropes holding the bar. He squeezed out into the full rush of the current sweeping past and snapped the tow line onto his shoulder harness ring. Worried the nurse shark might forget about the vicious bubble eviction and decide to return for a nap, he gated the bar back over the window opening. A few loops of cable lengths around the bar legs and through window ledge bolt holes secured the entrance.

Storm saw no sense in going through the whole bubble bath routine again with the stubborn nurse shark if he returned in the next day or two.

5:15 p.m. *Shit.*

At this rate he'd be trying to suck air from water before he hit the surface. Served him right.

Plan your dive, dive your plan, and unless you absolutely have to, never, never dive alone.

He'd even run out of time for self-denigration. He added valuable air from his tank to his buoyancy vest, kicked to gain upward momentum, and exhaled slowly to release the expanding air in his lungs as water pressure diminished with increasing altitude.

At the rate of about sixty feet per minute, he began a controlled ascent to the surface without even a glance down at the fading ship.

The first hint of trouble came on his controlled stop fifteen feet from the surface. He sucked on his regulator as if the air came from a straw as skinny as a toothpick.

He swapped his primary regulator for the yellow canister, and took its last breath of air just as he broke the choppy surface next to the flagged buoy.

When Storm climbed aboard twenty minutes later and unstrapped his gear with exhilaration breathing out of his pores, Cammy spoke first.

"Mario was starting to get worried about you," she said. "But I reminded him you are safer under water than above."

Mario read the pressure gauges on the main tank and the yellow canister. "My dear, if you see these numbers, you might also begin to believe our…your son is a fish."

"It was close," Storm confessed. "But worth every minute."

He recounted the dive, to Mario's almost teary-eyed disbelief.

"You saw the safe?" Mario asked.

"And your bar. I didn't see anything there to drink, but it's serving a useful purpose tonight."

Mario surprised Storm with a back-slapping embrace. "I'm glad you made it back."

Cammy stood watching with a smile that, for the first time, Storm could not read.

"Get your bag," Mario said to her. "Storm and I will have to get started on our trip in about an hour."

Cammy held both their hands. "You two will go alone. I'm sure you'll have lots to talk about and plan. I'll stay at home tonight so first thing in the morning I can go shopping for the curtains."

Mario turned to Storm. "While you change, I'll take her to the beach on the dinghy so she can drive your pickup home before it gets too dark."

"So we're going to Palm Island tonight?" Storm asked.

Mario beamed in the crimson sunset. "But of course, my son."

Storm chuckled to himself. Italian men sure know how to get emotional.

***

Cammy shifted Storm's pickup into first gear and it complained with a grinding sound. She reminded herself to always keep the clutch to the floor until the gear engaged, as Storm repeatedly taught her. But today she had a valid excuse for the bad gear shift. Her roller-coaster day on the *Carmen* with Storm and Mario ended with relief, as if someone had removed a useless weight she'd been carrying on her shoulders for years. The feelings she'd so long nestled for Mario now stood on real legs, not whimsical mists of wishful thinking. And he felt the same for her. This giddying distraction alone explained her rusty driving. In gear now, she raced in the dying sunset toward St. George's.

Her last wish today sat on the *Carmen*. Mario had asked her to let him break the news to Storm on their trip to Palm Island tonight.

Finally, Storm could claim a father.

For the first time since she lost Rachael thirty days ago, Cammy felt a glimmer of hope her wounded heart might be whole again.

She felt exhausted, but didn't expect to sleep a wink until the two men in her life returned safely to her arms tomorrow.

Fragments of life merged into perfection when hope and love filled the painful fissures.

She turned on the car radio for island music, but when the government 6 p.m. news came on, she quickly changed it to the Radio Antilles station in Montserrat, which usually gave more balanced coverage of the day's events.

"...the truck bomb collapsed the entire BLT Barracks on the Beirut Airport where the Marines were sent to help maintain a fragile peace."

She turned up the volume.

"So far more than two hundred dead Marines have been recovered. Few survived, and for the few who did, with the devastating injuries they suffered from fire and crushing concrete, observers gave them little hope."

"Oh dear God, no!"

Cammy sped home, locked the door behind her, and kept the lights off. Tonight, after the news, she wanted to sit alone at her window, with her thoughts and her bottle.

It took two quick shots of rum for her to absorb what the Beirut bombing meant to her. She mourned for all the mothers awaiting the horrible news about their sons tonight. Cammy still had her son, but the blessing tasted bittersweet.

She reached for another drink, and then changed her mind. She no longer needed it. She emptied the bottle down the kitchen sink and returned to her window.

Storm will need her more tomorrow than she needed another drink tonight.

What would he do when he heard the news of the bombing? Would he remember that if Rachael had not died a month ago, he would be in Beirut tonight—dead?

* * *

At 7:00 p.m. Jackie pulled to a stop at the turn leading to a house partially hidden in a nest of wind-blown trees. A razor-thin light sliced from behind thick drapes in one corner of the house. At the other corner a small lamp spilled light onto a neglected flower garden. A stone walkway disappeared into the backyard.

Hallam's red Mazda sat in the driveway a few yards from the front door.

She turned off her lights and coasted down the rough driveway, cringing each time her worn shocks squeaked her arrival.

She stopped behind Hallam's car and turned off the engine. Her heart drummed like the Atlantic surf pounding the Barbados shoreline.

She scanned the darkness for signs of people, or trouble.

If Steve was also here, did he park his car in the garage to her right? If not, he might be miles away, without a clue Jackie was about to walk into danger.

Should she just back out of the driveway and return to her apartment in Bridgetown thirty minutes away? But if Steve had indeed arranged a briefing and she failed to show up, he might reconsider trusting her in their plans for Grenada, plans she hoped would free her father from prison. She hated the thought Storm would be disappointed in her if she caused the plans to unravel.

Jackie decided to go up to the house and ring the doorbell in a sequence Hallam had instructed.

She held her keys with the longest one protruding between her fisted fingers. If Hallam answered the door in a threatening manner, she would stab him in the eye and kick him in the groin. Then race back to her car and get the hell out of there.

Jackie hadn't taken Taekwondo over the past five years for nothing.

A steady breeze, thick with sea smell, greeted her when she stepped out of the car. Her shoes crunched on the gravel driveway in hesitant steps toward the front entrance.

She crept up to the door and listened.

No voices from the inside, just the sound of wind rustling through the trees behind her.

The lamplight suddenly went out.

This isn't good.

She backed away from the door.

Maybe she should go around the rear to see who else was in the house. If Hallam was alone, she would quietly retrace her steps to the car and go find Steve at the embassy.

She'd just reached the corner between the flower garden and the house when footsteps raced up in the dark behind her. A metallic sound clicked at her head before she could turn around.

"Freeze!" Hallam said.

She tightened her grip on the keys and thought of her father.

***

Seated on a frayed leather armchair next to Mario, Storm watched the hillside lights of Grenada drift past like constellations against the dark sky. It should have felt weird motoring north on a ninety foot yacht with a one-eyed stranger he'd met only thirty-six hours ago.

It didn't, probably because Cammy knew him a long time. Yet, Storm had known some of her other friends and none exuded the natural companionship Mario possessed.

Mario also exhibited a level of leadership and decision-making Storm admired. Maybe Storm had experienced similar leadership styles in the Marines. Gather all relevant information before a decision. Weigh the advantages and disadvantages. Make the decision and follow through with a crystalized commitment to achieve the goal. And foremost, look out for your men.

Mario looked very much like a man in charge of a fleet, even on his aging yacht chugging along at twenty-five knots with a crew of one, having given his men a couple days off on Grand Anse Beach. The panel lights at the helm glowed blue on his face, highlighting the relaxed certainty of a man who knew what he wanted and how to get it. Storm hoped his dive this afternoon helped to boost Mario's confidence. The reason for his twenty-year wait now lay within reach.

Cammy had persuaded Mario to make the four hour dash north, despite his initial skepticisms. Now, he manned the wheel as if getting to Palm Island had been his decision all along. He even responded to the earlier radio message from Barbados with an equally cryptic response: *Rendezvous confirmed.*

Meeting with the Barbados contacts might not only get them more gear for the dive tomorrow, whether they needed it or not. More importantly, they would finally learn what dangers awaited once the contents of the *Bianca C* safe landed on the *Carmen*. And what Mario's little treasure had to do with Colonel Bravo and the Grenada Revolution.

The thought of holding Jackie again raced excitement through Storm's veins.

Mario must have sensed Storm's preoccupation with the dive and the night ahead of them. "Not tired after today?"

"A busy mind keeps the body awake."

"I am proud of what you did today," Mario said.

Storm restrained the gratitude that welled up in him. "Thanks. All in a day's work."

"Cammy was right," Mario said. "I was worried sick about you."

"I'll plan better tomorrow."

"If your friends deliver more gear tonight, I'll go down to the *Bianca C* with you."

"I thought you said you don't dive anymore," Storm said.

"I used to. Not as much anymore. But it would mean a lot for both of us to do the dive as a team."

"You're the boss."

"I am more than just your boss, Storm." Mario reached into a drawer under the dashboard and pulled out a folded paper. "Take a look at the pictures before you read the note."

Storm recognized Cammy's handwriting, but skipped reading the note. He placed the two pictures next to each other under the overhead light. He recognized himself in the picture he'd sent before leaving North Carolina for Beirut.

"Who's this?" he asked, pointing at the other picture.

"That's me at your age. See any resemblance?"

Storm's hand shook with the note and his throat tightened as he read it.

Storm, my love,
We didn't know how else to tell you this.
Mario is your father. Your only father. He loves you like I love you.
Cammy.

Mario turned to face him. "I am your father, Storm. I want you to be my son."

Storm's lips trembled. He searched for words but his dazed mind froze, leaving him speechless. The part of him drowning years-deep in bitter disappointment resurfaced with a thirst for air.

A river of emotions raced through him. Anger for not knowing a real father all those years. Relief he now had one. Apprehension Mario might also reject him, as all the others had.

Stunned, he did the first thing that popped into his mind.

He grabbed Mario by the shoulders and locked him in an embrace that ended only when both their collars grew damp from tears.

CHAPTER TWENTY-ONE

With the cold metal of a handgun against her head, Jackie decided if she were to die in this desolate place tonight, she would die fighting. Hallam's treachery would not take her down easy.

She swung around, elbowing his handgun away from her head.

Fisting the key firmly between her fingers, she threw a punch at his face.

He ducked and grabbed her arm. "Jackie? What're you do—"

She kicked at his groin and nailed him.

"Shit." Groaning, he doubled over and collapsed to his knees, just as the lights came on and swept away the darkness.

Another man rushed out of the front door and into the light. "Jackie, is that you crawling around out there?"

Steve?

Had she just made a dreadfully embarrassing and dangerous mistake?

"What are *you* doing here?" she asked.

He rushed toward her. "I told Hallam I wanted to meet with you both."

She held her head. "Oh no. I'm so sorry . . . I thought—"

"You thought?" Hallam stuck his handgun in his waistband.

Steve helped him to his feet. "We saw your car pull up but no one came to the door. It looked like the location was compromised, so Hallam decided to do a quick foot patrol around the house."

"You could have gotten killed," Hallam said to her. "We need you now more than ever."

Jackie handed Hallam a glass of water from the kitchen tap and sat on the couch across from him in the musty seaside cottage. He still grimaced occasionally, but she felt relieved he'd not retaliated with his handgun. If he'd wanted her dead, he could have shot her, or crushed her to death with the muscular arms that stretched the sleeves of his black t-shirt. Either way, her attack on him would have made a perfect self-defense case.

Her runaway suspicions almost got her killed.

"Sorry about the kick."

"It comes with the territory." Despite his obvious discomfort, Hallam's sincerity showed in his smile in the dimly lit room. "I'm just glad you're on my team."

"I became suspicious of you at the Grenada hotel," she said. "When I overheard your phone conversation with Colonel Bravo, I thought you were with the enemy."

"Bravo is still the enemy," Steve said. "But not the way you think."

Smoke drifted out of his thin nostrils while he crushed a smoldering cigarette butt in the ashtray. His crew-cut hair looked as if it still received daily meticulous attention, but his eyelids puffed with fatigue Jackie had not seen at the last meeting before the Grenada trip. He wore a loose white shirt with sleeves rolled up past his elbow. When he spoke, his wire-framed glasses magnified his focused stare to make him look more like a philosophy professor at the Barbados Cave Hill campus than a CIA operative.

"Hallam and Bravo have known each other for seven years," he continued. "They investigated the bombing of Cubana de Aviación Flight 455. The plane crashed eight miles off this coastline on October 6, 1976, killing all seventy-eight people onboard."

Jackie had read about the plane crash in the newspapers when she attended the Anglican High School in Grenada. Many of the passengers were teenage members of the national Cuban fencing team, gold medal winners in Central American and Caribbean championships. Her stomach tightened when she tried to imagine the horror of being a teen strapped into a plane fully aware death waited with a violent embrace in mere seconds.

Hallam added, "The Barbados government assigned me to help track down the bombers. And Cuba sent Bravo to work with me. We traced the plot to two Venezuelan men who purchased tickets on flight CU-455 from Trinidad to Havana, with a stop in Barbados. But they'd gotten off the plane here and returned to Trinidad on another flight. When CU-455 left Barbados, the bomb exploded at eighteen thousand feet. The radio transmission showed the pilot tried in vain to get back to Barbados, but it was too late."

A breeze rattled the living room windows. The house trembled and a draft parted the drapes facing the driveway.

Steve leaped from the couch and marched across the living room, the shag carpet muffling his footsteps. He halted at the window and peeked out the slit separating the drapes. He tugged them back together until they overlapped.

When he returned to the couch, he rolled his sleeves up another fold—just past the lower half of a tattoo on his arm. It displayed a red anchor bordering the left base of a globe, and beneath them, strange words she'd never seen before: *Semper Fi.*

Steve lit another cigarette and blew smoke rings toward the ceiling. "Hallam was the one who first revealed to us the bombers were working for Cuban exiles connected to the Venezuelan secret police. One of the plotters worked for us fifteen years ago. It was one of the most embarrassing and painful failures for our intelligence community. To prevent this from happening again, we asked Hallam to join us. The Cubans made him the same offer. Since then, he's had the most dangerous job in the world, working for two governments that hate each other."

Hallam chuckled and glanced at Jackie. "Three governments. Don't forget I also work for Barbados. And after your kick, I am due for a pay raise."

"I feel like a fool," she said.

"You did what you had to do with what you knew," Steve said. "We should have told you Hallam would be making a call to Bravo. In this business our commodity is information. We guard it jealously and dole it out sparingly. Like medicine, a little is good. Too much can be fatal."

Hallam stared at her. "The less you know about Bravo, the less you have to worry about him. At the beginning, we wanted you on the team for one very specific purpose. Link us with Storm Butler. Thanks to you, we say mission accomplished."

"As soon as Hallam got off the plane yesterday, he wrote us an impressive report about your performance in Grenada," Steve said. "You're highly motivated, young, and, with your permission, attractive."

A blush warmed her face.

Hallam laughed. "And don't forget, clever."

Clever?

Had Hallam figured out she'd spiked his rum punch and left him on his bed in a sleeping-pill coma? No way in that state could he have known she'd climbed out of their hotel room, and rowed to St. George's in a stolen boat to warn Storm about Hallam and Bravo.

No way.

"All excellent qualities in our profession." Steve sat next to Hallam and leaned over the bamboo coffee table toward Jackie. "That's why we want to bring you into the full plan. But you must be aware that you and Storm will now be in greater danger after tonight."

"I'll do what it takes to free my father," she said. "And I believe... I know Storm feels the same way."

"You have to trust us. And we must trust you."

She struggled over how much she should tell them in order to earn their trust. So much had happened in Grenada that night, where should she begin?

Steve saved her the anguish. "We already know you left the hotel and stole a boat to visit Storm."

Her jaw dropped. "You do?"

"Nothing happens in Grenada without Bravo's knowledge." Hallam chuckled. "It was convenient for him because he used the boat you stole as an excuse to send Reds running around chasing rabbits."

She sighed.

"Bravo told me you must have a special love for Storm," Hallam continued. "The only thing he hasn't figured out yet is how you got me to sleep through the whole night while you were on Park Lane romancing with Storm."

Jackie sheepishly told them how she'd doped Hallam's rum punch with sleeping pills so she could leave the hotel undetected. "I overheard Hallam mention *Bianca C* and Storm on the phone call. But Storm and I still don't understand the connection between him, a sunken ship, and the Grenada revolution. And where does Bravo fit into all this?"

Steve glanced at Hallam then back to her. "Bravo holds the key to Soviet-Cuban strategy in all of Latin America, including Grenada. If he goes, we can roll back Marxist gains in this hemisphere and send the Soviets back to Siberia where they belong. If the Grenada revolution collapses, all political prisoners, including your father will be freed."

"Are you planning to assassinate Bravo?" She hoped any plans to free her father would not require bloodshed.

"Not at all," Steve said emphatically. "We want him very much alive. We want to know everything he knows."

"But how can you get him to talk?"

"We're setting a trap for him. He's devoted twenty-five years to Communist revolution, but has nothing to show for it. He's a treasure trove of military and political intelligence, looking for a comfortable retirement so he could hang up his hat and smoke his cigars in peace. His best friend, another colonel, was recently tried and executed by firing squad in Cuba for dabbling in the ivory and diamond trade while serving in Angola. Castro controls all wealth to all Cubans, legal or illegal. Bravo knows if he's caught, a firing squad will be waiting for him in Havana. We want to set up a cookie jar on the *Carmen*. When we catch him with his hands in the jar, he'll have no choice but to come with us."

"And what do you plan to put in the cookie jar?" she asked.

Steve lit another cigarette. "Diamonds or rare gems. We know Mr. Costa converted a lot of his assets into rare stones even before the *Bianca C* sank, and before his divorce, apparently to keep his wife's hands out of his wealth. He had just a few stones, easy to carry, and easy to hide on the ship. We still don't know how many or how valuable, but we should be hearing from our friends in Italy soon. Bravo believes they're valuable enough to risk everything for it."

Hallam leaned forward and gritted his teeth in obvious discomfort from Jackie's kick earlier. "The bait is set. We have Bravo fixated on the *Bianca C* as the gateway to his future."

"Bravo really trusts you," she said to Hallam.

"I like him, and respect him, but he's on the wrong side of history," he said.

Steve blew another round of smoke rings toward the ceiling. "We've also given Bravo some cover in case things unravel to his disadvantage. He's reported to his superiors that he's uncovered a U.S. Marine working with the CIA off the *Carmen*. He and his Havana bosses believe Storm is using his diving business to install underwater listening devices around the island that could monitor arms shipments to Grenada."

"Storm is Bravo's excuse for keeping a watch on the *Bianca C*," Hallam said. "The *Bianca C* is his retirement bait. Now all we have to do is turn Mr. Costa's yacht into the trap."

"And Reds?" she asked.

Hallam shook his head. "He's a loose cannon. Bravo only let him in on the CIA story, in case Reds decides to complain about Bravo's offshore activities higher up the Soviet chain of command."

"We believe the Cubans recently got wary of his ambitions," Steve said. "Reds wants power. Bravo wants money. It's a delicate balancing act to keep the two men from tripping over each other."

"Is Mr. Costa aware of your plans?" she asked.

"Not yet," Steve said. "Bravo called Hallam an hour ago to let him know the *Carmen* is on the way to Palm Island. That's why I wanted to talk to you both. In a couple hours we'll be on a helicopter to meet them."

***

Reds washed down his lobster dinner with two glasses of Bulgarian white wine and asked his house maid to prepare his newest set of dress uniform. Within twenty-four hours, reporters from around the world would flock to his press conference. As Commander-in-Chief and Prime Minister, he wanted to give the shiniest example of the kind of leadership aspiring communists should look up to. His victory and his image would surely guarantee him official invitations to Havana and across the Eastern European capitals to Moscow.

Reds returned to his study and called his key military officers to help cut the tension that might keep him awake. His lieutenant-colonel, who manned the Fort Frederick command center, reported all elements on standby. The major at Camp Calivigny had his company in place to take over the radio station, and another major prepared to move into the most powerful government ministries. Reds' paramilitary squads pre-staged to arrest targeted government ministers and central committee members.

Prisoners already filled available cells in Richmond Hill Prison, so conditions might be a little tight with new incoming tenants.

Served them right.

They should all get a taste of what he experienced in the year he served in the sweltering boxes, all because of Storm's incompetence with the bomb four years ago.

At the given time, Reds' plan would shift into gear with precision across the island. He would charge with the tip of the sword, a company of loyal hand-picked infantry accompanied by three eight-wheeled BTR-60 armored personnel carriers.

The timing could not have worked better for him. The truck bombing in Beirut would surely keep the Americans busy scrubbing off embarrassment and incompetence from their bloody faces. Too bad Storm had not remained back there.

But that mattered little now.

At dawn, a new chapter in Caribbean history and international solidarity would greet the island and the world. The request for Soviet troops to solidify his new government would be a simple formality. The flight from Havana to Point Salines took less than four hours.

Despite his painstaking military plans, Reds' attention drifted to Cammy and her motley crew.

He dialed the phone number to the St. George's intelligence unit. When the officer on duty answered, they spoke briefly about general conditions on the ground.

"Nothing unusual to report, sir," the officer said. "All quiet."

"Anything on the Park Lane house?"

"No movement in the house. In total darkness all night. Our latest report said both occupants of the house are all on the *Carmen* with the yacht owner. Heading to Palm Island."

"Great. Just like I expected. The Cuban might finally get something done tonight."

"Pardon me, sir?"

"Oh nothing," Reds said. "Nothing at all. Stay alert."

***

When the meeting ended at 8 p.m., Steve walked Jackie to the door of the oceanfront cottage. "We'll pick you up in the airport parking lot at 22:30," he said.

She still hadn't adjusted to the military time. "Is that 9:30?"

"Glad you asked. It's 10:30 tonight."

Other concerns needled her. "I've been thinking though, suppose Mr. Costa refuses to let you use his precious stones to catch a Cuban spy?"

"We'll rely on Storm to convince him," Hallam said. "Mr. Costa will be dead and his *Bianca C* treasure gone if he doesn't team up with us."

"We have to be very careful with Bravo," Steve added. "He learned from his friend's deadly errors in Angola. Bravo told Hallam many times over the years, 'the best kept secrets are held by dead men'. If we make one mistake, or if Mr. Costa tries to recover those valuables without us, Bravo will swallow him up like a shark. He will take the goods and then kill everyone on the yacht."

Something big was about to happen—soon.

She felt it in Steve's urgent tone and Hallam's pensive silence, in contrast to his vivacious mood in Grenada. They asked her to pack a change of clothes for two days because they needed her to return with Storm to Grenada on the yacht.

"I would love to go with him, but I get the feeling there's more you're not telling me," she said.

"Did you listen to the radio news today?" Steve asked.

"No."

"A suicide bomber blew up the BLT barracks in Beirut today with a truck bomb. Storm may not know it yet, but he lost a lot of his brothers, over two hundred dead."

She covered her mouth with her palm. "Oh no."

"Once he gets the news he'll be in turmoil," Steve said with the certainty of a fortune teller. "Especially after losing his sister just a month ago. We need his presence of mind for the next thirty six hours. If he's to recover the stones tomorrow, he'll need your help to stay focused."

"I'll try," she'd said.

Jackie hurried to her car and headed back to Bridgetown as fast as the thoughts racing through her mind.

Steve and Hallam had asked her to pack enough clothes for just two days, but didn't discuss plans to return her to Barbados.

CHAPTER TWENTY-TWO

Confusion marred Storm's thoughts in the calm bay as he watched a helicopter roar out of low clouds and into scant moonlight over Palm Island. He'd stood next to Mario on the *Carmen*, expecting Hallam and his anonymous contacts to show up on a boat. Instead, Storm immediately recognized the darkened U.S. Army's UH-60A Black Hawk helicopter with its signature dragging-tail landing gear. The five-million-dollar twin-engine helicopter, capable of carrying eleven-man squads on special ops missions, took him by surprise.

Why did the U.S. Army have this helicopter on peaceful Barbados, a hundred and thirty miles north east from here, and a hundred and fifty miles from Grenada? Could there be more helicopters parked right now in Barbados?

While the Black Hawk circled the tiny uninhabited island, Storm and Mario climbed into the dinghy and sputtered up to the shore. Storm manned the throttle while Mario stood at the front with one hand tucked into his shirt in a Napoleonic stance.

The helicopter kept its lights out and probably used advanced avionics and its night vision cockpit to find safe landing in the dim moonlight peeking past thick clouds. It landed in a swirl of leaves on the field between a grove of waving coconut trees and the white-sand bay. The engines sighed relief with a belch of fuel-scented exhaust, drowning the sea-salt aroma that greeted the yacht when the *Carmen* pulled in from Grenada an hour ago.

Dark figures scampered out of the helicopter and hurried down to the beach.

Storm and Mario dragged the dinghy up the sandy shore and awaited the approaching group. Storm immediately picked out Jackie's curved figure and bouncing hair among the men in black t-shirts. Two of the men carried M16 rifles.

She rushed up to him and they embraced like it had been a lot longer than two days since they last saw each other.

"Okay Marine," a gruff voice barked from the group. "This is not a Parris Island swamp picnic, dammit."

Storm looked for the source of the drill instructor imitation and a lean man in wireframes glasses grinned his way out of the gray night.

Jackie made the introduction. "This is Steve."

Steve gave Storm a back slapping embrace. "How you doing, Leatherneck?"

"Just improvising, adapting, and overcoming, sir," Storm said.

"Don't call me 'sir.' I work for a goddamned living."

"Let me guess, son," Storm mocked. "You're Hollywood Marine from San Diego, right?"

"How did you know that, *boy*?" Steve asked.

"Boy? How would you like to tell your mama a boy kicked your ass?"

They chuckled as Jackie continued the introductions. Hallam's silver tooth and solid build gave him away immediately. Storm embraced him and then introduced Mario to the group, without revealing their newly discovered father-son relationship. Earlier, they had agreed to keep it out of the Palm Island conversation.

"Okay, gentlemen…and lady," Steve said finally. "Let's get on board. We have work to do while the rest of the world sleeps."

While one of the armed men raced the dinghy back to shore to retrieve the new dive gear, Jackie helped Steve and Hallam scan the *Carmen* for electronic bugs like the one discovered on Storm's Halon22. In the meantime Mario and Storm cranked out cups of coffee and hot cocoa in the galley.

Thirty minutes later, having found nothing suspicious, the five of them gathered around the table on deck with their steaming cups.

Mario sat at the head of the table with Steve on his right and Hallam on his left. Storm sat next to Steve, facing Jackie and struggling to keep his mind off her parted lips and the twinkle in her eyes when she smiled at him in the soft light.

"Mr. Costa," Steve began. "I want to personally thank you for trusting us tonight. We considered giving you this information before you arrived in Grenada, but didn't want to scare you back to Italy too soon. We believe your *Bianca C* treasure is in jeopardy and your life is in danger."

Storm admired how Mario held his composure with his response. "How did you come by this information?"

"About six months ago, the Soviet KGB picked up your phone calls from Genoa to Trinidad about the *Bianca C*."

"A Port-of-Spain company salvaged the bronze propellers a few years ago," Mario said. "I called them first to see if any of their divers were still around. Couldn't find the original divers."

"When the KGB forwarded your innocent calls to their Cuban counterparts, we piggy backed on the chatter. Seems they are nervous about any diving around the island. Probably because of all the arms they'd been shipping there."

"Why the arms buildup?" Storm asked.

"Three possibilities. One might be frontloading for a permanent Soviet combat brigade. They failed in their secret quest to install nuclear missiles in Cuba in 1963. They again lost international prestige when they were forced to downplay the role of a training brigade there in 1979. It infuriated Castro that the Soviets capitulated yet again on his soil, without his consent."

"But why Grenada?" Storm asked.

"Grenada is fifteen hundred miles from Miami, significantly more than the ninety miles separating Cuba from the U.S. Maybe the Soviets think Washington D.C. will ignore a Soviet brigade based more than arm's length away. But another possibility for the shipments is to use Grenada as a storage depot to foment revolutionary movements across the South American continent. And a third possibility might be to bolster another coup on the island, which would firmly entrench a Soviet controlled military regime under a new ruler."

"Reds?" Storm asked.

Hallam nodded. "All indications point to him as the Soviets' choice to replace Duncan."

"Sounds like there could be a fourth possibility," Mario said. "A combination of all three."

When Hallam leaned forward and clasped his big arms, the table creaked. "All of these scenarios trouble Caribbean neighbors like Barbados. The Grenada PRA outnumbers the military of the entire Eastern Caribbean islands combined. That's why my government is working closely with the Americans."

Mario tugged at his eye-patch strap. "So we have arms shipments going to Grenada. The Cubans and Soviets are concerned about diving in the area. Why didn't they just turn me and the *Carmen* away from Grenada waters, or arrest us?"

"You're right. A diving expedition conducted off Grenada by a U.S. Marine trained in underwater demolition is probably causing them to have kittens. Hallam provided Bravo just enough information to convince him the dive has two purposes."

Storm leaned forward. "Two? I only know of one."

"We'll get to the second reason soon." Hallam explained that while the Soviets outsourced the *Bianca C* concerns to Bravo and the Cubans, the CIA conducted its own surveillance on Mr. Costa to determine his real reason for the dive. "That's when they discovered you sold many of your business assets in Italy and secretly bought up the rare stones now on the ship. We know your reasons for doing that were personal, and we apologize if any of this is upsetting to you."

Mario waved him on. "Go ahead. Even without the stones, I'm in a much better place today than back then."

Storm wondered if Mario meant having Cammy in his life—and Storm too.

Steve jumped in. "We know the real reason for the dive is to find those rare diamonds. But Hallam convinced Bravo you are here tonight not only to pick up some of the latest dive gear, but also to collect equipment from the CIA that Storm will install on the *Bianca C*. After you find the diamonds, of course."

Storm stretched his legs, clasped his hands behind his head, and made no effort to disguise the sarcasm in his voice. "I'm sure glad we made this little cruise up here tonight to find out the Soviets have a missile pointed at my back for messing with their shipping plans. Now, swimming with nurse sharks might feel like a dip in a bathtub with a golf fish. Hell, this is as much fun as keeping the peace in Beirut."

Jackie exchanged a quick glance with Steve then looked down at her hands.

"Forget about the Soviets," Steve said. "Forget about the Cubans. This is between us and Bravo."

"Who dreamed up this bullshit?" Storm asked with anger rising in his voice. "The same idiots in Washington who came up with the Beirut plan?"

Steve's demeanor took on a solemn tone. "Hallam and I designed this plan, with approval up the ranks. I would never be reckless with the life of a fellow Marine."

Storm's embarrassment made him feel like diving off the yacht into the sea and never resurfacing, but Mario intercepted. "Let them finish before we jump to any conclusions."

Steve continued. "Mr. Costa, there's a reason you've not been arrested or denied entry into Grenada waters. Bravo convinced his bosses that allowing the *Carmen* to rendezvous with this CIA agent in Grenada waters is part of his plan. They expect him to catch you in the act with top-secret devices. They believe him because he has a solid record of achievement. He's flushed out and eliminated some of our best in Angola and Ethiopia. But his main objective is getting his hands on the diamonds. And he won't make a move against you until you find them."

Hallam's silver tooth shone even in the dim overhead light. "Since I've been in constant contact with Bravo from the days of the Cubana Airlines bombing, he asked me if I could find out any CIA information on a plan to install devices."

"Like a double-agent?" Jackie asked.

"You could say that," Hallam said. "I gave him enough bogus information for him to believe there was a CIA plan. But I also let him in on the dive to recover diamonds. That's when he came to me with an offer. He said if I worked with him in a partnership, he would split the diamonds with me. It surprised us how quickly a self-sacrificing communist can become a resourceful profit-seeking capitalist."

Their laughter flowed over the water and echoed against the quiet island.

Steve joined in. "We realized then we could get Bravo to defect, if we catch him. He wants you to recover the diamonds. Mario knows where they are and

Storm has the skills to find them. Bravo has neither the logistics nor men he can trust to search eighteen thousand tons of ship. He's used Hallam's information to convince the Cuban embassy, the KGB, and Reds that he has a plan to catch a CIA agent in the act planting listening devices."

Storm leaned forward. "They know nothing about the diamonds?"

"Only Bravo," Steve said. "While they're looking at his left hand, he's busy with his right. His main plan is to get his hands on your diamonds."

Something still troubled Storm. "How did you team me up with Mario to do the dive?"

Steve lit a cigarette. "Again, we have to apologize to Mr. Costa. We intercepted all his diving offers from Genoa to Miami and from the Bahamas to Barbados. Our friends along the way found means to discourage those who felt tempted to join your expedition."

"And here I am thinking it was my bad English accent," Mario said.

"Not at all," Steve said. "The embassy in Bridgetown got word a U.S. Marine had requested a hardship discharge in Grenada, after losing his sister in a tragic accident…my condolences, Storm."

Storm nodded his appreciation.

Steve continued. "It turned out your training and experience was a perfect fit for the dive… and to help us entrap Bravo so he could defect to our side. We intercepted Mario's inquiries to Barbados, and gave him the name of your dive shop on Grand Anse. But we had to get to you first. And that's the reason Hallam and Jackie paid you a surprise visit two days ago."

Steve explained they planned to record Bravo in his attempt to steal the diamonds. If they got him in the act on audio and film, he would be too compromised to ever return to Cuba. "His only choice would be to defect."

"And if he defects," Hallam said, "the entire Soviet-Cuba strategy in Africa, the Caribbean, and South America could collapse. When that happens, it'll only be a matter of time for the Grenada revolution to reverse course and release all political prisoners, including Jackie's father."

Jackie's smile held Storm's attention for a soothing moment when the yacht rocked gently and the sea lapped against the hull. He glanced away, hoping his restraint did not offend her affections for him. He now realized the significance of what lay ahead in the coming days and he needed to fortify himself for danger and not awaken his desires for her.

But when she shivered in the breeze and pulled her sweater tighter, he stood. "Can I get you a jacket?"

"No thanks," she said emphatically and jumped into the discussion without skipping a beat. "Bravo learned from his friend's fatal errors in Angola. He won't make the same mistakes. He wants the diamonds, but he won't leave us as witnesses."

Us? Wouldn't she be back in Barbados?

Hallam agreed with Jackie. "Witnesses led to his friend facing a firing squad in Havana. Even though Bravo promised me a share of the diamonds, I know him too well to trust that. His motto is 'the best kept secrets are held by dead men.'"

Just then, the dinghy pulled alongside the *Carmen*. Storm helped the man offload several duffle bags and a bulky suitcase.

Steve lifted the suitcase onto the table and turned to Mario. "This has everything we need to catch Bravo. But we need your permission to turn the *Carmen* into the perfect trap."

Mario turned to Storm. "If Storm agrees to the plan."

"I'm in." This time he smiled at Jackie.

"By the way," Mario said to Steve. "You seem to have all the information. Have your friends in Italy calculated how much those rare stones are worth these days?"

Steve chuckled. "We got the financial analysis from Italy just before we left Barbados, and Hallam immediately contacted Bravo with the news to set the bait firmly."

Hallam grinned. "Bravo whistled when I told him. A hundred and twenty million dollars."

***

Reds shut off the alarm clock when it buzzed at 2 a.m. He shouldn't have even set it. He hadn't slept a wink, even with his cat Toompin at his feet. He moved silently in the big house. Except for the soldiers who guarded his compound and monitored his message center twenty-four hours a day, he'd dismissed his entire house staff and sent them home after dinner. Not unusual, especially since he had no travel plans which would have required them to pack his suitcases, cook an early breakfast, and drive him up the long winding road over the Grand Étang Mountains to Pearls Airport.

Another reason he looked forward to the completion of this new airport, its construction floodlights clearly visible in the distance when he drew his living room blinds. Just what he needed—a twentieth century airfield that he would link to the historical forces changing the world. Small Grenada, valuable for its strategic location and allegiance to Moscow, would become a major player on the chessboard of geopolitical competition between the USA and the USSR, between imperialism and communism, between the past and the future.

And Reds would control the Grenada moves on that chessboard.

Once Soviet boots landed on the island at his invitation, the Americans would not dare to intrude on his revolution. Then he would transform his innocent looking airport into a formidable tip in the Soviet spear.

He made a cup of coffee and sipped it at his desk, scanning his message box for any dispatches that might have come in while he lay in bed. If the duty soldier manning the telegraph machines in the communication center down the hall received an urgent message, Reds' bedside phone would ring immediately. All other incoming routine messages went into his in-box.

His watch read 2:30 a.m., but the urgent message he expected two hours ago had not yet arrived.

Why hadn't he heard from Bravo about the final fate of the *Carmen* and her passengers on Palm Island?

Even while his impeccable military plans snapped into place in the dark hours around the island, an anxious thread stitched onto his thoughts—and refused to untangle.

***

Cammy awoke with a jolt. Another bad dream? No, she always remembered the dreams. A car racing down a river bank toward a rock. A girl with a familiar voice screaming for Cammy—Rachael. Water, darkness, then a silence pregnant with loss would awaken her, and she would replay the nightmare again and again, until tears soaked her eyes back to sleep.

The silence awakened her tonight, but this time without a dream.

Dread made her sweat more than usual, even for a humid night.

She used the bathroom and shuffled her way in the darkness to the open living room window overlooking the harbor.

No breeze, only stillness in the sparsely lit town. She recalled a similar night hours before Hurricane Janet devastated the island in 1955. Only thirteen at the time, she was staring out the same window on a still night like this when her stepfather grabbed her from behind, his alcohol breath tightening her stomach, and her body screaming for him to die.

"This is the calm before the storm," he murmured. "Time for us to go to bed."

She cried. She denied him. She delayed him. Long enough for the winds to pick up. Rain drops blew into open windows and loose roof panels slammed overhead. He darted from one room to the next, shouting orders for her to lock this door and shut that window.

By the time the howling fury of the hurricane descended with a merciless lash upon the island, a full asthmatic attack had dropped the graying pot-bellied man to his knees. She often wondered if her repugnance for the man had unwittingly prepared her to welcome Reds into her life with his youth, athletic physique, and enticing fragrance of Brut cologne.

Regardless, she never forgot how the storm rescued her—for one night.

Seven years later, when another stormy night delivered her a son, she named him Storm. The sound of his name and his presence always gave her such deep comfort. Sometimes she worried that a mother should never need her son that much.

Even as he now had a father for the first time in his life, she wondered how news of the Beirut bombing might hurt Storm.

No fence, no wall, and no ocean could separate his pain from hers. The hole in her heart felt as large as the gunshot hole in the wall where her clock once hung.

She looked outside her window for relief, but the stillness offered none. This did not feel like the calm before another storm. No hurricane threatened the island tonight, or in the twenty-eight years since Hurricane Janet.

It felt more like the island was holding its tropical breath in fear.

Fear of the unknown.

***

Reds fixed his starched military hat on his head and eyed the company of People Revolutionary Army soldiers standing at attention before him on the sprawling parking lot facing his house. Behind the four platoons, six Bulgarian trucks and three eight-wheeled Soviet BTR-60 armored personnel carriers purred in anticipation, their headlights piercing the darkness. In his mind, he checked off the BTRs' specifications that had convinced him to add them to his shopping list when he visited the Soviet Union two years ago. Bullet-proof windshields, multiple firing ports, 14.5 mm heavy machine gun, 7.62 tank coaxial machine gun, and 180 horse power to deliver hot-leaded dominance over any hostile force at the pull of a trigger.

Even in the dull light, Reds sensed the eagerness in his troops. Their eyes gazed up at him in fixed admiration and loyalty. He had only to bark a command, and they would obey.

They awaited his words, so he marched to the center of his verandah overlooking the troops, planted his fists into his hips, and delivered. "Your children and grandchildren will one day read in history books how brave comrades like you stood on the side of historical inevitability and joined the vanguard for Marxist-Leninist transformation of Grenada, the Caribbean, and the world. Tonight you breathe the inspiration of the Glorious October 1917 Russian revolution. Even Lenin would tremble at your courage."

If he hadn't ordered them to maintain complete silence, their roar would have alerted the Cubans guarding the new airport in the distance and awakened the people asleep in the hillside homes behind him.

Reds barked. "Let's do it!"

The convoy exited the gate and rumbled north away from the new airport toward St. George's with Reds' car in the lead.

As planned, they split up at the Tanteen round-about. A convoy this long might sound like a train running down the middle of the city at 4 a.m. and attract unnecessary attention. One of the BTRs spun right up Lowther's Lane followed by three trucks. Reds continued straight with the remaining BTRs and three trucks.

His convoy split again where Tanteen Road ended. One BTR and two of the trucks veered left onto the wider Carenage road along the harbor.

Reds' car took the upper Tyrrel Street with a BTR and a truck in the rear.

The closer his car got to Cammy's house, the more the tension stiffened along his neck.

***

Cammy stood in the dark window in her nighty and watched the approaching headlights sweep aside the night. Not unusual at this time to hear patrol trucks rolling past. Even on the nights when she stayed up late to have slurping conversations with the bottle, she might see two or three trucks rumble by at the same time.

Something looked and sounded different this early morning.

A car led two heavy vehicles along Tyrrel Street. Three more trucks ran parallel to them on the Carenage along the shoreline. In the still night, she could swear she heard even more trucks from Lowther's Lane, on the hillside above her house.

The car leading the Tyrrel Street patrol slowed to a stop at the bottom of her street. Someone in the back seat rolled down the window facing Cammy.

She stood erect in the blackened house, hoping to be invisible to the eyes peering up in her direction.

***

"Do you see someone standing in that window?" Reds asked his driver, pointing up at Cammy's house. Reds could not believe Bravo would allow Cammy to escape. But then again, Bravo's behavior lately had left Reds wondering what the Cuban's true objectives were.

The driver scanned the windows. "They all look dark to me, sir."

"Not all the windows, stupid. Just the one in the middle."

"If you see someone there, sir, then maybe there is someone there."

"Let's go," Reds ordered.

The driver engaged the gear and started to drive forward.

Reds shouted. "Stop, idiot. I mean let's go up to the house."

The driver glanced at his watch. "But sir, we—"

"Don't 'but' me, soldier. We have time."

Reds jumped out of the car and looked up at the house. The outline of the figure he'd seen no longer stood rigid in the dark window.

He ran to the truck behind him. "Quick, I need six men."

Rapid boot steps hammered up the road to Cammy's house.

CHAPTER TWENTY-THREE

Once Steve and Hallam completed installing the recording equipment at strategic corners around the yacht, they bade a hasty farewell to Mario. Along with the armed helicopter crewman, they climbed into the cramped dinghy with their equipment suitcase. Storm shuttled them back to the beach, intending to return for Jackie.

A minute alone with her in a dinghy might be all he would get tonight, but he felt grateful just to see her again and to feel the warm rekindling of what they'd lost four years ago.

Hallam and the armed crewman raced across the field toward the Black Hawk, its turbines now in full scream for liftoff.

Storm held out his hand to shake Steve's, but instead Steve gripped him in a tight embrace.

"Sergeant Butler," Steve said. "I need to have a word with you before I leave."

No one had called him by his rank since he left Beirut a month ago.

"If it's about my earlier blow up regarding the Washington paper pushers, I apologize," Storm said.

"No problem with that. Par for the course with Marines. It's something else."

"Talk to me."

"I can tell you haven't listened to the radio all day," Steve said.

"The last time was when I shut it off in my truck in the middle of some government bullshit. Why?"

"There was a suicide truck bombing in Beirut."

"That's not news."

"This time it is."

"Hurry up and say what you have to say." Storm said. "You only have an hour to get back to Barbados before sunrise."

"They got the Battalion Landing Team building."

"The BLT?" A rising wave of horror filled Storm's chest. "Oh shit. Casualties?"

Back in April, before Storm left North Carolina for Lebanon, a suicide bomber had killed sixty-three U.S. embassy staff in Beirut, including seventeen Americans. One Marine had died in the attack.

"It's gone," Steve said.

"Gone? Man, come clean. What the fuck are you saying?"

"They got us, Storm. Twelve thousand pounds of explosives. The largest non-nuclear explosion since World War II. They drove through the wire between posts five and six. The Marines on duty had their M16s disarmed, following the rules of engagement. We're still pulling bodies."

"No." Sharp fear slashed through Storm's gut. "Recon?"

Even in the thin moonlight, Steve's face paled. "Sixteen." He obviously had information on Storm's platoon.

"Gunny?"

Steve's silence gonged bells of terror in Storm's head.

Storm was afraid to ask, but he had to. "Cooper, the Iowa kid?" Cooper's grandfather's quips about sausage making used to trigger fever-pitched laughter in the platoon.

Silence.

"Doc?" Storm especially liked his Navy medic, a hard core sailor from the Philippines.

"Missing." Steve looked out at the yacht. "They're still identifying bodies. Over two hundred. They were asleep."

His friends, his brothers, killed while asleep instead of fighting like they'd been trained, and wanted, to do.

The horror seized Storm like a full-body cramp. He bent over and rose up with a howl that jolted every cell in his body. "Those motherfuckers in

Washington did this. They did this. And now you want me to team up with you on another of their plans? Hell no. I'm out of here."

Storm turned toward the dinghy.

"Sergeant Butler, you're on orders from Head Quarters Marine Corps," Steve yelled after him.

Storm whipped around. "Bullshit. Give me my goddamned discharge papers. I'll sign them right now."

"There are no discharge papers. You're now on special assignment with us. HQMC extended your enlistment. You're now on active duty."

"Tell them all to kiss my Grenadian ass. You people are good, so good, you make me want to puke."

It seemed at the moment the strained facade of normalcy he'd built around himself over the last thirty days came crashing down. Rachael's unexplained death, Reds' threats, Bravo's deceptions, and now the Beirut debacle, with Steve dropping bad-news bombs on Storm like he was a goddamned target.

Steve held his ground. "Your mission is for Grenada. For your sister. Do you realize if she hadn't died a month ago, you would have been in the BLT when the bomb went off?"

Storm's brain felt like an engine blowing its head-gasket. Whoever stood in its vicinity would feel the heat.

He turned and charged Steve.

Steve stepped aside and too late, Storm walked into a head-on crash with the former Marine's knuckles.

Storm collapsed to his knees. He struggled back to his feet in feigned shock. He grabbed a handful of sand.

When Steve moved in to deliver another blow, Storm let loose a spray of sand to his face.

But Steve was no fool. With eyes shut and face turned sideways, he went for the right roundhouse to Storm's head.

Storm saw it coming. He blocked the kick with his left hand and slammed a home-run fist into Steve's solar plexus.

Steve crumpled to the sand like a weight bag and curled into a fetal position, coughing. "Shit."

Storm felt the exploding rage in him subside. Rational thought trickled back.

Steve was not the enemy. Marine Corps style, he'd allowed Storm to vent the fiery buildup with their clash. But they had a mission.

Now it was back to business.

Storm steeled himself for what lay ahead in the coming days. He had learned in Parris Island how Marine camaraderie stood on a solid core of trust—each man's life depended on the other. A card game of blackjack drenched in beer might end with busted lips and black eyes. But by the time the Marines fell out in formation at zero-dark-thirty for another day of training, camaraderie returned in force.

Semper Fidelis, always faithful, flowed in their blood.

"You made your point." Steve clasped Storm's outstretched hand and rose to his feet in a groaning slouch. "We have work to do."

"Semper Fi," Storm said.

"Semper Fi, brother."

When Storm climbed aboard the *Carmen*, fuel-scented dust and leaves breezed past him from the Black Hawk's speedy liftoff. Mario had already shut down the yacht's systems for the night, to catch a few hours of sleep in the gentle bay before heading back to Grenada.

Storm needed the shuteye too. Even with the security of the 9 mm handgun Steve had given him, the past few days left him as beaten down as the aging planks creaking under his footsteps. The news about the Beirut bombing really did him in. The ache in the pit of his stomach rose and ebbed with each passing minute.

A cloud of guilt descended. He should have been with his platoon in its darkest hour. They'd trained to fight next to each other. Their faces and moments of laughter ran through his mind like a slide projector. Now his platoon had sixteen less than a month ago. And the Marine Corps had two hundred less.

Tonight, Storm floated in a Caribbean bay without a scratch, just a crippling wave of guilt, fatigue, and doubt rolling in his stomach.

In his turmoil, his doubts about Steve's plans magnified. But he gave Steve credit for the one thing that kept Storm afloat, the only sign his soul still lived. A little light in him flickered when he walked into Jackie's open arms on the deck.

Much work and danger still waited in Grenada in the next twenty-four hours. But in the absence of his Marine camaraderie, he needed Jackie's—and his new-found father's— help to face the guilt and grief-demons lurking inside him and preparing to attack on the way back to the *Bianca C.*

CHAPTER TWENTY-FOUR

Cammy had raced out of her house in her nighty once before. The morning that had changed her life. The morning she'd ran barefoot to the little boat on the water front and rowed to save lives from the smoking *Bianca C.*

But tonight, she ran barefoot from her house to save her own life.

The boot steps stomping up Park Lane toward her front door left her one exit. Her open bedroom window.

It took seconds for her to squeeze through and land softly on the grassy pathway outside.

Reds' barks to his soldiers on the street side of the house chilled her. "You, take the side. You, take the back. The rest come with me to the front door."

She ran through her kitchen garden and climbed over the barbed wire fence into the Marryshow House property. A vine caught her foot and she rolled down the hillside, coming to a rest at the base of the huge mahogany tree, which extended branches over her roof. She pulled herself behind the tree trunk and lay still.

***

Reds rushed up the steps to the front door and twisted the knob.

Locked.

He turned to the soldier behind him. "Break it down."

Two slams from the butt stock of the AK-47 and the door rattled open into the dark living room.

The Bianca C Still Burns

Reds pulled his 9 mm Makarov and stomped into the house. He knew exactly where the light switch hid on the right behind the same flimsy curtain. The single bulb hanging from the ceiling lit the small room.

He ordered his men into the bedrooms. "Look everywhere, under the beds too."

The living room looked almost the way he remembered it. The floor, though showing splits from age, still held its polished shine. A painting of a ship remained on the opposite wall despite the countless times he'd told her to move it. Cammy still had the same pale brown couch, sunk in the middle where the children used to jump when he was not around with his belt. But now, wooden splinters and clock springs lay scattered across the couch. On the wall above it, a bullet hole opened into Rachael's bedroom. Reds had laughed when the soldier told him about the incident.

If only Cammy had stuck to his side, she wouldn't still be boxed into this little rat-hole that could probably fit in the living room he now enjoyed in Point Salines.

Reds last stepped in here four years ago, the day after Storm mangled Reds' plan to assassinate the minister.

Reds had painstakingly crafted the bomb in his garage for Storm to plant in the car. The explosion he designed to start the revolution. Reds' revolution. He would have stood, taken credit for the patriotic act of courage, and accepted the gratitude of the masses as they ushered him to the top of power.

Sure, to get Storm's agreement, he'd promised the boy to stay out of Cammy's life after the bombing. Big deal. The end justified the means. "By any means necessary," Malcolm X had said.

But Storm's juvenile incompetence, inherited from his mother, led him to bungle Reds' plans. And by the time Reds showed up the next morning to eliminate his teenaged accomplice, the neighbor informed him a taxi had just sped off with Cammy and her children.

The old neighbor scratched his bald head. "Probably going on a trip."

"Why do you think they're going on a trip?" Reds asked.

"They leave in a hurry, and Storm had a suitcase."

What the neighbor lacked in hair, he retained in powers of observation. Storm hopped a boat that morning to Trinidad, and a week later flew to America where he joined the sharpest edge of imperialism's sword, the U.S. Marines.

Less than a year later, Duncan came along with his group and overthrew the government while Reds slept in prison for Storm's incompetence.

Duncan had become the Prime Minister, not Reds, all because of Storm and his bitch mother.

Now, for the first time in four years, Reds returned to the house, to even an old score before he reclaimed from Duncan what rightfully belonged to him.

A soldier marched up. "No one in here, sir."

"Have your men look again. Everywhere."

Reds remained skeptical. He walked over to Cammy's favorite window table where she always left her bottle and glass at night, next to her stacks of yellowed Readers Digest and National Geographic magazines.

She must have been standing on this exact spot when he spotted her from his car minutes ago. He ran his finger across the glass rings, stained onto the wooden surface from her years at the table.

Dry.

He knew she still drank. Nothing about her ever changed. Her youthful figure, her infectious laugh—her stubborn determination to live by her rules and not his.

If she'd spent the night in this house, she would have left her bottle and glass on the table. His imagination had gotten the best of him.

"Let's get out of here," he shouted.

One of the soldiers rushed up. "Sir, the first two teams just radioed to report they're already in place and awaiting orders."

Shit.

Cammy had intruded on his plans once again. Maybe he'd just seen her apparition in the window, confirmation Bravo had indeed destroyed the *Carmen* tonight.

On the way out, a light came on in the old neighbor's house across the yard from Cammy's front door.

Reds banged on the window and the old man poked his head out.

"Seen anyone here tonight?" Reds asked.

"No, sah," the man replied, rubbing his eyes then his bald head. "Not since the soldier shoot a hole in the house yesterday morning. Lights been out all night."

Reds turned to one of his soldiers. "Shut the door. I don't think anyone will be returning here, ever."

He hastened his soldiers back to their vehicles. They sped down Tyrrel Street and then made a sharp tire-squealing turn up Lucas Street toward Mount Royal, soon to be his official residence.

He noted on Lucas Street, house lights glowed from just one house, where Carl Marrow lived. The PRA soldier who'd served in the American Army. The soldier who'd accompanied Duncan to the Cuban embassy the previous day at the same time Reds' soldiers reported Storm showing up as well.

He glanced at his watch. Ten minutes behind schedule, too late for a second stop on the way to his prize.

The thread of concern started two hours ago tightened now with the strength of rope.

If indeed Cammy had been killed tonight, could her ghost have returned so soon to haunt him?

***

Cammy lay flat on the damp earth behind the mahogany tree until the lights in her neighbor's house went out and the squealing tires from Reds' trucks faded up Lucas Street. She pulled herself past the tree, crawled over the fence, and climbed back through her bedroom window.

Fear trembled her hands and her heart. Next time she saw Reds, one of them would die.

She'd been running from him so long, she'd forgotten a time ever existed when she thought she needed him in her life. Maybe the time to stop running had finally arrived.

She didn't know how yet. She prayed that when the time came, she would have the courage to do the right thing. For her sanity. For Storm and Rachael.

But then Storm would need to know the truth about Rachael.

A truth he might hate. And once he knew the truth, he might never forgive Cammy.

***

Reds marched between the rumbling BTR-60 armored personnel carriers facing the gate to the Prime Minister's Mount Royal residence. His second in command, the young lieutenant-colonel, approached him with a snappy salute.

Reds returned it. "What's the status?"

"Since you were delayed, we surrounded the entire compound, disconnected all phones, and disarmed the guards as planned," the officer said. "We have a squad inside with the Prime Minister. He's in custody along with his mistress."

"Good job," Reds said, absorbing the significance of the moment. From here on, there would be no turning back. "Where are his guards?"

"We disarmed and dismissed them."

"You did what?" Reds shouted and slammed his fist against the side of the BTR-60. "I said detain, not dismiss."

"They left on foot, sir," he said with a tremor in his voice. "They couldn't be far off if you want us to round them up."

"Was that American-trained soldier with them?"

"Yes. He was the Sergeant of the guard when—"

Reds punched his fist into the other palm. "Dammit. Do I have to think of everything myself? Send a squad to his house to pick him up immediately. His lights were on when we drove by a few minutes ago."

The officer passed along the order and turned to Reds. "We're fifteen minutes behind schedule, sir. I have the papers. Shall we proceed?"

"Yes, let's get it done."

Reds shook his head at the sight of Duncan in the Mount Royal residence. The Prime Minister already looked beaten in the sprawling living room crowded with Reds' loyal soldiers.

The tall British-educated lawyer, normally charismatic with well-manicured beard and hair, slumped on the couch with his demeanor and appearance in disarray. His eyelids puffed in defeat and a cigarette dangled from ashen lips, while long boney legs stretched like a skeleton's out of washed-out shorts unbefitting a leader.

His pregnant mistress sat next to him holding his hand.

Duncan dragged on his cigarette and blew smoke into air already thick with tension. "I trusted you when others warned me," he said to Reds. "They said letting you out of prison for that sloppy bombing and giving you military rank would come back to haunt me."

Reds wiped a film of sweat off his brow and barked. "Enough. The way forward requires the kind of leadership you do not possess. You've taken us this far, now the Central Committee has decided it's time for you to step aside for—"

"Who on the Central Committee decided? The ones you threatened with imprisonment, or those you promised big promotions?"

Reds thrust a sheet of paper on the coffee table in front of Duncan. "It's too late for this discussion. The decision was arrived at by Democratic Centralism, the highest principle of Marxism-Leninism. Just sign here."

Duncan read the paper briefly and laughed. "Let's see how this works. I sign power over to you. You put a bullet in my head. And in the morning your radio says 'the Prime Minister, concerned over deteriorating conditions on the island, signed power over to Colonel Reds Slinger to continue the march forward. Sadly, Prime Minister Duncan chose to end his own life in despair.' Nice and clean. Is that it?"

"You're jumping to conclusions. No one wants you dead. We tried to keep this internal, but you had to take it to the Cubans."

"Forget about the Cubans, how about taking it to the people and having them decide who they want as their leader?"

"The people?" Reds' agitation twitched his eyebrows. "What do the people have to do with this?"

Duncan's laughter accelerated to a coughing fit. "What do the people have to do with this? Are you serious?"

"You and I are made from the same cloth. Did you think the people mattered when you signed prison orders without charges or trial?"

"It's not what I did. It's what they think that matters."

"You controlled them with deceit. I'll control them with strength."

A soldier squeezed into the crowded living room. "Colonel Slinger, I have information you need to know in private."

Reds glared at the soldier. "Is there anything more important than what we're doing right now? Let it wait."

"But sir, the—"

Reds snapped. "Get him out of here."

The lieutenant-colonel and two of the officers escorted the soldier out the door.

Reds glared at Duncan. "You have exactly five minutes to sign this. Whatever your choice, it won't change the outcome."

A few moments later, the lieutenant-colonel returned, his face pale with concern. "Colonel, this is important."

Reds rose from his chair and walked over to the officer waiting out of Duncan's earshot. "What's so important?"

"Sir, we just received updates from our posts around the island."

Reds glanced out the picture window overlooking the city. "All good news I hope. Get on with it."

"None of our arrest targets were at their locations. Looks like those ministers had advance warning and went into hiding."

Reds snarled, "Operation Gallows was top-secret. How the hell could this happen?"

"Maybe this could be the explanation. The telephone exchange reported a call from a Lucas Street address to the Cuban Embassy, at about the time you were at the Park Lane house."

"That American-trained traitor. Did you get him?"

"He already disappeared when the squad showed up at his house." The officer swallowed hard. "But it's what happened immediately after the call that is cause for concern, sir. The call lasted just a minute, followed immediately by six outgoing calls from the Cuban Embassy. One to each of the six parishes lasting just a couple seconds each."

"Must be Bravo." Once he consolidated power, Reds intended to request Cuba replace its entire embassy staff, with Bravo on top of the list.

"It gets worse, sir."

Impatience and anger scorched the edge of Reds' voice. "Don't you have any good news?"

"The telephone exchange reported the switchboard lit up after the outgoing calls from the Cuban Embassy."

"Didn't they shut the phones down?"

"I just ordered it done. But it might be too late. The word is out that the Prime Minister needs help. There are rumors people are now going door-to-door to spread the news. It's not sunrise yet, but crowds are already gathering in the streets, some just down from the gate. We may need to move everyone, including Duncan, up to the Command Center on Fort Frederick to execute the rest of the plan."

"Dammit." Reds thought for a moment, twirling his moustache. "No, taking him to Fort Frederick will appear too harsh too early. You stay here with two of the APCs. I'll get out the new word to the radio station that Duncan is under house arrest for conspiring with a foreign government to defy our Marxist-Leninist principles and to bring chaos to our streets. We have the Cuban embassy calls to prove it. I'll return to the Command Center to take control of the Armed Forces. That's our most important card."

"What do we do with him?"

Reds stared at Duncan who sat puffing on a cigarette. The woman laid her head on his shoulder sobbing, one of those soft-headed women who deserved to be with Duncan on the final breath of his political life.

"Don't let them out of this house," Reds said.

"What if he won't sign?"

"Not every farewell note has a signature."

***

It started like a distant hum. Cammy stepped out of the tub and dried herself in the dark, trying to figure what made this strange sound just before sunrise. She did not want to poke her head out the window to attract uninvited attention, so she stood against the wall and held her breath. The sound came from the waterfront, like angry bees buzzing around a hive.

But she had more pressing concerns. She needed to get out of the house before daylight. Reds could still have spies in the neighborhood. She changed into clean clothes and packed a bag in the graying light, still puzzled by the sound growing in intensity.

Loud bangs at the front door. She froze.

The broken door squealed open and a woman called out. "Hello in there."

She held her breath, afraid even a shift in weight from one leg to the next might awaken her creaky floor.

"Nobody home," Cammy's neighbor shouted. "Them soldiers break the door an hour ago looking for them."

"Just spreading the news," the woman said.

'What news?" the man asked.

"Reds trying to take over the country. He has Duncan's house surrounded with soldiers. We're getting ready to march up there."

That devil, Reds. The rumbling of heavy vehicles Cammy had heard an hour ago now made sense.

"How many people marching?" the old neighbor asked.

The woman's footsteps shuffled away from Cammy's front door to the neighbor's house. "You can't hear the noise from the waterfront? People jam packed. Come down and join the march. We want Duncan, but we don't want no Reds' communism."

***

Storm jolted awake and sat up on the cabin bed. Jackie's embrace assured him he'd just emerged from a bad dream, but his psyche still reverberated like he'd just fallen into a lifetime abyss of pain.

"Stormy, it's okay," Jackie whispered in his ear. "It's just a dream."

"I hope you're not just a dream," he said.

She kissed his neck, sending goose bumps down his back "I'm not a dream my love."

"You're a life saver," he said. "I was dreaming about Rachael."

Hallam had told him Bravo might have information about Rachael and her friend, the young captain. The captain must have told her about Reds' plan to seize power. So far, this best explained why Rachael might have been killed.

To keep secret Reds' Operation Gallows. The captain apparently committed suicide at the Grand Étang camp, the day before Rachael died.

Storm turned to Jackie. "Can I ask you a question?"

"Of course."

He wanted none of this to remind Jackie how he'd almost killed her father. "If I get rid of Reds, would you feel different about me?"

"I always loved you. And I always will, no matter what."

***

Cammy left the house through her bedroom window again, this time with a scarf over her head and a plain loose-fitting dress, the best she could find in the dark house to pass as a disguise. Her large sunglasses remained in her bag. She climbed over the fence in the gray morning and hurried along the trail behind Marryshow House. Across Tyrrel Street a narrow alley led her to where she'd parked the pickup along the Carenage. By the time she'd arrived home last night, she found no parking space along the closer Tyrrel Street. That might have saved her since Reds would have recognized the pickup.

She now knew the sound she'd heard earlier came from people gathering to protest Reds' attempt to seize power. The size of the crowd filling the streets at the first light of dawn surprised her. It stretched along the waterfront road from the Cable and Wireless building past the Nutmeg restaurant. Lines of customers spilled on to the streets from shops, surrendering to the enticing aroma of freshly baked bread, rich *cocoa-tea*, and salt-fish souse. The flavor in the air lifted her spirit.

Then she remembered the feeling of dread that had awakened her earlier.

She'd marched with crowds against the old dictator. Back then she felt like an anonymous face in a sea of protestors, even when police attacked with tear gas and charged the crowds with axe handles.

Today felt personal. She knew Reds, better than the thickening crowds around her knew him. Out here in the open, she felt exposed to the man she loathed. The sound in his voice this morning always led to blood, from her lips, her children's backs, or even a stranger unfortunate enough to cross paths with him. She hoped these people, young and old, students and teachers, workers and unemployed, did not get to know the animal beneath Reds' skin.

Would anyone listen if she warned them? Their whispers still spoke of her as a woman foolish enough to bring Reds into her life and bear his children.

She jumped into the pickup and squeezed her way past the growing crowds toward the city to wait for the stores to open.

While she rushed to buy curtain fabric for the *Carmen*, the people marched away from the city and up Lucas Street to face Reds' temper.

CHAPTER TWENTY-FIVE

Jackie insisted that she alone control the galley to prepare breakfast, so Storm seized the opportunity to climb up on deck to inventory the duffle bags of equipment delivered overnight. Steve and Hallam left nothing to chance. When they boarded the *Carmen* from the helicopter last night, they brought two sets of everything Storm had asked for—and more.

They carefully secured in Mario's reinforced closet topside an M118 block demolition charge along with underwater blasting machine, caps, and electrical detonating cords. The closet, which also held Mario's plastic explosives, sat behind the pilothouse, well away from the galley and the engine room.

Mario must have well remembered the dire consequences of an engine room disaster. In case of a fire, he would have time to dump the explosives overboard.

They now had enough shit to blow more than just a safe.

Storm had also trained with the high-cost M118, perfect for underwater demolition. The block came with four half-pound sheets of flexible explosives, more than enough to rattle the steel door off the safe. Designed for small controlled breaching tasks like cutting steel, one sheet carried the kind of punch he thought would do the trick without scattering precious stones all over the Caribbean Sea. But he decided they would carry two sheets down to the *Bianca C*, just in case.

With a relative effectiveness factor of 1.14, pound for pound, it carried about fourteen percent more explosive power than TNT. But Storm liked its flexibility and its pressure-sensitive adhesive back that allowed it to attach to irregularly shaped targets, except wet and rusty surfaces like the safe. He'd just have to improvise.

The duffle bags also had two sets of the twin-tank harnesses he wanted in case they needed extra air in Mario's *Bianca C* library. Hallam and Steve had even tossed in a heavy duty crow bar. New regulators, pressure gauges, snorkel gear, skin suits, and fins of several sizes completed the collection. If Storm had gone shopping for the latest and best with an unlimited budget, he could not have selected better equipment.

"Breakfast, anyone?" Jackie stepped on deck balancing three plates with fruit, toast and steaming eggs scrabbled with diced tomatoes.

"Yes, my dear," Mario said.

"How did you climb up those steep stairs with plates like that?" Storm asked.

"My Taekwondo legs come in handy sometimes," she said. "Just ask Hallam."

Storm chuckled. "Yes, he told me."

Storm headed down to the galley to retrieve coffee. When the three of them sat at the table in the early morning light, he used the occasion to pass along the news to Jackie that Mario was his father.

"My goodness." A dumfounded look froze on her face for a few moments before she left her seat and gave both Mario and Storm a hug each. "Amazing. I thought I saw the resemblance too, but didn't want to say anything."

"I feel lucky," Mario said. "It might take some time for us to adjust to the idea."

"From the look of things," Storm said. "We'll be spending lots of time together in the next couple days."

After breakfast, Storm spent an hour with Mario in the thirty-foot water off the bay to get acclimated to the new equipment. Mario's early diving experience showed. He quickly adapted to the new single-hose breathing apparatus from the double-hose technology he'd spent time with in his early years. He cleared air pressure and maintained perfect buoyancy control throughout the exercise. The only difficulty came when his eye patch created leaks into his facemask. Mario removed the eye patch and continued to dive.

Storm avoided looking directly at him, after an initial glance at the sealed eyelid, scarred with rough skin. Strangely though, he felt a fond connection with the man he found kneeling over his mother just two nights ago. Maybe because Mario also knew pain and loss.

Back on board, Mario cranked up the engines. "Ready or not, Grenada, here we come."

Storm felt some relief. He now had a capable diving partner in his new-found father, and Jackie's embrace when he needed it. Storm's memories of friends lost in Beirut landed a little softer on his conscience, but anger still lingered. They had died in their sleep, next to Storm's empty rack, on a peacekeeping mission in a blood-soaked city.

Jackie must have noticed his thousand-yard stare. His jaws throbbing each time he clenched his teeth.

She leaned over and pointed to where the bow parted the gentle blue water. "Look. Dolphins."

Storm grabbed her hand and they headed up to the front.

From behind the windshield inside the pilothouse, Mario smiled like the morning sun and saluted.

Storm locked his body at attention and returned Mario's salute like he would to an admiral on a battleship. Storm might never have his comrades with him again, but Mario filled much of the painful vacuum they left behind.

Jackie grabbed Storm around the waist like she used to, the way he liked it, and pulled him toward the bow. Several dolphins rode the waves rushing away in the boat's wake. At home in their element, they almost seemed to smile in harmony with the ocean. Storm could only hope his fellow Marines had gone to a resting place where they too would find this bliss.

He'd already left all his tears on his pillow below deck, but Jackie must have seen the devastation building in his eyes.

She held him as Mario watched from behind the wheel.

***

Too late, Reds realized he'd forgotten a key element in all his military plans to seize power. He paced the communications room at the Fort Frederick command center, congested with ringing phones and clicking teletype consoles.

He'd forgotten the people.

Power, he'd always known, didn't really exist in government ministries, military camps, or radio stations. These were just symbols. And symbols only exuded strength when people remained cowering behind locked doors.

Real power resided with the people, whether they chose to exercise it or not. The art of political power belonged to the illusionist.

Reds studied the art and mastered it. At least so he thought.

Until today.

He'd expected the population to pay subservient homage to his control of menacing machines and loyal soldiers. But instead, something triggered them to make predawn phone calls and bang doors to alert others. Before dawn, they flowed out of their homes in droves. Now thousands flooded the streets in angry protest against him.

He'd also mistakenly left out Bravo in his calculations and underestimated the Cuban's capacity for deception. Bravo, the crisis architect, must have crafted this outburst of civil disobedience with Yankee-trained Carl Marrow and Storm as his *agent provocateurs*. How Cubans and American-trained agents could hold hands in such an ideologically despicable conspiracy, he hadn't quite figured out yet.

The communications officer handed him the phone.

"From Carriacou," the officer said.

Carriacou sat about five miles due south of Palm Island. If Bravo had delivered as promised, evidence of a destroyed yacht would have washed up on the shores of Grenada's sister island, a key station under Reds' control.

Finally, news of the *Carmen's* demise. "Colonel Slinger here."

"Colonel," the Carriacou commander said. "We have unusual activities up here."

Unusual activities? Reds hoped the man had news about floating debris and bodies, but his tone carried little assurance.

"Get on with it," Reds ordered.

"A few people camping on Union Island last night reported sounds like a helicopter over Palm Island, a mile away. It had no lights and it was too dark to tell for sure. When they awoke this morning, a white yacht left the bay heading south."

That SOB Bravo. The boat and passengers should have been in splinters.

Reds' suspicions deepened. "What else?"

"The yacht made a refueling stop in Carriacou, and filled up scuba diving tanks."

"Did you identify the passengers?" Reds asked.

"The captain had an eye patch. One of my soldiers recognized Storm Butler from their school days. And a young girl, early twenties."

Reds knew Cammy's youthful figure fooled people. "Are you sure she was not his mother?"

"We're sure, sir. No man would kiss his mother that way. His mother was not on the yacht."

Dammit! That was Cammy he'd seen in the dark window from his car. She must still be around town. He'd find the bitch and make her pay. "Where are they now?"

"Just left the jetty," the Carriacou commander said. "Already at twenty-five knots, speeding south toward you."

It all made sense now.

Bravo, Storm, and Marrow had worked with Duncan and the CIA to set a trap around Reds. The *Carmen* must have rendezvoused overnight with CIA operatives on Palm Island to plan how to capitalize on the rising tensions they seeded in the capital.

Reds felt the growing rift between the Cuban and Soviet's enthusiasm for his climb to power. Yet, he never expected ideological comrades would betray him so. Even if the Cuban embassy balked, no bears stood taller than the Soviets.

And they would stand by Reds, especially with Sergei as his intermediary.

No fool, Reds knew how to play the game. He still had a few cards up his sleeve. First he would take care of the pesky crowd gathering at Duncan's gate. In the meantime, he would have a few soldiers scout the city to find Cammy. She must have remained in Grenada overnight in their plan to alert people before dawn. She would be the key to unraveling the plot. By the time the *Carmen* pulled into Grand Anse, Reds would be ready to play his next card.

He slammed down the phone and turned to his communications officer.

"Add Cammy Butler to the top of the arrest list and spread the word. Find her, now!"

"Yes, sir." The officer turned to leave.

"One more thing," Reds said. "We still have that girl locked up, right? Pauline?"

"Yes, sir."

"Bring her here immediately. I have an urgent mission for her."

***

The Anglican Church clock hammered nine times into the unsettling silence hanging over the city. Even the morning humidity felt denser where Cammy waited on the sidewalk for the Syrian general goods store to open its doors. Rows of buses—trucks with colorful wooden canopies and padded benches—lined the outer perimeters of the market square across the street, but few people mingled. Most workers, shoppers, and students who usually congested the streets and square at this hour had probably skipped their daily routines to join the protest march up to Duncan's official residence. Vendors wore masks of disappointment behind colorful mounds of fruit and vegetables, waving cardboard sheets to chase away flies, their only customers.

A couple of armed soldiers faced her direction, but looked bored leaning against the brick pillars at the entrance to the square.

Cammy adjusted her sunglasses and tightened the scarf over her head. Given his security concerns this morning, she doubted Reds still had her on his mind. But she didn't want to take the chance one of his soldiers might want to be a hero.

The locks behind the closed door clacked and a white-haired man shoved the doors open. She pulled from her bag the list of sewing materials and measurements she'd jotted down on the *Carmen* and entered the musty store. A few customers followed her in. Less exposed in the narrow aisles, Cammy set to work scrutinizing fabric for the curtains.

A few minutes later she jumped when a low voice plucked her out of her shopping moment. "Miss Butler?"

She turned and came face-to-face with one of the armed soldiers. "Yes?"

"Trust me," he said. "Follow me to the back of the store."

If he'd planned to arrest her, he would have done so immediately. Her instinct guided her decision to follow him.

He strolled off with a rifle in one hand, and inspecting goods with the other. She followed at a distance, also pretending to shop in case anyone watched them under the quivering fluorescent lights.

He stood in a back corner when she caught up with him.

He held up a pair of jeans to the light while she rolled a bale of cloth on the shelf behind him.

"They're searching for you." His whispers struggled against the squeaks from the ceiling fan. "You must leave."

"Leave town?"

"Leave the island. Take Storm with you. I went to school with him."

"But why?"

"Reds. There's going to be trouble. I must go."

"Thanks," she whispered.

He took two steps away then turned to face her. "I heard what happened to the clock in your house. We're not all like that."

She smiled her understanding to him in case her nervous voice cracked. "I know."

He marched off and disappeared out the front door.

The commotion outside the store surprised Cammy when she lugged three bags of materials into the blistering sunshine an hour and a half later. An electric crowd of about eight thousand swelled the market square. People poured in from the converging streets carrying signs and chanting. Angry voices punctured the air. To battle the rising heat, some lapped rainbow-colored snow cones. One man clung from a telephone pole, tightening a gray loudspeaker overhead. Another man stretched wires to a microphone stand in the middle of a platform overlooking the crowd. Flocks of students in school uniforms, dark skirts and pants with white shirts and stripped ties, energized the crowd with youthful exuberance.

"We get we leader back." A group of female students chanted outside the store. "We get we leader back."

Cammy rushed over to them. "What's going on?"

"We freed Duncan," one said.

"While Reds' armored personnel carriers were blocking the gate," another said, "people jumped over the back fence and stormed the house."

"He's in a car now, leading the march down Lucas Street," yet another student said. "He's coming to talk to the people here."

Cammy debated whether to stay to hear Duncan's speech. This moment could be decisive in Grenada's future. Two strong-willed men poised to spring on each other. One she hated. One she distrusted. Where was Duncan while Rachael died alone on a river bank?

Her watch said 11:05 a.m. The *Carmen* would not pull into Grand Anse for another hour or two. She had time.

It took her less than ten minutes to deposit her bags in Storm's pickup two blocks away.

When she returned to the market square, Duncan had not yet arrived.

"Where's he?" she asked a man.

"He should be here by now. They say he stuck in the crowds on Church Street."

She hadn't seen much of Duncan in the past year. During the early days of the revolution his larger-than-life speeches from public platforms had magnetized the island behind his revolution, sweeping away young minds like Rachael's. He made fewer public speeches now. He hadn't even showed up to Rachael's funeral.

Cammy wanted to get a glimpse of him. She tightened the scarf over her head and adjusted her sunglasses. Up ahead, a thick crowd chocked the intersection of Church and Young Streets where a policeman with white gloves usually directed traffic with snappy hand movements. The marchers would likely carry Duncan to the market square from that direction. She hurried up to the intersection and squeezed to the edge of the curb.

She didn't have to wait for long.

A car inched forward, surrounded and trailed by a jubilant mass of people. A carnival atmosphere, fueled not by steel drum music and glittering costumes, but by celebration. The people had freed Duncan from Reds' grasp.

But they did not know Reds the way Cammy did. At this moment, Reds would be plotting his next move. And it might not be pretty.

The car drew nearer. Duncan and a woman in the back seat. A pregnant woman.

Kester, Cammy's long-time friend, sat behind the wheel.

He had been there for her for so many years. He'd wanted more than her friendship, but she never felt the compulsion to turn her life over to another man after Reds. Kester, so young then, had led her and Mario into a private office while the *Bianca C* flamed offshore. Kester had also helped her when he sold his boat and pickup to Storm.

Today he was helping yet another friend, a Prime Minister under siege.

"Kester." She removed her sunglasses and blew him a kiss when he looked her way.

He waved at her. Duncan did too, but like a school boy caught in bad behavior. A womanizer with no loyalty.

Rachael had fallen for Duncan and now Cammy wondered if her daughter had died because of him.

A reporter squeezed up to Duncan's window. "Mr. Prime Minister, what do you have to say about all this?"

"Today belongs to the masses," Duncan shouted with a hoarse voice.

Kester slid the car forward.

Chanting marchers followed. "We get we leader. We get we leader."

The car reached the intersection. Down the hill to the right, thousands waited in the market square for Duncan. But the car did not turn right as Cammy expected. Maybe the excitement had pushed Duncan's mistress into early labor.

The car kept straight, and up the hill toward Fort George and the General Hospital.

Unable to resist the momentum of the crowd, Cammy replaced her sunglasses over her eyes and turned to follow.

Someone grabbed her wrist.

***

Reds' fury burned at his temple. "Those fools. How could they let him escape?"

The communications officer rushed up. "Sir, it's Fort George. The crowd has taken over the operations center and Duncan just ordered his ministers to arm civilians with AK-47s."

"He's crazy! Get him on the phone."

"Who, sir?"

"Duncan, dammit."

The officer hurried to a bank of phones, but returned a minute later stoned-faced. "Sir, Duncan won't talk to you. The minister who answered said Duncan's position is no negotiation, no compromise."

Reds' twirled his moustache. "Then this is war."

***

"Look at the crowds around the city," Storm shouted, holding the binoculars to his eyes where he stood on the side rail of the *Carmen*. Radio 610 from Trinidad had announced earlier that massive demonstrations flooded the St. George's streets to protest Duncan's house arrest. And now the latest bulletin said Duncan had been freed by the crowd and taken to Fort George.

Jackie peered through another set of binoculars. "What do you think will happen?"

"I'm worried," he said. "It's not a good thing when you have so many civilians overrunning a military compound. Even looks like some are armed with rifles. If shooting starts, no one can tell friend from foe."

"I hope your mother is not in that crowd," Mario yelled from the pilothouse.

"Me too." Storm glanced at his watch. "She's supposed to meet us in Grand Anse in an hour."

"Oh gosh, no." Jackie pointed to the top of Lucas Street.

Storm adjusted his binoculars at the green hills, crisscrossed with sagging telephone wires and peppered with red-roofed houses. Three BTRs and four trucks filled with soldiers raced down Lucas Street from Fort Frederick toward Fort George.

Storm's chest pounded.

***

Damn. Cammy stared at the PRA soldier holding her by the wrist, not sure what to do. He must have recognized her when she removed her sunglasses to wave at Kester.

An American accent glazed his strong words. "Don't go up there."

She tried to disguise her fear with innocence. "What...what do you mean?"

"My name is Carl Marrow. I know Storm."

Maybe she should jerk free from his hold and vanish into the crowd. She played along, waiting for his grip to loosen.

She shouted over the chanting. "What's wrong with going up to the fort?"

"Too many guns and too many young, jittery soldiers." His tone communicated concern, not what she expected from an arresting soldier. "I already told my mother to go home."

"Reds didn't send you?"

"No." He shook his head and released her. "I just happened to see you."

She relaxed a little. "Maybe I'll wait down—"

Screams from upper Church Street. Several armored personnel carriers and trucks rumbled their way through the crowd. People scattered from the road and squeezed onto the sidewalk to make room for the intimidating machines.

The lead carrier screeched to a stop and the convoy halted behind it.

A hush descended over the throng. The growling vehicles spewed fuel-scented exhaust into the air.

Cammy slipped behind Carl in the thick crowd. She tightened the scarf around her head and peeked past her dark sunglasses.

A young officer jumped off the lead carrier and marched up to Carl.

They saluted.

"Lieutenant Marrow," the young officer said. "We need you up there with us."

"Why me? I am no longer trusted and accepted in the PRA."

"We know you called the Cuban embassy last night to alert them about Duncan's arrest."

"I was trained to obey lawful orders from my Commander-in Chief," Carl said.

"It looks like on this island today we have two Commanders-in-Chief."

"Which one are you serving?" Carl asked.

The young officer glanced around. "The people. But not everyone in my company feels the same way. Let's pretend you and I are the only ones with cool heads on the island today. We need you to talk some sense into Duncan and his ministers. We need to disarm the people and get them off the fort so negotiations can begin."

Carl shook his head. "I am not sure there's anything I can do."

As dire as the situation appeared, it did not surprise Cammy. Reds had been on an ambitious course since she first met him. When people and situations did not quite fit his mold, he would carve them out and discard them. She knew him down to the bones. Now after Rachael's death, she wondered how much Duncan's own demons contributed to the caustic atmosphere threatening her once peaceful island.

"Duncan trusts you," the officer said to Carl. "This has escalated from a political to a military situation. You're a professional military man. That's a start."

Carl pondered a moment. "Okay. I'll give it a try."

"It's all I'm asking."

They shook hands. Carl followed the officer without looking back at Cammy.

He and the soldier climbed to the top of the armored personnel carrier. The engines revved. The eight-wheeled machine crawled through the intersection and gassed up the hill toward the fort.

The rest of the convoy snaked past. Machine gun barrels poked out from open firing ports. Young scared eyes peeked from shadowy windows along the side of the armored personnel carriers. Trucks loaded with soldiers followed.

She watched as Carl, seated on top the armored personal carrier, disappeared up the hill and around the corner toward the fort.

He had just done what he'd warned Cammy not to do.

When the last truck passed, she headed down the hill away from the fort. Premonition tightened her stomach.

She'd just crossed Melville Street to the seaside esplanade when an explosion rocked the hilltop fort.

Screams filled the city air.

CHAPTER TWENTY-SIX

"Oh shit!" Storm adjusted his binoculars. "Looks like a car just blew up. All hell is about to break loose."

Smoke billowed from the car. People scattered. A wave of them rushed toward the back of the fort. Gun fire from the upper verandah of the operations building directed at the convoy.

Two soldiers fell off the top of the lead BTR-60 and remained still on the street.

A third soldier emerged from the turret and sprayed the operations building with bullets from the fixed 14.5 mm machine gun.

Wood splinters and glass powdered the air. Bodies fell on the verandah floor. People scattered. Gunfire from all directions.

People ran. People fell.

Could this really be happening?

Storm's gut tightened in horror. A massacre was taking place in front of him. But these were people he knew. His neighbors. His classmates. Friends. Teachers. People he passed on the street every day.

Nothing he'd trained for prepared him for this moment. He felt like someone had tied his hands behind his back and now forced him to watch an unfolding nightmare.

Soldiers poured out of the vehicles and charged into the fort complex.

Two more soldiers dropped. Gunshots raked the stone walls, impacting in showers of powdery puffs.

Mario held the *Carmen* on a steady course past the mouth of the St. George's harbor, allowing a rear view of the fort.

People by the hundreds leaped off the eighteenth century stone walls, ten, twenty feet high. Like a waterfall torrent, in a steady flow, they crashed through trees and landed on the rocky terrain below.

A scene from a nightmarish movie.

Jackie's wail reminded Storm this was no dream and no movie. "Oh God, no!"

She collapsed at his feet on the deck with a gut-wrenching shriek that tore at his heart.

***

Cammy glanced up at thick black smoke rising against the blue sky over Fort George. A flood of dread seized her.

Rapid bursts of heavy gunfire. People scampered in wide-eyed panic.

Cammy knew Reds would trigger a reprisal against Duncan. But against the people?

A block away, a male voice pleaded for calm on the public address system.

"Remain in place," the voice shouted. "Keep cool. Don't let them scare you away."

Despite his pleas, people ran from the market square. Overloaded buses and cars sped north away from the city. Away from the fort.

"Stand firm." Hollow words echoed from the loudspeakers over the thinning crowd. "Our respectable Prime Minister will soon be here to speak to you."

An army truck filled with soldiers rumbled toward the market square.

Screams.

Panicky footsteps shuffled down the narrow steps from the fort. Female students struggled, carrying a classmate with bloodied white shirt.

Cammy ran to them. "What happened?"

"She's been shot," one said.

Cammy helped the students lay the girl flat on the sidewalk and unbuttoned the soaked shirt. Thick blood pumped from a hole on the right side of her chest. Cammy pulled off her scarf and stuffed it over the hole.

A part of her wanted to scream. She wanted to surrender to the fear gripping her throat. But the girl needed medical attention. Fast.

The only ways to the hospital was back up the steps, against the tide of fleeing people, or a suicidal drive past the gunfire reigning over the fort.

Cammy had another option. She pointed to Storm's pickup down the street next to the Children's Shopping Plaza. "I'll get my car. Stay here with her."

Cammy rushed down the street with the stampede.

A woman cried. "A lot of people dead today."

More explosions from the fort.

Cammy jumped into the pickup and raced it toward the students, blowing the horn to alert the tide of people flowing against her.

She pulled up along the sidewalk and tossed her shopping bags into the back of the pickup. "Quick," she shouted at the students. "Get her in the front seat."

They squeezed the wounded girl into the middle of the front seat. One of her classmates sat at the passenger door holding the scarf against the wound. The other students jumped into the back.

Cammy made a hasty U turn and sped toward St. John's Street. She made a sharp right and raced up the hill toward the Catholic Church. A flow of people ran in panic up Church Street. She turned left away from them, squealing her tires over Cemetery Hill and down Old Fort Road to Lucas Street.

She raced across Archibald Avenue, and down Lowther's Lane toward Belmont. Cammy was half-way along Belmont Road before she felt relaxed enough to talk to the girl at her shoulder.

Please God, don't let this one die too.

"What's your name?" Cammy asked in a soft motherly voice, struggling to keep her despair under control for the girl's sake.

The girl's head bobbed on Cammy's shoulder. "Gemma…"

Cammy glanced at the young beautiful black face. "Gemma." Cammy swallowed hard. "Gemma. I like that name. What's your mother's name?"

"Mildred."

"You know, Gemma, your mother loves you. You know that, right?"

"Yes," Gemma whispered.

"Your mother will be so proud when she finds out how strong and brave you are."

No answer, just a head lying heavy on Cammy's shoulder.

She screeched to a halt in front of the Grand Anse campus of the St. George's School of Medicine. One of the students in the back of the pickup ran screaming for help from the medical staff. Americans in medical uniform rushed to the pickup with a stretcher.

A doctor felt Gemma's pulse. He shook his head.

Gemma was gone.

Cammy bawled like she'd just lost another daughter.

***

Reds explained the situation on the phone to his Bulgarian contact, Sergei. "Things got out of hand, comrade. I didn't want this. Our Cuban associates have some blame as well in inciting the crowds to invade the streets. Duncan's mistake was to take his supporters up to Fort George."

"And your mistake, comrade? Duncan had the gasoline. You lit the match."

"Duncan left me no choice."

"Where is he?" Sergei asked.

"We have him and his ministers under custody at Fort George. The troops are cleaning up and getting the injured to the hospital. But we're not sure what to do about Duncan."

A long sigh blew from the other end of the phone. "You're calling me to see how Moscow might feel about the next step?"

"As an internationalist, you've always given wise counsel."

"Let's pretend you were hunting a snake," Sergei said. "But the hunt goes bad. The snake now knows you're hunting it. It might strike back and turn you into the prey. It's you or him. You both can't live in the same hole anymore. It's too late, comrade."

"What about the people?" Reds didn't want to underestimate them again.

"Consider Duncan the head of the snake. The body represents the people, stretching from the fort down to every street and into every home on the island. You can try to regain control by starting from its tail, but you don't have space in Richmond Hill Prison. If the head is gone, the body loses its power. It's your decision, just be prepared to take full responsibility from here on. It's the burden of leadership. Good luck, comrade."

The phone went dead.

Reds understood exactly what Sergei recommended. Reds knew all along he had one option left. He just needed to hear it from a fraternal friend, joined at the hip in the struggle for historic inevitability.

If he had to exercise full authority over the island, he must dispatch his enemies. And he had no time to waste.

The American-trained soldier was already dead, along with Kester, Cammy's bourgeois admirer.

Duncan and his ministers were next.

Then Reds would be free to deal with the *Carmen* and its traitorous passengers. His gut instinct told him the yacht held the link between the CIA, Bravo, and the uprising. And why did they fill up scuba tanks? Something else was about to happen on the *Bianca C*.

Reds had given them the rope Bravo always asked him to give. But now Reds, and Reds alone, would decide when to pull the noose.

Cracking a major CIA plot with Cuban complicity right offshore would fit perfectly into his plan to blame the bloodshed on foreign agents. He already had enough evidence and suspicions to lay out on the radio. Bravo had allowed a suspicious Barbados couple to meet with a U.S. Marine and then to escape the island. He also arranged for the Marine spy to sail to Palm Island where a mysterious black helicopter waited in the middle of the night.

And why did Carl Marrow, an American-trained soldier and Duncan sympathizer, meet with the Marine and the Cuban ambassador just yesterday? This same soldier had called the Cuban embassy in the predawn hours. Minutes later the embassy phoned counterrevolutionaries across the island to enflame the people and to free Duncan from a Central Committee's house-arrest order. They drove him to the fort where armed anarchists waited to trigger the worst bloodshed in Grenada's history.

Reds could still emerge unscathed and victorious. It would be so easy to blame the shootings on a devious plot to destroy the revolution. The road ahead looked smooth and unobstructed.

His confidence on the rise again after Sergei's phone call, Reds dialed the number at Fort George.

"We're ready," the voice at the other end said.

"Do it."

***

When Cammy pulled up alongside Storm's dive shop, her eyes fogged in tears, Pauline was waiting. Rachael's friend looked as though she'd just survived a hurricane. Her hair hung in thick unruly braids. Her dark face barely hid circles around her eyes and one side of her lips bubbled out in a discolored bump.

"My child, who did this to you?" Cammy held her tight. "Were you on the fort too?"

"No, Richmond Hill Prison." She wore the same light dress she'd worn two nights ago when she visited them on Park Lane, though in the daylight it screamed for a wash. She stood in the same pair of black slippers worn thin at the heels. "They just roughed me up a bit because I was down by the port at night."

She clutched a green canvas shoulder bag, the only thing on her worth saving.

Pauline glanced down at Cammy's dress. "Is that blood?"

"I'm so glad you were not on Fort George." Cammy briefly told her all that had happened since morning.

"When they released me, I took a bus here to find Storm," Pauline said. "I saw people with bloodied clothes, some limping, some crying. What has become of our peaceful island?"

"You're coming with us," Cammy said. "You can't go back on the streets. Reds just announced a shoot-to-kill order on the radio."

They hurried down to the jetty with Cammy's shopping bags just as Storm pulled up with the dinghy. He secured a rope to the jetty and jumped off. A thin smile swept past his face when he saw Pauline.

He embraced her. "You'll be okay now."

At that moment, heavy machine gun fire echoed from the fort. It lasted two minutes. Then an eerie silence reclaimed the island.

Cammy stared at Storm on the dinghy ride back to the *Carmen*.

She'd never seen such quiet rage burn in his eyes.

CHAPTER TWENTY-SEVEN

Storm checked his pressure gauge and wristwatch as he began the slow descent feet first toward the *Bianca C* with Mario just behind him. Mario held the tow line, locked on his shoulder harness ring. The line trailed up to the flagged buoy on the surface where Jackie had just dropped them off from the dinghy. At 3:30 p.m., they had enough daylight to set the charge, blow the door to the safe, and return to the *Carmen* with a hundred and twenty million dollars in rare gems—Bravo's bait.

Mario had not said a word after the horrors they'd witnessed on the fort today. For sure, he must be in shock. How could people who'd risked their lives to save six hundred and seventy strangers from his cruise ship, turn guns on each other with such callous abandon?

Storm had the same question, but without an answer.

And how dare Reds get on the radio to claim Duncan, his ministers, his pregnant mistress, Kester – had all died in the deadly cross fire. Storm saw a couple people fall on the verandah of the operations building where Duncan stood with his key supporters. The survivors made a hasty retreat into the building. The last volley of machine gun fire, long after the chaotic shootings ended, sounded more like an execution.

The radio had also announced the names of soldiers killed, including Carl Marrow, probably one of the first two who rolled off the lead BTR-60 armored personnel carrier. Denver would be devastated at his younger brother's death. Storm wondered too about all the civilians who were forced to choose between bullets and the painful leap off the fort walls to the trees and rocks below where severe injuries or even death awaited them.

The radio had not yet announced how many, or the names of civilians killed.

Many would be students. Cammy had already lost one in the front seat of Storm's pickup.

The loss of his fellow Marines in the Beirut bombing, followed by the bloodletting he'd witnessed on the fort, left Storm numb. He'd also tried to comfort Jackie, but she'd stopped crying only to help him and Mario strap on the twin tanks earlier. The naked brutality on the fort raised a harsh new reality for her imprisoned father. An even more vicious regime held him today than the one that held him yesterday. Freeing him alive from prison just went from difficult to impossible.

Storm had considered going ashore to conduct surveillance on the fort, even if he had to leave the *Carmen* vulnerable for a few hours. But the message from Barbados arrived just in time.

"Stay the course," it said.

Stay the course?

How could the U.S. Embassy expect him to stay the course when Grenada and 800 American medical students were imprisoned under a twenty-four hour shoot-to-kill order? Storm doubted Reds would do anything more to endanger the Americans who attended the St. George's School of Medicine. Such a move would immediately provoke the fury of an American invasion. But then again, he hadn't expected that Reds' troops would inflict such murderous fire on the very people they'd sworn to defend.

In an atmosphere seething with grave uncertainty, 'stay the course' meant completing the dive, securing the gems, and entrapping Bravo on the yacht—if he showed up.

And then what? Steve had left the next steps vague. With Reds now in control of the island, the U.S. Embassy in Barbados would be busy redrawing its plans, even as Storm and Mario descended to the *Bianca C*.

The ship greeted them with the same majesty she had yesterday, untouched by the calamitous events darkening the island. Her vegetation waved green from the deck and playful fish darted around the foremast. A school of yellowtail snappers raced them to the cabin windows and then glided away in the steady current.

He glanced back at Mario.

Mario's single eye held an unblinking focus on his ship. Turmoil must churn in his stomach at his first view of her since the fire. He'd returned to the island with one mission. Maybe two. Find his diamonds and Cammy. He'd found Cammy, but then he also learned he'd fathered a son with her while his ship burned. Now, even before he laid his sights on the safe that protected his diamonds underwater for twenty-two years, Mario had witnessed a massacre and became entangled in a dangerous CIA defection plan.

Storm didn't know how yet, but Steve still expected them to capture Bravo and escape Grenada waters—before Reds shifted his murderous focus from Fort George to the *Carmen*. Hopefully, Reds would be too busy cleaning up today's fiasco to intrude on the dive.

Storm fought the current and reached out to the window ledge. Cable loops still held the bar frame securely against the window, reassuring him that no three-hundred pound surprise lurked in the cabin like yesterday's nurse shark.

Mario helped him untangle the cables and let the bar fall onto the cabin floor. Storm showed him where to hook the tow line on the window ledge.

They pushed through the current and entered the cabin.

Mario held a flashlight to show the way. Everything looked exactly as Storm had left it the previous afternoon. He brushed past the hanging cables toward the safe, tugged aside the sink, and pointed to the combination dial.

Mario nodded and gave the index finger-to-thumb okay signal.

Storm unleashed from his waist the heavy duty crowbar Steve and Hallam delivered with the scuba gear the night before. If the bar could remove the safe door, Storm might avoid the use of demolition charge. An explosion would destroy plant life and coral that had taken years to develop.

He jimmied the sharp end into the narrow gap between the door and the steel casing. Three jams of his weight, and the safe door held firm. He braced against the ceiling frame and tried with his heel on the crowbar.

Same result.

Aware strenuous underwater activity consumed more air than a casual dive, he decided to cease struggling with the crow bar. He reached into his hip pouch for the M118. Earlier on deck, he'd prepared the charge. He made a hole on the end of the demolition block for the M8 blasting cap holder with its three slanted teeth to prevent slippage. Next, he inserted an electric blasting cap into the holder, until the end of the cap pressed against the sheet explosive, and wrapped a string around the explosive to hold the blasting cap in place. Now in the cabin, he used electric tape to fasten the M118 block between the door latch and the door. He connected the firing wire to the blasting cap and covered the demolition charge with the sink to minimize collateral damage to aquatic life in the cabin.

Unraveling the firing wire as he went, Storm filtered through the hanging cables and headed out the window. He turned right and swam into the current toward starboard with Mario pulling the tow line in his wake. They stayed a safe distance from the windows, a likely launching pad for irate nurse sharks, and stopped after passing about eight cabins. Storm expected the current to take shredded debris blasting out of the window away from them and toward port. They swam above the cabins and held on to the metal supports for stability.

Storm connected the ends of the firing wire to the hand-held blasting machine and gave Mario the okay signal.

Storm pushed the plunger. The ship trembled and the sink shot out of the window like a cannon ball. A river of greenish brown flushed out behind it and turned a sharp left to port with the current.

He gave Mario a high five, and they let the current carry them toward the window. Silt fogged the cabin and a few fish floated upside down. They waited a few minutes until visibility increased. Then Storm led the way over the littered floor to the rear bulkhead. The door on the twisted safe still clutched to the bottom hinge but left enough room for the crow bar to finish the job.

He pushed the door away from the open safe and turned to Mario with a wave of his hand, as if to say "all yours."

Mario dove up to the safe, reached in, and pulled out a metal box with a rusty key lock. Storm wrapped a few feet of electric tape around it, just in case, and tucked it into the mesh bag. He placed the harmless blasting machine into the safe as a calling card for the next visitor.

He let Mario exit the window ahead of him and paused to look at the mangled bar frame pushed into the web of cables. He pulled out the battered remnants of the bar and dragged it along the floor, from the window to the rear bulkhead, sweeping away dislodged cable pieces and shredded plant life.

Mario watched with a puzzled look from behind his dive mask.

Storm realized he would have to explain when they reached topside. If he died trying to entrap Bravo with these diamonds, his final act of human kindness would be to a nurse shark that called this cabin home.

***

Aboard the *Carmen*, Storm marveled at the colors of gems tumbling out with murky water from the rusty box Mario held. Intensely pink stones rolled out with greenish-blue, black, red, and white gems into a salad bowl on the breakfast table as Cammy, Pauline, and Jackie looked on. Even with the blinds shut to block prying binoculars from shore and after all those years in sea water, they sparkled in the soft light hanging over the lounge's teak table.

Several diamond rings lay among Mario's collection.

He held up a clear crystal stone to the light, almost the size of one of the large marbles Storm used to play with in the dusty field on Park Lane.

"This is a *jeremejevite* from Siberia," Mario said. "One of my favorites. Bought it in a secret sale from a collector in Brussels. And this one is an Australian black opal. The aborigines used to wear these around their necks. They were millionaires long before we came along."

He pulled on a pair of kitchen gloves and placed the stones one at a time into a jar of hot water he poured from the coffee maker.

Cammy looked on, but it appeared the demands of the past couple days, and apprehension about what awaited them in the next few days, had begun to dull her spark. She glanced at Storm with a meek smile. And then, probably needing to escape to the comfort of a routine she knew so well, she returned to her Singer sewing machine next to the bar. Almost hidden behind stacks of curtain fabric, she foot-pedaled the sewing machine to a steady hum.

After a shower and change of clothes, Pauline looked renewed. She sat across from Mario, clutching her canvas bag. Cammy had braided her hair and given her a clean dress. One side of Pauline's lips still showed discoloration. She bit her finger nails down to the flesh. The trauma she suffered in Richmond Hill Prison lingered in a silent tension that soured her otherwise attractive face.

But she did have one bit of news to brighten Jackie's mood. Pauline had seen Jackie's father from her cell two days ago. Two guards were escorting him to the mess hall, a little feeble and with the help of a cane.

While Mario let the stones sit in the water for about ten minutes, Storm turned the radio dial to the government station.

Reds barked the same pronouncements. He blamed Duncan and foreign agents for the fort 'incident' that led to deaths in the 'crossfire', and reminded listeners of the grave consequences awaiting those who left their homes during the next four days.

This time, however, Reds had new curfew rules. "All boats," he said, "are strictly forbidden from leaving their current positions in every port, bay, or beach. Any boats moving along our coastlines will be sunk immediately."

"He's got us trapped too," Storm said.

Mario nodded. "Glad we stocked up on food and water in Carriacou."

Storm, Jackie, and Pauline helped him spray window cleaner on the gems and buff them with lint-free cloth on a beach towel spread across the table.

Once cleaned, Mario put the gems in a velvet pouch that resembled the one Cammy stored in the sewing machine.

He handed the pouch to her. "You're now in charge of these."

"That's a lot of trust," she said.

He kissed her. "Since *Bianca C* sank, I trusted you more than any other human being on the planet."

Mario's words obviously touched her. Cammy's lips trembled and she covered her face with her hands.

Storm turned away and headed out on deck. He'd already seen too many tears today. Grenadians were shedding many more this very minute, in pain, grief, and fear—and probably all three at once.

Storm's heart wrenched. Any elation he expected after the *Bianca C* dive now faded. Helplessness boiled at his temples.

Why didn't he take care of Reds earlier?

Jackie must have seen the anguish on his face. She followed him on deck and held his hand in the dying sunlight. Her return on the *Carmen* proved to be valuable in ways they hadn't anticipated. Since Mario ordered his crew to remain in the hotel during the shoot-to-kill order, Jackie filled in. She had piloted the dinghy in choppy waters over the *Bianca C* and retrieved Storm and Mario after the dive.

She leaned into Storm and squeezed his hand.

"I am concerned about you," he said. "Right now you can be considered an illegal foreign agent. You still have a fake passport and you're not registered with immigration."

"Don't worry," she said. "I doubt Reds expects anyone to visit his immigration office during the curfew."

"We have to get ready for Bravo," he said. "By now, Hallam would have told him we have the gems. Hallam said he might surprise us anytime between now and dawn."

Storm sat on deck in the midnight darkness and waited with the cold Sterling semi-automatic 9 mm in his hand and a pair of binoculars on the table. A steady breeze swept across the deck and thick clouds shut off any hope of moonlight. The boat rocked in choppy waters and he wondered if anyone got seasick downstairs. The aroma from Cammy's baked salmon still floated up from the galley hours after dinner, with mouth-watering reminders of her magical touch with island spices.

Most houselights remained off, deserting the hills to a mass of black. Yellowish streetlights dotted meandering coastal roads. Heavy military vehicles owned these roads, searching the night for counterrevolutionaries. Dogs howled their displeasure at the occasional gunshot echoing against the hillsides.

Armed resistance to Reds' takeover, if any, appeared sporadic.

Grenada shivered in complete lockdown.

The *Carmen's* stairwell creaked. He expected to see Jackie climb up from below deck. She'd fallen asleep two hours ago, probably exhausted from the emotionally taxing day.

Instead, Mario and Cammy crossed the lounge and pulled up chairs next to him.

Cammy hugged Storm. "Hard to sleep?"

"I'm okay," Storm said. "Go back to bed."

"I doubt any one can sleep," Mario said. "Your friend has been in her bed crying all night."

"Who, Jackie?"

"Pauline."

"She's had a tough life." Storm remembered to keep secret Pauline's rape. "Just hate she has to be here to see this Bravo business going down."

They discussed the plan a few more minutes.

"When I spot the boat," Storm said. "I'll come get you."

Hallam had informed them Bravo's approach would be relaxed and disarming. He might even suggest a private conversation with the men in the pilothouse. Enough time for either Storm or Mario to casually flip one of several hidden switches around the deck to initiate the audio-visual recordings.

When Mario and Cammy returned downstairs, Storm resumed watch.

He knew others watched the island as well. One reporter with Radio Antilles had announced that an American invasion to rescue medical students seemed imminent. The Organization of Eastern Caribbean States released a statement calling Reds and his clique a bunch of "murderers, outlaws, and illegitimate renegades." Even Castro chimed in with an announcement stating no doctrine or revolutionary principle could justify the atrocities witnessed on Fort George.

Finally, others saw Reds the way Storm knew him to be.

Everyone except the Soviet Union.

They dismissed the shootings and executions as an internal matter to be resolved only by Grenadians. Tonight gave little indication the Grenada people had the means to resolve their predicament. Reds controlled the island with Soviet armaments.

Storm felt sure the Cuban embassy must be in lock down mode just like the rest of the island, in communication with Havana to ponder their next steps now that Castro's favored son, Duncan, had fallen in a hail of Soviet bullets.

Duncan's loss must surely pain Castro, politically and personally. Castro had invested generously in Grenada's well-being, in medical clinics, university scholarships, and in the new airport. Storm could see few face-saving options to rescue Castro from the quagmire Reds created.

Storm expected Bravo would be juggling his options too, with cunning and daring calculation.

The *Carmen* sat offshore with a hundred and twenty million dollars and, Bravo probably believed, evidence of covert electronic devices. With Duncan gone, Castro might be reluctant to squander more resources to scuttle a CIA plot against Reds.

Bravo would certainly agree. CIA and Reds be damned. Bravo must be licking his chops, waiting for his window of opportunity while Reds remained busy hunting his opponents.

At 5 a.m., a truck turned off the main road and headed down the driveway toward the beach. Storm rolled to the deck and squeezed the binoculars to his eyes. The headlights went out but the outline of the truck disturbed the shadows on the way down to the stretch of white sand. The truck stopped. Three figures jumped off with rifles and hurried across the sand. They climbed onto the jetty and marched past several moored boats.

A few minutes later, one of the boats backed out. When it turned toward the *Carmen*, Storm recognized the outline of his Radon 22.

He remembered Hallam's warnings about Bravo. A highly suspicious man, anything out of the ordinary would set off the alarms wired in Bravo's brain.

Storm retreated into the lounge and down the stairwell with his binoculars and 9 mm pistol. He alerted the others to remain in their cabins and to keep all lights off as planned. When he pushed open the door to Pauline's cabin, she was already seated in her bed in the darkness.

"Stay here," he told her. "Whatever happens, just stay here with your door shut."

He thought he'd heard her say "I'm sorry," but by then he'd shut her door.

The Radon 22 engine sputtered alongside the *Carmen's* aft deck. Low voices topside. The floors above him groaned under heavy boot steps.

Storm called out, pretending a lazy voice, as if he'd just awakened. "Hello, anybody up there?"

A voice he didn't recognize answered. "Yeah. Come on up with your hands in the air."

It sounded like a Grenadian. Bravo must have brought along local help.

Storm tucked his handgun into the back of the shorts, covered it with his t-shirt, and barefooted it up the stairwell.

At the top of the stairs in the graying morning, combat boots led up to PRA uniforms, and then to the muzzles of AK-47 rifles staring at him.

Even before Storm saw the face of the soldier in the middle, he recognized the voice.

"Surprised to see me?" Reds asked.

CHAPTER TWENTY-EIGHT

Storm sat at the table with the others on the deck of the *Carmen*, his thoughts racing to figure a way out of Reds' trap. Hallam and Steve's defection sting just got blown. At the point of the AK-47s, neither Storm nor Mario had the opportunity to turn on the cameras and video transmitters. Now they all had their hands tied at their backs with deck ropes the PRA soldiers had hastily cut with their 12-inch bayonets.

All except Pauline.

Reds had not ordered his soldiers to tie her.

She stood aside, at the entrance to the lounge, gazing at the floor and biting her nails, her canvas bag hanging from her lean shoulder.

"Now I have your attention," Reds barked. "Who wants to be the first to tell me where you hid the *Bianca C* diamonds?"

Silence.

How the hell did Reds find out about the diamonds? Did he finally outsmart Bravo? If so, Bravo was probably already dead. This whole defection idea stunk from the beginning.

Regardless, Storm had no idea what Cammy did with the diamonds after Mario handed her the velvet pouch.

Cammy snapped. "What diamonds are you talking about?"

Reds marched over to Pauline and grabbed her canvas bag. He pulled a black box with a silver antenna and wires from her bag.

"I am no fool," he barked. "Thanks to Pauline, I heard every word since yesterday."

Damn. Pauline had the *Carmen* bugged for the last twelve hours.

But why did she do it, especially for a man she despised so much?

Storm had written off her tense demeanor as the aftershock from prison, but she had more on her mind. Reds must have cajoled her into this. She now stood at the entrance to the lounge staring at her feet in what probably felt like the lowest point in her life—except maybe the day Reds raped her.

Reds laughed. "All this time Bravo had me believing you were here to install underwater devices. I am sure he will be very surprised when he finds out he's not the only clever fox on the island."

So Bravo must still be alive. But where? They'd expected him by dawn, any moment now. Maybe he would arrive in time to foil Reds. If so, Bravo had better come with more than a Makarov pistol to outgun Reds and his two soldiers with their AK-47s.

But what if Bravo sensed a trap and never showed up?

Storm could not wait. He stretched the weathered ropes holding his wrist. When the soldier had disarmed him of his 9 mm and tied him in the dark, Storm had stiffened his wrists and arms out behind him just enough to create some wriggle room without the soldier noticing.

With such fast and sloppy work, it seemed Reds planned for an easy getaway with the diamonds— and maybe a quick death for his captives.

"I don't have all day," Reds said. "You have five minutes to get me the diamonds, or you'll go up with a bang. Give me the diamonds, and you're free to leave the island."

Storm doubted Reds intended to let them escape alive. This was a do or die situation. Storm had better come up with a plan in the next few minutes. Or they would all die.

Reds nodded at one of the soldiers. The soldier jumped on to Storm's Radon 22, tied to the rear of the *Carmen*, and returned with an ominous bundle. A full block of C4 and a receiver, wrapped together with electric tape.

"This is timed to go off in five minutes." Reds turned to the soldier. "Place it in the engine room downstairs. With the full tank of gas they got in Carriacou, all of Grenada will see it when it goes up."

The soldier rushed past Pauline, into the lounge, and down the stairs with the bomb.

Shit! Storm had to figure something out fast.

Steve and Hallam, wherever they were, would have no idea how quickly their well-conceived plans just got flushed down the shitter. Now Storm and everyone else who mattered in his life stared into death five minutes away.

He suddenly realized something—the bomb had a receiver and mini-antenna. Not a timer, as Reds implied.

He would have to set it off by remote control. A safe distance from the yacht. He must have a battery operated transmitter either on him, or on Storm's boat.

Reds' five-minute warning was a ruse. He wouldn't leave and destroy the boat without retrieving the diamonds first.

Storm might have some time to plan his next step—but not much if Reds started to hurt somebody.

Reds turned to Cammy with a snarl. "I've waited for this moment a long time."

She spat at him. "How could you stand there like that after killing all those innocent people? You work for the devil."

He slapped her hard. "Shut up, bitch."

Storm felt it to his bones. Like he'd felt the slaps she received all those years ago. Back then he would cover his ears and cry silent tears. No more.

Mario stood and yelled. "Stop it."

The other soldier slammed his rifle butt into Mario's gut. Mario collapsed into his chair groaning.

Reds shouted, "Somebody better start talking about the diamonds."

Years ago Storm promised himself Reds would die. But he lived on. And because Storm had not kept his promise, Reds continued to ravage lives and the island Storm called home.

Today Storm would keep his promise, or die trying.

He glanced at Jackie. Raw terror blazed in her eyes.

He couldn't afford to let his mother's pain or Jackie's fear trigger his anger at Reds. Anything he said to aggravate Reds further might lead to an incapacitating blow from an AK-47. And then what?

He bit his tongue and wriggled the ropes a little looser, but not soon enough.

The other soldier stomped back up the stairs without the bomb and stood next to Storm.

Cammy recovered from the slap, but kept fighting with the only weapons she had, her words. "This island is too small for your hatred."

Reds came within inches from her face, his moustache twitching. "Take a lesson from your quiet coward son over there. It's your kind of mouth that got Rachael killed."

Cammy exhaled and sank into her chair like a balloon losing its air. "*You* killed her didn't you?"

Reds snickered. "She died because she had a big mouth like yours. She just about convinced her lover-boy captain to expose our plans for Duncan. She even tried to get him to tell the Americans about our secret treaties with the North Koreans and others. Bravo sniffed her out like a cat finding a mouse. She's dead and you will be too if I don't get some diamonds soon."

Storm knew it all along. Rachael had assimilated Cammy's ways with perfection. A fighter and a lover energized by passion. In the end, it had gotten Rachael killed.

Reds had to pay. And Bravo would have some explaining to do, if Storm ever got to see him again.

Cammy's anger at Reds seemed to cleanse her spirit and reenergize her will to fight. "You stupid bastard. She was your daughter."

"What?" Reds wide jaw snapped open.

Despite the tears rolling down her cheeks, Cammy shot her words straight and hard into him. "You killed your own daughter!"

Storm doubted Cammy just made it up to antagonize Reds. If she said Reds was Rachael's father, no lightning strike would change it. Reds was Rachael's father. If only Storm had known earlier, but what difference would it make now? Through the pent-up emotions blazing through him, Storm held his focus on Reds.

Reds straightened. "You told the whole damn island she wasn't mine."

"You fool." She yelled. "I only said that to get you out of my house. To get you out of our lives. You killed your own flesh and blood with your hate, you worthless pig."

Reds pointed at Storm. "I know for sure this traitor is not mine." He glanced at Mario. "I wasn't gone a week and you had another man in my bed."

Cammy's voice slowed. "That's because you don't know what it's like to be a man."

Storm wriggled the rope a little looser.

Reds' breath snorted through his moustache. "Diamonds or not, today you die."

"I don't care," she shouted. "At least my conscience is clear."

Cammy always chained her spirit with secrets to protect her children. But today, even with her hands tied behind her, Storm had never seen his mother so free. Even with Reds' palm print on her cheek and the trickle of blood on her lip, she never looked so brave. And in Mario's rumpled *Italia* t-shirt, her untidy hair blowing across her forehead in the sea breeze, Cammy never looked so beautiful.

Storm glanced again at Jackie. Despite her fear, the love in her eyes filled him with all her hopes and dreams for them. He knew then, dead or alive, no one could take her place.

It had to be now.

She probably thought he'd gone crazy when he smiled and winked at her. But she must have written him off for dead when he leaped from his chair and knocked over the soldier in front of him. Storm hurdled over the rail and dived into the water.

***

"Storm!" Cammy screamed when her son disappeared into the water with his hands roped at his back. It felt like a red-hot stake piercing her heart.

Next to her, Jackie wailed uncontrollably.

Reds' soldiers rushed to the side of the boat, preparing to fire their rifles where Storm disappeared.

"Don't shoot," Reds ordered. "Let him drown with his hands tied. The coward deserves a slow death."

"You're going straight to hell." Cammy howled. She let her head hang forward, and wept even as a fluttering memory reminded her Storm faced danger better in water than above it.

Reds ordered his soldiers to undo the captives' ropes and retie them— to their chairs.

"I don't want to lose them all overboard before someone tells me where they hid the diamonds."

While the soldiers worked on Mario first, securing his arms and upper body to the chair with extra lengths of rope, Cammy glanced at Jackie. When their gazes met, Cammy smiled at her, hoping Jackie would understand—Storm was up to something.

"Storm is already dead," Reds shouted when his soldiers finished roping Jackie and Cammy to their chairs. "Someone else is about to die, unless I see some diamonds in my hands."

Jackie's wail pained Cammy.

The seconds ticked by.

Pauline shuffled toward Reds. "I know where the diamonds are. I'll get them for you."

***

Storm tugged his hands out of the loose rope. He dived ten feet deep and turned sharply to the left toward the *Carmen's* hull, beyond the deflection range of AK-47 rounds. No silvery tracers followed him so he figured the soldiers might not have had enough time to fire. Either that or keeping his hands behind his back had convinced them he'd committed suicide.

It took him about ten seconds to dive under the yacht to the rear. He resurfaced in the hidden shadow of the deck with a slow rise to minimize water disturbance. He took deep steady breaths. To hide evidence of his survival, he submerged to the propeller a few feet beneath the surface and looped the rope around the blades.

He floated back to the shadows. On the deck above him, Jackie's sobs rose over the sound of choppy water slapping the hull. He wanted desperately to let her know he was still alive, but that would have to wait.

Pauline's voice cut the morning air when she told Reds she knew where the diamonds were hidden.

"No, she doesn't." Cammy aggravated Reds every opportunity she got. "I alone know where they are and I will die before I tell you."

Reds yelled back. "Shaddup."

If Storm died today, he promised to let his final thought be that he'd had the best mother in the world.

Even he had no idea where Cammy concealed the diamonds, so how did Pauline know where to find them? She was shrewd enough—or broken enough—to sneak the electronic bug aboard for Reds, so maybe she was also watching Cammy when no one else paid attention.

But it didn't add up.

If Pauline knew where Cammy hid the diamonds, why did she wait this long to tell Reds? Did she have a plan to double-cross him, to avenge the animal that stole her teenage innocence and ordered her brutal imprisonment? If Pauline decided to turn the tide against Reds, she might help Storm with his plan.

First, he had to get the bomb off the *Carmen*—without being seen.

He swam the length of the ninety-foot yacht to the bow, away from the commotion. He tiptoed up the aluminum step ladder to the walkway and peered down to the other end of the yacht.

The one soldier visible to Storm towered over Mario where he sat, bareback, roped across his hairy chest, and tied to his chair. Mario kept his head upright in defiance, even though Storm suspected the AK-47 blow still hurt.

All the others were to Mario's right, outside of Storm's line of sight.

Just behind them, the unoccupied Radon 22 bobbed against the *Carmen*.

Angry voices rose above the yacht. It sounded like Cammy needling Reds again. Exactly the distraction Storm needed to make his way into the lounge undetected.

But the closest entrance to the lounge awaited him thirty feet ahead—thirty exposed feet closer to the soldier who might turn around at any moment.

Even if he made it into the lounge without alerting the soldier, Storm still had to cross the open living area to the stairwell, climb down to the engine room, and then retrace his steps to the bow undetected—with the bomb in his hand.

And then what?

He hadn't thought that far.

Also troubling, if Mario happened to look down the length of the yacht, any surprised reaction at seeing Storm might unwillingly warn the soldier.

Storm quickly dismissed the concern. It amazed him how quickly Mario moved from just another of Cammy's aggravating acquaintances to a father, a comrade Storm could trust with his life like he would a fellow Marine. Mario would maintain control.

Storm swept the cool water off his t-shirt and shorts to reduce the sound of drips. He licked the salty sea water off his lips, afraid a single drop might sound like a bowling ball crashing to the floor.

He stepped off the ladder and on to the wooden walkway.

The planks creaked.

He paused and held his breath. The yacht rocked and the sea slapped the sides. Raised voices continued unabated. The soldier kept watch on Mario.

Storm took another step on bare feet. No creaks.

More silent steps. He picked up his pace.

The soldier glanced to the side and shifted his position, allowing Storm and Mario to lock gazes. Just as Storm expected, Mario's face remained stoic and unresponsive, partially hidden behind his black eye patch.

What Storm did not expect was what Mario did next.

He looked up at the soldier and began to shout—in Italian.

The soldier faced Mario's outburst in what must have been a bewildering moment—long and loud enough for Storm to stretch his remaining footsteps down the walkway and into the lounge without being heard. He sneaked along the interior wall behind the couch and the bar. He ducked into the shadows behind Cammy's sewing machine and peeked through the open doorway to the deck just as the guard recovered from Mario's verbal flare-up.

The soldier yelled back. "What the hell you saying?"

Mario responded in perfect English. "I said I would like to have a glass of water, please."

The soldier laughed. "You will soon have all the sea water you want."

Storm still needed to cross Mario's aging floors to the stairwell, without Reds and his soldiers hearing him. A more daunting task from where Storm now crouched within earshot and view of the deck.

Cammy and Jackie also remained roped to their chairs, while Reds and his soldiers stood with their backs to Storm.

He wished he had his pistol, now tucked into Reds' belt.

Three shots would end the dilemma in seconds.

This close, Reds' words became clear again as he turned from Cammy and snarled at Pauline. "Why are you just now telling me where the diamonds are hidden?"

Pauline played the subservient role again. "I was thinking if they told you, you would spare their lives, sir."

"I do the thinking around here." He poked her forehead with his finger. "I'll send one of my soldiers with you to find them."

Pauline shouted. "I don't need a damn baby sitter. Haven't I done everything you've asked? You and your soldiers need to keep your eyes on these people. I am not one of them."

Two days in Richmond Hill Prison must have really changed her from when she met with them in Cammy's garden a few nights ago. Storm hoped this was an act.

"Go," Reds ordered. "And you better have some diamonds when you come back."

She turned and hurried into the lounge, bare feet carrying her thin frame quietly toward the sewing machine.

Her mouth opened in surprise when Storm lifted his head and waved her over to where he hunkered.

He placed his finger to his lips. "Shhhh."

"How—"

"Quickly, bring me the bomb." He whispered directions to the engine room, down the ladder to the left, past the galley and rest-room.

"I can't." Her eyes seemed to plead. "It will go off any minute."

"It won't go off." He held her hand. "Trust me. Reds lied. It's already been ten minutes. It's not on a timer."

Her lips trembled. Storm could not order her to do it, like he could a Marine. She was his only hope. He had to be gentle.

He smiled. "You can do it."

Reds' barks filled the air from the deck, twenty feet away. "Hurry up in there, woman."

Cammy raised another barrage at Reds. "Every time you open your filthy mouth, I want to puke."

Reds stomped over to her, his hand raised. "Why bother?" He dropped his hand to his side. "You'll be gone soon enough."

While he and Cammy traded loud condemnations and threats, Pauline firmed her lips, crossed the lounge, and disappeared down the stairwell.

Storm peeked out to the deck just as Reds turned to Jackie.

He growled. "And you, my mouthy friend from Barbados."

She looked away, her eyes moist in the softening morning light.

"You can quit the games," he said. "I know who you are now. When I'm finished with you today, I'll personally visit Richmond Hill Prison to deliver the unfortunate news to your dear father."

Reds must have also heard Pauline tell Jackie last night that she'd seen her dad in Richmond Hill Prison.

Reds continued. "I can't believe you're still in Storm's company after he tried to kill your father."

"If I remember correctly," Jackie yelled, "he saved Daddy from *your* bomb."

Storm resisted the urge to leap onto the deck and strangle Reds with his bare hands. Storm could almost smell his own rage oozing from his pores. The seconds ticked by as he waited for Pauline's return.

Soft hesitant footsteps climbed the ladder, across the lounge from Storm—too soft for Reds and his soldiers to hear over the slaps of waves against the yacht. Pauline's head rose slowly out of the dark stairwell, at the floor level of the lounge.

Reds glanced back. "What's taking her so bloody long?"

She slipped back into the stairwell like a turtle withdrawing into its shell.

Cammy yelled at Reds. "Maybe she's praying for your miserable soul."

He seemed unable to resist her hook. He turned away from the lounge and bellowed at her. "Prayers? Your prayers didn't put food on your table. I did."

Cammy roped him in. "I never needed you."

Their verbal barbs allowed Pauline to emerge undetected out of the stairwell with the bundle in her hands. She side stepped across the lounge toward the sewing machine and handed Storm the plastic-covered bomb.

Reds looked over his shoulder at Pauline. "Where are my diamonds, bitch?"

She leaned across the sewing machine, covering Storm's escape from his hiding place. "Somebody moved them," she whined, opening the drawer. "Ha! Here they are."

With the bomb in one hand, Storm crawled back along the shadowy wall the way he'd traveled minutes earlier, past the bar and behind the couch toward the walkway entrance. He glanced back as Pauline shuffled out onto the deck toward Reds—with a velvet bag in her hand.

He hadn't decided what to do with the bomb, except get it off the yacht. But now he knew.

He hated that their loot might return to the bottom of sea, but survival—and Reds' demise— meant a lot more now than a hundred and twenty million dollars and Bravo's defection.

When Storm stepped back onto the walkway, Mario resumed another charade of hysterical Italian that distracted the soldier until Storm made it to the bow, out of view from the deck.

He crept past the pilothouse steps and gently opened Mario's locker. Inside, the remaining C4 blocks sat in a plastic bag. Storm slipped Reds' bomb on the remaining stack in the bag. He twisted the top of the plastic and knotted it. With the bag firmly in his hand, he headed down the bow ladder into the water. He held the bundle above his head to protect the battery-powered receiver from leaks, and side stroked along the *Carmen* toward his Radon 22.

The engine sputtered in neutral gear, muffling Reds' voice and the squeak of Storm's bare legs on the fiberglass swim platform as he crawled toward the fish hold.

He peeked past it. Just the top of Red's hat where he stood on the deck. No one would see Storm this low in his boat.

Storm inched open the fish hold cover, glad he'd lubricated the rusty hinges with WD-40 a few days ago. He gingerly placed the bundle into the box, located directly above his gas tanks, and shut the cover.

He glided down the swim platform and returned to the sea.

Reds gave him no choice.

Storm never thought he would gladly see his Marine Corps savings go up in smoke.

***

Cammy could not accept she'd seen the last of her son, especially as she watched Reds scoop glittering stones from the velvet pouch Pauline handed him.

Storm's loss seemed too fast. Too easy for her to believe. Even Mario seemed oddly composed, like he knew things she didn't. She wondered what was behind his confusing barrage of Italian. He knew enough English to ask her for a gin and tonic, much less water.

Reds offered to take Pauline ashore with him, but her fatalistic mood seemed to sweep over her again.

She spat. "After all you stole from me I'd rather stay here and die with them."

Reds ordered the soldiers to tie her to a chair.

"Goodbye, dogs." He turned to his soldiers. "Let's go."

Reds waited until his two soldiers turned away from him. As they worked to untie the Radon 22 ropes, Reds pulled Storm's handgun from his belt and shot both soldiers in the back of their heads. They crumpled over and splashed into the water.

Pauline screamed.

She would have received the third shot had she not elected to stay on the yacht.

By bullet or bomb, Reds intended to return to shore alone. He'd become a more vicious beast than Cammy had thought possible.

He tossed the handgun on the table and snarled. "I learned well from our Cuban comrade. The best secrets are those held by dead men."

Cammy sighed and resigned to her fate.

She turned to Mario. "I love you. Always did. Always will."

He nodded and smiled. "I love you too. Don't lose hope yet."

Reds released his ropes, stomped into the Radon 22 pilothouse, and shifted the motor into gear. The boat pulled slowly away from the *Carmen*.

Pauline whispered at Cammy. "Storm is alive."

Cammy released a long slow breath. Pauline must have cracked from the turmoil. If Storm had survived, he'd be here by now.

Maybe this was Cammy's time to meet her children. The best part about dying now would be that, finally, she would never see Reds again.

***

Storm had just swum up to the bow ladder when two gunshots and a scream came from the other end of the yacht. His heart sank, thinking Reds had begun to shoot the others—or at him. He ducked into the hull shadow and caught a glimpse of the two soldiers splashing into the water. Their uniform shirts ballooned at their backs with air caught in them, and they floated motionless next to the Radon 22.

If Reds had shot his own men, clearly he intended not to leave anyone else alive out here.

Storm could not see Reds, but the Radon 22 gear engaged and the engine roared. Smoke coughed out of the exhaust pipe and blew over the soldiers' bodies. Storm held on to the ladder, preparing to submerge if Reds headed in his direction. Instead, the boat disappeared behind the stern and the sound of the engine faded to the seaward side of the *Carmen*.

Distant hums—not his boat— caught Storm's attention.

Bravo?

Storm had little time to speculate. He refocused on freeing the others. He climbed the bow ladder, still cautious in case Reds had more surprises. He crawled along the floor to the place where Mario had secured the dive buoy.

Storm squeezed behind it and watched for Reds' next move.

Reds steered the boat about a hundred feet away from the *Carmen* and slowed the engine. The gear shifted into neutral, the familiar puttering sound amplified over the vacant water between the two boats. He exited the Radon 22 pilothouse and stepped onto the fish hold, facing the *Carmen* with his arms akimbo.

Like an emperor savoring his grandest moment of victory, Reds glowed in the early morning rays peeking over the mountain tops. He probably thought he was standing on the pinnacle of his life. Obviously he had no idea he was really standing on enough C4 explosives to turn the boat into toothpicks and him into shark food.

Storm imagined that Reds was in a heightened state of glee. *His* green, mountainous island sat before him, subdued under the weight of his guns and the people's fear. Center-stage, the exhausted *Carmen* floated with the last of his enemies, roped and ready for his fiery pleasure at the push of a button.

Even from this distance, Storm recognized a slow grin spread across Reds' face as wide as his red moustache.

Then Storm heard it again—a rising drone.

Overhead?

Reds probably heard the same sound. He jumped and hollered, his words booming across the open sea between the Radon 22 and the *Carmen*. "I knew it! I knew they would come. My fraternal comrades are here. Long live international solidarity!"

Had the Soviets really decided to move troops in to support Reds and his bloody coup as they'd done in Afghanistan?

The noise clearly came from large planes closing in on the island. Low cloud cover hid them from view. If yesterday's trauma still paralyzed Grenada, it appeared more turmoil waited minutes away.

Was this a Soviet, or an American invasion?

Storm backed out from his hiding place and sprinted down the walkway to the lounge, on the island side of the yacht and out of Reds' view. The others remained tied to their chairs around the deck table.

Storm dropped to his knees and crawled across the squeaky floors to the table.

"Storm!" Cammy's relief brightened her face.

Pauline chuckled. "I told you he was alive."

"Stay seated." He untied their ropes. "Reds can still see you if you stand."

"Oh Stormy." Jackie embraced him.

Still on his knees, he pulled the last of Mario's rope loose. "Thanks for keeping the soldiers busy with your Italian lessons."

Mario groaned, in obvious pain from the blow of the rifle butt to his stomach. "You don't know how happy I was to see you sneak down that walkway. Pauline said you placed the bomb on your boat?"

"Yep," Storm said. "Reds has a surprise coming. I gave him the rest of your C4 as a present too. I hope he doesn't have a reason to open the fish hold."

Pauline's mood changed. "I'm so sorry for all the trouble I caused."

Storm kissed the tears from her cheeks. "You did well. You saved our lives."

"Those diamonds I gave him. Those were the carnival decorations me and Rachael used to play with."

Relieved, he kissed her again. "Rachael would be proud of you."

A formation of planes roared out of the clouds and descended toward the Point Salines airport.

Reds' exaltation intensified from the drifting Radon 22, his thunders rumbling through the distant chorus of planes. "Long live international solidarity."

In his elation, might Reds forget to trigger the bomb hidden in the fish hold?

Storm grabbed a pair of binoculars off the table and scanned the planes.

He had seen and flown in enough of the portly C-130s to recognize them immediately. He always thought these American workhorse planes looked like pregnant whales with wings. But these planes were not about to deliver calves.

Reds had been dreadfully mistaken.

Storm leaped to his feet and yelled at him. "Those are Americans, you idiot."

He couldn't be sure Reds heard him. Through the binoculars, Reds looked frozen in shock. Maybe from the sight of Storm alive on the yacht, or maybe he too now recognized the planes were not Soviet aircrafts. An American invasion would deliver a disgraceful end to his one-day rule.

Reds' delusionary flight of grandeur must have crashed onto the unyielding rocks of reality. His mustachioed face recoiled from the impact with a contorted mixture of dismay and torment.

His distorted facial expression gave Storm raw guiltless pleasure.

For a fleeting moment Storm searched for memories to inspire some sympathy for Reds. But on every memory lane Storm turned down, Cammy cried with swollen eyes and busted lips. In each doorway he opened into the past, Rachael embraced him with her toothy smile, her silence pleading for retribution. In the open fields of his Grenada memories, Pauline wept for her lost innocence, while Grenada wailed in agony from senseless killings.

Reds had become a vulture, cloaked in the promises of communism, while engorging on a steady diet of human pain, lost freedoms, and crushed hopes.

Now, death awaited him with violent, impatient clutches reserved only for the evil.

Storm too could wait no more. He grabbed the Sterling 9 mm off the table and shot two rounds over the Radon 22 to reignite Reds' venomous contempt one final time.

Reds pulled out a flat elongated instrument from his uniform shirt pocket and pointed it at the *Carmen*. His laughter crackled through the rising drones.

"Get down!" Storm pulled Jackie and Cammy off their chairs to the deck.

At that moment, an exploding ball of fire engulfed Reds and the Radon 22. The deafening explosion drowned out the sound of the incoming C-130s and sent shock waves across the *Carmen*. The flaming wreckage coughed thick black smoke and rained burning splinters over the sea. Smoke blew over the yacht.

Storm held his breath.

The last thing he wanted to do today was to inhale any of Reds' leftover contamination.

In the distance over Point Salines, American Rangers jumped from C-130s. Rows of parachutes opened up and drifted down to the airfield. An eruption of heavy gunfire and shelling rocked the island.

The world's largest superpower had just commenced a military invasion of one of the world's smallest countries.

CHAPTER TWENTY-NINE

"Have you lost your frigging mind?" Storm hollered over the radio at Steve. "You expect us to sit here with the *Carmen* in the middle of a goddamned war to wait for Bravo to show up brandishing a Makarov and demanding diamonds?"

"Affirmative." Steve's voice was calm and steady. "Over."

"You're shitting me," Storm replied. "Do you hear the anti-aircraft weapons and rockets going off? There's a war going on right in front our faces like it's on television. And all I have is a useless 9 mm with two clips. Over."

"Hold your position, Marine. Subject on the way. Over."

"Five minutes. That's it. Over and out." Storm slapped the radio on the console clip. "Dammit!"

Mario gazed out the pilothouse windshield at the fireworks rising over Point Salines. "If anti-aircraft rounds begin to reach us we'll have no choice but to take the yacht a few miles out."

"I agree." Storm headed out of the pilothouse to find the others.

Jackie, standing with Cammy and Pauline at the entrance to the lounge, pointed up to Richmond Hill Prison. "Look."

Two squadrons of Black Hawk helicopters charged across the sky. One squadron broke off northward and headed to the official residence of the Governor-General, himself a prisoner to Reds' PRA. Troops repelled from the helicopters to the tennis court area, where Storm as a young boy used to shoot birds with slingshots.

Rapid gunfire echoed against the hillsides.

The other Black Hawk squadron raced over the harbor toward the hilltop Fort Frederick and Richmond Hill Prison complex.

A prison rescue?

Jackie squealed a blend of joy and apprehension.

Storm recognized a problem immediately.

The first rays of sunlight peaked over the hills and reflected off the helicopters' windshields. The pilots would be blinded. The defending ZU-23 twin barreled cannons could pick them off like a turkey shoot. The Black Hawks held their advantage at night, not in the sharp glare of sunlight while racing into a wall of muzzle flashes spitting a thousand rounds per minute.

This had all the markings of a poorly timed and hastily assembled operation.

He held Jackie around her waist. "Not good."

The first helicopter shuddered from incoming fire and peeled off from the formation, trailing smoke. It reached over the harbor and took a vertical dive into the water.

The women wailed. "Oh no!"

Another smoking helicopter landed heavy on Tanteen field, still taking anti-aircraft and machinegun fire. A third, also smoking, raced toward Point Saline. The remaining six helicopters backed away and headed out to sea.

In its first minutes, the Grenada invasion had hit a catastrophic snag.

Storm scanned the action through his binoculars. To the south, anti-aircraft batteries hammered long trails of red at incoming American planes. To the north, PRA soldiers with BTRs surrounded the governor's official residence and his American rescuers in a nest of heavy gunfire.

Storm seethed. How could Washington, after four years of saber rattling about Grenada, send American sons into another quagmire like Beirut?

Proper intelligence should have pinpointed the antiaircraft guns for early elimination. Maybe their locations, embedded close to civilian houses, restrained military options. But no excuse could explain a mission that gave all the tactical advantages to the opposing side.

He did notice though, from the tracer patterns, the PRA soldiers manning the anti-aircraft batteries exercised skilled fire control. The Grenada invasion would not be a cakewalk for the Americans. PRA soldiers were putting up stiff resistance, maybe not for Reds, but at least to protect their soil from a foreign invader.

Storm now feared, with the Americans' nose bloodied in the early hours, they might escalate their fire power at greater risk to the innocent civilian population, alienating the very people who might otherwise welcome the intervention. Anti-aircraft barrages appeared to come from the midst of a housing cluster. Targets, like the Fort Frederick complex, snuggled uncomfortably close to civilian homes.

Storm hoped the American commanders also knew that the Fort Frederick complex included a mental hospital.

The "Crazy House," as Grenadians called the mental home, held a commanding view of Richmond Hill Prison and provided a safe home for some of the most entertaining personalities to walk Grenada's streets.

Storm expected PRA resistance would soften once Steve got the word to psychological operations that Reds was dead. *Psyop* units typically sent messages to demoralize the enemy through radio broadcasts and leaflets.

Mario yelled and pointed. "Cuban boat approaching starboard."

Sure as hell, Bravo's white launch cut water toward the *Carmen*, a large Cuban flag flapping above its pilothouse. Bravo had wasted no time.

When Colonel Bravo stepped on board the *Carmen* in his green combat fatigues, he looked out of breath. Storm noted Bravo had his Makarov holstered at his hip, its leather restrainer unsnapped for a quick draw.

Storm hoped no guns would be drawn.

But no mission ever executed precisely as planned. He stuck the 9 mm into his waistband and pulled his loose t-shirt over his shorts. And he never let his sights drift away from Bravo.

Storm shook Bravo's hand. "Colonel, I expected you to be fighting the Yankees at the airport."

Bravo got straight to the point, shouting over a barrage of gunfire. "We're not safe here. We must leave Grenada waters immediately."

"We?" Storm asked.

"Yes," Bravo said. "I'm afraid the conclusion of this fighting is already predetermined. The Yankees won't leave until they win. They're so rushed to restore the scoreboard after Beirut that they showed up with tourist maps. They will be bloodied, but they won't turn back now."

Mario stepped forward and shook Bravo's hand. "Do you think we can start engines and pull out without being stopped or shot at?"

Bravo had an answer ready. "Yes, you can with the Cuban flag. I have diplomatic immunity. I can get you anywhere you want to go." He glanced at the women and lowered his voice. "Let's speak some place private."

As Storm expected, Mario pointed up at the pilothouse. "We can go there."

Mario led the way, with Bravo next and Storm following.

When they entered the pilothouse, Storm shut the door.

Bravo drew Cammy's stiff new curtains across the windows. "Hope you don't mind."

Through the windshield they still had a clear view of the smoke rising from the Tanteen crash and planes landing at the Point Salines airport.

Mario sat on his weathered high chair against the systems console, a horizontal Christmas tree of lights and controls. A flashing red light Steve had installed on the dashboard behind the wheel signaled live audio and video transmissions. Microphones and cameras hid in strategic locations throughout the boat, including the pilothouse. The transmissions flowed through internal wiring to Mario's communication radar, which, through a secret wavelength Steve had calibrated, flashed live to a boat parked twenty miles off Grenada's shores.

Storm sat next to Bravo on the rattan chair against the rear bulkhead and prepared for the take down.

The windshield rattled from more explosions around the airport.

Bravo leaned forward. "Okay gentlemen, let's cut the bullshit. We have no time to waste. You and I know we all have reasons to leave safely as soon as possible. Let's make a deal right now."

"Colonel," Storm said. "You need to be clearer."

Bravo snapped. "The diamonds, dammit. The diamonds."

"Diamonds?" Mario asked.

"Listen to me, in an hour the Yankees will stop and search every boat in these waters. They will seize your diamonds as war loot. I have diplomatic immunity. I can get you all to Miami. Let's make a deal."

Make a deal? Steve and Hallam had warned that Bravo never made deals. He closed deals, leaving the dead behind—including Rachael.

Storm prepared the last hook. "How many of the diamonds would you need to get us out of here?"

Bravo grinned. "It's a fifty-fifty split now and whichever port you decide we should part ways, we can have one more cigar and say our farewells."

Storm debated when to pull the plug on Bravo. The invasion had obviously unraveled the colonel's previously controlled demeanor. His desperation showed. In just a couple minutes, he so implicated himself even Castro would lead the firing squad. Bravo had deserted his reserve troops and construction workers to an American airborne attack. While Cuban troops died within view, he proposed to give a U.S. Marine, suspected of espionage, Cuban diplomat immunity and safe passage out of a war zone. And for his troubles, Bravo demanded a payoff of diamonds from imperialist agents.

Steve, listening and watching from a video feed about thirty minutes away, probably wished Storm would shut up and read Bravo the riot act.

"Okay," Storm said. "We can work something out, but first I want to know what happened to Rachael."

Bravo chewed on his cigar stub. "Your sister was not supposed to die. She was good, with foreigners, politicians, and military. Her natural ways led men to trust her with secrets."

She learned well from Cammy, Storm thought.

Bravo continued. "We knew secrets were getting out, so I set up the network and found her. I told Reds I needed time to turn her. She would have been a great source, especially with you in the Marines. But Reds was more concerned about getting back at you and your mother. He shot her and made it look like an accident. We made a mistake trusting him."

Storm swallowed his rage. "It's too late for Reds now. But we still have time for you."

Bravo squinted at Storm. "Where's Reds? What happened to him?"

Storm glanced out the windshield at debris from his destroyed Radon 22 floating in the distance. "Shark bait. He played with fire once too often."

Worry lines furrowed across Bravo's forehead. "I wondered what that explosion was. Listen, Reds was never my associate. We at the Cuban embassy knew he could not be trusted with power. Too bad our Soviet comrades did not see it our way."

Storm had heard enough.

He rose from the creaky rattan couch, keeping his sights on Bravo.

Bravo glanced at his watch and aggravation seared his voice. "Let's get on with it. Where are your diamonds?"

"Colonel," Storm said. "There are no diamonds for you and we're not going anywhere with you."

Bravo launched out of the couch like a barrel on unsteady legs. He reached for his holster.

Storm pulled his 9 mm first and pointed it at Bravo's head. "Don't do it, Colonel. We don't want to hurt you. We just want you to talk to our friends before we make a deal."

Confusion twisted Bravo's face. "Friends?"

Right on time, Steve's voice crackled over the radio. "Flying Fish to Bianca C. Flying Fish to Bianca C. Over."

Mario released the radio from the console and answered. "Bianca C here. Over."

"Let me talk to the colonel," Steve said.

Bravo's color paled and his hand shook when he took the radio from Mario. "Who the hell is this?"

"Colonel, we haven't met, but we have a mutual friend who tells me we can work together. Over."

Bravo glanced from side to side like a man trying to buy time— and information. "What do you want? There's a war outside our windows and I might be in Havana by nightfall."

"Colonel, look at the vent in the ceiling above you. We have cameras and microphones everywhere. We've watched and recorded every move you made and every word you said from twenty miles away. Within hours we'll have video copies to hand over to your United Nations ambassador when they meet in New York to condemn this intervention."

Beads of sweat rolled down Bravo's face.

Steve continued. "If you return to Havana, Castro will have your head. But we have a safe future planned for you and your family. Over."

"Leave my family out of this."

"We care about your family too. A year ago one of your fellow colonels pulled your son Luis off a school bus in Havana and punched him unconscious for showing disrespect. You filed a formal complaint. But that officer had privileges and connections you didn't because of all your years working overseas. Castro promoted the officer to general, and shredded your complaint. That's when you and your wife started plans to escape Cuba. Are you still with me, Colonel? Over."

"Who the hell are you people?"

"We're friends. The *Bianca C* diamonds were your ticket to a secure life in Spain. But you and I know you need friends to cover your back. You know too much. Castro will find you. But if you agree to work with us, you and your wife can be watching the Miami sunset with your son by the end of today. Over."

"What have you done with my family? Where are they?"

"They're safe. We know you've been trying to call your Havana apartment since yesterday when Reds shut down the phone system. You haven't spoken to them since your son left for Mexico City two days ago to attend the annual communist youth conference."

Storm thought, probably a little bone Castro tossed to keep Bravo's loyalty.

Steve continued. "The student delegation has Cuban chaperones to guarantee their safe return to Cuba, of course. To escape them, Luis is now in a Mexico City hospital faking a severe case of appendicitis. The authorities gave your wife permission to travel on the first flight this morning. They figured you might be too busy in Grenada to plan a defection with your family."

Damn.

If the military planners had given the attention to the invasion as Steve had given to the Bravo mission, the Grenada invasion might have ended in five minutes with no loss of lives. Had the troops really landed with tourist maps, instead of the grid-lined 1:50,000 scale maps Storm had trained with?

Storm held his pistol pointed at the Cuban colonel.

Bravo's posture looked burdened, but his eyes gleamed with caution. "What if I don't agree? Over."

"Storm will disarm you and let you get back on your boat. But remove your flag. My helicopter friends flying around out there might consider you hostile. You'll be on your own. You will never see your family again. And the next time they see you, you'll be in a wooden coffin, buried with the public disdain reserved only for those who dare to betray the mighty Fidel."

Bravo grimaced. "And if I agree with your plans?"

"If you come with us, we call a payphone down the hall from your son's room in the Mexico City hospital. A janitor is waiting this very minute to answer it. Your wife is already in the room with Luis—her flight touched down at 06:30 a.m. Mexico time. The janitor will sweep by their open door and give them a signal to change into work uniforms. He will escort them down the cargo elevator to the loading dock exit. We have a car waiting to drive them to the U.S. Embassy in time for breakfast. In an hour and a half, you'll be able to call them at their breakfast table to ask your son how many eggs went into his favorite Spanish omelet. And then you can remind your wife to cut back her sugar in her coffee from three to two spoons. Your decision. Over."

When the two Navy fast-attack boats pulled up alongside the *Carmen*, Hallam was the first one off and the first one to shake Storm's hand.

"Great job." Hallam delivered a silver-toothed smile.

Storm didn't feel ready to debrief him on the last few hours. "We had a few close calls," Storm said. "But everyone one pitched in."

"Keep a phone close by," Hallam replied. "We might need the five of you again soon."

Storm handed him Bravo's Makarov and holster.

Bravo stared down Hallam, and a hint of pain dulled the colonel's eyes. "I trusted you, my friend."

Guilt needled Storm. He'd helped fracture the trust between the two friends. Broken trust between comrades, like broken trust between government and people, lead to pain. But these two men were professionals in the game, accustomed to shielding their humanity from the unforgiving rules of espionage.

Yet, Hallam seemed unwilling to let his friend walk away.

He nodded grimly. "It's the hardest thing I've ever done in my life. You were on a suicide mission. I did it for your family. I hope you get to thank me one day."

"Maybe one day I will." Bravo glanced around at Cammy, Jackie, Pauline, Mario, and Storm. "And they will too."

Bravo must have recalled his plan for the *Carmen*— a plan he'd shared only with Hallam, who relayed it by radio to Storm after Bravo surrendered in the pilothouse. Whether or not he'd gotten his hands on the diamonds, Storm learned that Bravo intended to blow up the yacht with all onboard, and return to the Cuban embassy to say he'd single handedly taken down a CIA operation that coordinated the American invasion.

Bravo turned to Storm. "Forget what you heard. I couldn't do it. Meeting you helped changed my mind. I hope my son gets to meet you one day."

"Me too," Storm said. "It's a small world. If I meet him, I will tell him his father was willing to die for him."

Storm realized then he still had no idea what Cammy had done with the real diamonds. He turned to her and whispered outside of Bravo's hearing range. "Where did you hide the diamonds?"

"Only Mario knew where I hid the real ones," she said, "They're stitched in the hems of the curtains in the pilothouse."

Storm chuckled.

The same curtains Bravo had pulled shut. If he only knew how close he'd come to holding a hundred and twenty million dollars in diamonds, it might give him a heart attack.

Storm embraced Cammy and stared into her eyes. "Have I ever told you, you're the best mother in the world?"

She grinned. "No, but I hope you say it every chance you get."

Just then, Steve, in military uniform, jumped off the Navy boat and bounced his way up to them with a sea bag slung over his shoulder.

He extended his free hand to Cammy. "Ma'am, I have heard a lot of great things about you."

They shook hands and Cammy smiled. "Just believe half of them."

Steve turned to Bravo. "Colonel, this is a wise decision."

Bravo sized him up. "A little early to say, don't you think?"

"Maybe." Steve shook Bravo's hand. "This first boat will take you to the USS *Guam*, and then on to Barbados for an early afternoon flight to Miami.

Your wife and son will be waiting there. I hope America becomes a good home for you."

"A man's home is wherever his family is," Bravo said.

Steve allowed little time to rest on his laurels. "Do you think you can ask your ambassador's American wife to join us?"

Storm recalled the enchanting woman in red dress with North Carolina memories.

"Never," Bravo said. "She loves Cuba as much as she loves America."

"Colonel Bravo," Steve said, "my wish is you get to love America as much as you love Cuba."

Hallam fitted an orange life jacket around Bravo and locked his wrists in cuffs behind his back. "You know the routine. This is temporary. Your family will never see you in these. We just don't want you to have buyer's remorse before you land in Miami."

A loud explosion came from Point Salines.

Bravo gazed at the airport. "You're fighting construction workers."

Steve nodded. "Yes. But they seem better with AK-47s than with shovels. How many of them are Angola veterans?"

Bravo chewed his cigar and smiled. "You're good. We'll talk in Miami."

While the *Carmen* followed the second fast-attack boat outside the range of anti-aircraft rounds, Steve pulled Storm aside and pushed the sea bag at him.

Storm recognized his name on the shoulder strap immediately. "How the hell did you get this all the way here from Beirut?"

"I've had it for two weeks."

"You knew all this would happen two weeks ago?"

"No," Steve said. "But we try to plan for every contingency. Reds caught us with our pants down. We're operating on old intelligence and tourist maps. The Navy and Army are communicating on different frequencies. It's a zoo out there."

"What's next?"

"Jump into your uniform," Steve said. "You have one more mission. You're going to catch a ride with Black Hawks off the USS *Guam*."

Storm glanced questioningly at Jackie.

Steve nodded, and Storm understood. The next target was Richmond Hill Prison, to rescue political prisoners, including Jackie's father.

Just then, a couple of planes roared overhead toward Fort Frederick.

"A7 Corsairs from the USS *Independence*," Steve hollered over the noise. "They're going to soften the perimeters before we go in."

Storm rubbed his chin. "I hope they remember there's a mental hospital up there."

"Yeah," Steve agreed. "Latest intel said patients were evacuated and all we have now are PRA soldiers using the hospital as cover to shoot at the helicopters. Don't worry. We have it in the bag."

CHAPTER THIRTY

Storm leaped out of the Black Hawk an hour later with Marines from the USS *Guam* and looked over his shoulder at the smoldering building that used to be the "Crazy House." Smoke drifted over the hillside in an eerie silence. Not even a chirp from the birds Storm used to shoot at with sling shots.

The Marines spread out along the street and Storm huddled with the platoon leader, a lieutenant. Storm pointed on the map where the narrow road led down to Richmond Hill Prison. Steve had said the mission required local eyes since the current maps were so inadequate.

Storm didn't need a map to find his way to the prison.

The lieutenant gave the move-out signal and the platoon moved forward. A Cobra helicopter flew unopposed overhead. The latest intel said PRA soldiers all over the islands had begun to disarm and surrender. Radio broadcasts and flyers about Reds' demise had begun to take their effect on the young men's willingness to die for a dead revolution.

The Marines rounded the hilltop next to the Lion's Den building. Storm led a squad into the round structure. Wind blew through open windows, scattering loose paper around the concrete floor. Piled in the far corner, PRA uniforms, and, strewn on the floor around the uniforms, about eight AK-47s.

The sight brought Storm some relief. Desertions meant fewer young men would die on both sides. He didn't know which thought he hated more, seeing the body of a classmate, or coming face-to-face with one holding an AK-47.

He tightened his grip on his M-16.

Once they cleared the Lion's Den, the platoon moved down the final stretch along the ridge to the prison gates. A breeze blew down from the hills, blackened with smoke from the mental hospital.

Flames crackled timber.

A woman wailed and it sent a chill through Storm.

He knew too well the nerve-shattering sound of a woman in loss.

He didn't know the woman bawling over the hillside. He didn't know why she bawled, and didn't have to.

To his bones, he felt every chorus of pain that poured out of her soul.

He knew then. In war, there may be victors, but no winners.

Human loss affected all.

The platoon inched toward the gates. No guards, no movement, just two open gates.

Once in the prison yard, the Marine at point signaled a halt. Urgent voices echoed around the courtyard. Storm moved up to the front. Through the foliage, several men in civilian garb held animated conversations.

Storm called out. "U.S. Marines. Move forward slowly with your hands up."

"We're prisoners," a man shouted. "The guards left an hour ago. We're the only ones here."

The platoon spread out while Storm moved toward the group of men, his rifle at the ready and his finger on the trigger.

One of the men limped forward with a cane. "Thank you."

Storm recognized him. "Mr. Benjamin?"

Mr. Benjamin squinted through glasses held by a crude wire frame. "How do you know...?"

"It's me, Storm." He'd waited four years to say three words to Mr. Benjamin. "I am sorry."

Mr. Benjamin's eyes welled up and his narrow chin quivered. He collapsed in Storm's arms and wept. The burden of guilty years vanished in minutes, washed away with tears.

Finally, Storm said, "Jackie is waiting for you."

Just then a woman scampered down the hill, her white uniform splattered with red. "Oh God, we need help at the "Crazy House." All you bomb the hospital with patients in there."

Storm looked at her in disbelief. "But I thought the patients were gone, PRA were shooting at the helicopter when—"

"No, no, no," she hollered. "The PRA soldiers ran away and left their rifles two hours ago. Those were mental patients playing with the rifles. We just couldn't get them to stop shooting in the air."

Epilogue

Storm lifted the scuba tank to the counter in his beachfront dive shop and inspected the O-ring, humming to his favorite Bob Marley rhythms from his cassette player. A steady breeze rustled through the coconut leaves overhead and blew in sweet scents of tropical flora. The gentle wash of Grand Anse waves blended with the rubbery smell of neoprene dive suits hanging behind him, a comforting reminder that redemption always waited one dive away.

He looked forward to the busy week ahead. A year after the American military had departed, sunglasses and bikinis replaced rifles and combat uniforms. And with increasing numbers of visitors, came divers who wanted to tour Grenada's pristine underworld. His blue and white Boston Whaler, purchased when the Americans refunded his Radon 22 as a casualty of the invasion, bobbed against the jetty on a sun-glazed sea.

Shoe soles crunched sand on the walkway to his counter, and he immediately recognized the footstep cadence.

Jackie bounced around the corner and dumped a stack of books on the counter. She leaned over for her daily kiss on the way to the medical school.

Storm happily complied. "Good morning."

She removed her sunglasses and the sparkle in her eyes told him right away she had good news.

"Guess what," she said. "The St. George's School of Medicine accepted me into their Marine biology program. Daddy's recommendation letter and Mario's big donation helped."

"Not true," he said, "I have inside information you had the highest scores on the application tests."

She gave him a suspicious glare. "Are you still in communication with Steve and Hallam?"

He traced her lips with his fingers. "Too much information can be dangerous." He thought about what her return to graduate school meant. "Will I get to dive with you every day?"

"Only if you like sharks," she said. "That's my specialty."

Storm grinned. "I can introduce you to the one I met on the *Bianca C*. But aren't you afraid of sharks? They bite, you know."

She teased him with a shy look. "I am not afraid of *you*."

"Hey," he protested. "I nibble. I don't bite."

She giggled and glanced out to the sea. "Where are your parents today?"

"They left early this morning for a trip up the Grenadines. My father is thinking of buying Palm Island and turning it into a honeymoon resort."

She eyed Storm. "Maybe because they're still on their honeymoon."

"After a year of marriage? It's a little uncomfortable staring out at them on their new yacht everyday wondering what they're doing."

"Exactly what you and I might be doing."

They laughed.

"So is he serious about handing over the *Carmen* to you?" She asked.

"Yup. And the upgrades are complete. New floors. New galley. The painting is next."

"Maybe you can use her to take Palm Island visitors on *Bianca C* tours."

"I like that idea," Storm said. "Pauline says she can run the galley, since Mario's staff returned to the Mediterranean."

He gazed out at the inviting blue water. Now that peace had returned to the *Bianca C*, she would be a great attraction for visitors. She no longer burned with secrets that burdened Cammy, or with diamonds that tempted Bravo, or even with devious suspicions that imploded Reds.

The *Bianca C* finally rested.

Acknowledgements

I am thankful to many, whose ideas, suggestions, and inspiration contributed to this novel. I am especially grateful to my critiquing partners, Joan Upton Hall, Sylvia Dickey Smith, and Joy Nord for their many hours of generous discussions and thoughtful editing. I deeply appreciate my wife, Susie, and daughters Malia and Crystal for their boundless encouragement and patience, especially during the long hours I spent in isolation to write this story. Jerry Hagins, your final touches and thoughts made a valuable difference. Mikey Steele, your artistic talents and eyewitness experience with the *Bianca C* event really captured the drama of that day on the book cover like no one else could. Finally, my profound admiration goes out to the many brave Grenadians who rescued *Bianca C* passengers and opened their homes and hearts to them. The event exhibited the noblest in the humanity and hospitality of the Grenada people.

About the Author

Dunbar Campbell is a writer, public speaker, director of a research group, and a former U.S. Marine.

His earliest writing skills were honed in danger when, as a teen-aged student activist growing up during turbulent years on the Caribbean island of Grenada, he contributed to and distributed antigovernment newspapers in support of a revolutionary movement. When secret police brutally crushed the organization, Campbell migrated to the United States and enlisted in the U.S. Marines.

The revolutionary group eventually reorganized under the leadership of Maurice Bishop and overthrew the government in the 1979 revolution. Another violent coup in 1983 led to Prime Minister Bishop's execution and the U.S. invasion of Grenada.

Among Grenada documents the U.S. military seized and stored at the National Archives is a passionate letter of congratulations to Prime Minister Bishop, written four years earlier and mailed from halfway around the world in Hawaii. It was signed Dunbar Campbell, U.S. Marines.

Campbell is a certified scuba diver and runs an occasional marathon. He has a bachelor's degree in political science/economics and a master's degree in economics.

He channels into his writings the dangers, secrets, and intrigues that shaped his life.